SAPOGONIA

DATE DUE

AP 14 '97			
NO 22 99			
MY 5 '00			
A 03			

Bilingual Press/Editorial Bilingüe

General Editor
    Gary D. Keller

Managing Editor
    Karen S. Van Hooft

Senior Editor
    Mary M. Keller

Assistant Editor
    Linda St. George Thurston

Editorial Board
    Juan Goytisolo
    Francisco Jiménez
    Eduardo Rivera
    Severo Sarduy
    Mario Vargas Llosa

Address:
Bilingual Review/Press
Hispanic Research Center
Arizona State University
Tempe, Arizona 85287
(602) 965-3867

SAPOGONIA

(An Anti-Romance in ⅜ Meter)

ANA CASTILLO

Bilingual Press/Editorial Bilingüe

TEMPE, ARIZONA

Library of Congress Cataloging-in-Publication Data

Castillo, Ana.
    Sapogonia : (an anti-romance in 3/8 meter) / Ana Castillo.
        p.   cm.
    ISBN 0-916950-95-6. — ISBN 0-916950-96-4 (pbk.)
    I. Title. ·
    PS3553.A8135S27   1989
    813'.54—dc19   89-933
                                                      CIP

PRINTED IN THE UNITED STATES OF AMERICA

Cover design by Robin Ravary
Back cover photo by Rubén Guzmán

Acknowledgments

This volume is supported by a grant from the National Endowment for the Arts in Washington, D.C., a Federal agency.

A Marcel Ramón,
querido ser que me sostiene
en esta tierra

This is the story of make-believe people in a real world;
or, if you like, the story of real people
in a make-believe world.

anti-hero *(ant-ē-hē-rō)* *n.*, *pl.* *-roes.* 1. In mythology and legend, a man who celebrates his own strength and bold exploits. 2. Any man who notes his special achievements. 3. The principal male character in a novel, poem, or dramatic work.
—as defined by Pastora Velásquez Aké

PROLOGUE

Sapogonia is a distinct place in the Americas where all mestizos reside, regardless of nationality, individual racial composition, or legal residential status—or, perhaps, because of all of these.

Their cultural roots may be traced back further than 7,000 B.C. In the gradual and inevitable process that eventually contributed to the world at large chile, corn, beans, and chocolate, not least among their agricultural developments are variations of something fermented and concocted from a root, plant, or cactus. These, owing to sheer human imagination, are used for the sole purpose of altering daily reality.

The Sapogón is besieged by a history of slavery, genocide, immigration, and civil uprisings, all of which have left their marks on the genetic make-up of the generation following such periods as well as the border outline of its territory.

The Sapogón whose family background has been one of a certain wealth and class status, like the one in our story, speaks fluent French in addition to his native Spanish—which aside from being the national language is considered by his kind to be the tongue of the less civilized and cultured. The truly updated Sapogón, however (also as in the case of the one in our story), will attain fluency in English. While he may maintain sympathies with the intellectual credences of certain European states, he perceives that international achievement now weighs almost exclusively on recognition by the United States of America.

Whereas he may, by affectation, acquire the mannerisms and the idioms of the North American with the intent of assimilation, his genetic make-up immediately sets him apart, for his European ancestry, which may be either Spanish or French with the invariable contribution of indigenous blood, makes him shorter in stature with dark features not *characteristic of the Aryan or Anglo. For his own ends, he may fake an entire Latin-European background or Mediterranean autobiography. Any acknowledgment of indigenous American ancestry causes him almost immediately to be relegated to the world of Sapogonia.*

Sapogonia (like the Sapogón/a) is not identified by modern boundaries. Throughout the Americas, Sapogones, those who are wholly or in part descended from the indigenous peoples of what was erroneously named "The New World," continue to populate, breed, and therefore dominate the lands of their ancestors. Due to present political conditions decreed by the powers that be, the Sapogón pueblo finds itelf continuously divided and reunited with the certainty of the Northern winds that sweep across its continents to leave evershifting results.

A.C.
July 29, 1985
Chicago, birthplace

one

His lips touch each eyelid light as breath. He steps back, arms raised over his head. Momentarily he is distracted by the sound of laughter on the street, a girl's voice and the deeper sounds of male companions. She is inebriated with life.

A hundred sparrows awaken and sing from the tree outside the bedroom window. Sunrise against violet chiffon curtains casts a hue on the brown body breathing softly before him. His head tilts and his being is filled with a certain tenderness for her whom he loved through the night and left limp, like an overused thing.

And like a thing, an abstract idea, he prayed to her. He worshipped her as he soldered metal and bent it into any likeness but hers. Her image, this one before him, consumed his brain until it burst like a circus balloon, pained him into nothingness, and he went back to find her, again and again, in other women, taller women, fairer, women of porcelain faces and transparent eyes, women with melon asses and women with cash to spend on a man such as he.

He escaped from her to every woman as unlike her as he could find. Women who drank hard whiskey and fucked him in the men's toilet. Women who'd travelled the four corners of the world, who spoke more languages than he, who dressed in silk camisoles and garters, who lived in big houses and high-rise apartments with doormen and a privileged view of the city. The women who would lay down their lives, who used their minds to scheme for him, who handled his contracts, negotiations, who wore tweed suits and carried briefcases, whose parents hosted dinner parties for him.

Meanwhile, he remembered her. He remembered her especially when he worked, when he welded, when he stared at what might be no more than the beginning of a wall, a crosspiece for an iron fence, and in his mind's eye saw it take form.

While he thought it cliché, he saw her in the eyes of the cat, because it was with her that he discovered how seductive that

7

animal was, indifferent and capable of attack when disturbed, so unlike the dog, unlike his own obedient animals that watched his house and his back on the street. And what good was a cat if not to be adored and stroked in this fashion, as he had done to her all night?

Once, he lured a yellow spotted cat into his house with a fish fillet. He left the kitchen window open all summer. At the same hour every day the yellow spotted cat would jump through and have its dinner, leaving without so much as a thank you. But if he happened to be sitting at the table, he was allowed to reach a hand out with ever so much finesse and pet its thick coat, causing the cat to stretch its back into a hump and close its eyes for three intimate seconds. Then it jumped back out the window. His Five-Minute Cat he called it.

By the end of summer, he had been conditioned to have the cat's fillet waiting, and he sitting quietly at the table, if he were to stroke it at all.

For several days the cat stopped coming.

Surely it had found another window to crawl into, or else it had become bored with its fillet, its daily stroke.

One evening he came back from walking the pit bull, Siquieros, and saw Five-Minute Cat waiting on the kitchen table, paws tucked under its body. It winked at him. Siquieros barked and pulled at its chain. The cat watched its familiar enemy, eyes steady, motionless. He let his fingers go limp on the leather strap and the dog headed straight for the cat that leapt like a jackrabbit out the window in one movement.

It never returned.

You are a damned alley cat, he wants to utter under his breath as he continues to watch her, who has just moved so that her breasts part and the sun-toasted shoulders, neck, and face contrast the flesh color of her breasts. The voices fade outside. In the distance, a car horn honks impatiently. Someone is on his way to punch a time clock. Another Saturday begins. He has appointments, too.

In one thrust his clenched fist holding the scissors from her sewing table comes down to pierce the hollow spot between the lumps of nippled flesh. Her eyes open and are on him. Her face is wild as she inhales with the thrust and exhales when he pulls the scissors out.

His hands are wet and drip red,
he wipes the sweat from his brow
mixed with tears.   ¿Estás muerta ya, puta?

Her body heaves and she writhes with agony. She moans but says nothing. She stares at him, quivers, writhes, holds her wound like a child clasped to her bosom and says nothing.

Still holding the scissors in one hand, he drops to his knees and kisses her bloodied hands over the new mouth of her chest; he kisses her navel, the line of sparse hairs down to the abdomen, his mouth burying itself in the pubic hair, and already he knows this is not what he wants.

"Mejor que yo me muera," he sobs. His eyes search with unexpected self-recrimination in hers, still staring, blank, darker now with death inhabiting her body. Knowing he doesn't want to die either, he turns away from her, and when his eyes return to her face, the yellow spotted cat leaps out at him, claws dig into his brow and cheeks, catch in the delicate skin of his eyelids, and yank them with loud screeches.

The scissors still in his hand can't find the cat to stop its excruciating attack. "¡Cabrona! ¡Te mato, cabrona, te mato . . . !" he screams, falling on the floor that is no longer the carpeted one of her bedroom but a cobblestone street, and somehow he knows that one's life is a full circle and he is about to die thousands of miles away. . . in the village of San Co at the steps of the house where I was born right after the war, during another war, and before the next; for in my country, a war has always gone on with peacetime falling in unpredicted intervals or at designated times, such as Christmas and Holy Week.

My father was not present at my birth. As my mother told it, he had been called back to Galicia to be at his mother's side during her last days. A stern matriarch, she had demanded that her only son return to take his rightful place as head of her estate.

This story fascinated me so that at the age of six, having tired Mamá with relentless questions as to the whereabouts of my father, who by then I believed was a grand man in or about Galicia, Spain, an enchanted place way across the body of massive water that separated us, she finally told me she wasn't sure about my father's story after all.

In fact, she had reason to suspect that he may have not had a dying mother to return to, but perhaps a wife. As it was confirmed to me by my father himself years later, he indeed had had no mother to return to, and least of all any inheritance, but left San Co to where he had gone to seek his fortune in gold mining, to get out from under the crossfire.

It wasn't long after he returned home that he married and for the time being forgot Mamá.

two

All my life has been divided into two realities: dreams of revelation and prophecy, and those dreams that manifest my present. In each case, the dreams take two forms: those that beg for fantastic flight and those that are nightmares without recompense.

Although you might think me a complete idiot, it has taken me almost all my life to know this. It is a fact that I'd often had a sense of awaking in my sleep when I was presumably awake, susceptible to those same occurrences of *déjà vu* as anyone else, or having those frustrating dreams in which one struggles with desperation to wake up and does so repeatedly before actually awaking.

It is also a fact that my Mamá Grande, a tiny Mayan woman, took me aside when I was an adolescent and told me several things that didn't make a bit of sense to my young and inattentive ears, and as young people tend to waste all attempts of our elders to relay to us wisdom accumulated over the decades, I thought my Mamá Grande had a few mice in the attic.

My tata, el señor Máximo Mireles y Macías, forbade his Mayan bride, whom he took from her home in Santa Agueda Quetzaltenango at the age of thirteen, to wear her native costumes, except, of course, when she went home on visits.

She was not allowed to pray to her rows of clay statues. He made certain his diminutive wife was a God-fearing Roman Catholic, and built a shrine in the garden for a life-size statue of the Virgen de los Remedios, where my Mamá Grande was permitted to go for solace and meditation daily. It was the only place outside that my Mamá Grande was ever permitted to go alone. Even though it was just in the back of the house, I think the privilege meant a great deal to Mamá Grande.

Then there was the period of repeated discovery of the little statues about the garden, in the house, the linen, and the chicken coops, servants turning up tiny baked men and women in Indian clothing of real cotton and wool.

Finally, out of sheer tolerance for the persistence of the Indian determination to keep her culture thriving, or because my tata knew when to give up, he allowed Mamá Grande to place all of her statues alongside and at the foot of the statue of the Virgen, which she did and which I believe caused her to have more reason to visit her shrine daily.

It was Mamá Grande who told me, not once but many times, the stories related to her people, their history, and her own ideas about their traditions, all of which are really quite entertaining and which I may somewhere along this discourse share, but for now, I will only tell of how she was the one who insisted that my life was merely a series of dreams.

three

When I was very small I suffered from a recurrent nightmare in which I dreamed I was drowning and, sometimes, that I had drowned. I told Mamá in hopes that she might save me from these nocturnal tortures and Mamá, after trying various teas and placing soothing potato skins on my forehead before I went to sleep, turned me over to Mamá Grande's care and wisdom.

Mamá Grande pulled out her little sack of tobacco and rolled herself a cigarette. She was almost done with it before I finally got a response. At a young age I tended to be an impatient fellow and I remember distinctly hanging on with every puff of her scandalous-smelling cigarette until she finally looked me in the eye. It was a whole minute later when she spoke.

"Mimo, tú eres un alma mu-uuy vieja. A mí me parece que en una de tus vidas te ahogaste . . . o si no, tú ahogaste a alguien . . ." Mamá Grande had just said an outrageous thing, judging from the reaction of my mother, who threw her hands over her mouth to stifle a gasp. As for me, I didn't understand a word of it.

Many years later, when I was an adolescent, I forced myself upon a girl. Her brothers were like mad dogs when they caught up with me. If it wasn't for my grandfather, who had approached and shot his gun in the air, they would have killed me. My grandfather turned around and went back home, leaving me half drowned on the river bank.

That night as my mamá fed me chicken consommé in bed, Mamá Grande rolled up a cigarette nearby and said, "You see? I told you."

In all honesty, I hardly know why I took that girl by force. It wasn't as if I couldn't have had any other girl that I wanted without a struggle, but somehow it occurred to me to choose this one and once I realized that she didn't love me, that she didn't even like me, it was too late. I was committed to having her. I think my grandfather understood this and I believe so did her brothers.

It was all part of the ritual. I never resented that they tried to drown me. I expected something of that sort to come after I'd left the girl by the side of the road. Afterwards, we became good friends, her brothers and I, probably because of mutual compassion, forgot about the deflowered sister, and gave ourselves up to fraternal esteem for each other.

The next time Mamá Grande gave me one of her nonchalant prophetic warnings was right before I left home and, in fact, the warning was the catalyst for my departure. Again, I was plagued by feverish dreams in which each one ended with my death.

"Quiere decir que te vas a casar, Mimo . . . aunque en este caso, tal vez sería preferible si te murieras," Mamá Grande stated simply with a punctuating sigh. I laughed because I had no intentions of getting married and this was only a week before I met Marisela.

To put it in a nutshell, Marisela said, "Jump, cabroncito!" and I asked, "How high, mi vida?"

Marisela was very dark and her legs were slightly bowed, so my mother wasn't impressed. My mother, who'd wanted to marry a Spaniard to produce light-skinned children and who was deserted before the birth of her only son.

I heard, because one never lacks those who are only too glad to be the bearers of bad news, that Marisela was slipping off into the night with one of my best friends. I went out to Mamá Grande's shrine and prayed to her Virgin Mary and all the little indio statues to help me to forgive Marisela and they did. But I also figured that since it was apparent she was already a woman of some experience, there was no reason to wait until the wedding. I too, took Marisela to slip off into the night.

She brushed the grass out of her thick, plaited hair, hair that was so black it contrasted with the field's shadows in the moonlight. We had just made love for the first time. I had given all of myself to my love, Marisela, and now, she busied herself with a handful of grass, which she used to wipe the semen from between her legs, not without a certain unhidden trace of disgust.

"What's the matter? You didn't like it?" My voice actually held a tremor in anticipation of her response. Marisela looked at me with eyes blacker than her hair. "Your friend is much better than you,

Máximo, but he's a poor fool. And I would rather marry a rich one than a poor one."

You might not believe that a girl of fifteen could have the audacity to be as cruel as my Marisela was that night and neither did I, which is why I flung at her, my hands like iron rings around her neck. She gasped for breath when I came to my senses and left her alone.

It was right after that that I decided to leave home. Mamá Grande was sitting up in my room when I came in that night. "¿Te vas?" she asked. I nodded and went about putting my things into a satchel. Mamá Grande sighed. She sat in a corner on a trunk in which I never knew what had been concealed. "Didn't I tell you you would rather die than get married?"

I stared at Mamá Grande. I assumed she must've heard the same rumor I had, about Marisela and my friend who had been putting the horns on me before I even got married. "*I* didn't want to die tonight, Mamá Grande! I wanted *her* to die!" Mamá Grande shook her head and laughed a little. "¿No sabes, hijo? Es la misma cosa."

I kissed Mamá Grande on the forehead of fine, wrinkled skin that was cool to my lips and smelled of the moss in her garden and asked her to kiss Mamá for me in the morning. I was a good distance from my grandfather's ranch before I realized I didn't know yet where I was headed. What I didn't know then was that no one ever does.

four

The power with which each individual was born could be measured by one facet, which was the quality of his or her soul. That is, the result of the progression of each cycle of life determined the individual's control over her or his circumstances.

Some individuals were extremely advanced. These persons were known throughout history as geniuses for the gifts they left humanity. While a soul might have been advanced intellectually, it might not always have been at the same level with regard to other aspects of human make-up. When honestly examined, these geniuses could have led twisted, dark lives.

By the same token, there were advanced souls, in everyday life, the bagboy at the local supermarket, the old man who kept the newsstand on the corner of our workplace, a woman who had borne many children and seemingly had accomplished nothing else. Advanced states could be observed by the purity with which they regarded their lives as they interacted with others. It was not a matter of humility or a sense of servility that marked the pure spirit. It was the inborn awareness of equality with other living things on earth.

"I was so filled with love for her I did not notice my effect on her."

—*The Diary of Anaïs Nin*, Vol. I

five

It wasn't that he had fallen in love with her. He hoped to latch on to the opportunities she was bound for with her celebrity status. Diego Cañas fancied himself an artist, too, although in an entirely different genre. But like Saúl, her accompanist whom he sensed didn't give a damn about her politics, Diego also wanted the glory and riches of fame—to be recognized for the special talent that he believed he possessed.

In November, he had heard that Pastora was not performing, that in fact, no one had heard anything about her. He shrewdly deduced it to be the time to tap this particular resource of variegated skill, in addition to having a creditable name, and ask her to help him on the gallery he was planning to open.

When he went to Pastora's flat, he was struck with the depression that consumed her. Her brown skin held a yellowish pallor. She ate sparsely and smoked far too much, which was detrimental to her voice. He was touched by Pastora's fallibility, something that had not occurred to him before about her. She had become a wounded tigress, a great bird whose wings had been injured, flight interrupted by the hateful bullet of sport.

Pastora went with Diego to the abandoned factory building where he had leased a floor to convert into the gallery/performance space. It was disastrous. Diego walked about explaining where everything would be, like Don Quixote pointing out the vastness of his region to Sancho Panza. Pastora agreed to help him. Like Sancho Panza, she needed to believe in something, too.

Diego surmised that, with a few decent meals and a binge or two, Pastora would be possessed again by the will she was known for, but by midwinter, he realized she had been punctured through to her soul. When she drank and when she was sober, she wiped her eyes every so often, hardly restraining herself from reflecting on the child she would have had that spring.

He didn't understand this sentiment. He had had women whom he had allegedly impregnated, whom he had accompanied to the clinic, and with whom afterward, he felt all was as before. At times he had resented their pregnancies because he thought it had been done as a ploy to trap him into marriage, or at the very least, into a monogamous relationship. But Pastora's mourning touched him. He remembered each occasion when he had almost become a father. He felt a tug at an absent womb in his lower abdomen and he cried.

In the same building, other artists began to flock in to roost and create. Just below, Perla and two roommates, Jesús Valle and Francisco Godoy y Sandoval, were art students and they, upon meeting Diego, who was somewhat older than they, became influenced by his contagious enthusiasm and supposed confidence. They came up often to lend a hand, or to just sit and dream with him.

One night, Pastora worked late on a proposal for funds for the future gallery. By dusk, Diego had decided to get some wine. He had whipped up chile and refried beans and they devoured it with corn tortillas, heartily and with high spirits.

Later, Godoy strutted in through the secret passage that connected the two floors. They had discovered it recently and although it was easier to come up the freight elevator, the obscurity of the passageway lent itself to Godoy's character. Pastora studied Godoy as he went on about his miserable day and the singeing cold he had endured without the benefit of gloves or boots. He wore his hair like Rasputin. Almost all of his paintings were self-portraits. He was a kind of masochistic narcissist.

They played Godoy's tango records. He had all of Gardel. Godoy preferred to dance alone. In a while, Perla came up, using the freight elevator and entering with the flare of a guest and not someone who lived directly below. She wore a red kimono under her coat, with paint-splotched jeans. She carried a gallon of wine left over from a party the previous weekend. Jesús Valle followed right behind her, but Jesús was innocuous and settled in without anyone noticing.

The two women had met before but had not had the opportunity to socialize. As she talked with Pastora, Perla's voice grew shrill. Her adrenaline had begun to flow and nothing could explain it but the excitement of having met the transfixing Pastora. Perla's eyes, which appeared black beneath the harsh fluorescent lights of the loft, sent out high-volted sparks.

Perla found herself recounting the battle she had been undergoing as the single mother of twin boys, the rejection from her family for not having gotten married to their father, who had mistreated her. All this she confided in the serene woman whose eyes engulfed her with compassion. Pastora hardly said a word, and yet Perla knew that Pastora was with her, understanding the tragedy of her young life.

When Perla had had enough to drink she lost all inhibitions and began to sing. Pastora encouraged her, assuring her that she had a lovely voice. They forgot about the men they had been dancing with, tangoing across the massive, dusty floors. Eventually, with the excitement and the alcohol, Perla had to dash to the bathroom. When she returned Pastora and Diego were out of sight. "Where did they go?" She tried to sound casual. In effect, she felt let down by their sudden disappearance.

Godoy and Jesús sat heavily on the couch with exposed inner springs. Each seemed suddenly sober. They held male secrets. "Upstairs," said Jesús, who was known for saying few words. Perla was not resigned to the end of the evening. She turned to Godoy, who was always game for the lascivious. "Want to go upstairs?"

Godoy lit up. Without hesitation he nodded, smiling broadly. It was Perla, however, who made the first move. She picked up the bottle of wine in which remained a few good swallows and tiptoed up the stairs that once led to the factory's offices. She heard Godoy stalking close behind. "Yoo hoo!" she called out. It was quiet up there. "Hey, you guys!" There was no reply. As Perla reached the landing, she heard a low sobbing and realized it was Pastora. She turned abruptly and faced Godoy. "You know, querido, maybe we ought to leave those two alone . . ." Godoy, who hadn't been close enough to overhear the crying, was obviously let down but didn't protest. Perla wondered at herself. She was disappointed too and she knew it had nothing to do with her curiosity about Diego as a lover, who always made it known to her that he was available.

Perla put an arm around Godoy's shoulder and drew him close. She whispered in a conspiratory tone, "But you know, I wouldn't mind *two* men tonight . . ." Godoy's eyebrow arched. His eyes gleamed. He went over to talk to Jesús. Perla watched from a distance. Jesús rose suddenly and, without turning to look at Perla, he left by way of the freight elevator. Godoy turned around and shrugged his shoulders at her. He shook his head as if he could not begin to account for Jesús's reaction.

19

Godoy and Perla went on exploring their passion—in subway trains, the freight elevator, on the floor of the kiln room at the art school—into late spring, but even those closest to them had not been aware of its boundlessness. Jesús, the third roommate, was the sole witness to their otherwise discreet behavior. Godoy had been intent on possessing Perla. Ever since that night in Diego's loft when Godoy had come and whispered to him to get lost, Jesús had had the impression that Godoy was crazy in love and wanted her all to himself. But now, Jesús did not understand his obsessive friend at all.

This is what weighed most on his mind one evening when he went to see Pastora. He had been hoping she would sit for him for a portrait. He had listened to Diego's stories of Pastora often enough—a gothic blend of the private and public personas—so that he felt compelled to capture the image on canvas even if, as Diego alluded, the woman herself was unattainable. Jesús believed himself to be falling in love with her. He had never been in love before and Diego teased him mercilessly for it. He warned Jesús that he was out of his league. But who could know? Pastora might be receptive to the novelty of such an inexperienced lover.

Jesús had accustomed himself to talking on these sporadic visits, an activity unlike his nature. Pastora listened well. He felt she understood even the most bizarre ideas. He told her on this occasion about his roommates. He was financially dependent on their living arrangement, but he was afraid the trio was on the verge of breaking up.

"You should have seen what happened at school today." He shook his head, his long hair tied back with a string. Pastora watched him intently whenever he spoke. His thick mouth and hooked nose were a transfixing testimony to his ancestry. He was aware of her eyes on him, which made him more timid, so that he looked at his feet as he talked. "Perla made a big scene . . . whew! She was fit to be tied, boy!"

Pastora didn't ask, but he continued with the details. "I guess they're going to end it now . . ."

"You mean Godoy and Perla?" She, like most people, had only guessed that they were lovers.

"Yeah. He said that he doesn't want it that way, but she does."

"Does Perla have someone else?"

"No. It was Godoy. He's been sleeping with one of the other students at school. She's Jewish with lots of money. He thought he could have them both . . . but Perla said nothing doing. She got Godoy and his girlfriend together in the cafeteria and really let them have it! There was a crowd and everything . . . !"

Pastora closed herself to the gossip, feeling Perla's humiliation and the rude disregard for her pain by this man who had come to transform it to community information. She got up and went to light a cigarette.

Jesús watched her lithe movement from the corner of his eyes. "You'd better go, Chuy," she told him firmly. And although Jesús didn't understand the sudden banishment from her apartment—could not have begun to understand the vulnerability of a woman like Perla, whose desire was like an unhealable wound open to the world—he left without another word.

Not long after, Perla called. As always, her voice was light and tinkled like glass ornaments. The words clinked together and were bright as Christmas lights. Pastora heard distinctly, however, only part of Perla's narrative, which began with, "There's just no code of honor among women!"

Pastora invited Perla over and let her into her life.

six

Pastora propped a knee up on which to balance her guitar. She waited for Saúl and Perla, who were coming to practice. Perla, a soprano, and Saúl, low as a swordfish beneath the ocean. She hoped the harmonious combination would have appeal to a new, however small, following. Saúl accompanied her on vocals and strings. An immigrant without papers, he had the tacit hope that fame and fortune awaited him in the U.S. He had heard Pastora's album and was flattered when she had approached him to accompany her. She was all business when they rehearsed and he was sure that that kind of dedication would bring its rewards.

Pastora struck a few chords as she tuned up, trying to remember the melody that had come to her that morning. It was melancholy and appropriate for the approach of fall. She allowed herself this sentiment when alone. Her repertory was of protest music, never a frivolous song of love and its follies. She hummed softly to herself as she waited.

She was disturbed by Saúl, whom she suspected was succumbing to that irrepressible urge of men of her culture to feel compelled to come on to women. They believed once getting to women's emotions, they could string them along like marionettes. Cast to a salted wind were the promises that *together* they would seek their fortune. Cynical at twenty-five, aren't you? Or perhaps as idealistic as you were at fifteen? She muttered to herself without considering an answer.

She was glad for Perla, who reduced the tension during rehearsals. Perla, whose skin was as flawless as the gem for which she was named. Perla of countless talents, all of which she was aware and ready to exploit. Pastora enjoyed Perla's comradery, the empathy of those born of the same sex. She already sensed that the notion of performing was only that to Perla, a notion, and that soon she would become bored. She would go on and try her clever hand at something else, challenge the fortuitous star under which she came into the world.

Pastora glanced at the clock at the far end of the studio apartment and saw it was a quarter of an hour before either was due. She put the guitar aside and got up to go to the bathroom.

She changed sanitary napkins. Although it was barely a trickle, she continued to bleed the final vestiges of the fetus she had eliminated. Her face was sallow. The abortion, the alcohol and lack of sleep, not enough nourishment, a steady and continuous direction toward self-destruction. It had to stop. She could not pretend to care about the salvation of humanity and care nothing about herself.

If she could cry. If she could cry as she had done so easily before. Then nothing. Dry as a gourd.

On Saturday the trio was as ready to perform before the gentility of Chicago's Latin American community. Pastora Velásquez Aké had been invited by it to give a concert at the Blackstone Theatre. She was to follow a woman castanetist.

They watched the castanetist from the wings, who wore a black dress, arms waving to the accompaniment of a pianist. She had a practiced smile and twirled her skirt like ribbons of crêpe paper. She had travelled around the world. A truly famous woman. Strange, Pastora thought, one becoming famous and earning one's living because of a cultural appreciation for the sound of clattering teeth in the winter cold.

Pastora and Perla wore white. Perla, with her fiery eyes and wild hair tamed into a chignon, had on a Victorian-styled dress. She was reminiscent of a Spanish maiden. Pastora had donned a hand-woven Huichol costume, while Saúl's Indian head stuck out beaming in a black tuxedo.

The performance went remarkably smoothly and afterward, as with the castanetist, Pastora was called back and presented with a bouquet of roses. She returned her gratitude spontaneously with a kiss in the air and immediately felt self-conscious about the prima donnesque gesture.

At the reception, the castanetist waited for her adoring public that had brought her to that cold American city, but the crowd encircled the trio. Some had brought with them copies of Pastora's album for her to autograph and the local Spanish papers' reporters pushed through to interview them. Pastora was occupied with the polite introductions to the consuls and such, while Saúl and Perla spoke with the reporters.

The consul of Spain was brought before her. He took Pastora's hand and kissed it. "The honorable consul," said the man who was in charge of the protocol, "has declared the Señorita Pastora Velásquez, the next María Félix." Pastora smiled, uncomfortably aware that the consul's wife hadn't come to meet her, but coolly kept her distance. María Félix had in her day been throughout Mexico and Latin America to her public what Elizabeth Taylor in hers had been to the Anglo population. Pastora kept a polite expression, hiding her disappointment. The honorable consul and his entourage had missed the point of the concert. She wasn't seeking stardom, a contract with a movie company. She had hoped they had come to hear her message.

In the back of the room her escort for the evening sat sipping a drink with an expression of irritation with the whole affair. Like the consul, like Saúl, he wanted something from Pastora that wasn't satisfied by sex. As a scholar, he pretended to be fully supportive of her efforts in the Latino movement, but it was the woman that remained reticent who disturbed him. He had consented to come only to demonstrate how unimpressed he was by her popularity. Pastora understood this and chose to ignore it.

She continued to smile and to sign albums and answer questions, but burdened by the pretentious atmosphere, she wished that she were somewhere other than there, despite the smug expressions on Saúl's and Perla's faces that said this was what they had wished for. The paradox of being an artist, especially a performer, was that the private side of her, so introspective, battled against her public's demands.

Máximo Madrigal, in a fresh suit, stood like a newly erected statue watching with an air of objectivity from across the room. He had come upon the invitation of his friend, Jacobo, an aspiring actor and someone who managed invitations to such events with the purpose of advancing his yet-to-bud career. Máximo had thought the castanetist to be mediocre and a bore. She was a fairly unattractive woman on the decline toward being a pretentious hag.

I was brutally judgmental of those who had reached the peak of success while I continued to hobble like a seven-legged spider.

I had never heard of the other group, although I knew they were

24

simply local talent with as much ambition as I, but at the moment I couldn't help feeling envious of their attention. The two women were equally lovely, although in opposite ways, but the male was a baboon in a monkey suit. I remained, hands clasped behind my back, cool and indifferent, planning my strategy. Comandante Madrigal. I leaned over to Jacobo and whispered, "What do you know of those two women?"

"They're both conceited as the devil. You can't get anywhere with them, believe me, my friend. I've known plenty of men who've tried. I think they're lesbians," Jacobo replied generously. It seemed to me, however, that there were women who were puzzles to Jacobo and this complexity was too much for my poor friend, who thought life was as two-dimensional as a script.

It was incredible to me that I could not persuade one or both with my unfailing charisma. If I was to get anywhere with any one of those pinhead guests that evening, it was going to be through those two women. In analyzing the situation further, I studied the attributes of each one to make a motivating choice. Pastora Aké was tall and slender, with a terrific aloofness. Apparently, she despised her public as much as I was despising it. But our reasons were different, of course. Had they come to see me, this would have been another tale altogether. I would not have to be here telling you now with great reluctance how in the next minutes Pastora yanked off my testicles, figuratively speaking.

The other woman, with skin like café con leche, was gaiety and celebration, but less provocative. In any case, Pastora, who was the leader of the group and the center attraction, was the one to approach.

I went to the table where wine and appetizers were being served and asked for two glasses. I took deliberate steps and methodically broke my way through the crowd. I was about one meter from Pastora when suddenly I caught her eye. I went cold.

Was it possible to castrate a man with a glance? She had looked up at me and at once chewed my existence and spit me out. I shuddered. I knew she had noticed I stood out from the crowd of garish idiots and she had spitefully chosen to reject me.

I handed the glass meant for her to the woman closest to me instead. I made acquaintances with this woman, who up until that instant I had not noticed. I hoped that that Pastora woman would see how mistaken she was, how vain to think that I was among her nameless admirers. That night I went home with the woman whom I had given the wine to at the reception. I don't even remember her name, but I thought it was the least I could do since she had inadvertently saved me from the jaws of a bloodthirsty female vampire.

A month passed and October had transformed the humid city I had arrived at into a nostalgic heartbeat and cradled the hopeless romantics like me. I was out one Saturday evening with a woman I had recently met. Later, I would go home to entertain two women Jacobo and I had invited over, a pair of cooperative ladies whom we had found to be fairly entertaining themselves on a previous night. It was past ten when I called my friend to tell him to make my apologies if the women arrived on time, but I was trying to get away from my date with a certain amount of gracious discretion.

Jacobo was breathless when he answered the phone. "What's the matter with you, man? Have you been out running or something?" I secretly wondered if the women had arrived and Jacobo had started the party without me.

"I've been dancing, sambaing . . . ! When are you coming?"

"Are they there already?" I inquired in Spanish. We almost always spoke in Spanish, a convenience language for conspiratorial behavior, especially around gringas.

"No . . . ! You'll never guess who's here! They came with Mauricio, who's here in town, but Mauricio left with his woman to get more beer. . . well, actually wine, because you see, they don't drink beer, only wine . . ." Mauricio was a friend of Jacobo from Texas. He was passing through Chicago and we had been expecting him to stop by to see us.

"Mauricio from Brownsville doesn't drink beer?" I was really confused and growing irritated with the fact that I was missing something perceived to be substantially gratifying.

"No! Of course Mauricio drinks beer. What's the matter with you, man? It's Pastora Aké and her friend Perla who drink only wine! They've been here all evening, talking about the theatre, this, that, and drinking like we were old friends. We just put on samba music and I'm dancing with both of them . . . *both* of them, man! When are you coming home?"

"As soon as I can." I hung up.

By the time I arrived at the flat, the women we had expected were waiting, like pigeons nesting on the couch. Perla and Pastora were on their way out. Pastora wore a long poncho of earth colors. Her hair was disheveled. She was flushed and when she brushed past me, I was aroused at the thought of her having been dancing and drinking uninhibitedly with her friend and Jacobo in what might have been a prelude to a wondrous night. Yet, I no sooner caught her look when I was reminded of her arrogance. It was more than I could stand.

I tried nevertheless without luck to persuade them to stay.

seven

Máximo lived in Barcelona for three months before he decided to look for his father. It wasn't an original idea. It came to him one night when he was watching a film on television. Except for one scene, which without any obvious explanation made him suddenly sentimental, the whole thing had been a waste of two hours of his life. As it turned out, that sappy piece of entertainment was the top that sent him spinning into one situation, then the next that in the end became his destiny.

The dawn that he walked off into the sunrise, as it were, while his grandmother like the guardian angel over one's shoulder watched as the sole witness to his departure, he decided rather quickly that the ranch and even the nearby village of San Co were not enough to hold a young man of his curiosity and enthusiasm. Among vegetables and poultry, Máximo made his way down highways until he reached Puerto Sapogonia, the capital.

Shortly thereafter, he enrolled at the university. Although not certain as to what in particular he wanted to study, classes in philosophy and literature sustained his interest for two years. His grandfather approved. At least his grandson showed interest in learning, and he sent on a regular sum to maintain Máximo's expenses.

During his second year at the university, Máximo became involved with the university periodical. The motivation came mostly from his friend El Tinto, who was managing editor, and El Tinto's brother, Horacio, a medical student and the editor-in-chief.

Horacio was his young brother's and Máximo's idol. He excelled in his studies, as well as being a star soccer player. Of course he was well-built and had a smile that melted women at his feet. To add to this, Horacio's charisma was based on an innate sincerity and no one was able to dislike him.

Whatever it was that Horacio set his mind to do, he did well. Whatever he started had a logical purpose and had to be finished.

Máximo and El Tinto followed him around like two sheep faithful to their shepherd. Max had no genuine interest in journalism to be sure, but being caught up in the drive that the two brothers displayed for their work, he went along, as the Spanish saying goes, siguiendo la corriente.

The last few months before Horacio disappeared, Máximo, despite his apathy toward the political ambience in his country, became aware that drastic changes were taking place at the university. Several faculty members were fired without sound reason. Courses once given as a matter of fact in the philosophy department were abruptly stopped. Now and then, visible government agents roving about the campus stopped to question students at random. Horacio was advised to stick to reporting cultural and sports events in the paper. There was no reason for witty editorials, much less direct comments on what did not concern the university students.

Horacio did not stop his editorials. He had known students dedicated to their studies who had been intimidated into not going to school any longer. He had had stories cut out of his paper without his authorization or awareness, but brought that way back from the printer. One evening after a date, he was beaten by three young men pretending it was a case of robbery, but who hadn't bothered to take the wallet. To the rational Horacio, he was engaged in a war of intrigue and disconnected ends against a faceless enemy.

Then it happened that Horacio had been inexplicably gone for days. It wasn't like him to go off for more than a night without saying anything to his brother. The second night of his absence, El Tinto began to ask around. He called Horacio's girlfriends, he went to his favorite hangouts. After the third night, he and Máximo did not say it, but they already knew. And without knowing exactly why at the time, either, they did not think to go to the police for help.

It was late when El Tinto came to the room upstairs from Max's godfather's funeral parlor. Max stayed there in exchange for helping to keep the place tidy. As he noticed business increasing at an astonishing rate lately, he began to tire of the arrangement and contemplated whether he should write a letter to his grandfather and ask for an increase in his monthly stipend so that he could rent a place outright.

El Tinto's forehead glistened, although it was a cool night. He had obviously been running from something or someone; fear labored in his black pupils. Just the sight of him frightened Máximo.

He knew his friend came to bring a horrid truth about Horacio. "They've killed my brother . . ."

"You're crazy, man! Who? Who would do such a thing?"

El Tinto, who leaned against the door as if to prevent some abrupt intrusion by a nameless pursuer, slid down slowly until he was seated on the floor. His head tilted, and with no warning he began to sob. Máximo felt his own eyes burn. Horacio was dead. They had known it from the first night of his disappearance. The beating a few weeks earlier had been the warning.

"How do you know?"

"I know, believe me. I know." El Tinto answered between sobs. He looked at Max directly, like a small child who awaits a response, a word of consolation from the wise parent. What could Máximo say? His heart pounded. It was all true then? All those things that Horacio had told them to the effect that the country was headed for civil war and that countless people were going to die whether they wanted to be part of it or not? Máximo banged his fist against the wall. "Fuck! It can't be! How do you know, Tinto? Did you see the body?"

El Tinto only buried his face in his knees and encircled his head with his arms. He was on the verge of hysteria. Max left him alone. He went to sit on the bed and waited until El Tinto got a grip on himself. Máximo asked again in a hushed voice, "Tinto, man, did you see proof?"

El Tinto lifted his eyes toward his friend. They were sullen but bright as marbles. Mucus ran down his nose. "Do you want proof? Here! Here is the proof they gave me that my brother is dead! Here!" He reached into his jacket and threw something toward Max that landed on the bed. It was grotesque and at first unrecognizable, and Max picked it up to examine it. He dropped it and, leaning over the edge of the bed, he heaved until he vomited.

Horacio's finger with the initialed university ring still intact rested on the bed in the room upstairs from the funeral parlor that would never lay out his body because no body was ever to be found.

Máximo helped his friend make arrangements to leave the country. They agreed that as Horacio's brother and an editor of the university paper, it would be dangerous to continue on in Puerto Sapogonia, but probably no less dangerous if he returned to his hometown. It was only a question of money to obtain false documents, as El Tinto did not feel secure in requesting a passport under his own name. A few nights before El Tinto was to leave, the two men got drunk in the long tradition of parting friends.

"Listen, why don't you come along?" El Tinto suggested. "You've never been to Europe! Paris awaits two assholes like us to just go there and get ahold of her titties! Think of the French girls!"

Máximo *had* thought of the French girls, and although it had already occurred to him to go, this was the first moment he actually considered it as a real possibility.

"Don't worry. We have a place to stay when we get there. We defend ourselves in French. We'll manage. Come on! What do you say, compadre?"

"And what about my passport? It'll take weeks to get it and all those questions they ask you. They could easily make a connection and discover we're going together." Máximo had made an obvious point. His friend was drunk, but not without common sense. El Tinto reached into his pocket and dropped a bulky envelope in front of Máximo.

Max picked it up. There was a full set of documents inside. They belonged to a university student. "Who is this guy?"

"'Who *was* he?' you should ask." El Tinto corrected him solemnly, taking a swig from the bottle. "A relative of his passed that on to me. No one has seen him for a while. This was delivered to the family by the post office carrier. No explanation," El Tinto said with a grunt. He went on to hypothesize. "The assumption is the poor asshole was mugged in some dark street, perhaps left to die. Some good samaritan finds these documents just lying around in the gutter and delivers them to the post office or drops them in the mailbox to be returned to their owner, but the owner is never coming home.

"The police know nothing. The family gets the message, or is supposed to get the message, but they go on hoping . . . Maybe he's eloped with Elena or Martita and they don't want to say anything because she's pregnant. Maybe he's hiding out from some guy he owes money to, or maybe he got it into his youthful inconsiderate spirit to just go off and have an adventure. Not everyone is as lucky to receive a finger to end the cruelty of hope."

Max put up his hands. He couldn't bear to remember the mutilated finger of his friend. "Fine, fine. I'll go with you, but not because I really believe things are as bad as you say. Sure, a couple of guys playing with dirty politics are getting into trouble, but it's all right if you keep your nose clean. I'm not involved in anything to make me afraid of going about my business . . ."

El Tinto looked disgusted. "You're an asshole and an idiot, but I'll let you come with me anyway." He slapped Max on the head and took another drink.

When it came time to travel, Máximo and El Tinto both let their beards grow so that it would be less noticeable to the casual eye that neither looked like the photograph on his passport. Although Max found El Tinto's precautionary measures an exaggeration undoubtedly borne of paranoiac tendencies and the trauma of having lost his brother, he also went along with his wish to take separate seating on the plane and not let on that they were travelling together.

At the airport Máximo spotted a pretty woman, who turned out to be from Belgium returning from her vacation on the beaches of Puerto Sapogonia. With his stilted use of French, he passed the authorities with her seemingly as his companion. He looked around for El Tinto and saw that he had as well latched onto company, not to a woman, but to an entire family—parents, grandparents, children. El Tinto was carrying a small child as he handed the customs agent the passport.

It was the middle of the school year when the youths dropped out to leave their country, one out of a courage that was presently disguised as fear, and the other because the unknown and unventured were inherently more attractive than the boredom in what was already secured.

They both wore jackets, but as Puerto Sapogonia was by northern standards not cold at all, the jackets had no lining. It took no time for the two to deduce after landing in Paris that there was a deadly chill like nothing that either had ever known, threatening to pull at their very lungs. They searched through their bags for sweaters and shirts, and in the men's room layered their bodies until they felt they could make their way out into the bitter rain that made Paris a dreary land of greydom.

El Tinto had an address on Rue Daguerre where he was told he would find a place to stay with a compatriot in self-exile. He had never met Alberto de la Torre, but he was told in the strictest confidence that de la Torre could be trusted and counted on.

They found their way to Rue Daguerre and coming upon the market, lingered a while to make a few purchases. They were hungry and ragged with need of a good rest. They were on their way to find the address when El Tinto was abruptly pulled back by a grip that came from behind. A couple of policemen were eyeing him up and down and told El Tinto they wanted identification. Before he was able to reach into his jacket, they yanked him toward a courtyard. Max, hesitating at first, caught up with them. El Tinto had been pushed against the wall.

He produced his identification and the police counted his money as well. Almost all of it was still in Sapogón currency. "This doesn't look like you," one of them said to El Tinto, examining the passport picture. "With that beard, it's hard to tell," the other remarked. El Tinto said nothing.

They asked several questions. Why was he travelling with so much cash? What had he come to do in France? Was he a native of Sapogonia or naturalized? From what country had his parents originated? They hardly glanced at Max, who remained outside the portal until they left.

"Well, just look at us," Máximo said with a nervous laugh, "We look like a couple of derelicts—these beards, and not even dressed decently . . ."

"They didn't stop us because we look poor," El Tinto gave Max a cynical glare. "In fact, they didn't harrass *us* at all. They harrassed me, only me."

"Now don't jump to any conclusions." Max gestured to stop his friend from continuing the thought, but El Tinto went on. "Why do you think they wanted to know if I was born in America and from where my parents came when they immigrated there? Why the hell should they care what my ancestors were? My people don't live in this country!"

Máximo wasn't prepared to answer the question, but he sized up his friend. El Tinto with Lebanese blood, dark as a field worker. Horacio had not been as dark as El Tinto, although both had been equally handsome. It was Horacio alone, however, who had been encouraged toward success, given the confidence by mother, teachers, women, to try anything. He had never been told he might fail. El Tinto, on the other hand, had been the problem child, the brunt of all his father's frustrations; he'd gone out into the world aware that he was not in the favor of those who counted.

They found the address only a block away from the market of fresh seafood, poultry, rabbits, cheeses, and bread shops. They picked up a loaf of bread and a bottle of wine to present to their new hosts. The address did not indicate the apartment number, but after much going in and out of doors in the courtyard, they finally found the Spanish name on the mailbox of a clean and quiet building. The wooden stairs were polished and the iron railings dusted. The door of the concierge was slightly ajar and closed without a sound as the two men went up to the fifth floor. After the encounter with the police, they now had a sense of being constantly vigilized by bodiless eyes.

They rang the bell a long time, afraid to face the possibility that no one was home to receive them, before a woman opened the door. She appeared to have been sleeping, although it was afternoon. Máximo and El Tinto introduced themselves and asked for Alberto de la Torre.

The woman told them Alberto wasn't there. El Tinto, in his broken French, explained that they had just come from Sapogonia and had been told that they could stay there, just for a few days, until they found something permanent. Wrapping her kimono tightly around her waist, the woman stepped back and invited them in.

They were in a small, crowded apartment, and from that vantage point one had visual access to the rest of the apartment: two bedrooms; the bath; and this room, a kitchen buried beneath books, plants, empty wine bottles, plates of hard crusts of bread and cheese. Letters.

"Are you hungry?" she asked in Spanish that was less discernible than El Tinto's French. They nodded and handed over the bread and wine. She thanked them and set about clearing the table and putting out glasses and bowls.

"What's your name, Madame?" El Tinto asked. He almost sounded timid in his earnest attempt to make a decent impression. She smiled. She was a woman of about mid-forties, but to Max, who was scarcely twenty, she was practically an antiquity. Her hair, a kind of auburn, was hennaed, and she was small, although one couldn't see what shape she was in underneath the kimono. "Sophie," she answered. She wanted to smile, but instead began a cough that kept up for several minutes.

She poured a mushroom soup that had been simmering on the stove and opened the wine. They ate and made light conversation during the meal. It was awkward as all three wondered about much more than anyone felt comfortable expressing. Finally, El Tinto inquired directly about Alberto. "Is he coming back soon?"

34

Sophie looked into El Tinto's eyes as she spoke. "I don't know. My idea is that he went back to his country." Max and El Tinto exchanged glances. El Tinto asked Sophie, "You're not sure? Why would he go back if it's dangerous for him?"

"I suppose he was worried about his family. It was important for him to do so. If he had told me, he knew I would have been upset. So he has gone off without telling me and I worry anyway. . ." She halted, not because her Spanish did not flow, but because the pain of her thoughts made it difficult. "When I saw you two at the door, I thought you had news."

The two friends sat feeling impotent. Max wondered if Sophie was not being unrealistic. It was possible that this Alberto de la Torre fellow had had a wife and children in Sapogonia and it had only been a matter of time before the idyllic affair with Sophie would end. He looked around. It was as good a place as any to have an idyllic affair. This Sophie was probably more upset by the fact that at her age she didn't have much time to wait around. "He'll probably be back soon," Máximo heard himself say without knowing why. El Tinto shot him a look.

"Madame, have hope," El Tinto told her, putting out a hand and covering hers that held the stem of a wine glass as if it were a raft. They exchanged a halfhearted smile. They were still at the table finishing their meal when the door opened and an adolescent girl came in. She was a much younger version of Sophie. Sophie introduced her daughter, Catherine, and told her to arrange the bedding so that the men could take one of the bedrooms. With the appearance of Catherine, Máximo felt his spirits uplifted. Sophie had been getting him down. She seemed so depressed and she had that terrible cough; he felt irritated by her. It was possible that he was simply fatigued from the journey. Now with Catherine moving about in those birdlike ways of young females, he had something to distract his attention.

The women, mother and daughter, set out to make their guests comfortable. They were polite rather than friendly and when left alone, Máximo and El Tinto slept deeply before being alert enough to decide on their first steps toward establishing their new lives in Paris. Without de la Torre, they knew they couldn't, or perhaps shouldn't, go on in the apartment. De la Torre, whom Max gathered to be a rebel of some sort, could show up unexpectedly and suspect something was going on behind his back. Or perhaps the landlady might object, or Sophie, heaven forbid, might get ideas, or the young girl . . . well, Max thought, that last possibility was the only realistic temptation.

Just before dawn, Max was awoken by the harsh sounds of Sophie's cough in the next room. He got up and in the dark found the bathroom. When he came out, he peeked into the bedroom where the women slept. Catherine was curled in a ball and her mother had wrapped herself around the girl. Sophie continued to cough.

Max and Tinto stayed on a few days with Sophie and her daughter when Sophie told them that the old woman who lived upstairs with her two terriers had a spare room to let. She was an invalid and needed someone to take out the dogs and to run errands for her as well. Sophie assured her that Max and Tinto were of trustworthy character and after a brief interview, they moved in with the old woman.

Max and Tinto investigated the possibilities of their surviving in Paris. Because they travelled with false documents, they could not apply at the university. It seemed that for the moment, their most practical objective was employment, which being unskilled and non-degreed, was extremely limited. Tinto suggested they work at the market as vendors. He did the necessary research, obtained a permit, and a week later Tinto and Max were selling vegetables on Rue Mouffetard.

They started quite early in the morning and were done by afternoon. Max didn't know where Tinto went off to most of the time. He was aware that his friend was ridden with his brother's death and that there was a good chance he was driven by a need for vengeance. How he would do this, Max didn't care to find out. There were others from Sapogonia in self-exile, who met each other, whose eyes made contact in the métro, who by chance spoke up at the market to confirm that they were of the same origin and not from Algiers or Argentina, but the language and the specific usage of it was Sapogón, American.

Unlike with Tinto, Max was never mistaken for North African, but always for European; if not Spanish, then Greek or Italian. Sometimes someone inquired discreetly if he did not have Semitic blood, the hook in the nose, the dark hair and beard. His French improved and in a matter of months no one asked about his origin at all. He had bought a wool coat and scarves, which he wound around his neck to further authenticate his European demeanor.

36

He met young women whom he always told one story or another—he was on vacation, or applying to law school. He spent his evenings in cafés and movie houses or in the boudoir of many a mademoiselle.

Max almost never saw Sophie or her daughter Catherine, although they continued to live in the same building. Once he met up with Catherine in the stairwell. She was coming in just as he was going out. Her face was flushed, perhaps from hurrying through the evening streets. Her hair was like smoke; soft rings floated about her oval face. He had a desire to kiss her, full on the mouth, but he suspected she was so inexperienced, she would panic and he let the idea pass.

It was spring in Paris and Max had become restless and tired of the demanding routine of their work. He had written to his grandfather several times and finally had received money, along with a letter of reprimand for his delinquent behavior for dropping out of school in Sapogonia. Max wanted to tell Tinto that the market partnership was going to cease. He no longer wished to rise at four a.m., to spend the day measuring les champignons by the kilo and making change for dowdy housewives. Perhaps El Tinto would come up with a more appealing plan to make a living.

One night when Max came home, he decided to wait up for his friend to discuss this. It was close to midnight. El Tinto had yet to show up and Max had lost his desire to sleep. He went out for cigarettes and as he returned, passing the door, he thought to put his ear next to it, wondering if Sophie and Catherine were up. He was expended by the loneliness of the homesick.

There were voices and he was certain one of them was El Tinto's. He knocked softly. Then he rang the bell, anxious to be let in, to be with friends. El Tinto answered the door. He was half dressed, or half undressed, depending on how one wanted to interpret the circumstance. Sophie was out of sight, as was her daughter. The first thought that crossed Max's mind was that El Tinto was screwing Catherine and he felt his ears burn with jealous anger.

He had been deliberate in not offending Tinto by making a move toward little Catherine, not to insult the friend of a friend— de la Torre, whom neither had met, but who was inadvertently responsible for their having a place to stay since their first night in Paris.

El Tinto didn't appear to be embarrassed or ashamed by Máximo's sudden appearance. He greeted his friend with a smile and moved aside to allow Max to enter. "Bonsoir, amigo," he told Max. "What brings you here at this hour? You were looking for me?"

"Well, I wasn't looking for *her*, if that's what you mean!" Max snapped with clenched teeth. El Tinto gave him a puzzled look. Catherine's door was shut, as was Sophie's. All appeared quiet in both rooms. "What does her mother have to say about this?" Max lit a cigarette and blew out the smoke, as if the smoke itself offended him.

"Her mother?" El Tinto repeated. He scratched his head and went over to the stove to put on the kettle for tea. "I don't know her mother, much less what she would think of me, but I am sure Sophie is of the age to make her own decisions." Max winced. It was impossible to him that it was not Catherine whom El Tinto was sleeping with, but Sophie—! She had just seemed much too mature for men their age. This bothered him even more than the fact that she supposedly belonged to another man, a man El Tinto professed to be a compañero, without a face to refer to in memory perhaps, but certainly by name.

"How could you, Tinto? Are you crazy? She could be your mother!" Max whispered in a gruff voice. He kept his cigarette locked between his lips. It dangled as he talked and the smoke caused him to squint. El Tinto prepared a cup of tea and without addressing Max's reproach, took it into Sophie's room. In a minute he came back out.

"If you like, we can go upstairs to talk . . ." he whispered to Max. El Tinto did not look insulted by Max's last remark, but he was solemn. Max was so upset by his discovery he couldn't see his friend was hurt. "Never mind. Finish your business here . . ." Max told him brusquely and went for the door. El Tinto put a hand out to stop him.

"Wait a minute, Máximo. At first you thought I was sleeping with Catherine, didn't you?" Max put his head down in acknowledgment. Tinto went on. "Why was that your first presumption? Because you couldn't conceive of an attraction to Sophie, but you could with the girl. Isn't that right?" Max didn't answer, but kept his hand on the doorknob, ready to leave at any moment.

El Tinto was so close to his ear as he talked, keeping his voice down but firm, that Max could feel his breath. El Tinto was a passionate man who had been taken out of the bed of the woman he was making love to only to be reproached for the fact; consequently, he diverted his passion to the object of intrusion.

"The problem with you, Max, is that when you see a young girl who is beautiful, because it is not enough to be young, you get an erection.

"You are here in Paris fucking every girl you can get your hands on and not giving a damn about what we left behind—not giving a damn about Horacio's memory." Tears welled in Tinto's eyes. He was deep crimson. Max felt him controlling a tremble that went over his body like an electric current.

"You admired Horacio because he was all that society tells us makes a hero. You want to believe you could be like him if you associated with him long enough.

"And what does all this have to do with your sleeping with that woman?"

"That you don't understand about loyalty, you don't understand the love that grows out of conviction. In the sixties Sophie was a student at the Sorbonne, she rallied, she protested. She didn't care if her father disowned her or cut off her allowance . . . She has worked with Alberto de la Torre to get people out of Sapogonia safely . . ."

"So she is an idealist, like you, like Horacio was. Where does it get you all? Where is this Alberto de la Torre now?"

"In all probability de la Torre is dead, like my brother," El Tinto answered him.

"And what are you doing—following the holy law and taking your brother's widow for your wife?"

"What is your problem, Max? What do you have against Sophie?" Tinto was exasperated.

"That hacking, the bloated face . . ." Max turned away. All the while, Sophie had been coughing furiously behind the closed door of her room. El Tinto waited for Max to finish. Without looking at Tinto, Max said, "It disgusts me."

El Tinto stared at Max for an eternal minute. Max was ready for a sudden swing. He could feel his friend's rage and he knew he should not have insulted him about the woman he was having an affair with, but he couldn't accept Tinto with such a woman, who in addition to her age, looked unkempt. It hurt Max's vanity by association.

"Max, get out of here before I throw you out. I don't just mean from this apartment. Get out of this house. I don't want to see your face again . . ." Tinto didn't hit Max because of his sentiment for the friendship they had shared. He regarded Max as a kind of brother, though not like Horacio. Horacio was so extraordinary, anyone could have loved him as a brother—even his assassins must have had to shut their eyes in order to kill him—but Max was like that brother one didn't ask for but got anyway, and like it or not, one couldn't help but feel responsible for him, and a compulsion to protect. Despite himself, Max needed someone to guide him.

Máximo left. He went upstairs to sleep. In the morning he made the old lady's espresso, took out the dogs, came back to pack his bag and left to find a new place. He wanted to regret what he had said to his friend, but he couldn't see El Tinto making a life with Sophie. He fantasized all kinds of consequences as a result of it. Sophie and Tinto marrying, Tinto regarding himself as Catherine's stepfather. The partnership, the carefree tone to their adventures would be over.

He found a cheap hotel also on the left bank and spent the next months doing little with his life that in retrospect he could account for. He drank considerably, having acquired a weakness for cognac. He tried his hand at writing, but was impatient, stared at the blank pages of a notebook and put it aside to go out for a drink or a rendezvous with a girlfriend.

He thought of returning to Sapogonia, to the university. After all, he had had no real reason to leave, but he was not motivated. He missed his friend. He wondered what would become of El Tinto, as he continued to delve into the politics of their homeland even from across the ocean in Paris. He left messages with Sophie on the telephone, and later, when it was always Catherine who answered, he asked her, too, to have Tinto contact him. El Tinto never responded.

One afternoon, Máximo wandered to the market on Rue Daguerre. He told himself he missed the familiarity of the street he had first come to know in Paris. He bought bread and cheese. In a pastry shop he selected strawberry tarts. He took them to the building where he had lived with El Tinto. He was going to take a sweet to the old lady who had rented him a room, he told himself. He would see how she was; perhaps she had missed him. He hesitated as he passed Sophie's door, but he continued on without knocking. At the old lady's door, he had no luck. There was no answer, not even a yap out of one of the terriers. He assumed she was gone, probably dead. She had been so pathetic. It was for the best.

On the way down, when he reached Sophie's door, he put his ear to it and listened. There were movements inside, an indication that someone was home. Sophie? El Tinto? They were the mouse sounds of one person shuffling back and forth to the bathroom, to the stove for tea. He looked down at his package, the bread, cheese, the tarts. They had really been meant for El Tinto and Sophie. An offering on behalf of one who had learned to mind his own business. His friendship with El Tinto meant more than a protest as to one or the other's choice of a lover. He rang the bell and a second later, the door opened.

He was taken aback by the pallor in the face of the girl who was once rose-cheeked and who had exuded good health. She looked drawn, troubled. Catherine smiled halfheartedly and opened the door to let Max in.

"Ça va?" he asked. He felt nervous about the possible confrontation with Tinto, but there didn't appear to be anyone else around. Catherine returned to the table, where she was having a bowl of café crème and crackers. She indicated with a gesture of the chin for Máximo to take the seat across from her. He looked around. There was something odd about the place. A sullenness devoured it. The plants looked less spirited. The windows were dingier. Dishes were stacked up in the sink. Most of all, Catherine was different.

She had been almost jumpy around Máximo, the signs of an infatuated girl. She giggled too often, moved away awkwardly whenever he came near. Now, she was indifferent. She took small bites from the crackers, occasionally dipping them into the bowl, and made no attempt to communicate.

"Where is El Tinto? Working?" Max inquired. He was inclined to whisper, although he didn't know why. Catherine shook her head. The skin beneath her eyes was dark and sunken. "Are you all right?" he couldn't help asking. She nodded without interest. "I'm only a little tired . . . I didn't sleep last night."

"Why?" Max grabbed on to the first effort she had made thus far to talk with him. "My mother is very ill. She's in the hospital. Tinto and I are taking turns sitting with her. He's with her now. He insisted that I come home to rest, but I can't sleep."

The news of Sophie's condition didn't surprise Máximo. Her body had been ravaged by a disease that wasn't going to let up until it conquered her last breath. He didn't feel anything for her—perhaps some pity—but he was concerned for his friend. El Tinto was probably going through a terrible time. His nature would make him feel guilt for her illness. Catherine, too, was suffering.

Max remembered the strawberry tarts and took them out of their dainty box. Catherine managed a smile and for a few seconds her eyes lit up. Max saw the radiance of her good looks; she was a girl of fifteen again. "Will you have one, too?" she asked timidly, reluctant to be the first to reach for the delicacies, unconscious of the fact that a moment before she had been so unhappy.

They ate the tarts. Max found an opened bottle of wine in the cupboard and poured a glass for each. She took his friendly gestures with a kind of feminine gratitude, offering lingering looks, a coy smile. When he placed his hand on hers, she placed her other hand over his.

"My mother is dying," she said. Max nodded. She took his hand and placed it under her blouse, against her heart. "I'm going to be alone . . ." The voice was that of a child, Sophie's child, a last wish for the immortality of the mother, a bridge now forming from mother to lover.

Max lifted her in his arms and carried her to the bedroom, where he placed her tenderly on her narrow bed. He kissed her lightly on every bare part of her body and only when she returned his kisses did he disrobe her and then himself.

I felt nostalgia for the virgin after penetration. Why couldn't I love her and let her remain whole, as she had been loved by the mother? Why in the process of loving the woman, did the man have to nullify something so profound that it was no longer physical? Catherine had longed for her mother's arms, her mother's breast to suckle as she made love to me. She accepted the trespassing of her body only as a logistical necessity to feel connected to another human being.

We dozed off. When we awoke it was dusk. I went with her to the hospital. Catherine asked me to wait outside the door of Sophie's room. Shortly, El Tinto came out. I could tell from the expression on his face when he saw me that Catherine had obviously not told him I was there. I offered him a cigarette, but he had his own. We said nothing for a while.

"Had you always known she was dying?" I broke the silence at last.

"Perhaps I did. I'm not sure." El Tinto was feeling philosophical, as usual. He turned to me, putting out his cigarette on the floor. "Why?"

"I wondered if you had felt sorry for her all along . . ." I said. I couldn't help myself. I was so fixed on the idea that I was right that I couldn't think of tact at that moment.

"It's possible that I'm just tired now, Max, but it is redundant to always feel so superior to you in character, so I will grant you this: yes, I have felt sorry for Sophie.

"When she couldn't swallow a morsel because she coughed it back up with blood, I felt sorry for her. When she was unable to sleep anymore because of that horrible cough, I stayed up with her. I felt sorry for her when her body degenerated before my eyes and she was skeletal, but still so filled with womanly pride that she was ashamed for me to see her undress . . ." El Tinto spoke as he did the last time we had seen each other, heatedly, as if the entire purpose for living was essentially tied to his words, his saying them as well as my hearing them. "We only made love once, you know, that night, after you left." He added cynically, "She was too ill, really, to exert energy in anything but making it through each night."

We fell silent again. El Tinto lit another cigarette and, after a time, went on. "When one is faced with one's mortality, one can only become anxious for death. I feel pity for Sophie because she has prayed for death so long now that even Catherine and I want her to die, to cross over to that other place, to who knows where, but away from this pitiless world.

"I've been thinking about my brother, Horacio, and how he must have been faced with that same agony, the anxiety that precedes death and the ultimate desire, which is to experience it, have its mystery revealed. After he was beaten, just before he disappeared, he must've known death was inevitable—that it had stalked him his last days. And if he suffered before they finally ended his life . . ." El Tinto was moved. "If they mutilated his body before he was killed, while his spirit was still imprisoned in his body . . ."

Máximo put his hands on his friend's shoulders. "Enough. Stop torturing yourself. This situation with Sophie is making you think about your brother again, but don't blame yourself. You sound as if it were your fault. You're not responsible for what has happened to them." Max, too, felt the need to cry, but his sympathy went out to Tinto. He wanted to pull Tinto away from the depressing atmosphere of the hospital, to drink, find some women, forget their mortality.

"Do you ever think of your death?" El Tinto asked.

"No."

"You don't? Why is that?"

"It seems to me before one dies, one has to live. And I think I'm just too young and know nothing in regards to life to be capable of dying yet," Max answered him openly. Max and Tinto embraced and laughed with a reluctant sob in between.

"Well, I think for once you're right!" Tinto kidded. "You are too young and too stupid to understand anything about life to die just yet! It would have been a waste of your mother's labor."

"And you? You think you have the answers, Socrates?" Max asked defensively. It was all right to criticize himself, but his friend didn't have to agree so readily. El Tinto put his arm around Max's shoulder. "Let's go, hermano." Max hesitated, looking back at Sophie's door. For a moment I imagined Catherine at her mother's deathbed. I put my arm around Tinto's shoulder and we left.

eight

Paris, true to its promise, had been a place of civilized indecencies, or uncivil decencies, a city of true enchantment to Max, who had wandered there from a ranch near a village not on its country's map. Had he not been such an oddity, a foreigner forced to be grouped among those who for whatever circumstances life had placed where opportunities to integrate into dominant society were scarce, he might have been happy there.

At times, he resented his friend for having convinced him to travel under a false name, so that when he had considered applying to the Sorbonne, he couldn't. He regretted the weeks they had worked at the market at Rue Mouffetard, when he had felt worse than the peasants of the country because he was considered a *foreign* peasant. But he also recalled that El Tinto had done his best, or rather, had done what he did in their best interest. El Tinto did not rely on checks from home as Máximo did, and he had to respect his friend for his determination to be independent.

The structure of the city was at once most impressive. Puerto Sapogonia, as the capital of his country, had an equally long history, once having belonged to an advanced indigenous civilization, and later the Spanish architecture of colonization dominated, so that present-day Puerto Sapogonia was noble with history. Yet, France went beyond demonstrating before the grandeur of the ages; it was intimate with it.

There was so much about world history that Max had to learn that what he was able to grasp in his twentieth year was tactile, rather than abstract concepts. He visited Notre Dame, and he felt proud about the crowning of Napoleon and sorrowful about the martyrdom of Joan of Arc. He sat in the back of the great church listening to the muted voices embedded in stone walls. He never prayed and he wasn't sure if what he did could be called meditation, but he sat without being aware of time, as one could only do in such a place.

Sometimes his eyes wandered upon the tourists, a busload of Japanese or a mixture of people with guides who spoke a variety of languages. At other moments, the place was as discouraging as an irrelevant museum. He would come out and stopping over the bridge gaze upon the muddy waters of the Seine, imagining the river that ran near his grandfather's ranch; it was so clear one could use it for drinking water. Max was terribly and heartfully homesick.

He wrote to his grandfather regularly. It wasn't only the fact that if he didn't write, he risked not receiving an allowance, but his grandfather always responded with such a keen sense of understanding rendered by a genuine talent for letter writing that Max was comforted. This was despite the continuous dispute regarding his grandfather's insistence that he return to the ranch and put himself to work. He was no longer a child, no matter what his grandmother and mother said, but a grown man and he would have to take responsibility sooner or later. When Máximo persisted in contradicting his grandfather's wish, there was silence. No sooner had the date passed when he would have received his monthly allowance than Max knew his grandfather had cut him off, most likely as a last resort, hoping to starve him into coming home.

"What do you mean—what will you do now?" Tinto asked sarcastically when Max told him. He had continued to work at the market, but Máximo had been depending totally on his grandfather's stipends. "You'll go to work. You're not maimed, are you? I mean, I realize you are a bit retarded, but you can always sell something. In Spain, the blind sell lottery tickets and so do the gypsies; in addition, they'll tell you your fortune . . . ! But if you want good news, it'll cost you more!"

"I don't want to go back to working in the market," Max whined. "I hated getting up those cold mornings . . . !"

"Well, it's not cold anymore . . ."

"The point is, I don't want to do it. But maybe you're right. Maybe I should go to Spain. It isn't my country, but at least they speak Spanish there."

El Tinto thought for a few seconds. Max had a point. Part of their cultural background lay just on the other side of the border. Why not go to Spain? There were surely markets where one could find work. It was possible that he might even come upon contacts emigrated from Sapogonia. They made immediate plans. The next night they were on a train destined for Barcelona.

46

"What are we going to do in Barcelona?" Max asked casually. They shared a bottle of bordeaux. They had splurged on the bordeaux as well as on the couchette, where each took a top bunk and passed the bottle back and forth.

"Sell. We'll find something to sell. Listen, you have to have an understanding of human nature. If you ever notice anyone on the street who's selling something, it doesn't matter what it is, you'll see all he needs is one or two people to take interest. After that, you have a crowd pushing to get whatever it is he's selling. Natural human greed. I could sell you that bottle filled with water by convincing you that the water tastes as good as the wine that came in it, is better for you, and that the only difference is that you pay less!"

Max took the bottle from his friend. He half listened to his friend's theory out of appreciation for Tinto's earnestness. In fact, he thought Tinto was talking foolishly, but didn't comment on it. Instead, he changed the subject. "You know, compadre, I am going to miss all the French pussy I had in Paris . . . each and every one." He smiled dreamily, lying back with hands behind his head. "You know, there wasn't one I wanted that I didn't have."

El Tinto didn't respond. It caused Max to sit up. El Tinto seemed to be glaring at him, although he said nothing. Max waited. "Catherine went to Lyon to live with her father," Tinto informed him without taking a steady eye off Max. "Would it matter to you at all if you had left her pregnant? A girl at that age gets pregnant practically with a kiss," Tinto continued.

Max answered him dryly. "Forget it, man, leave it alone. She didn't get pregnant, so there's no problem."

"But if she had, Max? Would it matter to you? Would you go to Lyon and claim your child, marry her?"

"Tinto, we are not talking about Tess of the D'Urbervilles. This is a modern world. I am sure if she got pregnant she would not ruin her life by having a baby. And who is to say, if she was pregnant, it was mine?"

El Tinto took another swig of wine. He watched Máximo until he was sure he had fallen asleep. With an agile jump, El Tinto came down from the bunk and stepped out of the couchette. Staring out the black window at his own reflection, he watched Spain vanquish France, like a nun slipping away from the quarters of the soldier she knows will be gone by morning.

nine

What I remember most about the Barcelona period are three
things. First, there were many, many long days in the metro stations
selling, as El Tinto foresaw, anything. I never sold lottery tickets,
but there was an occasion when I, after a drinking and drug bout,
put on a pair of dark glasses and wrote up a sign soliciting handouts. I
sat on the ground in the metro for hours and made, well, about as
much as I would on a regular day selling the Moroccan mirrors,
acrylic scarves, brass picture frames, windup toys, the hand puppets
in fluorescent colors to attract greedy tots who badgered parents into
making puchases against their better judgment as to the quality of
our merchandise.

I remember, not without some regret, the night El Tinto told me
he was going to Morocco with the compañero from Argentina who
was our wholesale connection. This guy knew how to get hold of
anything. He always had an irresistible price and usually made the
merchandise sound so good we could do nothing but fall to the
temptation of buying it by the box, barrel, or sack and hope in the
end that we could sell it as easily as we had bought it.

But he and Tinto got on so well that they went into partnership.
I must say that my feelings were never taken into consideration and
when El Tinto stated flatly that he was going on a shopping spree
with this fellow, I was driven with envy. Why hadn't they even
considered cutting me in on their plans? It was the least El Tinto
could do for someone he had oftentimes called a brother.

El Tinto was tight-lipped, and let me rant for a while before he
admitted he had asked his new partners about including me, but the
idea just didn't go over. I found out there were others involved, and
all had decided they didn't want me as a business associate; in fact,
weren't eager to have me come along on the trip at all.

This was not information I took lightly, and when the Argentine came over I started in right away. "So, Shylock, you're off to

make your fortune, eh? And I'm not good enough to deal with?" *The Merchant of Venice* had come to mind suddenly and I referred to the Argentine by the name of the wealthy Jew in the play. The Argentine said nothing. He rolled up a marijuana cigarette and proceeded to smoke it.

El Tinto was shaking his head at me from across the room. He knew my moods and he was only left to hope I was not going to make a scene and start a fight with the tío. I stood and walked around the Argentine, studying him who sat so passively as if I didn't exist, as if I were a bug, a cockroach walking across the floor without enough menacing effect to earn a squashing.

El Tinto was waiting for me to speak. I obliged. "You merchant, have you anything to say?" I addressed him and replied to myself, "But little, I am armed and well prepared. Give me your hand, Tinto, fare you well. Grieve not that I am fallen to this for you. Say how I loved you, speak me fair in death. And when the tale is told, bid her be judge whether El Tinto had not once a love."

My ability for memorizing verse had also served the weakness of my passion for theatrics. Any opportunity was good enough to show off a quote from Shakespeare, an excerpt from Jorge Luis Borges, even an occasional wise word from Plato, although in all truth, sometimes I didn't know what the hell I was saying. El Tinto mirrored my pose with one hand on a hip and the other pointing directly at the object of his speech and answered, barely suppressing his anger. "What are you talking about? The tío and I are going on a business trip! Don't act so much the offended one! You're getting sickening with your pathetic self-pity! This isn't a game! There are those of us who really must earn a living, who can't just sit around waiting for money from our families to pay for our marijuana! I've had it up to here with your Little Lord Fauntleroy shit! You're nothing but a bourgeois elitist! What do you know about anything?"

Naturally, I accused him next of homosexuality. It took the Argentine tío to pull him off my throat, which he had such a grip on, I had almost blacked out. There's one thing you don't accuse a Sapogón of, if you value your life, and that's homosexuality, whether or not it is true. There are, of course, plenty of homosexuals in Sapogonia. There's an especially large congregation in the city of Colón, the second largest city of my country. Many of them like to dress up. You see transvestites even in broad daylight. But at night, it's really tiresome. You can't tell some of them from the female hookers and you are left to wonder, upon seeing a familiar face, if that was not your barber or dentist in those pink hotpants and stiletto-heeled shoes going by.

El Tinto left that same weekend. He probably returned by the end of summer as he had said he would, but by then I had gotten bored of being drugged up, around people who I really didn't know, and peddling was not the most reliable income. My grandfather was still trying to starve me out. I had to make a decision on my own.

The third thing I remember was the night I saw that ridiculous movie that I mentioned earlier. It was at the Girafa's place. I was crashing at his apartment because El Tinto and I had never really been able to get a place of our own and always managed to make friends with guys who were willing to put us up for a while or put up with us, depending on one's point of view.

Girafa and I had smoked some pasto someone had brought from South America. We were just sitting there, drinking cognac, watching the black and white screen hour after hour when the movie came on. I think, by then, the marijuana had begun to wear off.

During this period I was a fanatic reader. I read everything, indiscriminately. I read labels on food products, match boxes, metro ads. I also read everything I could find on Shakespeare. Girafa was an interesting guy, I decided, after realizing he liked Shakespeare almost as much as I did, with Disney comics coming in first, and had quite a collection of his works—Shakepeare's of course—in English, which I believe is the only way he can be read. This wasn't an easy task for me since I didn't speak a word of English, with the exception of the rudimentary course given to all students in their first year of secondary school in Sapogonia.

As a result, I considered myself quite a critic of what was decent scriptwriting. The movie we were watching, we both agreed, contained absolutely no redeeming value, save the fact that it was giving our eyeballs something to do with themselves for two hours. We were finishing the bottle of cognac when this bullfighter character was told that his father was dying. The old man on his deathbed had asked to see his only son.

Now this pip of a guy had left home against his father's wishes to become the best bullfighter in Spain. Of course, the father, being a man of little faith, didn't know that his son could do any better for himself than to be the heir to his tremendous estate. He threatened the son with disownment, but the son went on to meet his calling.

50

The son felt remorse and a tremendous need to show up at his father's deathbed in order to hear the father say how wrong he was—and I believe, to give the old man the chance to reinstate him in his will. (Girafa believed the bullfighter went because he was a dutiful son and had truly repented, having made his father so unhappy by going against his wishes, and the money was only incidental.)

We debated as to what the greatest bullfighter in Spain would do if he suddenly became stinking rich through inheritance and didn't have to work for a living. Girafa said (Girafa, being an Argentine, didn't love the bullfights as the Spaniards did) he thought it would have done the bulls better to have inherited the money so that they wouldn't have to work for a living. "Or to go in for soccer," I suggested, showing some understanding of the Argentine mentality.

I got to thinking at that precise moment about my father. I remembered he lived in Spain. "My father is Spanish," I said aloud.

"Go fuck yourself," Girafa responded, waving his hand like I was a big mosquito.

"What? You don't believe me? Why?"

"All you light-skinned assholes from Sapogonia want to pass for full-blooded Spaniards." Girafa himself was of Italian descent.

"I didn't say I was a full-blooded Spaniard, you piece of shit! I said my father is a Spaniard and he lives in this country. Look at this nose, this ass of mine! What do I look like to you? A God-damned Indian?" I wasn't really angry with Girafa, but he had upset me. He was right. Light-skinned Sapogonians always tried to pass for Spaniards. Girafa looked disgusted.

"You look . . . you look like a Jew, man, now, shut up."

"My father lives in Madrid. He's a bloody gallego, but he's been living in Madrid for years," I insisted.

"Why don't you look him up?" Girafa jabbed at me. "Remind him about his long lost little boy. Who knows? If he's wealthy like that tío in the movie, he might leave you a little something in his will."

I stared at Girafa, who looked like a remnant of wasted humanity thrown on the floor. He did nothing but get high day and night. I never knew what he did for a living or how he managed to pay the rent. I only know he always got the best pasto I had ever smoked. It might've been because of that pasto or the cognac, but I bought a train ticket to Madrid the next morning, and a few days later I was on my way in the dramatic search for my father.

I was very impressed with Madrid as a city, I must admit. Paris was enchanting; Barcelona with its gothic architecture, Gaudí, gargoyles, its blond catalán girls . . . was vibrant; but Madrid was impeccable. At least at first sight. There was the dignity, the posture, a certain affection that I really admired and shortly began to emulate with facility. My talent for learning dialects caused me almost unconsciously to lose some of my original accent and speak the Spanish of the madrileños.

I took a room in a hostel near the Puerta del Sol. It was a narrow habitation with a small bed and a sink. The bathroom was down the hall and I was allowed one bath a day, if I paid extra for it. The old woman in charge didn't prepare meals.

I roamed the Sol for days. Near the Plaza Mayor, I joined a group of South Americans who solicited change by playing folk music. Someone handed me a drum and I beat it in time with the charango. A woman by the name of Isabel sang lead. She had a pleasant voice, but she smoked so many cigarettes throughout the day, it cracked. We split up the tips at the end of the night. Isabel and her man invited me to stay with them in their place in Vallecas and I went along. The tips were not enough to pay for the room *and* to eat.

We were forced to find another location to play and finally we gave up because the police kept hassling certain members of the group. They searched them, they asked all kinds of questions. Those who were being harassed finally gave up and Isabel, her man, the tío she lived with whose name I've forgotten, and I decided to find straight work. Isabel went to work for a lady on Calle Orense. Her man thought about finding work as a waiter, but in all frankness, I don't think he looked around. I wrote again to my grandfather and got into a little gambling. I was very good at cards. A few nights in jail for brawls while I was drunk led me to the types who could teach a thing or two about the game. Usually, I only played for cash, but on one occasion, some unfortunate jerk gave up his guitar.

I played a little, and once having this guitar I began to pick up lessons from guitarists in bars. Usually I just played a bit and sang the rest of the tune, because between the playing and my voice, the voice was undoubtedly the better of the two. But because I am the type who has never wanted to be defeated by anything that presents itself as an obstacle, I practiced fanatically. Some of the best flamenco guitarists ever heard went through those little bars and for a drink and tapas they would be only too glad to show off their tricks.

Isabel paid the rent and she had a lot of fights with her man because all he did was get high. At least I brought food now and then she told him, and that's when I got my cue. Isabel had her eye on me. She was a nice girl, nicely developed, nice teeth and nice hair, but she reminded me too much of the one who I almost married long ago and who had cuckolded me with my best friend. You remember, the bowlegged one, Marisela.

Isabel got blatant, walking around in her underwear, leaving the bathroom door ajar when she bathed, and her boyfriend started to take it out on me. "Why the hell don't you take better care of your woman if you're afraid of losing her?" I advised him, but he was too high on drugs to think with lucidity.

Isabel and I became lovers, but we never let on to her boyfriend as if he were the cuckolded husband of the trio. I don't know why we kept it from him. He wasn't her husband. He didn't support her. He only loved her. And I didn't. I think that's what we were protecting, the love that Isabel received from one person in the world. It was low-quality love, but true love nevertheless.

Meanwhile, I had no luck finding my father. I wrote home to ask for clues and the only thing I was told (my mother wrote to me, since my grandfather was once again withholding my allowance and not writing) was that my father had had a friend whom he had gone with to Madrid years before. She had heard, through the invariable sources of the scorned woman, that this man had become financially successful and owned a furrier business in the Sol. My task as investigator was made somewhat easier by the fact that she knew the man's name. A few times a week I went around, first, all over the Sol, and later, to any furrier I came upon inquiring for this man.

Finally, someone told me they knew of such a person and gave me the address. My heart pounded just at the thought that I was drawing nearer to my father, to a truth that suddenly became more important than it had ever been. I found my father's compadre only to be told he saw my father only now and then, and in the past years, even less than that. I was reluctant to tell him who I was and, therefore, did not ask too many questions. The man eyed me strangely, as if he suspected who I was, but I doubt that he knew for certain.

He eyed my guitar, which I always carried, and with raised eyebrows pondered, "Oh? You're a musician, too?" I nodded. "Why? Do you play?" Almost every Spaniard I met was either an aspiring guitarist or a bullfighter who'd missed his calling. Can you imagine going to have your appendix out by a guy who really wanted to be a bullfighter, but if it wasn't for his parents . . . ?

The man, my father's compadre, laughed. No, no, he said. "What? You don't know that Pío Madrigal is one of the best flamenco musicians in Madrid? He just drinks a little, you understand," the compadre added in a tone of confidence. Then he eyed me. "You seem as if you don't know el Pío."

I didn't know what to say. I was thinking at that moment how much better it would have been if this tío had been my father rather than some drunkard-flamenco musician. "No," I finally answered. "I don't know him, but I'm looking for him. We have some business to clear up." I walked out, leaving the tío perhaps regretful that he had talked to me at all if in the end it would do his compadre harm. But he hadn't given me a hint as to where I could find him. I had been to plenty of bars and nightclubs. I had gotten to know quite a few musicians, too. I knew some of the singers and dancers. No one had ever mentioned Pío Madrigal. It was possible my father's old friend was biased out of loyalty and that Pío didn't play half as well as he claimed.

One night things got out of hand with Isabel and her man. We were out having something to eat and he was, as usual, high on drugs. He got loud in the cafeteria and obnoxious toward Isabel. The woman behind the counter went out on the street to call the police. I was trying to calm him down when he took a swing at me and the police, seeing this, threw us both in jail.

I wondered how long Isabel was going to put up with this bean-head. In the meantime, I warned him to keep away from me, and fortunately we were separated when we got to the Cárcel de Diputación so that I didn't have to see his stupid face all night. I had my guitar, mi niña, as I called her, my lucky charm to keep me from getting lonely. It was never taken away from me whenever I was thrown in jail for the night. I suppose it was the respect the Spaniards had for their music. I played for a while, sizing up my fellow cellmates to make sure none was liable to get any ideas about me. Sometimes you got an asshole who didn't like your looks and therefore decided you weren't going to get out of there alive. Usually it was a lot of bluff, but sometimes I came out of there in worse condition than when I went in.

There was always someone who wanted to play your guitar, but any serious musician would never let anyone dare touch his instrument, and in this respect I was given support by others if the tío got persistent. They also liked my playing. I began a fandango. There was a tonadilla I had been working on and I showed it off to my ragged audience in that urine- and barroom-smelling atmosphere.

Then the inevitable cock who is bound to show you up and tell you how it should be played, opened his mouth. "That's not it, young man." His voice was gruff from decades of harsh tobacco and he was sitting away from the group so that I couldn't see his face. "Here. Give me that and I'll teach you."

I hesitated, naturally, holding on to my niña's neck. I took out a cigarette with one hand and lit it. The tío came out of the shadow. He was about twice my age. It was evident he had been through a hard time. One of his front teeth was missing, but I liked that distinguished look some Spaniards maintained despite these details. I don't know if it was in the squint of the eye or in the erect shoulders, but he had it. He put out his hand and waited. Someone said, "That's Pío de la Costurera. *Vale.*" The man who said he would show me the fandango kept his hand firmly outstretched. After a few tense seconds, I gave up my niña.

He smiled, smug as the bullfighter who was about to finish off the bull. He stood up and, despite the gap in his mouth, his smile had charm. He got the feel of the niña before he actually went into the tonadilla I had been trying to master. A couple of guys began to do palmas and el Pío de la Costurera made up lyrics, which he sang with his gravelly voice:

> You want to know
> you say you want to know
> how to play the fandango
> of Lucena, but what you don't
> see is that I was born beneath
> the moon and only I can teach
> you to play the fandango!

I was angrier than hell, but I smiled. He played a thousand times better than I did. Then another guitar materialized. It was handed to the tío and apparently belonged to him. "Why did you want my guitar, if you have yours?" I asked when he handed mine back. "You'll see now how well it's going to play for you! I have a certain touch with guitars, as I do with women. I taught her a secret or two, maybe now she'll behave for you." He laughed after his picaresque remark that caused the others to laugh at my expense.

But Pío de la Costurera had not exaggerated. La Niña did play as she hadn't played for me before and together with el Pío and his guitar, we played an old fandango while he sang:

> Los surcos de mi besana
> están llenos de terrones,
> y tu cabeza, serrana,
> está llena de ilusiones,
> pero de ilusiones vanas.
>
> Cuando la vi de llorar,
> creí de volverme loco;
> pero luego me enteré
> que ella lloraba por otro,
> y entonces fui yo el que lloré.

El Pío winked at me and went into the tonadilla. He finished the old cante:

> Y me tratas como a un niño
> porque te quiero con locura.
> ¡Tú me tiras por los suelos;
> que malamente me miras,
> tanto como yo te quiero!
>
> ¡Cuántas veces se juntaron
> tus labios sobre los míos!
> ¿Qué veneno me has pegao
> que me tienes consumío?
> ¿Pa qué tú a mí me has besao?

Everyone was in a good mood. El Pío put his guitar aside. "You play very well," he flattered me. I knew he was just making fun of me because, next to him, I was polyester next to silk. He seemed to read my thoughts and continued for the benefit of my intelligence. "If you want, I'll show you how to play . . . " I nodded. "Of course, if you dedicate yourself to playing, you must resign yourself to poverty.

I've never been able to live off my music and I am the best in Madrid." He grinned immodestly.

"The best in Spain," someone added and, had they had something to drink, they would have raised glasses in a toast.

Máximo remembered his father's compadre telling him that his father, Pío Madrigal, was among the best. "I've heard there's someone else who's the best in Madrid," he poked at Pío de la Costurera's ego. Pío de la Costurera grew indignant, lighting up like a match. His chest swelled. "What do you know? When you were still sucking your mother's titty, I was playing the guitar all over the country. You mean you've never heard of me?"

"Were you moving around the country because you were playing the guitar or dodging the army?" a voice muttered cruelly. El Pío de la Costurera didn't answer right away. The men were waiting. "I hate war," he said solemnly. "When I was young, there wasn't a place I went to that wasn't at war—what's worse, with itself! It's true, I left my country, my mother, whom I never saw alive again, because I didn't want any part of the war. At that time, I was a musician to contend with. I even made records. A friend told me of a country in America that reeked with gold . . . It sounds ridiculous, doesn't it?" El Pío looked around, but no one answered. "I must've thought I was a conquistador of the sixteenth century."

"Did you find gold?" Máximo asked. He wondered what country el Pío had gone to, but he didn't ask.

"I found more death, more men wanting to shed blood. I found more war in a country tinier than my asshole and more stubborn than a dung-carrying beetle. It turns over its natural resources to that avaricious beast north of it for the sake of protection and, in the process, leaves its people to starve."

"When I was a child, there were a handful who got rich from the gold found in the mines on their land. Of course, they were already landowners. My grandfather was one of them," Máximo told el Pío.

"That's the problem, the wealth always goes to the wealthy." El Pío was asserting his newly acquired socialist doctrine. "That means you have money, too, eh?" he almost sneered. Máximo shook his head. "My grandfather has cut me off. I'm a disgrace to him, he says. He believes I took after my father."

"Well that means that your father was probably not a fascist like your grandfather."

"My grandfather is not a fascist. He's a member of the Christian Socialist Party of my country." Máximo felt inclined to defend his grandfather. He was upset with the old man, but he didn't feel this drunk could insult him.

"And from what country are you, young man?" el Pío asked.

"Sapogonia," Max told him and waited for the response. He knew this character would have something to say, but instead Pío replied with a boisterous laugh. "What the devil makes you laugh like that?" Max was getting tired of this tío who used him as the brunt of his jokes. When el Pío stopped laughing he told him.

"That's where I went to when I left here! That's the country I went to find my fortune at and all I got was a kick in the ass by a fascist government. When it broke out in civil war, I came back. If I was going to die anywhere, it might as well be on the land where I was born."

"It's true that the president of that era was tough, but he had to be in order to straighten out the economy of the country." Max felt compelled toward nationalism, to defend his very being from this coward's redundant sense of superiority.

"*Vale.* It's your country so I won't fight with you about it. I can see your blood is as thick and as hot as the lava of those volcanos you have there," Pío remarked. "But I will tell you this: all the independent miners, of which I was one, had to turn in all the gold that was excavated up to a certain amount. Afterward, if the miners found anything, we were allowed to keep sixty percent and forty automatically went to the government—but I say, to Romero's pocket."

Max said nothing. His grandfather had detested the president of that era, who had dictated his power for nearly forty years. Most of the fortune amassed on his grandfather's land was to be turned over to the government. Fortunately, there remained a sufficient amount to keep his grandfather comfortable by Sapogón standards.

"Anyway, that's not why I left your country," Pío de la Costurera went on. He sighed. "I left because of the war. And by the time I returned here, things had calmed down. I often wonder if life would not have worked out better for me if I had stayed in Sapogonia.

"I was going to marry a lovely girl, a lovely *rich* girl, who by now may have inherited a good sum of money—like this tío is going to have someday, although he denies it now, trying to convince us ragamuffins that he is one of us." He indicated with his chin that he referred to Máximo. Máximo, in the meantime, had begun to brood. He was insulted by this man who talked about his country as if it were an old whore. He also reflected on some of what else the tío had said. He had an inkling of an idea, but he thought it was too absurd, a glimmer into a reality he wasn't prepared for in such an environment. "Why didn't you marry her?" he asked Pío. "Didn't she love you?"

"She loved me all right. She loved me enough to have my child. But her father and brothers insisted that I go and fight in their bloody war. If I expected to reap the benefits of their country, they thought I should defend their interests. If I wanted to die I would have done it here, I told you."

"You left because you were a coward," Max declared between clenched teeth. The other men grew still.

"I left because I had been born a poor idiot, the son of a seamstress who was widowed very young. All my life I was in search of the good life, the life the politicians and the bishops have, and those born with silver spoons in their mouths, like you! I don't trust politics. I never have. Why should I have given up my life for the sake of benefiting some cross-eyed politician, to supply his mistress with jewels? No, young man, not being a righteous idiot doesn't make me a coward!"

"I'm glad you can say that looking me in the eye, because otherwise I would have to knock out the rest of your teeth," Max said. The words barely made their way through his throat. He was one solid muscle. It was possible he was mistaken, but it didn't matter. This Spaniard represented everyone that had come to exploit Sapogonia for centuries.

"But why do you feel that way? Don't be so sensitive!" Pío told him. "I loved your country, its mountains, its waters. There was a river that I can still see in my dreams, clear as a glass of mineral water. And I loved its people. Its women are among the most beautiful in the world. And I was in love with that girl from your country. She was rich and out of my league, but she loved me, too. I have never forgotten her."

Max, unable to control himself any longer, lunged at el Pío de la Costurera. A few of the men placed bets and finally one or two took pity on el Pío or had remembered how he had played the fandango earlier, and pulled Máximo off his father. Máximo began to cry.

"Wait a minute, wait a minute, gentlemen," Pío said, catching his breath and collecting himself, but still on the floor. He got up and backed away from Máximo as if he were a leper. "What year were you born? Where exactly were you born . . . ?" Max stopped the tears, embarrassed and afraid that showing such vulnerability might earn him a beating. He straightened his collar and answered Pío Madrigal, son of the seamstress. "My name is Máximo Madrigal."

Pío was shocked. He ran a hand through his thinning hair, that curled at the ends just as Max's did. El Pío uttered, "¡Coño! ¡Hijo! ¿Eres tú?"

Max turned away. His eyes landed on those of one of the guards who had been sitting outside of the cell and who had enjoyed the music they played earlier, demonstrating by accompanying with palmas and a few dance steps. The guard gave Max a look of compassion. "What do you know! You are the son of el Pío de la Costurera!" He grinned. Máximo looked upon his father. "Yes, I am the son you left in that country smaller than the size of your asshole."

ten

The following day we went to Vallecas. Pío de la Costurera lived in the same area as the apartment building where I lived with Isabel and her lover. We took the metro and got off at the exact stop that I always got off at. My father pointed to a building. It was one of those newer constructions, with no style, no thought but to furnish housing for the poor. Clothes hung out on lines from terrace to terrace, children scurried about. Common Spanish lives clustered together in urban banality.

My father explained that he lived there with his wife and their four children. Cuca, his wife, like Isabel, also worked on Calle Orense. He said she was undoubtedly at work at that hour and the children at home, but we stopped at the café across the boulevard to have breakfast first. He sprang for the potato omelette, the espresso, the cigarettes, and the drink we each had to start the day.

"How many brothers do I have?" I asked out of curiosity. The prospect of not being an only child suddenly appealed to me, especially since I knew that this fact meant nothing to my relationship with my family in Sapogonia. Assuming my grandfather didn't keep the grudge he had against me at the present time to his death, it was a given that I would be the principal heir to his estate. My mother's two brothers died in the civil war my father refused to join. My mother and grandmother, naturally, would be provided for, but it was unlikely that my grandfather would leave women in charge of his affairs.

These new siblings were a novelty. The idea of a father was a novelty. The fact that he was a worthless scoundrel surprisingly didn't disappoint me much after all. I felt a new dimension suddenly reveal itself to me since the night before when Pío de la Costurera turned out to be Pío Madrigal, grand amour of my mother's sheltered life and my biological father.

My grandfather had been all the father I could have wanted in any man. He had been physically capable of raising a boy after his own sons were grown, and of doing so with a new strength when they were killed. He raised me with a strict hand, but with a guiding and protective one. I adored my grandfather, I tell you. I often thought he was larger than life, a man whom I could never replace on the ranch, nor would I have wanted to do so.

Curiosity and ambition drove me to find Pío Madrigal. I say ambition because I had had illusions that Pío was rich, that he might have had equal curiosity about me all those years of estrangement and, as an act of compensation for not having raised his son, would share his wealth with me.

While Pío Madrigal turned out to be impoverished, he had already let me know that there was a thing or two about life that he could tell me. He showed me up on the guitar, my newly found passion. His voice, gravelly as it was from alcohol and cigarettes, was better than mine. Perhaps what I needed was to drink and smoke more, I speculated, to get that effect so desired by flamenco singers.

My father was not afraid of life. Neither was I, of course, but I was barely past twenty and had been fairly doted on by my family. Why should I have been afraid? But my father had been fatherless himself at an early age. He had had to find ways to make a living, to eat. He had had no shoes until he was an adolescent. (Somehow, I don't quite believe all of this, but I liked the way it sounded when Pío told it to me that first day that I had a father. I could have accepted anything that spouted out of Pío de la Costurera's mouth, so smitten was I with the idea that we were blood.)

He remembered my mother vividly. From the photographs I had seen of her taken when I was an infant, his memory was accurate. Mother had had virginal hair, black like her eyes. Her smooth skin was the color of caramel. Mother always smelled of rosewater. As the only daughter, she had been pampered by her father and obsessively protected by her brothers. Her Indian mother guided her with watchful eyes that could never be deceived. But my mother fell in love and Pío gave her a child before the benefit of a church wedding.

"I knew you were going to be a son," Pío smiled proudly, as if I had just been born the night before. "I knew from the moment she told me she was pregnant."

"Didn't it interest you enough to stay?" I said, torn from one moment to the next with the impulse to reproach him and then to leave it alone.

"You didn't need me. You had your mother, the most important thing. You had your well-to-do grandfather, uncles . . ."

"My uncles died in the war against Romero's government . . ." I informed him, as if he should feel guilty about it. He lowered his head appropriately. I presumed it was a hypocritical gesture, but at least he made an effort to show sympathy. "Anyway, tell me, how many brothers do I have?"

"Four! And three of them are sisters," he beamed again. "No one was going to say that Pío de la Costurera was not going to have a son to whom he could leave his guitar. The little one is the boy."

After breakfast we went to my father's apartment. It was crowded with old furniture, the possessions of children, and their trails of cups and soiled clothes about the place. Pío ordered his oldest daughter, a girl of about twelve, to make up a bed for me. It was a cot and I believe two of the girls usually slept on it. "I can sleep on the floor, Pío," I told my father. I didn't call him father. We had only known each other less than twenty-four hours. He insisted I sleep on the cot and that was settled.

Cuca came in while Pío and I were taking a nap, catching up on the sleep we missed in jail the night before. I heard her gruff voice reprimanding the children for the mess they had made in her absence. I think she was yelling loudly to disturb her husband's sleep; when she discovered me, she lowered her tone. "Who's that?" She addressed the oldest daughter in a hushed voice; I sensed they were standing next to the cot. The girl must have shrugged her shoulders.

"You mean your father is bringing strangers to sleep in our house now!" This time she spoke loudly again, but Pío responded from his bed. "He's my son!" There was a pause. I pulled the cover over my head, suspecting Cuca was inclined to take a peek at me. Her footsteps went in the direction of their bedroom. Her voice was not discreet. "WHAT DO YOU SAY, PÍO MADRIGAL?"

"I tell you, woman, that young man out there is my son. We met each other for the first time last night." Pío's tone was challenging.

"And who the devil is his mother? ¡Coño!" Cuca demanded. "Tell me the gallega who gave you this son so that I can pack your bags and send them to her house!"

"Calm down, woman! She's not a gallega. She's in America and I haven't seen her since before he was born, and as you can tell, that must've been some time ago. It was an adventure of my youth. You remember! I told you I had lived in Sapogonia years before I met you!" Pío sounded as though he retained an outburst of laughter. Then I heard them both laughing. The front door slammed and the oldest girl was gone to the market. The infant was asleep and the younger girls played in the kitchen. Shortly, I heard a distinct moan from the bedroom. I went back to sleep.

Cuca, my new stepmother, received me as well as one could suddenly accept an adult child into her home. She served me as she served her husband. She was polite and attentive to my needs all the while I stayed with them.

I wanted to go back to the apartment with Isabel and her boyfriend, but my father prohibited it, or I should say, embarrassed me out of it. When I told him that Isabel was not really my woman, but the other's, he said she was making fools of both of us. "She has you both working for her, doing for her, and keeping her happy in bed to boot!" my father deduced. "What kind of fools are you? It's all right for a man to have two women, but a woman to have two men? You Americans are very strange!"

I explained to him that out of the three of us, Isabel was the only one who really made any money, but this only made him more critical of the situation. I had to tell Isabel it was time to tirar la chancleta and I left to live at Pío's.

Pío had for a time worked in construction in the area of Vallecas. He was a welder and while he had been unemployed more than employed in the past years, he was occasionally called back to work. Cuca changed from a mood of resignation to my presence to one of delight when Pío was called one day a month after I moved in and, taking me down to the site, got me a job, too.

Pío taught me to weld, mostly tack welding, nothing too elaborate. He introduced me to some of the others on the job who he thought were worth getting to know. Mostly, as a young, unskilled, able man, I was given the work that demanded lifting and carrying. During lunch break and after hours, Pío and I teamed up and gambled with our co-workers.

Some weeks we were lucky and doubled our earnings; others, we lost everything, save the pesetas it required for a good drunk. We didn't come home those nights. Without saying it aloud, we knew it would be best not to come home sober to Cuca with empty pockets.

After about six months, the job was completed and we were out of work again. I decided it was time for me to go, not only from Pío's home, although heaven only knew—the smell of soiled diapers, spoiled food, the crying of children at all hours, Cuca's invariable bouts of ill humor which encompassed carnival tricks having to do with flying dishware and small furnishings and Pío's artful dodging, Pío's own periodical dark moods when even my companionship kept him despondent—in short, all that comes with family life under trying circumstances made me yearn to move onward.

For a time I thought I might travel around Europe; I wondered what had become of El Tinto and thought I might find him in our old haunts in Barcelona. Then my grandfather answered my twenty-third plea to forgive my vagabonding, but as I had found a great need to know my father and having done so felt all the more a man for it, he sent on a modest but ample sum and advised that I use my own discretion regarding my life. He could only hope one day I would stop being such a gallego and come home. ¡Abuelo querido!

I held back the news from Pío for about a week. I wondered if he knew that I had been reinstated in my grandfather's good graces if he would expect that I help him out financially. The sum my grandfather sent was not enough to go around. Whatever I was to do with it, I would have to think it out wisely because my grandfather didn't indicate that another check would be forthcoming.

I also sensed Pío did not expect me to ever leave Madrid. We had become quite a team in bars, both in gambling and on the guitar. Pío would have to wait fifteen years before his snot-nosed infant barely learning to walk could take my place.

Finally, I told him. Pío was quiet. I knew he was scheming and I was prepared to hold on to my precious check. Pío sized me up. I was ready for any con. He surprised me. "Do you have enough for a new suit?" he asked. I nodded. I asked why I needed a new suit. "You'll need a suit to travel to North America," he replied as a matter of fact.

What business did I have in North America, I wondered. What business did Pío have in North America, I thought I should ask. Instead, I waited. He walked off. I followed him. "Why am I going to North America?" Pío looked at me as if I were a buffoon. "Do you want to go on living this life forever? In North America, maybe, just maybe, an imbecile like you will have some luck at life. You can't go on forever depending on handouts from your grandfather."

My father embarrassed me. He hadn't wanted my grandfather's

money at all. It must have brought back bitter memories. I didn't know much about North America, but I understood it to be a very modern nation where with initiative anyone could succeed.

I immediately fantasized the possibility of studying there, at Harvard. (It was the only North American university I knew by name.) The possibilities of making a life for oneself in such a place were endless. I might even become a famous musician, with the right manager, the proper connections.

"Where will I go in the United States?" I asked Pío. I knew of Texas, New York City, and California; the rest of the United States was grey area. "New York," he replied in irritation, as if there was no sense to my questions. "Where do you want to go? To North Dakota?" I stared blankly at Pío. I had no idea what that meant. "North Dakota is one of the states of the United States of North America," Pío informed me.

"That means there is also a South Dakota," I said, proud of my powers of deduction. He nodded. I went on, "But are North and South Dakotas two different states with their own governments, or are they one state divided into two geographical areas?" I knew by Pío's expression that he hadn't thought of this at all. "How the hell should I know? I'm not American!" he snapped, frustrated with my insolence.

Pío took me to a tailor, a trusted friend of many years, and got a suit made up for me at a reasonable price. It was four pieces; the jacket, vest and two pairs of trousers. We also went to the furrier friend whom I had gone to when I looked for my father. Pío asked him to give me a sheepskin coat. I didn't think I wanted to spend money on a coat. Pío insisted that it was much colder in North America than I realized.

I told Pío that, furthermore, I wanted to save my money for my trip, but the coat was a gift. Either my father paid for it or the compadre who owned the shop gave it to me. It didn't matter. The point was, it was given to me and with my suit, I was a well-dressed man. The suit was a light color because that was the fashion in Madrid at the time, but the rest of my clothes were black, which when worn with high-heeled boots were quickly identifiable as garb worn by those who play flamenco.

One night Pío made another gift to me, the gift of a woman. Her name was Hilda and she had been a girl of fifteen when he knew her in New York. He was there briefly after he had left Sapogonia on his

66

way back to his country. The girl, the younger sister of a friend, had fallen desperately in love with Pío, who considered her much too young to take seriously. "But she was sweet," he said, reminiscing, "tasted like honey . . . "

Hilda sent a Christmas card as well as a birthday card to Pío's hometown every year. Although the cards were no longer forwarded, he knew she was still sending them because his relatives always let him know. The cards were already a tradition. "You want me to believe some girl you knew over twenty years ago continues to send you cards and that she still loves you?" I couldn't believe it as much as I wanted to. Pío told tales that were too large for even me to swallow.

"I have a few at home, dated as recently as two and three years ago," he confided. "When my sister came to Madrid to visit, she left them with me. Of course, Cuca doesn't know. I save them as souvenirs of my youth." El Pío was suitably smug.

"Do you think she ever married?" I wondered, feeling sorry already for the husband of a woman possessed by Pío de la Costurera.

"Who knows? For her sake, I hope so. I never plan on seeing her again." Pío looked at me in such a way that indicated he would prefer that she had remained faithful to the love of her life regardless of his definite absence. He put an arm around my shoulder. "But don't worry. When she sees you, she'll love you with the same adulation she showed me twenty years ago. You're almost as good-looking as me."

With a leather satchel, la niña, dressed in the new sheepskin coat, the pastel suit, and new high-heeled black boots, I got on the flight departing for New York, the United States of America. Pío, Cuca, the children, all waving from below as the jet left the ground. I couldn't see them, but I knew they were doing this. I had to say they were the closest thing to having a family that I had known since leaving my country. At the time I was certain, as we are whenever we've been to a part of the world that manages to settle in the fabrication of our make-up, that I would return to Europe, that I would go back to Madrid, and that I would see Pío again, play fandangos together, get into brawls, aggravate his wife. But I didn't.

I saw Pío Madrigal instead on every face on New York City streets, every hustler, every immigrant worker in the subway; Asian-faced or East Indian, he was Pío de la Costurera gigging to make a living, to survive, to keep warm. I saw Cuca in America, carrying home two pork chops at the end of the day, thinking of how to divide them into six. I saw their children weaving in and out of crowds in the subway, on busy streets, bumping into someone who wouldn't notice the wallet being slipped out of the back pocket, giving a sob story to an unsuspecting pretty woman who would be inclined to reach into her purse for change.

I saw Pío in America as I had not seen him before in Sapogonia until the day came when I had to return there. Then I saw Pío working at the most menial jobs, the burdensome worker that kept my country barely trudging along with its burdensome multitude. I saw him abused and finally sent away, or he left on his own as he didn't always leave when in the north because, as unsavory as the reception might have been there, it was more promising than living in his host country.

I saw these things years later. Gradually, I realized why Pío went back to Spain without knowing if he would have to fight in a war after all or not. I saw Pío killing off his liver with liquor, destroying his lungs, lips, gums with strong tobacco. I saw him losing more teeth in fights and falling off a beam one day, ending paralyzed and having no way to support his family again.

For the moment I told myself that Pío was happy with his life. He had to be happy, otherwise he would live it differently. Otherwise he might have chosen to come to the United States with me, to claim his role at the side of this young Hilda who had not forgotten me. But Pío chose to give her to me instead.

I got off the plane on a humid day in April. I had to remove my coat at once. When I showed the cab driver the address where I wanted to go, he sputtered something that sounded like profanity being chopped up in a blender, which I took for an Asian dialect. We drove off to the most familiar of neighborhoods to the New York immigrant. I am certain that if the Statue of Liberty were capable of it, she would actually point from the harbor to the Lower East Side.

eleven

During their first months together they were not too unlike a pair of newlyweds, blissful within the tight cocoon they had woven for themselves.

Each morning, before Pastora went off to work, Perla prepared for her friend a cup of café con leche, dashed with cinnamon. She poured it into an earthenware cup that was painted with gladiolas. She knew this pleased Pastora very much.

Perla found dozens of small ways to please her friend, whom she now loved. She might prepare dinner, though out of a can, or save Pastora the trouble of warming up her car in the morning by starting out first to confront the cold. It made Perla uneasy, however, if she allowed herself to think of it, that she behaved this way with a woman, while having no patience whatsoever with the wishes of men.

She had a lover for each day of the week, or could if she chose, which lately she chose less and less. She was invited to dinner and each was only too willing to comply with her slightest caprice.

She felt uneasy, too, when she sensed that Pastora, who at times had the reserve of a queen, appeared to take her kindness in stride. Yet, she was happy. They were happy. Perla had moved in with Pastora. As there was only one bedroom, they shared the same bed, the only closet, each other's clothes, make-up, toothbrush. In their new relationship, they celebrated all the possible advantages of sharing life with another woman, while counting the disadvantages one had when sharing it with the opposite sex. Lovers were allowed to come by only when it was found necessary.

Their abandon to each other's pleasure was mirrored to them when in the presence of other women, as it was on the occasion of Fabiola's overnight visit. It was always an occasion when Pastora was able to visit with her childhood friend, since Fabiola now lived in Gary, Indiana. With the distance between them, Fabi's husband and her child, their contact was usually made by telephone.

As it was, Perla prepared a fried rice meal in her wok. She whistled and sang Mexican rancheras as she cut broccoli and diced pepper and onion. Pastora and Fabiola caught up on news in the living room. Pastora's friend was conscious of the novel element moving about with such gusto in Pastora's kitchen.

"Is she always like that?" Fabiola whispered, referring to Perla's enthusiasm and good nature. Pastora nodded as she lit a cigarette and Fabiola took the opportunity to study her. Pastora looked more at ease than she had in a long time.

After dinner Pastora and Perla invited Fabi to a jazz concert. Although the plans were spontaneous, Perla demonstrated one advantage of being a beautiful woman by arranging for tickets with the use of a name. It belonged to a man who had been asking her to dinner for some time; in this case, he was also the producer of the concert. Three tickets would be waiting for the women at the box office, they were told.

It had begun to sleet when they got into Pastora's jalopy. Her windshield wipers stopped working just as they turned onto Lincoln Avenue. Perla rolled down her window from the passenger side and, leaning her body halfway out in a perilous display of improvisation, wiped Pastora's window. They giggled and joked nervously throughout and Pastora sensed Fabiola's absorption of what life was like on a given evening with the most delightful couple she had ever known.

They shared expenses, they bought furniture together. On most weekends they had Perla's twin boys. The only factor that Fabiola could tell was not in the relationship was sex. Everything else was obvious; companionship, financial interdependency, as well as individual independence.

When had Fabiola driven the car with her husband as a passenger when he didn't nearly push her to tears with his constant criticism and commands? Pastora had gone the wrong way down a one-way street and all they had both done was let out screams and laugh until they turned off.

When had her husband cooked dinner for her last as she entertained a friend in the living room?

When had he said he was confident she was going to succeed in a goal that was outside of their home—and was actually prepared to be a shadow in her life as a result of it if necessary to keep her going?

When had he bathed their son and put him to bed and gotten up to give him his feedings at all hours of the night? Well, once or twice since the child was born. But her husband was from a family of one son and three sisters. He had not ever been required to help around the house. That about summed it up for Fabiola in their home as well.

The following day, Fabiola left feeling lightheaded, filled with all sorts of notions. She was excited by the dimension of life that the women had revealed inadvertently to her. She was innocent enough to believe they hadn't been aware of how she marvelled at them all evening.

A week before Christmas, they saw Fabiola again. Perla and Pastora had decided to have a potluck for women one Sunday after-noon. Fabiola had told her friend Rosario, who lived next door to her, about Perla and Pastora. They had sat in Rosario's kitchen drinking coffee and baking sugar cookies for the holiday gift-giving, and Fabiola went on in detail about her night with two women who lived without the prerequisite of men. They mixed, rolled out, cut, baked, and sighed, wondering what life would be like without the invariable question every day at the same hour: "Hi, babe! What's for dinner?"

Fabiola arranged for a baby-sitter for both her son and Rosario's two children and, promising Rosario's husband to have her home by dinner time, they drove to the potluck.

Perla and Pastora suspected Fabiola's mission when they saw her at the door with her friend. Each took time to sit and talk with Rosario, who seemed like someone not used to being asked an opinion or to elaborate on a thought.

When Rosario and Fabiola left, each agreed that it would take effort and a great deal of determination to be sure, but the solution had been tested and proven. They would leave their husbands. They would move out-of-state if necessary to start over. They might even move in together and raise the children without men who became ugly human beings when they drank, who fucked them without so much as a kiss and rolled over afterward to snore. They would find lovers like Perla's and Pastora's, who sent gifts for no reason save to be looked upon by them in a gracious light, who were taught their place, who were sent out of the premises when threatening to step out of line, just don't you dare . . . !

A year passed. Two years passed. One of the women did leave her husband. She moved to Arizona. The other stayed behind.

twelve

It was through one of his father's underworld connections that he secured a false set of documents that allowed him to pass customs at Kennedy Airport. His new identity made him a Spanish merchant whose visa was not to exceed six months.

None of this concerned Máximo. He would arrive, get lost in the Romanesque arena of anonymous characters and freaks found in the streets of Manhattan, and establish himself somewhere, a central point from which he could concentrate on seeking that promised fortune.

The cab let him out two blocks from the address he had on the crumpled paper he'd kept in the breast pocket of his suit. The cabbie, from what Máximo could make out, was afraid to drive into the neighborhood where he wanted to be taken. He indicated this by pulling over and reaching from behind the wheel to open the back door for Máximo to get out. He made a signal with his thumb and said, "Beat it, buddy!" Máximo got the message, although he thought the cabbie was a spineless pig and said as much in Spanish.

After all, how bad could a neighborhood be? Máximo had wandered more than once to neighborhoods in Spain that he had heard were treacherous. He'd gotten drunk and awoken face down in gutters, his wallet still in his pocket. Of course there was the time when the pretty girl he'd been following lured him into the corridor of a house where, once he had taken a step in, a keen sense of imminent foul play told him that someone awaited with unpleasant plans for him behind the door. He was deft enough to escape such a fate.

He muttered to himself, angrily throwing his bag over his shoulder, his sheepskin coat over the other arm, after straightening out the major wrinkles in his pastel-colored suit, and finally, by asking every Latin-looking face that seemed approachable, he was at last in front of the decaying tenement that bore the numbers he had on the paper in his hand.

There were three young men standing in the doorway, all staring at him with a kind of amused, taunting expression. Máximo couldn't believe it. Hardly an hour in the land of stardom and stardust and he was about to enter into a rumble with three hoods no different from those hanging out in the bars in Vallecas. Looking squarely into the eyes of each and sizing up the biggest, a black-looking fellow who nonetheless Máximo sensed spoke Spanish, he asked for Hilda Gálvez.

"Who?" one of the other fellows asked in English, mockingly, as if he didn't understand Máximo's Castilian Spanish. Perhaps he didn't. "¿Quién tú dice?" asked the third. Still, the one to whom Max had addressed his question said nothing, but folded his husky arms over his semi-bared chest and raised an eyebrow.

Max repeated his question when a young woman with a round belly and a small child came up behind him. She wanted to get by to enter the building. Max turned and moved aside for her. He knew, despite her downcast eyes, that she had noticed him, his fine suit, his neatly trimmed moustache. "Señora," he addressed her in a cavalier manner, the one reserved for breaking the resistance of the female gender.

She dared to glance up, only for a moment to meet his eyes, then she looked down, pretending to fuss over the child. She surprised herself at her sudden coyness, the unexpected timidity with the stranger.

She was dark, with very tight hair. To Max, new to the blends of races particular to New York City, she looked Moorish. He addressed his question to her, asked if she knew Hilda Gálvez. She said she knew a woman by the name of Hilda, but she thought that her last name was something else, something French-sounding. Anyway, she lived on the fifth floor.

"Grathias," Max told her with a great air of the gentility he was certain she was not used to and with a nod permitted her to start up before him. The three men who had been blocking the door didn't take their eyes off him, but decided to move and lean against the building. Max went up behind the woman, patient with her pregnant waddle and heavy breathing, and for some odd reason suddenly was embarrassed to be faced with her widespread derrière.

She shuffled herself out of the way on the third-floor landing, where she didn't lose the opportunity while getting out her keys to smile at Máximo, who returned it with a grateful one acknowledging the brief acquaintance they had just shared. Taking two steps at a time, he continued up to the fifth floor, where the pregnant woman had told him the Hilda she knew lived.

No one answered but the incessant barking of what had to be a small dog. The antagonistic yapping of the animal irritated him to no end. He stood impatiently before the bolted door, trying to decide what to do. He had a feeling that if he left at that moment, with The Three Muscateers waiting downstairs, he might not get very far without losing all of his belongings and suffering a broken rib or two.

He heard a door unlock on one of the flights below and it was the voice of the woman who had shown him up, "¡Señol!"

"¡Sí! ¿Sí, señora?" he called down to the voice. He was so anxious to put his bag down, he half hoped she would invite him down to her apartment.

"¡Hilda viene ahora! Okey?"

She was letting him know that Hilda would arrive soon. He sat at the top of the stairs, elbows on his knees, tentatively incognizant that he was soiling his suit on the filthy landing. In a few moments he brightened as he heard the clicking sounds of a woman's heels on the steps five flights down. He peered through the iron rails. In the center of the cornucopia of the stairwell was the top of a woman's head. He could tell next to nothing of her but that she had a mane of dark hair that went over her shoulders.

He closed his eyes and waited. Hilda was merely fifteen when she fell in love with his father. All that this meant was that she may have been a bit young to be Max's mother, but not too young for his father. Hilda had fallen crazily in love with the dandy gallego who had passed through Manhattan waiting for a ship to catch a ride back home and whom she never saw again. He left only his mother's address, as transient lovers sometimes do; Drop me a postcard sometime, in case you're ever in my part of the world, negrita . . . and she had faithfully and relentlessly dropped post cards and Christmas cards with glitter for snow and pictures of Santa Claus and North American candy canes. During the war, his father said, he received one of the diligent post cards from France and he worried that any day she might appear on his doorstep.

As she grew nearer, Max envied his father to have captured the ardent love of a woman for so long, as well as pitied the woman, who, as far as anyone knew, hadn't been left with a child but had wasted a good life on a man who hardly remembered her except for the persistent one-sided correspondence.

When Hilda reached the third floor, she stopped abruptly. Max knew the third floor tenant had called Hilda over to whisper to her about the man who waited at the top floor. A few moments passed before the hollow sound of her heels continued and just as she turned to go up to the last floor, Max caught the first view of her face. She was dark, as he knew his father liked his women, and although not very small, with those thick bones of women indigenous to the Americas, she seemed in good shape. For Max, who was still a young man, she was an older woman; not old enough to be matronly; nevertheless she had reached the age which his conservative upbringing had told him to treat with deference.

She stopped before she began the last series of steps to her door. By her hesitation he could tell that momentarily she had held her breath. She probably was not able to make out his face well because of the dim light in the hall and until then he had remained seated in the shadows of the railing. He stood up. Another moment of exceeding weight passed before she proceeded up toward him, haltingly, scrutinizing her guest. Once next to him, she jangled her keys into the locks in the door and opened it. She stepped in without saying a word, but left it open and he followed.

A scraggly poodle greeted its mistress inside a dingy hall. The stench of dog urine filled Max's nostrils and in one sweep his eyes absorbed the repugnant combination of vermin, foul smells, and human degradation.

She lit the pilot on the small stove with a match she pulled from a box on the shelf that served also as a breeding home for cockroaches. Max noticed the mangy poodle was not her only pet. A lazy Siamese stared up with its crossed eyes from one of the two kitchen chairs.

She began to boil a pot of water and brought out a pair of unmatched cups from the excuse of a cupboard that had lost its glass doors in a battle against vandalism. Every now and then she glanced at him sideways.

Max ached to sit down and get out of his tight boots, but the lazy Siamese (that later was to become a mortal enemy) remained stubbornly on the chair; and the dog, as if intentionally, jumped on the other and growled at Max. Its pink tongue hung between snarls in a look that showed it was also delighted to see Hilda.

Max watched her prepare Cuban espresso. Presently, she had rinsed out the cups and poured the coffee. Taking a sip from her own first, a maternal act to test its temperature or taste, she then picked up the other cup and handed it to Max. It was her first deliberate act that acknowleged his presence. He hoped this also meant that he was welcome to stay.

"You almost gave me a heart attack, you know." Her voice was unbecoming, he thought, to her who seemed she might have a mouselike voice and yet was coarse. Her Spanish was fluent.

"Oh? Why was that?" Max accepted the coffee. He saw that they were playing a game. Women and their endless games, he mused. She was in his league, for no other man could enjoy such games more, except perhaps the one who kept receiving cards sent with religious fervor for twenty years.

"The girl downstairs said there was a Spaniard waiting up here for me. When I first saw you, all dressed like a peacock, with those pointy boots and that moustache . . . !" She put down her coffee. Now, she studied him eye to eye, an open stare, uninhibited. She was making an evaluation and Max put his cup down, too, uneasy. He wasn't used to a woman's blatant appraisal of him.

The kitchen light was a combination of shadows and eeriness, while the sun set somewhere on the other side of the ozone. Her hair was thick and wild, the kind of hair that gives a person a fight all her life, charged with an electricity that had the strands vibrating like black currents around the head.

Her face was unquestionably attractive, a woman who, in Max's youthful mind, must have been pretty in "her day." Her clothes were odd, a series of mismatched layers, and he could only assume she was terribly eccentric, abreast of the ultimate in fashion, or pitifully poor. The impoverished apartment gave the third possibility a strong argument.

She came close to him, seemingly unaware that she made him self-conscious with her scrutiny. "You don't have his eyes, not just because yours are darker and his, as clear and as cool as water, but they're different altogether."

Max had his grandmother's eyes.

"But beneath that moustache, I can tell you have the same mouth, the same fullness of the bottom lip." Hilda was up to him now and he felt her coffee breath on his chin. He brought his mouth down on hers and she received him.

thirteen

As the months passed, Max gave up the regular use of his single suit for jeans and shirts, but kept faithful to the pointed flamenco boots.

Hilda turned out to be an actress, although obviously one who had never attained much success. She introduced her intense young lover to her contacts and he got a job playing in a Spanish restaurant-bar. For a while he kept alive the expectation that a powerful talent scout would appear in the dive that catered to Iberians and discover the terribly handsome, although perhaps not terribly adept, guitarist (Pío had demonstrated Max's shortcomings in this area by his own flawless musical ability) and put him on Broadway or even in films.

The owners of the club, a married couple, came up with the idea of adding a dancer to the act. Max had accompanied flamenco dancers now and then in Madrid, but only with reservation did he consent to the change. Hilda thought that if it made the owners happy, it shouldn't make much difference to Max, and who would know, he could be given better tips if the act turned out to be appealing enough.

La China, as she was billed, was a flaxen-haired gringa who'd studied with a famous flamenco dancer and had spent a summer with the same in Andalucía. Max was made to spend hours on end in rehearsal with the anarchist dancer, who was bent on high energy as the primary factor of her body's expression. She was in decent form, as young women in good health were, particularly dancers, with a certain tension in the hips and thighs that aroused Max's interest. If it was a game of fate, he mused, if she made the first move, he wouldn't frown on the consummation of their union as a performance team. Up until then, he had been faithful to Hilda, although he hadn't looked at his not having made love to another woman in months as being monogamous, but she had managed to satisfy him physically so that he didn't consider variety.

As the time spent between La China and Max increased and his time with Hilda diminished, Hilda grew intolerable. Her possessiveness was no longer guised in caring or protectiveness over a naïve foreigner. The obsession that motivated the string of cards sent to a man she had not seen in more than twenty years lapsed over to the fear of losing the surrogate. Every night after Max finished playing, he and Hilda went home battling. Although he never admitted he had been making love to La China, she sensed it, had an instinct for his betrayal, and followed it relentlessly, like a hound on a fox trail.

It wasn't until the owner's wife sat with a complimentary cognac in hand for him that he knew at last what he had to do. Before him she placed a few large bills neatly folded on the varnished bar. His eyes stared at the money and he looked at the woman who obviously had a plan in mind for him. He drank his cognac in one swallow.

"Buy yourself a new suit, Máximo," she told him. She had a kind of slow way of talking that was sensual to him, although the woman herself had never called his attention. He mistook the gift and, without yet putting his hand on the money, he reached over to kiss her lips, but she pulled away. She looked around nervously, as if someone may have been watching. The bartender was preoccupied with drying glasses.

"Buy yourself a new suit and find another job." This time Max knew exactly what she was saying, but he was puzzled. She continued, "Hilda loves you." Máximo remained silent; he didn't discuss his women with other women. "But she's bad for business. Maybe she's too in love for her own good, or for your own good. In any case, you'd better go and find another place to work and take her with you."

Max wanted to ignore his patrona's suggestion, and reached over to kiss her again. He ventured she was having a bad case of unsatisfied yearning and he would happily give himself up to the service. "Please, Max grow up." she insisted. "My husband doesn't need another reason to hate your guts. He sees how all the women that come in here drool over you and he's sick with envy. . . I like you, I think you have potential, maybe not as a flamenco guitarist. The United States isn't exactly loaded with aficionados, but you've got something special."

Max put his hand over the bills and in a deliberate sweep stuck them into his breast pocket. No sooner had he done so when the woman's husband came out from the kitchen. He joined them at the bar to have a drink and Max told him that he would regretfully be playing his last sets that night. By the way the patrón nodded and waved his hand in consent, Max knew the couple had already discussed the issue.

Hilda came in just in time to catch the first set and sat at the bar next to Máximo. The patrón discreetly changed the subject. "Hey, we had some nice people in from Chicago last night, Máximo," his patrón told him. "Some musicians and a singer, a woman . . . " He groped for the name in the air.

"Pastora Velásquez," his wife helped him.

"Yes, yes! Did you ever hear of her? They say she has recorded."

Both Max and Hilda shook their heads. The truth was, Max was hardly listening to the conversation. Hilda's appearance only added the spice to his anger for having been let go from his job. She had been the sole cause of it. Every night she sent dagger looks to the female customers, any woman who came near him was immediately put off by her. He understood now why La China had quit her job the week before.

"Ever hear of her?" his patrón repeated and again. Max shook his head. "Very nice-looking girl, dark, with long hair. I hear she's got a good voice, but she doesn't do flamenco. We couldn't use her here . . ." he said. The patrón was just shooting the breeze to kill time, a few polite minutes with the man he had just had his wife fire, and with his old lady who was the type who would kill to save her love.

Máximo's patrón's voice faded as his own silent rage grew. He knew, however, that he must not let Hilda know how he felt toward her, not yet. No, he had to go on as usual; perhaps he might be kinder than usual and in the end she would recall that the kindness was nothing more than the sugar-coating on a strychnine tablet. He would get his vengeance.

"Too bad you couldn't use her. She sounds wonderful." Hilda spoke in a tone that grated against Máximo's nerves, as he took it all as hypocrisy. He couldn't believe she meant she would like the idea of an attractive woman working in the same place as Máximo.

"Autre femme plus ravissante que vous?" He smiled at Hilda and put an arm around her tight waist. She almost blushed, so flattered was she by his unexpected charm. Max had begun to prepare his lamb for the slaughter.

His flattery throughout the evening suddenly turned into glumness when they were on their way home. By the time they were on the subway she was desperate to bring back his good humor. After she had made several attempts at probing him for what was wrong, without looking at Hilda, but keeping his eyes on his shoes, Max responded, "How would you feel if you had been insulted as I was this evening?" Of course, Hilda had no idea as to what he meant.

"The wife of my boss tells me to buy another suit! She tells me mine is too worn, too pitiful! As if her miserly husband paid me enough! But what offended me most was that she's right!" He sounded truly dejected.

Hilda was quiet. Max knew what she would say and he waited. "Amor, if it doesn't insult you for me to offer it, because I only do it with the best intentions, you know how much you mean to me, cariño . . . We'll get you a new suit tomorrow. If that bitch thinks she is bringing down the standards of her cheap joint by the fact that you aren't dressed up enough, tomorrow she'll see!"

The following evening as Max bathed and dressed in his new suit, extra new shirts laid carefully out on the bed, he asked Hilda to run an errand for him. He looked at his watch as if he suddenly realized the time and told her that afterward she should go straight to the restaurant-bar to meet him there. With a semblance to her mangy poodle, she obeyed without hesitation and left.

From underneath the bed, Max produced his leather bag. He opened all its compartments and shook it out violently to evict the cockroaches nesting within. He packed his things at once and went out the door, down the five flights of stairs, past the door of the woman who had had a miscarriage, past the hoodlums who stood like sentinels in the hallway but were now Máximo's compais, down two blocks to the boulevard where he caught a cab to the bus station.

fourteen

Max woke with a stiff neck as the bus broke its rhythm of steady motion and pulled into the bus terminal. He opened his eyes and could see his breath on the window. It was hard to believe he could be travelling south to California and the weather was actually getting colder.

All the passengers got off the bus in a sleepy stupor and Max followed all too aware that something wasn't right. He'd bought a one-way ticket to Los Angeles with the money he'd gotten from the patrona. But it was apparent by the snow on the ground at the end of the terminal, the pallid faces around him, that they hadn't been going in the direction he'd set out in the night before.

Once in the terminal, large and bustling, with the usual display of transients pertaining to bus depots everywhere, he saw on a terminal screen that they had arrived in Chicago. It was impossible! He had had a few drinks while waiting for the bus in New York, but he had asked for a ticket to Los Angeles and had furthermore boarded a bus destined for Los Angeles.

He went directly to complain to a ticket agent. Max pulled out the stub from his pocket and put it under the thick window for the agent to see for herself how he had been duped, a victim of her company's incompetency. "I bought a ticket last night for Los Angeles, Madam, and instead, it came to Chicago. What seems to be the problem here? I expect a refund!"

The woman took up the stub and, after examining it, pushed it back toward Max's side. "This ticket clearly states New York to Chicago, sir." Max snatched it. How was it that he had bought a ticket to Chicago and boarded a bus to Chicago and had in his conscious mind the idea that he was on his way to California?

He walked off staring in total bafflement at the ticket stub. He had to check his wallet now to see if he had enough money left to take him to L.A. Before he'd gone to sleep and awoken in this phenomenal predicament, he had had enough to carry him through until he got a job in California. He had the money for the one-way ticket and an agent told him a bus, although not an express, would be leaving shortly. He was completely disoriented and went straight toward the dark lounge for a cognac. He sat at the bar and put out of his mind what had just happened.

New York had driven him crazy. That had to have been it. He had arrived injected with all those pipe dreams typical of his father's and had found New York, America a grotesque circus, a Felliniesque nightmare, and that was what had him doing things now that he couldn't explain.

Sitting at the bar, he wanted to avoid conversation with the unsavory character two stools down who eyed him as if they were old friends, and he pulled out a book to read from his bag. It was one that had belonged to Hilda. Hilda, despite her shortcomings, he felt, had been a cultured person. Already he thought of her as something that had been rather than still existing somewhere else.

To Hilda, whose reality had not changed but for the absence of one factor, Max had left her only the night before. Until it occurred to her to look under the bed to check for his bag, she would have gone on expecting him home any minute. To Max, Hilda was non-existent. All that Max left behind ceased to exist, was unreal, like the celluloid on which a whole story was told; it was all imaginary, pictures contrived and pieced together for the sake of entertainment.

It was a book of poems by García Lorca. Inside there was an inscription: "To Hilda on your birthday, Luv . . ." The giver's name had been scratched out with a vindictive pen. The year in which the dedication was inscribed was the same that Max had had sex with a girl for the first time.

> Sí, tu niñez ya fábula de fuentes.
> El tren y la mujer que llena el cielo
> Tu soledad esquiva en los hoteles
> y tu máscara pura de otro signo.

"¡Pastora! ¡No se te vaya a olvidar tu mochila!" The woman's voice broke his concentration and Max instinctively turned about, hearing the familiar Spanish and curious to see who spoke it. He looked about as two women left the bar silhouetted by the bright lights of the station as they came out of the lounge as if from a cave. He hadn't been able to see their faces, but one, the one whom he thought had been called Pastora, wore a handwoven blanket over her body that came down to her knees. Its motif was reminiscent of the work done in his country.

Curious to know who these women were and believing that perhaps by having a brief exchange with someone who was reminiscent of the familiar might orient him back to reality, he picked up his bag, swallowed his cognac, and took off behind them. They were a distance away when he spotted them walking toward the rows of ticket agents behind the long counter.

At the same time, as if he were suddenly in the theatre watching a movie or a play in which every detail was presented intentionally for him to observe as part of the drama, there were two Caucasian men in dark suits also studying the women. At first Max assumed the men wanted to approach the women because they sought their company, but as he studied the course of events he realized the men were authorities of some sort and weren't necessarily friendly. Each woman dug into her respective bag, produced identification, and in a few moments was dismissed.

Máximo's heart pounded. The men were immigration officials and were scouting out the bus station deliberately for undocumented persons. The women, in their ethnic garb and dark hair, probably aroused the suspicion of the pair of idiots who actually thought anyone who was undocumented would dress in a native costume!

All during his stay in New York, Max had never once had such an encounter. He stood frozen, watching the men watch others, and for the present forgot the women who went on their way. He reminded himself that he looked Caucasian. He was dressed in denim pants and his sheepskin coat. There was nothing about him that could give him away. Appropriately dressed for winter weather, pale, how could those men pick him out of the crowd as they had done to the women?

He had to revive his courage. Taking sure steps, he went in the direction of the men who had hardly looked his way as he passed and continued unnoticed. Then one called out. "Hey, you!" He thought not to turn around, but what good would it have done? The man called again and came up behind him. "Hey, buddy, I think you dropped this." He handed Max the envelope with his bus ticket that had slipped out of his back pocket and Max thanked him with a nod.

His knee joints had locked and his ears burned but he had been able to get past the immigration officials, right below their noses without arousing the least suspicion. A sense of freedom welled inside that came to the person whose identity had been completely erased. He fit in the crowd inconspicuously.

Max looked about him and could not decipher one face from the next. There were ugly old women and degenerated men, in all probability much younger in years than their appearance. There were young black men with cocky looks that dared anyone's attempt to demonstrate human compassion. He took a seat along an endless row of plastic chairs and opened the book of poems again.

Lorenzo
Emilio
Enrique
Estaban los tres quemados
Lorenzo por el mundo de las hojas y las bolas de billar
Emilio por el mundo de la sangre y los alfileres blancos,
Enrique por el mundo de los muertos y los periódicos abandonados.

From the corner of his eye he saw the pair of immigration officers pass behind him. Max was no longer intimidated. He was secure in his disguise and with open curiosity followed with his look to see whom they were about to prey upon next. A small man with a mane of black hair and a windbreaker talked on the pay phone, his collar up, as if wishing he were invisible. He was yet unaware of the men who were descending on him. A flash of bravado passed through Max's head. He could hurry and warn the man, pretend to ask the time and in Spanish, in a low voice, warn the stranger, who most likely, from appearances, had just arrived in the city and may have spent what was to him a small fortune to get there.

For an instant of empathy, Max imagined himself in the role of the ordinary hero, who on any given day extended himself to his fellow man in need because preservation bound all humanity.

Max observed the men approach the dark one on the phone and when it was apparent they were about to take him away, suddenly another one who'd been standing nearby, perhaps a companion of the first, shot off; in fear of being taken too, he was attempting escape. One of the immigration men went in pursuit. The first dashed up the escalator and the one chasing behind took the stairs, two and three steps at time. Another agent appeared, one whom Max had not noticed before. He wore jeans and a pea coat, not the usual attire of government officials with their short trousers and white socks. He chased the one who was trying to get away too, as if they were after a viscious criminal, determined to take him in and see justice carried out.

The first one, the one who had been on the phone, stood expressionless. The agent with him kept a firm grip on his arm. Max continued reading.

> I will not see it!
> Tell the moon to come
> for I do not want to see the blood
> of Ignacio on the sand.
> I will not see it!
> The moon wide open.
> Horse of still clouds
> and the grey bull ring of dreams
> with willows in the barreras.

It was time for Max to board the bus. He double-checked his ticket and watched the bus driver as he changed the sign over the windshield to one that read a series of stops, the final one being Los Angeles.

fifteen

The sun in Los Angeles was a Spanish sun. It threatened to melt the brain, but it had been a long time since Max felt such warmth and he wallowed in its rays to the brink of sun stroke.

His first nights in California he slept in a fleabag hotel. He asked around for places where he could apply for work and mostly drank in an attempt to erase New York. To Max, Los Angeles was as different from it as the difference was between two countries. There was the question of the architecture. The houses in the Latino community, although crowded and rampant with licelike nests of children, were horizontal and didn't rise into the sky as did the tenements on the East Coast. The structures were mostly Spanish-influenced and that, too, reminded him of Puerto Sapogonia.

The year he spent in New York, he had dropped his Castilian Spanish, except at the restaurant-bar where he played, and picked up the accented one of the Caribbeans who surrounded him in everyday life. Hilda had reprimanded him for it. She thought he degraded himself in some way, pretending not to speak the language properly, as it was meant to be spoken. What Hilda hadn't observed was that Máximo changed with his environment as the chameleon became the color of a leaf or a rock to protect it from being detected easily by a predator.

At the end of the week, his feet burned from walking with his guitar from restaurant to bar, bar to restaurant, in search of a job. He let himself get slobbering drunk in the bar just two doors down from where he had rented a room until that day when he ran out of money and was unable to pay for another night. His new suit was unkempt, his beard was scraggly, and his eyes sunk in from the abuse the alcohol committed on his body.

"Well! Well! So from what far off place have we strayed, stranger?"

Max looked up through glazed eyes and saw an older man with a moustache and hair too black to be real. Max was too weary to insult him. This encouraged the man and he continued, moving over to the stool next to Max. "¿De dónde eres?" he asked. Max looked at him again. The character was well-groomed and neatly dressed, although Max didn't want to give him much credit considering the area they were in. He straightened up and ran his fingers through his hair. Putting on his Castilian accent, like a tuxedo one kept in the closet for just such occasions, he told the man, "I'm from Spain . . . a well-known guitarist there. I've been here only a few days . . ."

"A well-known guitarist in Spain, but no more than a miserable, hungry fool here," the other said, pretending to be unimpresed.

"Wait a minute, pansy . . . !" Max took him by the collar. The man didn't look intimidated, but stood up. "My house is a short walk from here . . ." Max nodded. With the gallant but clumsy motions of a drunk, he helped the man with his jacket. "Just remember something . . ." Max told him. The man turned and waited to hear what he had to say. "And what should that be, señor?" Max looked him in the eye. "Just don't fall in love with me!"

Max got excellent tips at Las Fuentes de Atotonilco Restaurant where he had worked as a waiter for seven months, and despite the white peon's pajamas the waiters had to wear as a uniform, he enjoyed his job. It allowed him free days to pursue other interests, and since he had not lost sight of the aspiration to become a well-known performer, he worked like an ambitious black widow on its web, making contacts through the Spanish-speaking network.

There were moments when hope was not ridiculed by his efforts. There was a brief, but what he considered to be important, spot on a popular local television show on the Spanish language station. His manager told him that the station had received numerous calls regarding his performance. He'd sung for a month of weekends at a Spanish restaurant downtown for a salary and tips.

He made friends with actors from a community theatre company. They advised him to study voice and to take his guitar more seriously. They thought he showed unusual promise for the stage.

He worked a rotating shift at Las Fuentes de Atotonilco. They flipped coins and as it was, he was usually lucky enough to work on the same day that Carmelita worked as a hostess. Carmelita, with the eyes of caramelos, was a Chicana he had been going out with.

Chicano was a new word for him. As his friends explained it, Chicanos had been in California, the whole Southwest of the United States so long, they could still remember when it was Mexico. Carmelita's people had been in California forever. Her Spanish was fragmented, but she was still Chicana.

It was the first day that week that he had come in to work and he was in an especially good mood. He was going to his first audition that evening. He'd never acted before, but he was confident he would get the part. It was a play by García Lorca and he knew there would be no man around who could do justice to García Lorca as he. Besides, there could be no other meaning to having picked the *Poet in New York* from Hilda's bookshelf at random. It had to have been an omen. Life wasn't a coincidence, after all.

Carmelita was standing by the podium near the entrance in her China poblana costume, her pale shoulders bare, the plastic gardenia pinned to her caramelo hair. She led a couple to a table when a Latino man with dark glasses came in, dressed in a sport shirt and jeans. His hair was a little short for the times, but I thought he was in the navy or something like that. In any event, there was something peculiar about him. I remember even now that I noticed him immediately, sensed that something was off, but I didn't know what.

He didn't seem to be waiting for the return of the hostess to seat him. As I said, there was something odd about him. I delivered the order I was carrying to a table and decided to take it upon myself to seat the man. The thought did occur to me that he was a pest after Carmelita's attention. As I was about to step toward him, Carmelita called to me. It was an urgent gasp sounding my name. I stopped dead in my tracks.

At that instant, three others stormed in and without warning went straight toward the kitchen. "¡La migra!" someone yelled and the place was in an uproar. Not only were there undocumented workers among the employees, but among the patronage as well.

In my best English I tried to explain that I was Spanish, not Mexican, but I had no identification. The merchant's visa I had entered the country with had expired. "Spanish, Mexican . . . It's all the same shit!" came the reply from the migra official. I looked in the eyes of the dark man that had come in first, who had to have also been Latino, maybe Chicano. It was an instant of mutual recognition before he threw me into the wagon.

After I was deported to Tijuana and had stayed to sight-see for a few days, I had the illusion that I would run into someone who could give me a ride back to the other side. I had little money and paying a coyote was out of the question. With my accented English, I proceeded with my plan as I befriended a lone American in a bar one night. We got roaring drunk together, the bartender filling our shot glasses with tequila and the North American matching each one I swallowed. I told him I was Mexican-American and lived in San Diego. Although the other was practically falling off his stool, he eyed me with suspicion. "How did you get over here? Take a bus or something?" I had just asked him for a ride back to San Diego.

I was ready with a story. "I came here with my girlfriend this morning, man. We were planning on getting married. At the last minute she chickened out and left me, just like that. 'Walk back, as far as I care!' she told me!" I said with great drama to convince the gringo in hopes of gaining his sympathy.

"Women!" the drunken americano said, waving a hand to show his disgust. "Mujeres! It's 'mujeres,' right?"

"Yeah, yeah, mujeres," I verified his Spanish, pretending to be drunker than I was. Finally, he decided to go home. He thought of spending the night somewhere in Tijuana because he felt just a "wee bit too loaded" to drive, he said, but I assured him that he was steady as could be and that anyway, in the kind of room he would get in Tijuana at that hour, he'd be lucky to wake up with only his pants, shoes, and wallet gone.

We climbed into his pickup and headed for the San Ysidro border. On the way, I subtly tried to prepare my new accomplice in the event that we were questioned. It crossed my mind that the gringo was so drunk we might be harrassed on that basis alone. "Listen, hombre," I told my friend, "if they ask you at the border anything about me, tell them I'm an old friend, all right? Tell them I work with you in San Diego."

The gringo got that suspicious look again, a look that should have warned me then that the man was not going to stick his neck out for me if the circumstances called for it. "Why do I have to tell them that, amigo? You don't got papers or something? Is that it?" He was making me nervous, but I managed to laugh. "No! That's not it! My girlfriend, man, the one who ditched me this morning . . . she took off with my wallet, too!"

"Some woman you got there, hombre!" the gringo said, handling his vehicle as if he were commanding a rocket. "Maybe it's a good thing you got rid of her before you got hooked up."

"Yeah," I agreed, wondering if he believed anything I had told him. "Women! They're all the same."

"Not mine," the gringo cut in. "My wife's a gem, a real beaut. She's home with the kids right now, waiting for me to come home with open arms."

I eyed the gringo. That's why you're whoring around in Tijuana, huh, you bastard? Your woman's probably put the horns on you so many times and you don't even know it, that every asshole on your street has had her. I got satisfaction telling the gringo off to myself while we rode in silence, and I held on to my seat praying that we just got to the border alive. The gringo drove like a maniac.

When we reached the border, the gringo guard, seeing the California license plates and a red-faced gringo behind the wheel, was about to let the truck pass when the asshole behind the wheel leaned his head out the window and threw up, just missing the guard as he stepped back in time.

I turned my face and pretended to be asleep. I heard the guard tell the American to pull over and to get out. I didn't lift my head or open my eyes. I hoped the guard would assume I was a gringo, too, and would let me sleep off my drunk. Then came the inevitable question, "Who's your pal there? He okay?"

My stomach became a ball of iron as I waited for the response, the verdict of my destiny. There were dozens of replies the gringo, who could hardly stand up, might have given, dozens that would have had nothing to do with my nationality or my place of origin. With the limitation of his gnat's brain, however, he thought of none of them. Instead, he said, "Some greaser that caught a ride with me is all I know," and threw up again.

sixteen

Finding it somewhat easier in the respect of crossing borders to travel south than it was to go north, I decided to return to Sapogonia to see my family. It had been over five and a half years since I left home. I was thinking that perhaps it had come time for me to consider my future seriously.

I had a talent for music and drama, but I'd already seen how little the performing arts were appreciated by the public and cultural promoters. If I were taller, perhaps, (if my English had been a tad better as well) or if I got into rock music, I could have made a name for myself. I needed assurance of financial support so that I could return to the U.S. with a student visa. I would have to tell my grandfather I was going to study medicine or law. The old man would never consent to paying for an education in the arts. Could I ever hope to make a living from it—assuming I had talent? And if I proved to have exceptional talent, perhaps even displayed genius, pity me. It would be certain that I was destined to starve. Society never recognized its creative geniuses until long after their deaths. The problem with this theory, my grandfather would readily point out, was that usually society also did not recognize its mediocre artists and no one in his lifetime knew for certain in which category he belonged.

It took me three days to hitch from the border to the village of San Co, which I thought as a boy was the epitome of sophistication and progress. In fact, it was then, and had remained a thumbnail-sized village, anachronistic and pathetic with its twenty-five-year-old fin tail cars and its aged square with the grandiose cathedral looming over the plaza, and everywhere traces of irreparable dilapidation.

What was new to my eyes, the eyes of a new generation of adults, was the foreboding presence of the military among civilians. The inhabitants seemed to be oblivious to the military installation at all its places of business, parked in front of the bank, the primary school where children passed in their starched blue uniforms ignoring the soldiers who smoked and joked with each other as if they were crossing guards.

When I left my country, there had been trouble in the South. I had only heard news through sources that travelled back and forth. It was nothing that was printed in the newspapers or, even less, heard on the radio or seen on television. Civil unrest had a way of being kept from the citizens of the nation. Talk of such incidents was discouraged and considered, at the very least, unpatriotic. Still one heard them, as rumors. A newspaper that was published in the city nearest San Co was closed after printing a photograph of soldiers attacking two men in the South who were thought to be organizers of field workers.

How casual, like an afternoon hobby, that kind of talk seemed to Máximo now, as he witnessed the frankness with which soldiers displayed their imposing status on the public. It seemed that at random they stopped people who passed just to insult them.

As I waited to cross the street, I heard one of the soldiers call to a woman who crossed in the opposite direction. "Don't you know that a woman has no business being out on the street by herself? Or is that your business?" The woman pretended not to hear the remark and kept walking steadily. I succumbed to the urge to see who it was who had insulted her. It was a boy, no more than seventeen, scrawny, with a rolled-up cigarette between his teeth. His dun-colored uniform hung over the shoulders. He caught my glance and gave me a fraternal grin. I smiled back and looked away quickly.

I managed to get to my grandfather's ranch without incident. It had startled me to see military in the streets. I'd kept up with the news printed in the U.S. It was said that the government was making every effort to keep under control terrorist attempts that threatened the well-being of civilians and guerrillas in the hills that sought to destroy the tranquility of the state.

From what Máximo could tell, there probably were terrorists and guerrillas organizing in the hills. There was nothing new about that. There were always bands of rebels forming for the sake of the poor or to pillage and plunder. It all depended on who was the national leader at the time. They never had been such a threat that, even as far north as San Co, there was need for military vigilance.

It was dusk by the time I saw my grandfather's house down the road, silhouetted by the flaming sun on the horizon. The house seemed much smaller and much older than it was before I left. There was a time when I'd thought my grandfather was the richest man in the world.

"Saturday your grandfather is going to take you to the city to order the finest little boots anyone has ever seen on a little man such as you!" I heard my grandfather's bellowing voice in my memory. It was the voice of a man with great stamina, superhuman strength and abilities.

He had inherited his property from his father and aside from having married an Indian, he had followed to the letter the norms of his class. He treated his workers and house servants fairly, never raised his voice or was abusive in any way. Unlike his own grandfather, who'd probably treated the slaves on his land no better than the animals that grazed on it, my grandfather listened to complaints, considered their legitimacy, and was even known for making an effort to remedy them.

The first familiar face that Máximo came upon was that of Paquito, a mestizo who'd been on the ranch since Máximo's childhood. He tended the horses. Paquito was strong despite his small size. Max had watched him lasso young bucks and dominate the most spirited steeds. "¿Quién va?" Paquito called out to Max as he stepped onto the front porch. It was understandable that Paquito did not recognize the young man who'd left as an adolescent. "Ha!" he laughed, coming over to shake Máximo's hand and embrace him. "It's you! Good to see you! Your grandfather's going to be happy to see you!"

Máximo entered the house that had shrunk in his mind. The main room was half the size as he remembered it. The dining room, with its table to seat eight, was also smaller than he had thought it. He was nervous about reuniting with his family, his mother, grandfather, grandmother—who alone stayed vivid like a flame in his mind; an eccentric, tiny and ancient, completely out of synch in her husband's home.

"So you finally decided to return home, you vagabond," the voice came from behind the armchair that faced a sizzling fire in the fireplace in the living room. Mixed with the smell of the burning wood was the smoke of a hand-rolled cigarette.

"¿Mamá Grande?" Máximo stopped, dropping the plastic bag that contained the few belongings he'd collected since his deportation. "Who else, cabroncito? Marie Antoinette? Come give me a hug and let me see how ugly you are!" Máximo ran over to the little body, fragile as a figurine of blown glass, and hugged his grandmother with all his strength.

She was smaller, too, than he recalled. In this case, he thought, age really was shrinking the old woman. Her tawny face was a myriad of wrinkles, like hundreds of roads all leading back to the ranch in San Co. She had all her teeth and her hair, combed back and plaited, remained as black as obsidian. She smiled. Her eyes were dots surrounded by wrinkled lids, and the whites of the eyes were yellowish red and moist.

"What is this?" She pulled at his beard. "Only goats have those things . . . and that's because they can't shave!" she teased him. "I guess beneath it, you're really a handsome boy! How we've missed you! You just don't know . . . your mother, your grandfather! He doesn't like to admit it, always pretending he is angry with you for leaving as you did, but you know how he always adored you!"

Máximo buried his face in the shriveled bosom. Tears ran down his face as his nostrils consumed all the smells of his childhood. He wanted to tell her he was sorry for having left so abruptly, for not having come back sooner, but he understood there were no apologies necessary for the old Indian woman.

It wouldn't be the same in the case of his mother or his grandfather, but he would have to reckon with them soon enough. He had enough time for a good cry and then his grandmother asked if he was hungry. He nodded. He was a little boy again and his grandmother was going to take him off somewhere and perform magic, turn a cloud in the sky into the shape of a bull or cause a hummingbird to land on his shoulder.

He helped the old woman out of her comfortable chair. "Come on, sinvergüenza! Let's see what we find for you to eat," she told him, insisting that he sit down at the table while she went to the kitchen. Máximo wanted to get up, explore the rest of the house, find the other members of the family. He was also beat and yearned for a hot bath. Yet he knew his grandmother was up to something unique.

She no sooner went into the kitchen when she returned with a large earthen pot. It was steaming. A stewed chicken with vegetables and a savory tomato sauce tantalized his hunger; and she sat with him while he devoured everything, right out of the pot. It was only with his grandmother that he had ever been able to get away with the absence of all table manners.

He was sucking the last tricky bone when he heard the door slam. "Es tu papá grande," his grandmother whispered, as if it were a warning rather than an announcement. "Get up and meet him," she coaxed Máximo. He rose and went to the living room, wiping his hands on his pants as he went.

Only his grandfather hadn't shrunk. He was actually bigger than Máximo remembered and it took only a few seconds of sizing each other up, Máximo waiting for his grandfather's reaction, when the two embraced, long and tearfully. "You little bastard! You almost killed your mother when you left in the dead of night!" He pretended to be angry.

Máximo's grandmother came in on birdlike legs and stopped to watch the reunion. "Don't use that word here!" she scolded her husband. She was the only woman Máximo had known in his life in San Co that dared to speak up to her husband and to any other man when she was displeased. "You yourself have said children come from God born to women, and we are all the same in His eyes. It's the men who fail to meet up to their responsibilities that are bastards," she muttered slowly, making her way back to her chair in front of the fire.

Her husband, with an arm around his grandson's shoulders, stared at the miniature dame of his household of more than fifty years. He gestured to Máximo as if to say, "We have to watch ourselves around the boss!" and took his grandson in his embrace once again to make certain it was not one of her aberrations.

The older man asked Max if he had eaten and then offered him a drink. Máximo accepted the idea and when he looked over at the chair where his grandmother had gone to sit, it was empty. He went back to the dining room table with his grandfather, taking a seat across from him with a bottle of firewater between them.

"The situation is very serious around here, son." His grandfather spoke in a low voice. "Did you see all the soldiers in town? It's like when we had that buey Romero all over again! Thank God you're back. I think the Lord has sent you back to us to take over the ranch . . . to defend what's yours. I'm not going to be here much longer . . ."

His grandfather looked almost identical to how he was when Máximo saw him last. Certainly, he was an old man, but even with his age, he was powerful and lucid of mind. In addition, Máximo remembered his grandfather as among the most respected figures in the whole area. Yet, he drank like a man condemned to be hanged in the morning.

"Papá Grande, señor," Máximo discreetly took the bottle from his grandfather, afraid that he would get drunk before they had a chance to discuss his future from his perspective. "What is it that you're afraid will happen?"

The old man yanked the bottle back from his grandson. "Me? I'm not afraid of anything! Who do you ask? I've never been afraid of anything in my life! When Romero was in power, I was the only one in the whole district who stood up against him, and I'd do it again if necessary!"

Máximo felt frustrated in less than an hour's time with his family's patriarch. "I don't mean to say you're afraid of anything, Papá Grande, but something is wrong and I want you to tell me! Have the soldiers been around here, or is someone threatening to take the ranch from you?"

His grandfather's eye bulged. "Threaten? Do you think those bastards bother to threaten? They just come and burn your place down with you still in it one night and that's that! You're finished!"

"But who, Papá? Who is it that comes?" The more Max talked and the more he drank with his grandfather, the more he returned to the familiarity they had had before he'd left, when he called him Papá, as he had been the father figure of his childhood.

"Who gives a damn if it's the half-starved soldiers or the half-starved rebels who come to take anything worth taking and killing innocent people! The point is that one day they can come here and I may not be here any longer—to defend the ranch!"

"Don't say that, Papá! You're not going to die!"

"What do you think, I'm going to live forever? I'm an old man, I'm tired!" His grandfather squinted. "Or what do you want to say— you're leaving again? You don't plan to stay?"

Máximo remained silent. He involuntarily lowered his head and reached for the bottle; his grandfather put a hand on it too and kept him from taking it. "Speak up! Are you leaving?"

Máximo felt the intimidation brought on by the man who was once total authority. There was no one in the whole area who didn't respect his grandfather. Even now, after all his wordly travels, he had trouble facing up to him. If Max were a man like his grandfather, he would stay. There would be no question but to stay and fight for righteous causes, freedom, and peace; but Máximo never cared for politics. His only politicking came from wanting to improve the economic and social condition of one individual.

He changed the subject. "And the Jiménez family? The brothers Jiménez?" He referred to his old friends, the brothers of the girl whom he'd raped and who had almost killed him for it. Their family owned and ran the ranch nearest his grandfather's.

"One went off with the army and died. The other joined the rebels in the South and got killed." The old man put up a finger as he accounted for each one. "The third stayed on the ranch with his father. He was already married, so he couldn't just go off. The ranch was burned one night and the whole family died. The animals, all of it, set ablaze and nothing left but charcoal."

"How long has this been going on, Papá Grande?" Máximo was somewhat ashamed of the fact that he knew so little about the chaos that had taken over his country.

"How long? About a hundred years!" his grandfather shouted back at him. "It was going on in the South since the turn of the century; only you were too young, too busy fucking every virgin in sight to be aware of anything before you left. Your godfather used to say, 'That little goat has his father's blood, destined to fuck and drink and waste his life away hustling whatever fool he comes across . . .'!" His grandfather wiped his eyes with the backs of his hands. Sentimentality showed through the tough exterior due to the drink. Máximo had never seen his grandfather cry before and he was stunned as the man buried his leather-skinned face in his big hands and sobbed.

"This is absurd," Max uttered, wanting very much to bring composure into the meeting. "We're in the twentieth century, we can't go on living like savages, taking the law into our own hands!"

His papá grande stopped crying to look at him. "Where do you think you are? This isn't gringolandia where everything is like Disneyland and just because the government says, 'Don't do this and don't do that,' people obey! Everyone in this country wears blinders or blindfolds. And you know why? You know why, don't you?" He was waving a finger in Max's face. Max didn't want to answer. His grandfather loathed the United States with a passion and he knew the old man blamed everything that went wrong in the country on the United States. Máximo didn't want to concern himself with that argument. "And my mother?" He asked for her in a funereal tone to calm his grandfather, who was once again taking a good swallow from the near-empty bottle.

"Ah! Your mother!" He sighed. Máximo imagined what criticism went on during those very seconds in his grandfather's head regarding Max's mother, the old man's only daughter, who had allowed herself to be seduced and impregnated by an unscrupulous Spaniard who then left her to have the child alone, like a miserable slave girl on a plantation. "Your mother, son, is fine. She got married . . . finally."

The day had been one of great surprises, none exactly pleasant, and this news came as no small package as well. His grandfather went on with the details. "She married a dandy and they live in Puerto Sapogonia. Even San Co wasn't good enough for him. I believe he's just waiting for me to drop dead so he can have all this. Your mother's a woman; she doesn't realize these things."

Max protested his grandfather's cynicism. "Don't think that way, Papá. This man might really love my mother. Anyway, you're not going to die . . ."

"What do you think? I'm made of stone? Of course I'm going to die! I'm going to die defending what my father left me, but I'm not going to go on forever. My sons have left this earth and you, I can tell, have no intentions of staying. Your grandmother was right. The earth is not in your blood. You liked the horses when you were a boy. What boy doesn't? But the labor of the ranch was like an insult to you. Your mother and grandmother protected you so I never made it a point to force you to work. It might've taught you some respect, made more of a man of you than only having your head underneath women's skirts—! In the end, it's my fault for not insisting. Now it's too late. You're leaving and the ranch is going to go to that imbecile your mother married. Although he's no rancher, either! Let's hope he doesn't throw your saintly grandmother out, being the son of a bitch that I know he is! I can tell he's a racist bastard, too! He claims he mistook her for a servant when he first came here! Imagine, him saying that about your mother's own mother to her face. 'I thought she was the servant!'"

Máximo heard his grandfather talk through the fog of his drunkenness. He staggered away from the table and tried to make his way to the front door before he spilled the contents of his stomach on the floor. His head cleared and he steadied himself against the wall. He felt his grandfather's sharp eyes, even though drunk, studying his actions. Máximo straightened up, or made an effort of it, and went to the bathroom.

That was the last he remembered of his first night home. He spent more than a week on the ranch before he left for the city to see his mother and to implore her to give him the money to return to the United States. He fully realized then what his father had felt when he escaped the turmoil of Sapogonia. Life was to be enjoyed; the comforts of modern society were to be made use of. He couldn't waste it in a shit-colored uniform, licking the boots of lice-headed officers or acting as a water boy for an egotistical self-anointed savior of the people.

Máximo's mother immediately consented to giving him the money to return to the United States to study. She, too, although ecstatic to see her son, didn't want him to lose his life for the sake of either side, but to escape, as one might have it, to where he could seek out a promising future.

Her husband didn't seem like much of a dandy, as his grandfather had called him. It was possible that to his grandfather any man who wore a suit when he was not conducting official business or going to church was a show-off. Yet, the man's clothes were not impressive to Max, who had seen what a good suit looked like, and what the man wore didn't come close. He did observe and concluded on that occasion, however, that his mother showed a weakness for men with a flair for *la vie*, hardly seen in San Co, much less on the ranch, where it was an occasion for men to bathe.

Máximo's mother was less critical than her son. She was proud of Máximo. She held his hand and showed him off to her husband. "Don't you think he's quite a good-looking young man?" She smiled. She ran a hand through his beard.

Her husband nodded. "Takes after his lovely mother, except that his skin is whiter, but it's not your fault that you're a little black." He continued, "You took after your poor mother, la indita." The man was aware that his remarks were offensive and Max noted that his mother was embarrassed. She'd always been self-conscious about her color, although she wasn't as dark as her husband made her out to be. Her cheeks reddened with humiliation, but she said nothing.

"La indita de quien Ud. habla, señor, is mi mamá grande," Máximo reminded his stepfather, hoping to make a point without having to go further.

"That's already known, boy," the man responded. "But you obviously inherited your father's looks. I know you didn't ever get to know him, but he was a light-skinned Spaniard, your mother said."

Máximo rose from his chair. "And how do you know, sir, that I never knew my father?"

"Your mother told me that he died when you were an infant. How could you remember him?"

Máximo exchanged looks with his mother, whose eyes pleaded he say nothing to contradict her. He bent over to kiss her goodbye and whispered, "You're going to give me the money to go?" She nodded. Máximo left his mother's new home without shaking his stepfather's hand.

A season passed before his mother sent him the cash to make it to Mexico and from Mexico to fly to the United States. (It was said that flights out of every airport were undependable and led to endless questioning before boarding.) At last, Máximo prepared to leave his grandparents' home again.

He planned to go away without giving notice, otherwise he anticipated a scene. His grandfather would call him a bastard, an ingrate, a coward. He was capable of hurling a fist his way. Despite the awareness that time had turned the tables so that he could easily take on the old man, Max trembled at the thought of such a confrontation. His grandfather had a courage about him that Max suspected would make the old man choose death to losing or giving in to anything.

"Do you know something? She's loaded down now with brats, lives in a shanty outside of town with a drunkard who uses her to wipe his ass with!" It was Máximo's grandmother who laughed from behind the opened trunk in his room that he had never paid attention to, but remained like a fixture.

At once he knew whom his grandmother was referring to, the cause for his infantile misery and fleeing his home years before. It was as if time had not passed, as if he had not travelled so far to return to hear what little imagination fate had had for his first love.

"Not only that, but she's more bowlegged than ever with having had all those children!" She laughed again. She enjoyed giving the word about the young woman's miserable life to Máximo, who had suffered the blows of feminine callousness when his ego was yet tender.

"I should have killed her," he half kidded, sitting on the bed, remembering the night he'd made love to a girl who responded by insulting his manhood.

"For what? You would've spared her of a miserable future but you would've ended up in jail . . . or hanged! Bah! You see how life resolves things?" The old woman brought out an item from the trunk. An infant's yellowed christening outfit. "You were baptized in these clothes," she said almost coyly. "What a pretty baby you were, Mimo!"

Máximo looked at the outfit with indifference. He put Marisela out of his mind with difficulty. "I'm leaving, Mamá Grande," he said.

"I know," she answered, but didn't look at him.

"I'll be back . . ." He didn't know if this was true, but he said it spontaneously, an effort to console or to excuse his self-preoccupation.

"Yes. You'll come back, Mimo, although we won't be here, your grandfather and me." She was sad and Máximo moved to hold her, a black dress over loose bones that threatened to crumble in his embrace. "Don't say that, Mamá Grande. Of course I'll see you again, both of you. You'll see."

His grandmother pulled away from him and motioned for him to sit. "Listen to me, Mimo," she said firmly, holding back tears. "Your grandfather always called you a bastard, but you know he didn't mean it. That's just his way. But I want you to remember something. Your father committed a great crime when he left a young girl here to have his child alone . . ."

Máximo turned away. He had heard this story all his life. It was partially the motivation for him to seek out the cretin he'd heard so many insults about and discovered that the man was no monster, no heartless creature bent on hurting anyone. He'd left to save his hide, as Máximo was doing at that moment. Nevertheless, he let his old grandmother have her say.

"My people believe that all children are the children of God, so you were not born without a father. You were God's child. The Christians say they believe the same thing, but they don't. They think if two people haven't taken vows in their church, the children who are born to them are sinners. That's very un-Christian thinking, don't you believe?" She seemed reflective and didn't intend to hear Máximo reply. "Don't deceive woman, Máximo. Do what you must and be happy, but try not to use woman like an animal who has no feelings, which by the way, animals do . . ."

Máximo interrupted his grandmother. "I know what you're trying to say, Mamá. I'm not going to get any woman pregnant and leave her just like that. Besides, the women I know are no innocents. They know what they get themselves into . . .!"

The old woman laughed cynically. "Máximo, son, no ordinary woman could ever know what she was getting herself mixed up in with you!"

Máximo left at dawn without saying goodbye to his grandfather and with the blessing of his grandmother's moist kiss on his forehead, knowing he would never see them again because his grandmother had foretold it.

seventeen

Let me tell you a story, one that was told to me on the first night my mother was in the United States. We stayed up until almost dawn informing each other of all that had gone on in past years. My mother told me of things that occurred during my childhood, when I had been oblivious to the goings on of the adult world; and finally, some things that happened before my birth, so that I couldn't have known of them.

I wished I'd known this particular story, one that neither my grandmother nor grandfather thought to share with me before they were gone. However, it would have undoubtedly made my grandfather, in my perspective, even more noble than I already thought him. It was hard enough to know he was one of those men on which great novels are based, leaving the rest of us mortal and bogged down with the infallibilities of being all too human and the fanatic determination to preserve our measly lives.

He was a young man, out to sow his wild oats, as one says. He was not wealthy, but his father was comfortable enough to have been able to send his son to study in Europe. After one year, the son preferred to return to his country so that he might learn the business of running the ranch. He wanted to have his hands blackened with the soil of his land. This pleased his father enormously.

When he was back home, however, he had a notion to take off one night after a few drinks with a good friend, to explore the North. They rode for days and nights, getting drunk, stopping along the way to see what mischief they could get into; nothing serious, a few fights, a couple of narrow escapes from the law or men who took their pranks seriously.

Finally, they reached the peninsula of Santa Agueda Quetzaltenango, a lush paradise, the precise region from where my country got its image-bidding name, the Spaniards being ever the symbolists that they were. The peninsula is known for the multiplicity of its amphibian-populated ponds, with particular reference to a creature that exists there and may be found nowhere else in the world. It is very similar to the toad, except for its phosphorescent skin. In the day, when the sky is the sister of the ocean, the creature in reference is generally thought to be an aquamarine color; while at night, especially when the moon is high and glowing, the ponds vibrate with live diamonds, all singing a pathetically out-of-synch chorus of gutteral sounds.

To continue with the tale, it was here that my father and his friend stopped to rest from their adventures. At the time, the area was still jungle. A few bold anthropologists were excavating Mayan ruins, but the jungle was so dense and miserable, no one else would have appreciated its buried treasures.

It was their third or fourth day. They had gone swimming in the cenote, said to have been a natural well where Mayan virgins were once drowned as offerings to the gods. My grandfather spotted two young women not far off. They were unaware of the two foreigners. These were young girls actually, not quite women, but the two men were barely men themselves, although old enough I suppose to have been responsible for their behavior. But they were out for adventure, and one suggested approaching the two inditas. "No, wait," the other said. He held his friend back and they both watched as the young women removed their tunics and, letting down their long hair, went into the water to bathe. Their dark skin was shiny like tide-beaten stone and their laughter incited the men to come as quietly as a pair of jaguars stalking their prey.

The young women had been virgins. The one my grandfather had, tried to run, but seeing she was done for, submitted without a whimper or complaint. It was afterward, when he was about to leave, that he heard her sob. "Don't cry," he told her. "It happens to everyone sooner or later. It wasn't that bad, was it?"

The girl shook her head; no, it wasn't that. Then why was she upset? "I was promised for marriage," she told him, half in Quechua and half in Spanish. "Now, I'll be returned to my family . . ." The rest of what she told him, he didn't understand, but he got the essence of her tragedy. Because she was no longer a virgin, she had lost her worth.

"Don't cry," he told her. He asked her to come back the next day and she did. It was then he made his decision. He told his friend later, "I'm going to stay with her. I can't leave her just like that." His friend responded to his sentiment with laughter. "What're you saying? Are you crazy? She's a little Indian! You can't spend the rest of your life with her! What about your father and the ranch? What about Florentina?"

My grandfather nodded to all of it; he'd thought of all of it, except for Florentina, whom he had completely blocked out of his mind until then. He had asked her father, Don Pedro Jiménez, who owned the ranch nearest theirs, for her hand. Their land wasn't as large as his father's ranch, but the marriage would've meant a profitable merger for both families. His friend had reason for opposing his decision and my grandfather left with him.

They travelled for a whole day and night when he stopped suddenly and told his friend, "I'm not going any further without her. I'll just have to bring her to my father's ranch." With that, he turned around, married his Mayan lover by the customs of her people, and then took her south to his father's house where he then married her by the Church. Surprisingly, his father's only stipulation in accepting the Indian girl into his family had been that she convert to the Church. He would not allow a pagan at his table, he said.

Their first child was born exactly seven months after that first time my grandfather took the girl. The baby did not survive. The following year she gave birth again, and that child lived until the government of Romero caused him to go to the hills to fight. The ballad "Mestizo Mireles" was written for him and went more or less like this:

"Mestizo Mireles"

Presten oído, señores
que les voy a cantar
lo del mestizo Mireles
que fue un hombre muy cabal.

No fue un peón, ni mucho menos
ni el hambre conoció
pero fue de los muy pocos
que al pueblo se ganó.

Llamó desde los cerros
a todo huelguista
¡Minero, tu piqueta!
¡Que se freguen los Romeristas!

Te llevaron al tribunal
los que jugaban a la justicia
sin hacerte una pregunta
anunciaron tu día final.

Mestizo, eras de humo o polvo
puma o buho que te fuiste
una noche sin que hombre
te viera volar—

    That's all that I remember of it, but you get the idea. Máximo put down his guitar and wondered why you didn't turn to the next page.

eighteen

The hot water bottle wrapped in a towel to keep her skin from scorching was placed carefully on Pastora's lower back. The second day of her period was the worst, which began the disintegration of the nest in her body with currents of physical and emotional distress.

It was attributed to the hormonal changes in the body, the sudden sensation that everything in life was defeated, as if instinctively, the body, void of mind and logic, concluded that the failure to be fertilized each month meant failure in life. The mind, unaware of the body's own determination, attempted to rationalize this apprehension, this concern with failure, by pointing to the external environment. Thus Pastora Aké submitted to the absorption and was carried by waves of turmoil throughout the body, the lower abdomen, the lower back, thighs. A fruitless labor.

The first day of her period usually began at dawn; a pinkish spotting, a persistent mild headache throughout the day, nothing intolerable. The night before, on that bed, she had made love. The essence of that lovemaking remained, not only in odor, the mixture of female and male secretions on the sheets which she hadn't changed in order to welter in memory. The presence of Máximo Madrigal was heavy, a substance more disturbing than blood.

Their interludes were rare and only for sex, a suspension of obsession for the other linked each occasion with uneven measurements of time. Each occasion returned them to the first night: Madrigal pulling from drunken memory, taking her first on the couch, waking in her bed, being sent off to walk home in the cold. In this way, they re-enacted the same scene.

She did not always throw him out; he chose to leave if she hinted that she wanted him to stay. "¿Ya te vas?" she would ask, a trace of regret in her languid voice. "Here you go again, about to crucify me," he would say defensively.

"Why not?" came her sharp answer. "You always bring your own cross and nails."

Each went her/his own way, parted without the vulgar promises and gestures of tentative lovers. No one knew when the next contact would be, neither dared to suggest it. It all depended on the other's will to resist. These were lovers who, instead of surrendering to the physical heat each felt for the other, engaged in mutual submission to the intrigue, which could only be sustained by the refusal of each to reveal more than one or two secrets with each sporadic meeting.

The recollection would remain the trophy: initial kisses; his beard mixing with her hair; the deliberate manipulation of fingers and tongues; the words exchanged; intimate childhood memories easing from a half-conscious state; references and homage to films, artists, symphonic movements, all so familiar to the other as to call up a quote, a phrase, a yes!, a momentary recongition, stillness, peace.

For Pastora, her attraction to Máximo lay at times more in their capacity to share their knowledge and the drive for such. On this level, their souls were equal, both had travelled many paths before this life and brought the capacity for such intellectual pursuits.

Pastora's resistance to Máximo Madrigal held itself in the acute differences inherent to their genders. Each was a prima donna, a matador, fearless with the kind of bravado inherent in those whose motives are heightened in the face of danger before a crowd.

Oh, there were times when one, in the pit of loneliness, utilized the telephone to call the other, but it ended there. Neither spoke of the wish that the other might satisfy his/her need of consolation. During such brief communication, it was certain that the receiver of the call would put the other off. "I have work." "I was asleep." Then silence, as redundant as the hum on the telephone line when the call ended.

For the length of fifteen days, Pastora would be consumed with Máximo Madrigal's last visit. She would not seek him out, ask him outright to come to her. Consciously fighting her skill in being able to bring him to her, Máximo would not come. "You're like poison," he told her, not just once. "I can only take you in small doses, if I am to survive you."

They were each sources of destruction for the other. While they might not hesitate to destroy other relationships, possible friendships, love affairs, they valued each other inasmuch as they valued the necessity of each to create, not wanting to obliterate the other completely, only enough so that each would be reminded of her/his own imperfection.

After the torturous two weeks, the intensity would diminish each day, until Máximo Madrigal became a name, inconsequential as an acquaintance one had met in a city passed through a long time ago. It didn't matter if they saw each other again. The idea that he was with another woman, women, meant nothing in relation to their involvement. For if Máximo Madrigal had the capacity to resist his need for Pastora, he could love no other woman. What he had as a man to deliver to a woman he reserved for her and gave up, at best, a few times a year.

Days would pass, a month, and Máximo Madrigal would be reduced to a microdot in the center of Pastora's brain, constant but controlled and certain as death.

nineteen

Undaunted in the face of perpetual obstacles, our principal character in this tale made two trips to the capital before he was issued a passport. His mother gave him a telegram to take along as proof that he had business in Mexico. Her cousin had left Sapogonia years before and now owned a used car dealership in Mexico City. Máximo's mother sent him a telegram that she wanted her son to work in Mexico. Yes, came the reply, there would be a job waiting for him.

The telegram with the promise of the job wasn't sufficient. Máximo greased several palms to expedite the processing of his papers before he crossed over to the next country and finally found himself on Mexican territory. Mérida was splendid, the tropical climate, the long siesta afternoons; then Máximo heard of the tourist resort being promoted by the Mexican government and he went to Cancún.

Unable to resist the fabulous beaches, outdone only by the European and American beauties basking on the white shores, Máximo stayed on in the peninsula for a month. He made himself available as a tour guide with the use of his French and English and for the present forgot about his uncle in Mexico City, who was waiting to start him off in the used car business.

Máximo eventually reminded himself that it was this uncle who was going to make arrangements for him to enter into the United States. He promised to secure evidence that Máximo was going to study in the U.S. and to obtain a student visa. It would take a little time, and a little money, but he assured Max's mother that it would be taken care of.

By the time Max arrived in Mexico City, his uncle was frantic. Everyone thought something had happened to him. He let three months pass, Max cleaning and waxing cars on the lot, before the older one put aside his anger at his cousin's son's inconsideration and gave him the news. Max had received a letter from the Chicago

School of the Performing Arts to come for an interview. "But is this sincere?" he asked his relative. The letter looked authentic and he really did want to study music, but he didn't think anyone, besides himself, would have been able to make such arrangements.

"Yes, of course it is!" His uncle patted him on the back, not unaware of his small miracle. "Congratulations!"

"But I don't understand . . . how did you know?"

"To be honest, your little grandmother called one evening before you arrived. She said, 'My grandson has an ear for music.' I tried to get an interview for you at the Julliard in New York . . . you've heard of it, haven't you?" Max was dumbfounded. He was impressed that a used car salesman had such American savvy. His uncle continued, "But, unfortunately, I couldn't. Still, I believe this school in Chicago is very good."

His uncle sent him on a direct plane to that city with his letter granting the audition at the Chicago School of the Performing Arts; a little extra cash to supplement what his mother had given him; and a sheepskin jacket and wool socks, because it was said that the cold up north was inhuman. Máximo told him that it had been plenty cold in New York City, too, but his uncle guaranteed that it could not compare to Chicago's cold.

Max spent several weeks in the home of friends of his uncle, who may have been the source responsible for his getting to the U.S. with practically an acceptance into a school he had not even applied at, but he never asked. They had a contemporary home, designed by the architect Frank Lloyd Wright, whose work did not seem anything like the only other architect Max knew by name, Gaudi. But, then, whose work did? They lavished it inside with antiques. It was situated north of the city and the distance was cumbersome for getting downtown to where Max had registered for only two classes until the new semester when he would be accepted as a full-time student.

He took up the offer of a fellow student, a Mexican-American, to move in with him and share the costs of an apartment. Jacobo studied voice, and piano for "dexterity" he said. Máximo opined his friend displayed little talent for anything but drama, which, of course, was Jacobo's true love. He wanted to be an actor, in the same vein as Sir Lawrence Olivier, his idol. Jacobo paid his bills by holding down a job as an employment counselor at a neighborhood center in the Mexican community of Little Village.

Jacobo persuaded Máximo to work in a play that was being scheduled for one weekend right before the holidays. All the cast, with the exception of the director, who only agreed to work with the company because of a prestigious grant, were Latino and Spanish-speaking. They were young, and their little, if any, experience was compensated by their enthusiasm for putting on a piece in their native tongue, or at least the language that reflected their cultural background.

Before Máximo joined in, the play, Rudolfo Usigli's *Corona de sombra,* had been selected. "But why don't you do something more popular, more relevant?" Máximo protested, over a couple of beers, to his friend. "Who the hell cares any more about that imbecilic Austrian who came to be the 'Emperor of Mexico'? He got what was coming to him for being such a conceit! Napoleon set him up and left him defenseless!"

"The director is thinking of casting you for the part of Napoleon." Jacobo dangled bait before his friend. Max winced with surprise, but recovered quickly, although he was pleased. "Of course! I'll make an excellent Napoleon! I'll take the part, but I still think something more popular should be put on." Máximo insisted on getting in the last word, although with the new knowledge of having such a role, his heart wasn't in the dispute any more.

"What would you like to see produced?" Jacobo humored him.

"*Yerma!*"

"*Yerma?* Are you kidding?" Jacobo wanted to laugh. "What kind of holiday spirit is that, a play in which a woman strangles her husband in the end!"

"It's a fantastic piece! Imagine me as Juan: A ti te busco. Con la luna estás hermosa! Then, egh! She tightens the grip around my neck and pas! I fall dead at the hands of a grief-stricken woman, barren as the land of my grandfather . . . !"

"You sound a tad masochistic, my friend," Jacobo put a hand up signaling for two more beers. "And those are not his last lines, his last lines are . . ."

"I know, I know! The point is García Lorca is infinitely more popular in this country than Rudolfo Usigli! And you want to fill the house, don't you?"

"Look, no matter which way we look at it, we are not going to fill the house. To begin with, we are producing a play in Spanish.

Who comes to something like that? Spanish professors, a few students taking a class in Spanish literature."

"And what were you thinking then? Let's put on something that will really pack them in—a play about Maximilian's woman who goes coo-coo. ¡Luces! ¡Traed más luces!"

"Don't be such a cynic! You are underestimating the patriotism and pride of the Mexican, hombre! They kicked ass! They make up the majority of the Latinos in this city, and they are the ones who are going to come!"

Máximo gulped down his beer and ordered the next round. He envisioned himself in costume, a strident commander, patent leather boots, hand ready at the handle of his sword. "Okay. As long as I play Napoleon."

During the rehearsals, which ordinarily took place in their apartment, Máximo insisted on challenging every one of the director's decisions. Jacobo pulled him aside with a mild warning. Other cast members were getting irritated with Máximo's arrogance. He complained that since his role turned out to be so small, he found himself with excess energy needing to pour forth into something constructive.

"Listen, do you have any talent for design?" Jacobo wondered, exasperated yet torn with the affection he had for his friend. He thought well of Máximo, but obviously not as much as Max thought of himself. Max nodded. "Of course! What do you need?"

"We need a stage designer. The guy who volunteered hasn't come through with sketches or anything, and the play is less than a month away!"

Max stroked immense sideburns (he'd grown them to achieve a believable image of the historical figure he was going to play for a weekend). "Do you have money?" "We have some left over from the grant, after we allot for the director's fee, the theatre, publicity, costumes . . . Yes, there's some. Why don't you take on the project? Do you think you can do it?"

Máximo grabbed his coat. He would go to the bar to brainstorm. "And I still think Carlota should fall on her knees before me when she says, 'Abandonaré mi orgullo entonces, si es lo que queréis, y os pediré de rodillas ayuda para Maximiliano,'" he said out loud for the benefit of the director, who threw down the script in response. Máximo laughed and slammed the door behind him.

"He's too much, I say! That little fellow's just too much!" the director complained to Jacobo, picking up his script again. "You must admit, he's the best actor we've got!" Jacobo whispered to the director with a wink. The director smiled reluctantly. "Unfortunately!"

Máximo set out designing props and scenery with fanatic fervor on the meager budget he was given. He bought layout board and spent days on end making drawing after drawing, meticulous about detail. His imagination soared and he spared no frivolous idea for the chance of showing off his ability. His music classes were abandoned for the time being, but he felt it was worth it. He might be on the verge of discovering a new field, a road that could lead to a profitable career.

Jacobo, the director, and the cast, were all pleased with the work Máximo designed. Everyone was so preoccupied with their individual tasks, however, that Máximo didn't get the praise he hoped for his endeavor. The greatest disappointment came after the third and final performance of *Corona de sombra*. The house, on its best night, was half full. Some of their publicity efforts weren't successful. The Spanish language radio claimed it never received the press release. The main Spanish language paper did not come to review or to cover the opening night and reception.

The only paper that did come was an English language cultural periodical, circulated in the North side of the city. They were all thrilled to discover there was a write-up, although a minor one, in the following week's edition. Apparently, the critic was a friend of the director's who wanted to help keep him in the limelight for consideration by other local producers for future work.

> . . . it was indeed an heroic effort on the part of the director, Stan Saks, to work with this new company of Latino actors for most of whom this was a professional debut. Unfortunately, the notorious sense of "Latino time" spills over into its dramatic timing as well. The señorita, Glady Torres, our deranged Carlota, missed her cue on more than one occasion and one could not help wonder if having played the part of a madwoman might not have had some personal effect. . . . It is understood that these ambitious amigos were work-

ing with a modest grant from the Belmont Foundation, but a sore absence of taste ran rampant in the area of costuming and scenery.

Máximo and Jacobo spent the following week on a binge. "I told you, you asshole, we should have done García Lorca. The gringos love García Lorca. What sympathy do they have for the Mexicans for executing a fucking Austrian Emperor? It's the fascists in Europe that fascinate them!"

"Oh, shut up already!" Jacobo retorted, letting his inebriated body slump over on the couch. "What the hell day is it, anyway?"

"Who the hell cares?" Máximo told him, getting up from his chair to aim for the bathroom. "Let's go out and find some viejas," Jacobo called out. "Until you finally came up with a good idea, idiot!" Máximo responded, laughing.

My dear Jacobo should have listened to me. Even I, who claimed to know nothing about the theatre and drama, knew something about the North American mentality. It was a question of common sense, for heaven's sake! García Lorca, *Poet in New York*, executed during the Spanish Civil War! As the years went on, what I had always thought was proven. There were popular films made of his plays, his poetry was resurrected from the lamentable obscurity of the literary urbane and heard commonplace again, as was being done in Spanish cafés.

It was sheer logic that if any cultural figure was going to gain prominence among the American status quo, it was not going to be someone like Rudolfo Usigli. Tell me, honestly, are you familiar with his plays? Oh, but of course, if you happen to know anything about the history of theatre in Latin America you would be ignorant altogether not to know the author of *Corona de sombra* and that wonderful piece of satire, *El gesticulador*. But what bloody gringo critic in Chicago would have given two peanuts to see his work?

Moreover, and the crux of my point was then and remains to be that the North American public culturally could only relate to Latinos insofar as their roots lie in Spain. Yes, the Spanish Civil War, the great battle against fascism; castenets, toreadors in tight pants, women with thorned roses between their teeth. But bring up our amigos just south of the border, conjuring images of gritty, snot-nosed children; women in dust-covered skirts squatting before a griddle over hot stones, patting the crude dough between their dark palms for the meal of tortillas; and their men, loathsome bandit types, with beady black eyes and those wretched bodies, tough like those of desert mules—and they wrinkle their noses as if someone had just passed air.

It was Jacobo's Chicano pride that doomed us, I'm afraid. I understand his sentiments; he went on infinitely about the long history of his people in this country, on what was their land, he said. But he was avoiding reality. If he wanted to be an actor more than anything in the world, as he claimed, he would have done better to keep his nose out of righteous social causes for justice and retribution and sought out the best avenues to display his talents.

Which is what he finally tried to do, but without much success either, unfortunately. There was the Hollywood movie that was filmed at a local high school. It was announced that extras were needed, and you can see Jacobo in one scene. He's one among two hundred Latino faces in a crowd the police were presumably keeping back at the onset of a riot. He got a free lunch of pizza and beer for his work.

We did not go back to the Chicago School of Performing Arts the following semester. I was impatient with the instructors and started working at North Side restaurants, playing flamenco/classical guitar for the listening pleasure of their patrons. On a busy night with the talk and hustle and bustle of platters and popping corks and the waiters and so on, even a microphone was defeated by the acoustic deficiency created by the atmosphere. It didn't seem to matter to anyone either; I was just part of the decor of the pseudo-European café.

I got to drink the wine left in purchased bottles in addition to a few dollars for my trouble and a brandy snifter for tips was sometimes noticed and made use of by the rare music aficionados who patronized the place. It was not a lifestyle that I wanted for myself permanently and, by midwinter, both Jacobo and I were depressed. We tried to remedy it with weekend binges and lots of healthy sex with muchas viejas, as my Texan friend called the lovelies who generated spirit into our lives.

You must remember I was in my twenties and in the prime of my male virility! I tried to remember Mamá Grande's warning. I made certain any woman I slept with had no illusions that I was her prince come to sweep her onto my trusty steed—there was room for only one on the back of my winged unicorn, Rosinante, and that one was me!

Of course there are always a couple of conniving women who, after you've seen them a few times, begin to get confident, possessive. They suggest dining together, that one should cook or the other take the one out to a particular place. If I was in the mood, I would say yes, yes, of course. I'll call you, I'll be there. And if I wasn't in the mood at the appointed time, I just went in the other direction.

More often than not, I went in the other direction. I much preferred using my money to buy Jacobo and myself a few drinks on the weekend or to purchase a case of Chardonnay. I had a favorite Argentine place where I got a generous churrasco, medium rare, served by the chef himself. I had so little money, I knew what luxuries there were to be found could only be afforded for one. After all, I had earned my money, hadn't I? Why should I have spent it on women I hardly knew?

That was the winter I first made love to Pastora. I never took her out, either. The thing about her was, however, that she always gave me the distinct impression that she didn't care about those things, that she might not even want to be taken out. Perhaps because she was so secretive, that she preferred not to be seen with a man. I can only guess why she was always so distant. That was all well and good with me because I didn't have to spend any money on her to get to sleep with her. She did occasionally suggest that I bring wine. Sometimes I did.

Sometimes I didn't.

twenty

Máximo Madrigal opened his eyes, flared his nostrils, and at once was caught up in the aromatic spell of mint. He remembered the field of yerba buena, a mint weed that was used for medicinal purposes as well as a calmative tea, that grew on his grandfather's ranch out near San Co.

He knew at once he wasn't in his own bed; the mattress was too soft, the sheets too crisp. He knew he wasn't smelling the yerba buena that sprouted in summer and whose scandalous aroma was an integral part of his childhood. Máximo did not know, however, if he had awoken.

He was also remembering something else about the evening just past; it had been filled with Coatlicue. Of course, that wasn't her name, but it was the only name he felt suitable for her. It hadn't been once, twice, or even three times that he tried to go to bed with her. In his first naïve efforts, (for suddenly with Coatlicue, he discovered there was still that about his character that was yet unexplored and could be termed naïve) he hadn't wasted overtures of seduction.

Why fool each other into the pretentious game of seduction with a woman as sharp-witted as she? First, he assumed she would have sex with him. Later, he entreated. Then, in the predictable manner appropriate for his type, he feigned having been offended by her persistent rejection. It never occurred to him to court her, to woo her, as he might have with a young girl, or someone of bourgeois society, from whom he would expect material reciprocation later.

It was quite unexpected that he found himself there and, to his own disgust, he couldn't remember how it had come about. Drunken confusion hadn't permitted him to remember how their lovemaking had been. He had gone about the motions, no doubt, but he could not for the life of him recall what she was like.

He sat up. It was dark and he made out all the objects in the room as shadows and silhouettes. He heard the small sounds of the tea preparation in the kitchen, which had to be adjacent to the bedroom as it seemed so close. A candle burned on the dresser and, for a moment, he was intrigued by the peculiar figurines surrounding it.

Then she returned, carrying a cup in a steady hand and taking calculated steps around the bed. Máximo was startled to see her face painted red and yellow. "What is this?" It wasn't certain if he asked of the painted face or the cup she brought him to drink. He brought the cup up to his nose and the steam disappeared into its narrow orifices. It smelled of mint. "Is it true that you're a witch? Dicen que eres bruja."

She smiled, but not a cynical or bemused smile. It was enigmatic. "Does that mean you're not going to have the tea? You drank a lot tonight. Don't you feel sick?"

"My head hurts, but I don't like this kind of tea," he lied and handed the cup back. "Where are my clothes?" She stood up and left the room without answering him. In the darkness he found his clothing randomly spilled on the floor. He dressed hurriedly. When he came out of the room, she sat in the kitchen, drinking tea. Her face was clean. A scrawny cat slept on her lap. "Can I use the bathroom?" he asked.

"Leave," she said, neither anger nor reproach in her voice, a demand simply put.

"It's snowing. I seem to have spent all my cash at the bar . . . Can you give me a ride?" He immediately regretted having asked her for the favor. He noticed that the black bulk lying across the foot of the door was a large dog that pretended to sleep, but that had one eye on him. Máximo's heartbeat accelerated. He was uneasy as hell and already angry with himself for having persisted in this conquest.

"Go, please, now," she repeated. Her voice monotone.

He took a seat across the table. "Why was your face painted like that, all yellow and red? Are you Coatlicue as I've dreamt?"

"Oh? Have you dreamed of Coatlicue?" she responded, as if offended.

"Why not?" He grinned. He thought the conversation was silly, a game, a bohemian artist's idea of fantasy. "Sometimes, I believe I am Huizilopochtli, 'Sun God of the Aztecs'!"

"Have you been so conceited as to believe Coatlicue your mother? You are less of a god than you think," her eyes narrowed, not amused by his lightheartedness with the topic. "Tonight you were the hand that held the flint."

Máximo closed his eyes; a sharp pain burned inside his chest, the pounding of his heart that had begun moments before was now an excruciating throb. He pressed both hands to his chest and bent over until he hit the floor face first. "Xalaquia," he whispered from a strangling throat. "Xalaquia, ayúdame . . ."

When Máximo opened his eyes, the syllables that clung to his tongue, "Xalaquia," meant nothing to him. He looked about the room and was relieved to find himself in the morning on his own hard cot. His works in progress sporadically placed across the area, tall windows bare and soot-covered, a thick layer of frost on each pane revealed the temperature. He pulled the llama blanket over his shoulders and let it hug his bearded chin.

Xalaquia, who danced and pirouetted, hair loose and flung about, whose face was painted to represent the colors of corn and harvest, who went on with the rite until exhausted, was carried up to the altar of the temple, disrobed and given up to satisfy Coatlicue's hunger and thirst. Xalaquia was a temporary personification of Coatlicue.

Máximo turned to face the wall. How had she appeared nude? Her skin was brown and smooth as coastal clay. Her hair tangled about him. She had swallowed him in his entirety and left him to suffocate inside her entrails. Máximo went to sleep the whole rest of the day and did not dream.

twenty-one

They stayed up watching an old late-night movie, Perla braiding Pastora's waist-length hair, so that the next day when she unraveled the dozens of plaits, her hair would be layers of fine spiderlike webs. Meanwhile, they discussed the final rehearsal that took place earlier that evening, reminding each other of meticulous details.

While Perla had already gone on to another interest, she consented to perform on this special occasion with Pastora. It would be only one number, but Pastora had written it especially for the fusion of their voices. Perla tried to hide her anxiety over the importance that all would go right; the concert was being taped and would be used for Pastora's second album. She'd worked on the music for an entire year. It was different from the first record that consisted of protest compositions. This one combined jazz with themes that professed not so much resistance through physical force, but a revolution of the mind and heart.

They were in their robes and ready for bed when a quiet rap was heard at the door. The two women exchanged glances. There was no doubt that if it was someone they knew, it was undoubtedly a man. Pastora automatically moved away out of view from the door. She whispered to Perla to ask who it was. Perla went and Pastora could hear her talking to someone. She detected a male voice, but didn't make it out. When Perla came back, she told Pastora it had been Máximo Madrigal. Perla told him Pastora was out and he went off.

"Had he been drinking?"

"It was hard to tell, unless you take into account the wavering and staggering as he went off. When was the last time you heard from Máximo, anyway?"

"Eight days ago; last Saturday, in fact."

"You weren't expecting him tonight, were you?"

"No!" Pastora's response wasn't convincing. Perla grew curious.

She knew very little about the relationship and Pastora always spoke of it as if there wasn't much to tell. Pastora seemed to read her mind. "He called last Saturday, as I said, asked how I'd been. I asked how he'd been. That was it."

"He didn't ask to see you?"

"Not at all, but I did invite him to the concert tomorrow." Máximo was among the few acquaintances to whom Pastora had personally extended an invitation.

Perla smiled, "Poor Máximo! Well, I guess he'll get to see you tomorrow. He does act like a man possessed, doesn't he? I mean, coming here unexpected at such an hour . . . ?"

Pastora shrugged her shoulders. She took off her robe and hung it on a hook behind the bedroom door. Before going to bed, Perla shut off the television that had been talking to itself in the living room. She frowned. She hadn't understood before then that anything so intimate was going on between Máximo and Pastora.

Pastora lighted the candle she kept on the bureau, with all those strange little artifacts she collected. Perla sat at the edge of the bed. "I suppose he couldn't help himself. Huh, Pastora?" Pastora blew out the match. "I suppose."

As it turned out, whatever brought Máximo Madrigal through the dark streets in a drunken state to Pastora, kept him away from the performance the next day when he was sober. Pastora was reminded that Máximo's interest in her was principally physical. She respected his musical opinion enough to have invited him and knew he was sufficiently vain to have given it without being asked, but his lack of support in this effort showed that they both remained at the level of beasts when it came to how they treated one another. Máximo was under the impression that Pastora was his sexual counterpart in every sense, that she was as much a manizer, a Jezebel of a thousand lovers, as he was the Cortés of every vagina he crossed.

He lent an ear to each word of gossip related to her associations with men. She didn't know what it was he heard exactly, or if any of it were true; he was never specific with his insinuations that sounded vaguely like the reproaches of a jealous husband. This, too, she knew was characteristic of the polygamous lover. He wanted to possess each of his women and be without competition. He was either supremely jealous or pretended it to get his desired results. It didn't flatter Pastora to hear him degrade himself by bringing up rumors and pressing upon her all the times he felt she'd rejected him before she'd finally let him make love to her.

They could never be friends.

He had an extremely susceptible soul. Willing him toward her, he came. He left the country, he could be gone for months, a year. He no sooner landed in the city but had it in his mind to see her. Only once. Then it didn't matter if he stayed in Chicago. She would not hear from him for a long while. She didn't look for him.

Perla thought Máximo was terribly vain and that her friend went beneath her standards to allow such a man even the small space he had in Pastora's life. Still, it was Máximo whom she pitied.

Perla was raised Catholic. Therefore, she also knew that the little figurines on Pastora's bureau and the persistent devotion to the candle, the glass of water, the white flowers, was not capriciousness. Pastora was too much of a somber person for rituals that didn't have meaning.

Perla couldn't say she'd seen or heard anything that would give testimony to her suspicions, except, of course, for the rumors. The same rumors, undoubtedly, that Max had been exposed to: Pastora was a witch. Pastora always laughed, cynically, when they were brought to her attention. She said Latino men always thought that a woman who allowed herself to be thought of sexually and denied any reason to feel shameful of it and had none of the inhibitions or insecurities with relation to commitments as it was considered women should—had to be a witch. Likewise, she said, men had similar distorted and archaic perceptions of their own sexuality.

Max did not pretend to be sincere with women. Rather, he had his own blend of sincerity. He showed uncontrollable passion for Pastora, but only when it suited him to do so. All this Pastora explained to Perla and Perla accepted. It made more sense than believing that men like Máximo Madrigal, Jesús Valle, and others she'd come to know who had been with Pastora were really hexed.

Perla decided she would pay no heed to it. She opted not to believe Pastora had such powers. Even when Pastora meditated before the candle or when she read the Tarot cards with such accuracy, Perla cast it all off as superstition. She told herself to humor her friend and to stop the rumors whenever they passed her way.

What did bother Perla, what had disturbed her from the first, when she and Pastora began to share their lives, was how devoted she herself was to Pastora. Perla cried when alone at times (for no one was like her in having such a dread of being alone) for fear that one day Pastora would reject *her,* might think her too trivial, abandon her. Perla decided she would find a man who would love her as Pastora was loved.

twenty-two

What has bothered me most about my "encounters," let's say, with Pastora Velásquez Aké, is that persistent, almost innate, way of hers that warns me of her incapacity to surrender herself. Why? I've asked myself over and over again. When it even seemed (because I am not all that myopic on this subject, as it may appear) that if it were not for that quality, if one can fairly call it that, she would be as any other woman.

I'd go as far as to say, less, in specific ways, than other women. After all, when I met her, she was no spring chicken. Although she was not one whose beauty quickly fades, who is striking at a tender age, but whose looks are superficial.

No, I am the first to admit, Pastora's physical attractiveness had the character of infinity. It was chilling. A man could guess she was, oh, say, anywhere between sixteen and thirty when we met, although at times she behaved as old as the Sphinx. The taut legs, her firm breasts, the lean torso, were such that any young girl would've been envious. Her beauty put me off, because she wore it like an heirloom pendant. One could view and admire it, but was not allowed to handle it. Ha! I said, Ha, again!

So, in the beginning, I watched her from afar, from the other side of that smoked pane she kept up before the world. I came across her several times, always making sure I was ever the cavalier; a tilt of the head, a pleasant greeting, hiding my disdain for her type. That's all she was then, a type. I knew, knowing from being aware of my unusual talents, that when and if I wanted, I could easily shatter that glass shield.

I saw her a good many times so that finally I felt I had never seen her for the first time at all, but had always been aware of Pastora on the periphery of my existence. It seemed her name had come to me in veiled images, a presence, the resonance of her voice, in fragments, perhaps in dreams or conversations I'd overheard. I don't know when precisely, but I knew I couldn't treat the situation with indifference any longer.

I was still confident, despite that terrific façade, that she would be mine. For it was becoming clearer during those last months or weeks when just before I approached her that I realized consciously how often I wondered about her. She seemed an enigma and no one I broached on the subject could give me a full account, so that she was even more of a curio.

"Would you like a sip to warm you?" I offered the aguardiente in the silver flask as a kind of friendship offering. Those were not the first words I ever spoke to her, but they were the first that went beyond polite salutation. She had attended an exhibit in which I'd participated, although I must admit, my work was in good company on that occasion, so I had no reason to believe it was specifically to see my sculpture that she was there. I tried to make myself visible while in the gallery, but she didn't seem to notice. Each time I neared her, she stepped away.

She was leaving the building with her friend, the pretty one, (whom Jacobo was certain was her lover) when he decided to follow them. Max gestured to his friends Ricardo Luna and Jacobo to come out, too. They followed, true admirers of the ardent lover, to study him at his best. October nipped at their faces as they stepped out on the street. Pastora wore the knee-length poncho from which, Máximo observed, peered out riding boots of expensive leather. She took the flask and swallowed once. Her face screwed as she returned it and went off.

Máximo was offended. Had she thanked him? It was excellent aguardiente, guaranteed to keep the cold away, and the expression the haughty woman had made seemed as if she would spit it out. He caught up with the women. Ricardo Luna and Jacobo were close behind, like a newly formed pack of dogs. As this image came to Máximo, he wished he were alone and that Pastora, too, was not with that woman. "Listen, where are you going from here?"

The two women stopped. Perla jingled a large ring of keys. Máximo wondered if she wasn't a prison guard with so many keys. He didn't notice that the women knew full well right off which one it was he pursued. "We hadn't thought of it," Pastora said, expressionless. She had a way, Máximo noted, of concealing her thoughts. She responded; there was no visible hostility, but no tone of amiability either.

"Would you like some coffee, a plate of black beans, perhaps?" He turned and bid his friends near, "We're on our way to a Spanish restaurant to get a bite to eat." He made this up at that moment. Jacobo and Ricardo Luna caught up with them, but now they stood around like shy schoolboys, smiling awkwardly and not able to look at the women directly. Pastora asked where the restaurant was and the women agreed to meet them there.

Jacobo and Ricardo gave me a pat on the back congratulating my work. The dice were rolling, they said; before morning Pastora would be mine. Although both of them were equally attracted to the women, they resigned their fate that night to their empty pockets and the inability to persuade women without so much as cab fare to offer for their trouble. I scoffed at all this. I was just as penniless, I said; worse off, because they at least had steady employment. I hadn't sold a piece in months. I assured them that with my credit at the restaurant (always good for a night of playing my guitar in exchange for the sum owed), we could manage to buy the women a drink.

Pastora and Perla were already at the bar. The restaurant was about to close, but the owner (who always had an eye for pretty women) said they could have a nightcap, which they had already had when we arrived. I played a number, one of the tightwad owner's favorites, which reminded him of Asturias, and he locked the doors and said we could stay a while longer. So the women joined us, picked at bread, like sparrows, and had a few glasses of wine. Finally, it was time to leave.

I invited everyone to my studio. Perla took out her weighty keychain and said she was tired. Jacobo and Ricardo Luna then said they had other plans, (the insinuation was that they had women to meet—or to find!) but would join us at the studio. Pastora, who was admittedly not ready to retire but in an uncharacteristically relaxed mood caused undoubtedly by the wine, agreed to go with me.

I can't recall what, if anything, was said on the way there. All I know is that it seemed I'd gotten her to come to my place with much more facility than I anticipated. Well! If only I'd known before! I told myself, smug and assured that that October night was not going to catch me shivering beneath the covers with nothing to embrace.

She wasn't like those women who came to an artist's studio and take on the appearance of collectors or, heaven forgive them, critics. She didn't show the least curiosity about any of the work in the whole place. She took a seat after removing the blanket, pulling it over her head with a confident flair, and sat down on the couch. Yes, she accepted a glass of wine—which I materialized like a sideshow magician. A wonderful Chardonnay of a very special year. But, then, who am I kidding?

The Chardonnay had been wonderful, but I'd finished it alone the evening before. What I served her was an off-the-shelf grocery brand, something that passed itself off as Chablis, poured into the bottle where the Chardonnay had come. She had had, I deduced, enough to drink at the Spanish restaurant and wouldn't be able to tell the difference.

I picked up my guitar, remembering how well this worked with women, and offering up an impromptu serenade. I began "La Mala-gueña."She looked around impatiently. "Do you think your friends are coming?" she asked, not paying attention to the music at all. "Yes, yes," I answered, striking the cords furiously, annoyed by her distraction. I put the guitar down. I was equally annoyed by her air of superiority.

"Where does your family reside?" I asked. Suddenly I was the one impatient. We were wasting time and I felt that this spoiled woman who had been given enough attention all her life should not expect it from me. She should know that at once. "Why?" she asked. She sipped the wine in her glass and let it dangle between the most delicate fingers I had witnessed in my entire memory. I forgot what I had asked, much less why. I poured more wine into the glass, not losing sight of the hypnotic fingers.

"Well, I've heard your album. I've heard a lot about you, in fact, and I always thought you were the daughter of a wealthy Latino family, privileged to do the things you do, rather than apply yourself to serious work." I hoped she wouldn't turn the tables on me, who as an artist was always in question as to the legitimacy of my efforts. "What?" she asked with disbelief. I saw her face flushed from the wine or perhaps the presumption I'd just made.

"You have a fine education, an elitist's education, let's say. You attended the Julliard, didn't you? You play the intellectual, your taste in clothes . . . although you're always careless about your hair and you wear those atrocious jeans, but those boots. They're costly. I can tell because I have my own boots made and I know what I must pay for that craftsmanship."

Pastora let me go on. I, too, had been drinking, and I'm certain it won my personality no honors. I was behaving boorishly, but I was too far gone. She had set something loose and I felt bullheaded and justified. She finished the second glass. I went ahead and filled her glass again, which emptied the bottle.

"I put myself through school," she said, with such reluctance that I felt it was a strain for her to admit it. "Or, rather, I attended on a scholarship. My parents are factory workers. They don't even know about my album." She stopped, as if all at once she knew she had no reason to give me an account of her background. "Haven't you ever listened to the words of my songs?"

"Yes," I partially lied. I'd heard, but didn't find them distinguishable from the endless peña singers in my country. What set this woman apart from them was the opportunity for success she had in the United States. English, of course, was her strongest language, and she was a citizen. I gritted my teeth with envy. "Well, I just thought you were a spoiled niña who played at being communist or something . . . I myself wasn't always a miserable artist as I've become in this country. I worked all my life, too . . . I had to take care of my mother." I don't know why I told her this, but as I said it I was committed to the farce. Besides, I began to enjoy our discourse, whether we were both loading each other with lies or not.

Pastora looked distracted again; for a flash it even seemed she was miserable. Máximo was uncomfortable with this. He couldn't put her off any longer by pretending they were still waiting for his friends. She asked for the time. He lied, saying it was an hour earlier than it was. "I think I'll go," she said, rising.

"Wait." Máximo put a hand out and then got up to dash into the other room. When he emerged he was wearing a pair of pointed-toe snakeskin boots; his pants rolled up so that the V-cut tops were exposed. "Didn't I tell you I have elegant boots, too?" Pastora didn't respond. She sat on the arm of the couch with an unrestrained grimace. She had gone pale. Her contempt welled up in a tightened mouth. Máximo didn't notice, too preoccupied with the display of his ostentatious footwear.

So it was that when he confidently took a seat next to Pastora he made his gravest error by trying to seduce her. His arms went around a statue of chalk, that neither reacted to his kisses nor was in the least receptive to his suggestion of her staying that night. "Will you give me a ride home?" she said, pulling her blanket down over her head, an act to determine the scene's end. He knew she knew then that his friends had never intended to join them.

"What's the matter? Why don't you stay?" he whispered sensuously, or what he hoped sounded sensuous rather than desperate. But she was so peculiar, it was difficult to tell how she interpreted him.

"Will you give me a ride or not?" she asked.

"And if I say no?"

"I'll call a cab. That is, if you permit me to use the phone."

"And if I don't have a phone?"

Pastora headed for the door. "I'll walk."

Máximo grabbed his jacket and went out behind her. He would take her home. All the way he complained. She didn't know what that kind of rejection did to a man, he said. It was hard on a man to be told so unabashedly that he wasn't appealing. He was ridden with the rejection and didn't think to ask if he might have offended her or considered if his ego hadn't got the best of him. He'd done nothing wrong. He'd offered her a drink from his silver flask, silver, he emphasized, it had belonged to his grandmother . . . (At first, Pastora thought he'd meant grandfather, but when he repeated it, she held back a smile.)

He reminded her that she had made a face after tasting the aguardiente as if he'd given her insecticide. Then he'd invited her to eat at the restaurant. Fine, it was only a place of black beans and bread, but none better could be found anywhere. She refused his offerings as if they were dog's turds, he ranted. She treated *him* like a dog turd!

Once she spoke up, squeezing the statement in edgewise between the raving. "Maybe some other time you could call, we'll have a drink, maybe then . . ."

"You just don't understand," he said stubbornly. He did not say he would call her or attempt to see her. As far as he was concerned she wasn't worth it. She'd had her chance.

This, of course, was how I felt until the next time I ran into Pastora, which, unfortunately, was all too soon.

twenty-three

It rained all day, not hard, but the throbbing rain of alienating cities. Máximo remembered similar rain, like an incessant pulse, in Puerto Sapogonia. It probably was raining there, too, at that moment. He went out.

On the street he pulled up his collar and walked north on Milwaukee Avenue. Without thinking, he headed toward the drugstore where Josephine worked as assistant to the druggist in the back of the Polish-run business. As he passed, he realized it was after six and she would be home in the small bungalow where she lived with her parents.

He turned off Milwaukee into an angular one-way street and headed for her house. She would have something on the stove, those delicious dumplings or homemade leek soup. Her nearly deaf mother in the living room, knitting or reminiscing by herself, her senile father staring at the television set. He would knock at the back door. This way the pair of mostly incognizant parents wouldn't be aware of his presence at all.

Josephine would have on her white smock, reluctant to remove the one symbol of respectability of her bland existence. She had come from Russia via Poland as a child and had lived in this neighborhood all her life. Neither her mother nor her father had ever learned to speak a word of English. She worked at the same pharmacy her father had worked at until he began to lose track of general perspective.

Máximo began to talk to Josephine in the drugstore just a month or so before. She was about thirty-five, in his estimation, and bound to never marry. Her nose was an exaggeration and her breath persisted with stagnancy. Her body, on the other hand, was the saving grace, abounding but restrained.

As Máximo neared her house, he was thinking about the confinement he felt with regard to his life. For two months he'd lived in the room upstairs from a Polish dance hall. Josephine's home cooking spared him from the local deli, where he, without means to cook in his place, limited his meals to sausage, fruit, and bad wine. He had drinks in the local European bars, where, because of his pale skin and deceptive features, he passed easily for any of a slew of European nationalities. He was incognito and in hiding.

Jacobo had gone to seek his fortune as an actor in New York. Máximo continued playing classical guitar twice weekly in a pretentious café near Rush Street. He'd given up studying music. His student visa had expired. There wasn't an instructor around who could teach him what Pío de la Costurera had in Spain. Not one had the true gift of the musician that Máximo felt he'd inherited. What's more, despite his love for the genre, what might he do with his proficiency that could bring him the ends he sought? He wanted a life of comfort, to travel; he sought fame. He had little expectation of joining a symphony. Had he been a violinist, a pianist perhaps, ah! To have become a conductor!

He reached into his pocket. There was the card he'd been carrying since the last night he played at the café. At the end of his first set a woman came up to him. She was an American, a white woman to be sure. He found them to be the most aggressive in these cases. At least, initially. Later, they withdrew, behaved even timidly, with an insecurity on the edge of neurosis. Máximo was not attracted to her. Indeed, he might never have noticed her, although she was pleasant-looking. She had regular features, an average figure, dressed well, conservatively, but well. She smiled. He nodded.

"You have the hands of a true artist," she said. He could tell she was nervous, but attempted to hide it. He raised an eyebrow and let her go on. "I don't mean a musician, but an artist . . ."

"How do you know I am not a sculptor or a painter?"

"Oh, I think you are, but you haven't explored those possibilties yet."

"How can you tell?" She had his attention. Anyone who took an interest in him usually did. "They're much too smooth." Her eyes traced his fingers; they caressed his hands.

"Are you an artist?" He wondered on what basis she spoke with such authority. This might only be a clever prelude to a seduction.

"I have a knack for nurturing artists, let's say. I teach at the Institute."

Máximo had heard enough for the time being and asked her to

stay until he finished his last set. Later, while the waiters and busboys scurried cleaning tables and putting up chairs, the couple sat intimately at the bar. He did not put away his guitar, but continued to strum randomly. He knew this had a certain effect on women; his playing struck their sensual chords. "Laura," he said, his voice deep and rich, his eyes downcast. He continued to play softly. "Laura," that was her name, Laura Marie Jefferson. "Do you think you might nurture me into a respected artist?"

"Yes. I knew from the first when I heard you play. You have the hands and the heart for it. I'd go as far as to predict that in a year you'll have your own show at the Museum of Progressive Art."

Max forced a pessimistic laugh. He pretended to doubt her, although he already found it plausible. "And how are you so sure of that?"

"I have very strong ties on its Board of Directors. My father is the chairman." She smiled, but her eyes were dead serious. Máximo laughed a little more heartily this time. He put down the guitar and looked at Laura Jefferson with an expression that told whatever it was she wanted to know.

Máximo reached the bungalow where Josephine lived with her eccentric parents. He pulled open its gate and went past the rows of geraniums to the back, where Josephine opened the door with its windowpane and ridiculous bell that rang lightly with any movement. She pulled Máximo in out of the rain. The smell of homemade dumplings, the wax on the old furniture, the alcohol on her hands, and that persistent stale breath, which he sensed had to do with bad teeth, welled up in his head.

He let her draw him into the pantry of spotless shelves and neat rows of cans and canisters. He pulled up her skirt and felt that she wore no underwear.

If Máximo went to study at the Institute he might be eligible for a government loan. He could get his student visa renewed. He could move out of the shabby room with its late-hour accordian music and foot stomping downstairs. He could thus come out of hiding and return to mingling openly with his Spanish-speaking friends.

Máximo penetrated Josephine, coming almost instantly. She pretended to have an orgasm, or perhaps she actually did.

twenty-four

Thirteen months after Máximo Madrigal met Laura Marie Jefferson he had a one-man show in the sublevel of the Museum of Progressive Art on Chicago's Michigan Ave. It was decided by Laura, upon advice from her father, that for this to be accomplished without provoking opposition from suspicious parties, Max would have to have reputable exhibits to his credit.

Within that year, he studied as an apprentice to an eminent Japanese sculptor whose work was recognized from the East to the western world. Máximo proved to be not only a prolific student, but immediately soared with demonstrations of his unique capabilities. Regardless of the artist's talents, it was a vicious world and it did not satisfy him that what Laura had set out to do was sheer nepotism. Unlike those masters so highly praised post mortem, Max intended to reap his glory while on earth.

He exhibited in a group show in a gallery on Superior; later, with one artist at another important show on the same street. It was made important by the fact that the painter who exhibited with Max had defected from Rumania and had been given immense publicity, so that by proxy, Max, too, was mentioned in the reviews. Afterward, Max was given a one-man show in a gallery on Soho. When he returned, he was scheduled for the museum.

During his exhibition at the museum, Max spent part of each day happily greeting his new public. There were catalogs to autograph and potential patrons to meet and impress with all the wit and wiles of his incorrigible charm.

His show coincided, or perhaps it was not all that coincidental but a strategic move as part of the board's endless effort to practice cultural diplomacy, with a festival of folk music of the Americas. A program was scheduled for each Wednesday of that month. Groups were brought in from Argentina, Uruguay, Bolivia—to Canada. There were several names representing various U.S. regions.

One Wednesday afternoon, Jesús Valle, a young artist whose work Máximo had become familiar with at the Institute, but whom Max felt at best showed promise, came in to see his exhibit. The two men talked in the fashion of protégés, but Max sensed the other's contempt for his conspicuous burst into prominence. Just as Jesús was about to leave, he stopped to read the evening's program listed plainly at the entrance. Máximo asked him if he planned to stay. He thought to invite Jesús for a beer afterward. Perhaps with a few drinks Jesús would relax and accept some advice from Máximo, who now felt very much in the position to give it.

Jesús frowned. His thick Indian lips tightened. Beneath his breath he cursed. "What is it, man?" Max asked in Spanish. Although the other's first language was English, he understood Spanish perfectly. "I didn't know she was on the program! Damn, damn," he muttered. His eyes were filled with turmoil, although his lips curled into a tense smile. Max recognized that look in men. "Who do you mean? Is there someone performing tonight that you know?"

"Pastora Aké? Who doesn't know her?"

"What's the matter, man? Are you in love with her?" Max patted the other's back with fraternal consolation. Jesús withdrew, uneasy with the knowledge that his feelings were so transparent. "You know how it is. She's got that face," his cigar fingers covered his own, as if he described a mask, "that way about her . . . I asked her to sit for me and I did her portrait. Afterward, I couldn't get her out of my mind."

Max laughed. He pretended to be objective about the other's confession, but already his heart had begun to beat rapidly. His palms sweated. He had felt that same way the last time he saw her. He thought it was simple animal heat, that after the conquest it would be gone. He would think of her no more. "What happened? She didn't pay attention to you?" he asked Jesús.

"On the contrary, man," Jesús replied; now the turmoil surfaced and he had to rid himself of it. "She'd let me come see her . . . I couldn't sleep; I'd drive around for hours at night. I'd have to stop somewhere to call her, after a few beers, didn't care if she was busy or asleep. Finally, she told me to stop bothering her. I guess I can't blame her, but I think she's a witch . . ."

Max started. Jesús was in fact talking like a man possessed. After all, what mere woman could have this effect on men? Jesús spoke as if to himself, "She's real strange . . . quiet, but with a fire inside. You get too close and you burn; but you have to . . . you can't help yourself." Jesús laughed at himself pathetically. He wondered why he was telling this conceited bastard the biggest woe of his life. Jesús chose to be kind to himself and did not stay for the program.

Máximo decided he would remain, sit in the back where he wouldn't be easily noticed. He wouldn't stay afterward, as he had done the week before, to meet and go off to drink with the touring performers. On second thought, to hell with that woman! If he felt like it, he would do as he pleased. He would ignore her. To the devil with her spell casting. Let other men be her marionettes.

From the shielding darkness of the back row, Max watched the program that evening. He anticipated Pastora's repertory was to be nothing he hadn't heard or seen before. When she came out on stage, not with her friend, Perla, and that monkey in a tuxedo he had seen her perform with before, but alone, again he felt anxious. His first thought of her, a conscious battle of emotional will power, was that she was insidious.

She was no longer in the silk skirt and white shawl look of the fifties Latin American movie star. Instead she wore the traditional costume of the Mayan woman. The tunic, stark white, splashed along the bodice with hand-embroidered flowers; the skirt, ankle-length, also embroidered at the hem. Her small feet were sandaled and her abundant hair braided with colored ribbons. She looked like a quetzal, an aberration from the Central American highlands.

Pastora was in good form, held her own without accompaniments. She kept the audience captive, number after number, and left when the allotted time was up. There was no pretext to steal a number, knowing the audience would not have been displeased, but she left with consideration for the group that waited in the wings, that'd travelled from its village where this night in the U.S. was to be the highlight of all its career.

After the program, Max hurried backstage. He was told that several of the performers had decided to meet at a bar known for its artistic patronage. Many of the performers recognized him as the distinguished artist who was currently exhibiting at the museum. They shook his hand; he patted their backs and congratulated them on their talented renditions, for Max prided himself on a good first impression and winning as many fans as he was able. His eyes scouted for her.

Coatlicue, he said to himself, tonight she was a goddess incarnated. Whereas the first time he saw her perform she would have been María Félix at the beginning of her stardom, tonight Pastora was magic dust particles and ether. When he saw her, the woman of flesh and bones, she was smiling politely at a Brazilian, a snake, he was sure, who already had his fangs ready for her. When he neared them, he heard them conversing in Portuguese, the only romance language he did not speak.

He begged their pardon and handed her a copy of his impressive full-color catalog. "Miss Velásquez," he said in Spanish. He didn't know why, but he preferred her Castilian surname to the Indian one of her mother. "I don't know if you've had the chance to come to my show downstairs. I'd like you to have this; I've autographed it."

He mentioned nothing of her performance, how it had carried him to heights and depths he had only recalled during his childhood in Sapogonia, the thrill of riding bare horseback, when his grandfather took him out to hunt deer. She had brought tears to his eyes with the reminder of the great tenderness certain women had shown him when he was a boy. He thought that by giving her the autographed copy, one exceptional artist paid homage to the other. Those songs would echo for some time in his head and he would hear them when he went back to work in his studio.

She was gracious, accepted the catalog, and with scarcely a glance at it, let it disappear in the straw bag she carried over her shoulder. She turned to go. He stopped her. "Are you going to the bar? Perhaps you'll let me buy you a beer?"

She looked at him impatiently. "Well, I don't know whether I am or not." Then, as if she felt obligated to give an excuse, "I have to work in the morning."

Then another performer came up to her. This one was tall and dangerously handsome with refined features. Máximo saw him for what he was, a Valentino, a garish gigolo; but without a doubt, his interest in Pastora was physical. She turned to him with the same gracious but curt manner which she had used with Máximo.

Max waited on the steps leading out of the museum. She was leaving alone. "Have you decided to go to the bar?" he asked as if they were old friends, with his usual forwardness. "Do you need a ride?" She didn't stop her descension, but replied she had her own car. Máximo didn't. "Well, perhaps you can give me a ride?" Without stopping, she answered him she hadn't decided yet if she would go to the bar and continued out to the street. Máximo was behind her. He was dazed. Nothing drove him harder than a challenge. He took hold of her arm. "Why don't you go? I would like to talk with you. I'll buy you a beer."

She was no longer courteous, but impatient. "I don't drink beer, but we'll see." With determination she shook off his grip and went off. Máximo found someone to give him a ride to the bar with its liquor-soaked floor. What the place lacked in decor it made up in atmosphere. The group was gay and thirsty. The jukebox played until closing time. Pastora, after having wine, seemed amiable; she danced and he heard her laugh aloud. She let her hair loose, the ribbons tossed precariously to the floor.

He waited his turn, but took each opportunity to dance with her, to hold her to his chest, to smell her, to take hold of her eyes like jewels he possessed. He was set on having her that night. He didn't forget the pitiful Jesús, who at that moment was drowning himself in the memory of her. Her indigenous background was prominent, but she wasn't as dark as a full-blooded Yaqui and was tall with subtle bones. When he'd had enough to drink, he whispered, "India grandota, india bonita." She gave him a haughty look, as if he were repulsive to her.

As the lights went on, she put on her coat and her car keys appeared. She started to leave. He grabbed her. He was drunk. "Take me with you." He didn't realize the force which he used to restrain her, but it was enough to pull her down onto a nearby stool. She scarcely looked at him.

She may have worried about a scene, whereas Max was in that drunken state which bade one on. A small woman, one in the group of actors who had appeared in the Usigli fiasco, came to Pastora's defense, as if Pastora of all women needed defending. "Listen, cabrón," she tried to be threatening. "Don't treat her that way! ¡Ella es un dama!"

Without a thought to his actions, Max lifted the actress with one arm around her waist. "How dare you tell me what to do?" he scowled at her, who dangled like a rag in the air. She begged to be let down and he did so just as Pastora started for the door.

He followed her outside. Someone came up behind him. "Hey, Máximo, need a ride?" Max looked at the man and then at Pastora, who, for some reason, now hesitated. He knew then the battle was won. "Well, what do you say?" he said in a tone loud enough for her hearing alone. She had a grave look. "You're drunk."

"I'm not drunk," he spoke with the true obstinance of a drunk.

"Well, fine. Let's go."

Máximo turned to wave his friend off, and the other man winked. He went with her to her car. It was a cold night; bitter northern winter had approached. They said nothing to each other in the car, but he was confident, satisfied that he was about to dispel the myth, defy that opaque wall from which behind she observed the world and all its inhabitants, as if they were there for her private amusement.

twenty-five

Xalaquia was bronze and approximately a meter in height. Her delicate arms rose, and tapered fingertips nearly touched above the tilted head. The eye furious with secrets. The mouth was firmly closed and suggested a smile. Xalaquia had no heart, but a void in the area of the chest and abdomen, and as Máximo created her, he remembered the severe sensation of pain he had felt the only night he had been with her.

Before he completed Xalaquia, he heard from her, or rather from Coatlicue—as he referred to Pastora in the private realm of his thoughts. It had been a good day for the artist, having received a call that told him he would be exhibiting in a reputable gallery in Ontario. He wouldn't show alone. Another artist whose work the curator felt complemented Máximo's would be exhibiting with him. Let him bring a hundred artists to the gallery! His work would stand out above them all, survive and surpass all competition and what's more: sell!

It gave him energy the rest of the afternoon to work on Xalaquia, but when he heard the foreboding introduction of *Der Ring des Nibelungen* on the radio, the world was no longer his residence. Wagner was an old friend, the figure behind a wistful desire to conduct symphonies. Máximo quivered, imagining the tragic Siegfried, whose fate was to love his own sister.

He ran his fingers through his shocks of dark hair and jumped on the nearest chair to assume the conductor's pose. He had to be spry; the symphony had begun without him. The prissy soprano had already made her entrance. He gave Brünnhilde a look that warned they would have words later, after the performance. But she *was* beautiful, a luscious Fräulein of flaxen hair (although he knew that she was fat, as was characteristic of sopranos, in his opinion). It was 1876 as he proceeded to make history at Festspielhaus.

His arms waved frantically in the air, but the hands remained taut, the wrists firm, the baton directed subtly, the fingers gave hidden messages—no, no, baboon, soft, soft now we go up, up. WE ARE SOARING NOW FLYING OVER OCEANS MOUNTAINS LOVE HAS STRUCK OUR WEARY HEARTS WE ARE OMNIPOTENT GODS OF THE UNIVERSE, MY LOVELY, HERE TO OBSERVE THIS SPECK OF A PLANET AND MODEST EXAMPLE OF TRANSITORY EXISTENCE!

He did not let up and the radio, airing a live concert, played the entire opera, leaving Máximo utterly drained. Returning to the world of mortal men, he realized he had not fed his stomach the entire day. He took mental note of the freezer. It was a waste of effort to reach for anything there since he hadn't bought a morsel or brought leftovers from the restaurant or Laura's in a week. Still, the demands of his capricious stomach urged him on. He gave it its way far too often, he muttered to that part of his body as he dragged his feet across the dull baseboards to the kitchen area. It was akin to gratitude what he felt when he found a black-skinned avocado in the cupboard and proceeded to cut it open and devour the overripened fruit, digging his teeth in the blackened substance that, despite its bland taste, teased the entrails. The telephone rang.

It was Friday. It had to be a friend inviting him out to drink; if not, with any luck, it was a woman who would have him to dinner or to drinks and once at her home, he would help himself to her food. He would persuade her to prepare something for the devoted artist who so deserved the compassion of the public. But all these musings ended when he realized it was not a friend or a woman in the ordinary sense of the word, but Coatlicue a.k.a. Pastora. He stopped himself before actually uttering the pet name he had for her.

"On the last occasion I was with you, you threw me out," he spoke with indignation, determined to receive retribution.

"I know, I'd like to make up for it by inviting you to have a drink with me. We could meet at the same bar where we were that night."

Máximo felt stubborn. "It's cold and my car isn't working. I haven't any way to get there." The words pared their way through his teeth. He couldn't resist the anger that surged whenever he recalled the long, dizzying walk that dawn when she made him leave her apartment without so much as a duro in his pocket. He agreed to let her come for him. He would be gentleman enough to allow her to make amends, although Máximo knew himself too well. The insults and rejection that woman had hurled at him effortlessly were unforgivable.

He would be polite. He would make certain that he wouldn't drink so much that, utterly intoxicated, he would lose track of how he ended in one place and woke in another. Above all, he would assume her game. He would play indifferent. He would go on that night about
the beautiful ballerina
in Paris
who had been *soooooo*   Once upon a time . . . in love
with him.

He would go on in tragic detail how he had to leave her behind in Paris with a promise to return as soon as he had tended to the issue of his dear father. Then, as fate would have it, he contracted a deadly fever. It would take months to recover. All the while he was driven by one concrete belief, that his ballerina awaited him, hanging to the silver thread of hope that he would return soon to marry her.

He recalled her beauty (much more beautiful than the Brünnhilde in the opera that afternoon) and the knowledge that he was truly a fortunate man to have her adoration and loyalty to help him back on his feet. He told all this to the dark woman who sipped a sol y sombra and listened shrewdly as if every word that came from his mouth was being delivered to a place that would eventually determine his fate. Undaunted by such skepticism, he went on. Believing he would never return to her, such a humble girl, she had given up on him shortly before he actually arrived and married a wealthy man.

Máximo sighed and in one swallow emptied the double shot of scotch. Pastora was buying that evening. He signaled to the bartender for another drink. He was certain Coatlicue would be affected by this account, and possibly made envious. His story had let her know he had been loved by a beautiful woman, far more beautiful than Pastora, who pretended she could have no rival and who, of course, was overestimating her qualities. Although one had to say at that moment she was attractive. Some might call her beautiful.

He had let her know as well that the woman who'd loved him had been of a certain class and culture and not a half-starved cabaret dancer with peroxided hair and penciled eyebrows, but a woman of elegance and discipline. And she had loved him. He had emphasized that point, hadn't he?

Coatlicue, whose expression was sometimes as fixed as the

bronze Xalaquia in his studio, (of which he didn't dare speak for fear that it would add to her insupportable arrogance) sighed as well. Máximo was certain he had moved her.

"How did you expect her to wait months on end without a word from you?" She held the snifter with her sandstone fingers, swished the drink before she took a sip. He noticed on the middle finger of her left hand she wore a silver ring with an indigenous figure with coral eyes and turquoise wings. "Did you actually expect her to wait months without a word from you?" she asked.

Well, of course, I knew I should never have expected the woman I'd left without warning in Paris to wait for me with no reassurance during that time that I would come back. I glared at Pastora, who so coolly had assessed that great loves belonged to the stage and balanced works of fiction and not in the acts of living men and women.

Had I written, instead of presumed that my dancer (because, although she had studied ballet as a child, she had not actually ever worked in that capacity. Instead, when we were together she contemplated the better life we might have if she took to the streets and, in fact, I believe she may have done so on occasion. Although I would never have permitted it had I known for sure. Since she didn't tell me where she had gotten the francs to pay for our expensive meals and the silk shirt she surprised me with once, I accepted it all as one very well should accept gifts from a lover, with grace and without question) would wait for me, there may have been a reason to return to Paris. But friends who met up with me in Madrid let me know she had returned to past paramours. One aspect I had not had to improvise to this stone-hearted woman by my side was of the dancer's beauty. She may have looked very much like any young, country girl, only painted up and hennaed, but she was lovely.

How was it that I had expected her to wait without a call or a letter for so many months? Pastora asked cockily.

"Because she knew that I loved her," I replied simply, with great sobriety. I ordered another double scotch. The waiter was Mexican and his English was worse than mine. We spoke to each other in English, with vowels that mellowed extreme sounds, and understood each other perfectly.

My sole wish was to embed the flint into Xalaquia, twist it and make her writhe with envy with the awareness that I could love a woman, really love her, not simply adore her for the moment, for the sake of a conquest, but want her forever and deliver myself up to her as I would definitely not allow myself to do with Pastora Velásquez. I had loved the ballerina I left in Paris and she had loved me, I insisted. She had succumbed to family pressure, I said, inventing spontaneously for good measure, and had married the entrepreneur without love for him.

Coatlicue lit a cigarette. I was sure that I had succeeded in disrupting her self-confidence. She was not about to let me go on my way so easily that evening. She wouldn't dare send me out in the cold like a cheap streetwalker she had picked up for her entertainment. She went into her bag and left some bills to cover our drinks on the table. Her actions indicated she had decided to leave. Of course, she was the one driving and, as such, had no need to consult with me as to whether we should remain a while longer. I was scarcely finishing my fresh drink.

I knew enough not to risk having to walk from the bar back to my studio in the freezing temperature or chance a deadly wait at the bus stop. I put on my cashmere coat with the raccoon collar I had worn for the occasion. I may have been a half-starved artist, but I had style and knew how to present myself before a lady, scholar, stone diety, or rumored witch.

twenty-six

Pastora made her way to the apartment of the woman named Alicia with less difficulty than she had anticipated. Her friend in Chicago, Teresa, had given her Alicia's address and assured her that she was a person with whom it was all right to stay for a few nights.

Alicia received her pleasantly enough, if not without a certain reserved manner which Pastora couldn't decide whether it was shyness or a troubled mind. Alicia said that Teresa had played one of Pastora's albums for her during a visit a year or so before and she had enjoyed it, but she displayed no enthusiasm. In any case, Alicia demonstrated solidarity with Pastora as a woman artist and took her into her tiny abode on the Lower East Side.

Pastora had come to New York to attend the American folk music conference at the New School, where she had been invited to perform as part of its ongoing three-day program. Her performance was well-received, although she was treated as only one among eighty-seven performers who had travelled to the congregation. The auditorium had been filled, which was always gratifying, as she had too often performed in sparsely peopled cafés and pitifully empty auditoriums.

After the program that evening, Pastora, with her performance behind her, relaxed. She invited Alicia, who had come to see her that evening, for a drink. Pastora was disappointed that Alicia refused the drink; she didn't care for the taste of alcohol in any form, she said. Pastora toasted to their new friendship, clinking her wine glass to Alicia's ginger ale.

Pastora studied the patrons of the Village bar talking loudly and interacting animatedly. She lit a cigarette. The adrenaline from her performance continued to rush through her body. She wanted to mingle with other lives, tell them about how she sang Lennon's "Imagine" in Spanish. She had translated it herself. Could they imagine it sung in Spanish? She glanced at Alicia, who had finished the ginger ale. Alicia was waving her hand at the smoke from Pastora's cigarette.

"Tomorrow morning I have to turn in photographs I took for *Visión Magazine*. You've heard of it?" Alicia said suddenly. Pastora smiled and nodded. She had heard of the new Latino magazine, the first of its kind to be distributed nationally.

"Do you work for them?" she wondered.

"I do free-lance assignments." Alicia sipped the water from the melted ice in her glass and grimaced at Pastora's cigarette. Pastora put it out. Alicia continued, "I told one of the editors that you were in town and that you're staying with me."

"Yes? Do you mean he had heard of my music?"

"Yeah." Alicia smiled briefly, relieved by the cigarette's death. "He said he had your album, in fact. He asked me to bring you down to the offices."

"Why do you think he wants to meet me?"

"Because he likes your music, I guess." Alicia shrugged her shoulders, indicating that she had not really questioned the invitation herself. "It's a possibility that he wants to write something up on you . . ."

"Teresa writes for them, doesn't she?" Pastora thought she remembered hearing that about their mutual writer-friend. For the present, she didn't want to get her hopes up. The notion of her first national coverage in a non-underground context was more exciting than having come to perform in New York. "Yeah. She's written an article or two, one on Mexican migration to Chicago and one on something else, I can't remember," Alicia said, sipping with a slurping sound.

"Do you want to come with me tomorrow?" Alicia asked. Pastora said she did. She finished her own drink and thought to order another and to invite Alicia to a second ginger ale, then, overcome by the fatigue of the traveller, changed her mind and, as she suspected, Alicia did not protest her suggestion to leave the bar.

The suite of Visión Magazine was located in a high-rise near the Rockefeller Plaza. The secretary told the women to go directly into the editor's office. He seemed to be a genuine sort. For all that Pastora had heard of New Yorkers, she found that they were actually quite friendly, if one overlooked the persistent air of those who were assured by the world that the future of culture depended on their definition of it.

148

Pastora hid her disappointment when she realized the editor wanted nothing more than to meet the singer and suggested nothing by way of publicity for her in the magazine. He said only that someone was covering the music conference and he settled his business with Alicia. The meeting was over. The women were ushered out of the plush office and past the secretary, a dark Latina with fantastic burgundy fingernails. Pastora wondered how the woman could hold a pencil much less type a letter with such obstruction.

Just as they were leaving the office, Pastora thought she heard a familiar voice, but she found it hard to believe it could belong to whom she thought. "Pastora? Is that you, babe?"

Pastora stopped in her tracks. It could be none other than Diego Cañas, who was the only man she knew who referred to her by such names. Pastora suspected that Diego knew that "babe" and "honey" at the very least annoyed her, but he persisted as if he wanted her to say she wanted him to stop, so that he could persist with more reason.

She turned in time to catch the bear hug he lavished on her. Alicia stood by, smiling despite the hunch that Pastora had that Alicia had not liked hearing how the stranger addressed her. Babe. It was a name for baseball players and strip teasers. "Honey" and "dear" were reserved for the exclusive use of diner waitresses and old ladies with mothballs in their pockets. Pastora made the introductions.

"What're you doing here?" Pastora asked first.

"Oh, you know, some business, that's all," Diego responded evasively. This kind of vague response disturbed Pastora. She never understood why individuals who seemed to be friends could display so little trust when it came to their ambitions. "What are *you* doing here?" Diego reversed the question.

"Alicia does free-lance work for the magazine . . . we came to drop it off." Pastora, equally evasive, didn't mention that the editor was a fan and had wanted to meet her. The first thing Diego would ask was if the magazine planned on doing a feature article on her and Pastora would end by saying how disappointed she was that it had not occurred to the editor. The mention of Alicia as a free-lancer for the magazine stirred Diego's interest, who until then had scarcely given the woman a glance. He proceeded to bombard her with questions as the three made their way to the elevator, down to the main lobby, and out to the street.

"I'm on my way for a few drinks with friends in Soho. You guys wanna come along? C'mon, vieja, don't be a party pooper!" Diego pulled Pastora by the arm toward the subway entrance.

Pastora was eager for adventure. "Want to come?" she invited Alicia, already certain of the answer. "No, I'm kinda hungry. I think I'll go home and eat," Alicia begged off. The two women looked at each other oddly for a moment. For an instant, Pastora started to respond to Alicia and not go on with Diego, then abruptly decided against it.

Pastora went down to the subway with Diego, arms locked. They were old friends reunited and ready to explore new frontiers. He led her to a nondescript corner bar in the Soho district. She had never been anywhere near that area and realized that if she had too much to drink and Diego left her stranded for any reason, she would be at the mercy of a cab driver to lead her back to Alicia's.

A couple waited for Diego at a table near the door. The man, whose name was Gerry, was fat; not very fat, but his protruding belly gave him a Buddha effect as he sat with a mug of beer before him. His woman, whose name was also Gerry, was equally unappealing. She wasn't fat like her lover, but she looked like someone who had had enough good years of hard living. She was loud and abrasive. Pastora disliked them immediately. It wasn't a conclusion based on their appearances, but she sensed a lack of respect from both of them for her, for themselves, for life in general.

Gerry the Woman had sized her up. With her eyes she let Pastora know that she saw her as one of Diego's fly-by-night girlfriends, or more aptly put, lays. She called Pastora honey, giving the dozen-year difference between their ages a stretch of decades. One an ancient sage and the other, Betty Boop.

Diego ordered a glass of wine for Pastora and a mug of beer for himself and his friends. He was in high spirits and without hesitation entered into a pedantic discussion on the history of American art. Pastora remembered an exhibit she had seen at the Chicago Historical Society. Eighteenth-century portraits. She had never been inspired less. Could she say she had expired?

"Robert Henri," Diego was saying, "he pronounced it Henry, because, as an American, the painter had wanted to emphasize his patriotism." The rest of Diego's speech was blurred because either his pronunciation had already been impaired by the beer or she found the talk so pretentious that it was tedious to hear.

Occasionally Gerry the Man would interject a ludicrous remark meant to be hilarious, as hinted by his laughter that followed, but which was really a cheap shot or a simpleton's play on words. Gerry the Woman was worse. She interjected rude remarks that had nothing to do with the conversation at all. She had a tendency to jab her partner's ribs and slap his shoulder each time he made one of his offbeat jokes. They're a regular Punch and Judy, Pastora thought facetiously, letting her mind drift to other directions.

Outside, as dusk settled over New York, a light snow fell, giving the street an innocent quality. There truly was magic in New York incomparable to other cities. It was that kind of snow that one saw in picture books, silent and cool enough to wet the tongue and stick to eyelashes. New patrons kept coming and the place filled. After exhausting the possible contemplations of the atmosphere, she found her paper napkin to be of interest, shredding it with concentration. She had finished her drink and had not been able to get the waiter's attention. Diego, meanwhile, went on with his soliloquy.

Gerry the Man was the first to call out the name. He faced the door directly, while Pastora had her back to it. "Hey, Max! Amigo! ¿Cómo está?" His Spanish held a distinct Yiddish accent. By the look on Gerry the Woman's face, Pastora had only one guess as to which of all the Maxes in the world that could've walked into that corner bar of anonymity in Soho it was. All that was needed were ceiling fans and a black piano player. Gerry the Woman straightened up and thrust forth her chest. She patted her hair. She licked her lips to give them shine. What was it about that man that had such an effect on women? For heaven's sake.

Pastora didn't turn around. She knew Diego would invite Max over to the table and she knew there was only one thing that would be more surprising than her seeing Máximo Madrigal at that moment, and that was him seeing her. She kept her head tilted, pretending to be devoted to the ball of tissue that was once a napkin. She poured a little of Diego's beer into her wine glass and took a swallow.

Max's hand reached over to shake Gerry the Man's. He patted Diego on the back. He was already wondering who the woman was with Diego. She had long dark hair and probably, he could guess, she was Latina. It didn't matter. She could be blond or brunette. Máximo showed no preference, himself, for types.

She could no longer keep her face averted without it seeming deliberate. She raised her gaze. For an infinitesimal instant, but it happened nevertheless, his self-assured demeanor diminished. He blinked twice with thin eyelashes then recuperated. He reached out a gloved hand to shake hers.

Diego continued to dominate the conversation and he invited Max to a beer. "So how are the plans for the show going, Máximo?" Gerry the Man asked. Pastora listened. She found Gerry the Woman's transfiguration amazing, from wench to a vestal virgin. Máximo told her he was having a reception in two days. "Please come," he invited both Gerrys with his eyes. He didn't look in the direction of Pastora.

He hadn't removed his sheepskin coat and had just pushed back the Cossack hat. Pastora saw that he, too, had come to New York prepared for Chicago weather. He seemed exaggerated in his dress. Nonetheless, she regretted it when he chugged down his beer and left. They had scarcely exchanged a greeting. Anyone would have thought they hardly knew each other. But that was the point, wasn't it?

Neither had ever made their relationship public. Moreover, neither had allowed her/himself to accept it as actual. It had been a fantasy until they had just accidentally crossed time zones and without notice, found themselves face to face. It was not meant to be; they had not really seen each other in this bar in New York in front of someone like Diego Cañas, herald of Latino artist gossip. Máximo left like a fugitive on the run.

Pastora was disturbed. Injected with his presence, she was reminded of the pleasure that they were depriving each other of—if only they permitted themselves to wander into the realm of everyday folks. Fleeting images went through her mind, making love in New York, on the subway train, wherever it was that he might be staying, in the toilet of this bar if necessary, anywhere, as long as that inevitable physical connection of the species was achieved.

She watched Diego, comparing him to Máximo. Diego, with his drawn-out jaw and colored teeth, was not necessarily bad-looking. Weighing the physical debilities of both men, they came out about even. Why was it that Max alone had this uncanny effect on women—and men? The Gerrys were testimony. Both now returned to their slouchy selves. She, poking at her lover's ribs on cue to punctuate each of his remarks. He, acting like a slob.

Diego announced he was hungry. They all agreed. No one mentioned Máximo, but they all felt his absence. Food seemed a natural consolation. They decided on a Cantonese restaurant only a subway ride away and as a group they left and made their tracks on the new snow on New York's gritty asphalt.

They were halfway through their meal when Pastora wished the night wouldn't end so uneventfully. She had a desire to sing, to play her music. She had had enough beer and wine to make even the Gerrys tolerable. She hinted at taking the party on to someone's studio. The Gerrys ignored her, so that she concluded their place was probably as atrocious as they were. Diego said he was staying with a guy who was fastidious about his work and would not be open to strangers coming by to have a party.

"Who is Max staying with?" Pastora asked, as if the thought had just occurred to her at that moment. With the effect of the alcohol, she was not ready to release the image of Max to mesh with the density of New York.

"He's staying with the owner of the gallery where he's going to exhibit his one-man show," Gerry the Man said, clearing his throat. "It's just down the block from where we were earlier."

"That's what he is all right, a one-man show," Diego muttered half to himself, revealing his rivalry. Pastora overlooked the remark. She smiled, "Well, do you think they would mind if we came by? Just old friends from Chicago?" Pastora sounded persuasive.

"Ha!" spouted Gerry the Woman. No explanation, no need to elaborate; a simple, singular "ha" sufficed to confirm Pastora's suspicion. The proprietor of the gallery was a woman and Máximo had used his cobralike charm to get that exhibit.

"Why don't you give him a call? Ask him if he would mind?" The suggestion came from her friend Diego. Gerry the Man held out a coin. Pastora didn't hesitate to analyze the plan; she took it and went to the pay telephone. Her trim figure weaved through the tables, her snug jeans showed the contour of a slight ass, her hair brushed to one side, a serpent over the shoulder. She was conscious of this image of herself as the three pairs of eyes watched her and waited for the results.

They had silently conspired to use her as a tool; an attractive female thrown as bait to Máximo Madrigal, to louse up a cozy arrangement, an exhibit that neither Gerry the Man, Gerry the Woman, nor Diego the Friend would have ever been able to claim for themselves as none of them exuded the sperm-odored allure that was natural to Máximo. They were reduced to two envious men and one disgusting woman out for blood. Here Max, you snake, here's a little tadpole. Take a chance, Max. Gobble her up. Go for it, boy! Risk it! Maybe the woman you've been laying to get that exhibit at her gallery will let you get away with it . . . or maybe not.

Pastora took the challenge. Her gypsy heart had gone up to the yearning for music, for more wine, for laughter, for Máximo's kisses. She was drunk. A woman answered. She sounded as if she had been asleep. Only then did Pastora consider the time. "Excuse me, I'm a friend of Máximo Madrigal's. We're friends from Chicago . . . We were wondering if we might come over to say hello."

There was a pause. Pastora wanted to hang up. She smiled back at the group that watched her. "Máximo is not here at the moment, dear," the woman answered sternly, a million light years in superiority to Pastora, a voice from Máximo's list of cunts. She knew all the tricks. She knew Max. She was not allowing any female friend over to party at her place.

"Oh, well," Pastora didn't know what else to say. "Do you expect him back soon?"

"Yes, of course," came the reply strewn with matriarchal authority. "But I'm already in bed. We'll probably be asleep soon."

Pastora got a grip on herself. Who were these people maneuvering her like the cue ball on a pool table? "I'm sorry to have disturbed you, madam," she told the woman, hanging up. She had not left a name. When she returned to the Gerrys and Diego, who had the look of irrepressable pranksters who can't face the teacher who's just sat on the thumbtack, they pretended to be preoccupied with the bill. No one wanted to pay for a grain of rice s/he didn't order.

Pastora went into her bag. She left a few bills on the table, certain it was enough to pay for her meal and her share of the tip, and handed Gerry the Man a coin. "That's for the one you gave me to make the call," she told him. Her voice was not pleasant, but she also restrained her irritation. He took it and did not look at her.

"Well, how did it go? Are we going over there?" Diego asked. She could refrain from showing a stranger that he had made her angry, but not Diego. "How do you think?" she muttered. She tried to keep her voice down, but the others were all ears. "I don't know," Diego pretended not to have an idea that having a woman call Máximo might cause problems for him.

Pastora sighed. "He wasn't there. *She* was sleeping. No, we can't come over to party. Satisfied?" Pastora gathered up her things. She was about to set out into the streets of Manhattan, angry at men, at the lack of integrity among human beings, and at women who hurled their resentment at the world's inhabitants for having been given life.

"Hold on, I'll get a cab for you. Unless you know your way back to Alicia's on the subway . . ." Diego said, fishing in his wallet for his share of the bill and flinging it on the table. The Gerrys were still counting up their money.

Pastora didn't wait for Diego, who came quickly behind her. "Are you mad? Why are you mad?" Diego put his arm around her. She shrugged it off. "You know damn well why I'm mad, jerk." Pastora held back the tears that were either due to the alcohol or the enhanced loneliness. Why did a cad like Máximo have a woman ready to set him up both with her home and connections in New York City and Pastora couldn't count on a friend to invite her to a decent meal? "Assholes!" She wiped a tear with her glove, at the same time searched the street for a cab.

"Who?" Diego asked. "You mean those people back there?" Pastora didn't answer. Instead she ran out to the middle of the street as soon as she spotted the light of an available cab. "Hey! Do you need some money for the taxi?" Diego asked. He didn't expect Pastora, especially in her mood, to accept anything from him. She surprised him. "Yeah," she said spitefully. He took out his last bill. "I don't have change," he hesitated to hand it over to her. She snatched it from his hand. "That's fine," she said, sticking it in her pocket and running across the street where the cab had stopped for her.

Once on her way, Pastora remembered her hostess, Alicia, who was warm and safe, tucked into bed in a dreary apartment where men who called women babe and who fucked for the sake of ambition without feeling were not allowed. Pastora cried softly in the cab. She had had too much to drink and not enough to eat.

twenty-seven

Max came in from the street with the wolf upon him. It had followed him through the rush-hour traffic, onto the elevated train platform, from the train down the five blocks to Laura's apartment. She recognized the wolf the moment he entered. He reeked of it. She smiled, feigning oblivion. Schubert played on the stereo. *The New York Times* was spread out on the oriental rug where she relaxed after a bath with a glass of Kir.

"Max, amour! Look, your show's in *Art Forum!*" Her vice was cheery, but he knew she had tensed with his glum entrance. "And? What do you want me to do? To thank you? Do you expect me to get on my knees with gratitude for everything you do for me, my manager par excellence?"

Laura tried to overcome his intimidation. His anger was sometimes frightening, so rash and irrational. Her therapist had reminded her that she was to disassociate herself from it, create distance. She was not to blame for the discontent of others. It wasn't a crime to help those one loved. "What's wrong, Max?"

"I just came from the restaurant where I used to work. There was a raid just before the place opened. Two of my friends who worked there were taken by immigration."

"Why are you so upset? They didn't bother you, did they?"

"They didn't bother you, did they?" he mocked her. "They sniff out an illegal like dogs I was thrown against the wall and searched. My bloody accent was a dead giveaway. What do you think?"

"But you have credentials . . ."

"My bloody student visa; that's almost expired. Of course, that's why they let me go, the bastards. But now they know me by name. I'll have to keep away from there." As he neared her, she could tell he'd been drinking. He removed the wool scarf from around his neck and let the suede jacket she had picked out with such care for him drop on the armchair. He scrutinized her, the artist's acute eye searching for flaws, her defenseless imperfections.

Laura was small-breasted and slender everywhere but at the hips and thighs that'd won against all her efforts to diet since adolescence. She wrapped the robe tightly around her, pretending she was chilled and not insecure. "And why are you wearing that ugly rag? Haven't I asked you a hundred times to get something else? You have the money. Why don't you buy something silk, blue—that would go with your coloring, so you won't look so pale and anemic!"

Laura said nothing. Instead she rose. She was recoiling to the refuge of her bedroom. He had asked her before to wear sexier things at home, it excited him. She had made such purchases, but they waited in her closet, up on the top shelf in their tissue-lined boxes to be brought out like the trousseau of the virginal bride, for the perfect moment. Something about dressing up for him for the mere object of his sexual arousement disheartened her. Suddenly, she was depressed, from the deepest part of her spirit to her bulging thighs.

The wolf stalked her. "What do you think—that you can keep men by buying them? Is that how you got your husbands? You paid them off? Well, maybe so. But you see now that that wasn't enough, was it? They used you and they left when they had wrung you dry. When are you going to learn, Laura? When are you going to have some confidence in yourself and learn to love a man?"

He had hold of the towel on her head just as she reached the bedroom, and he yanked it off. With an exaggerated response, she let herself go back, as if the act had pained her physically, not only emotionally. She continued toward the bedroom, hoping he would stop his antagonizing pursuit. She had become the despising symbol of all he aspired but had to work for, beg, steal. She untied the robe and underneath she was naked.

Máximo pushed her on the bed, where she fell face down, crossways. He mounted her. "What do you expect from me, Laurita?" His whisper was harsh, he was excited by her humiliation. "Do you want me to be your puppet, your personal toy? You pull strings for me, and in turn, pull my strings?"

The coarse texture of his jeans was rough against her backside. She felt his hardening. "Well, not me, chiquitita. This is one man you're not going to possess like something you buy with your bloody money. No one buys me." He reached for a pillow and shoved it under her abdomen. He pulled her up by her hips. She held back an urge to cry, to resist. "Max, please . . ." "What? Isn't this what you want? You want me to take you like this, don't you, to fuck you like a common bitch. Don't deny it."

He held her firmly but without need as she didn't fight. She bit into the satin quilt to stifle her cry. It would be over soon. Afterward, he lay limp inside her. His fingers caressed her head. Laura lay motionless. Máximo kissed her tenderly on the neck, in the ear, whispered, "Marry me."

twenty-eight

He halted at the bedroom door, so as to examine the collection of figurines in deliberate arrangement on the bureau. He pretended the study was brought on by curiosity rather than real interest. Without looking at Pastora, who he knew watched from behind, arms folded a few feet away, he spoke wryly. "Your pantheon has grown. Once it was no more than a few clay figurines, now you have a menagerie of icons." He turned with a cynical smirk. "You probably have a pantheon of men's souls you've been collecting, too."

Pastora ignored him.

Máximo, his coat over his arm, went to the door. He continued with the game. "What do you do—rip out their hearts and throw their trembling bodies out in the alley?"

"Someone should do you the favor and rip out your tongue," she retorted, letting him know that she found no humor in his teasing.

"Don't you understand? All of that is what holds one back. Worshipping idols! It doesn't matter the name you put on it, what religion it is, it's nothing but a method employed to make common people understand their place."

"Which is where?" she inquired, arms folded.

"Which is nowhere, with nothing. 'Religion is the opium of the people' and all that."

"Look who's quoting Marx." Pastora threw her arms up in exasperation. "The Pinochet of the art world."

"No me compares con ese cabrón," Máximo's teeth shut at the end of the demand like steel clamps. "He's a despot. Whom do I have to dictate?"

Pastora was more reticent than a prisoner of war who had to be tortured to speak. He went on probing. "Tell me, do you believe those things have power?" He referred to her makeshift altar of statues. "For a woman as sophisticated as you, it is very disappointing to see your flaw is the weakness of common people."

"No one is a common person." She smiled sardonically, a direct rejoinder to his implied superiority. "All persons are complex. What I have been doing over the years is separating parts of myself, the so-called energies that my soul has carried into this life, and given them names, manifested them into clay figurines, not unlike the Mayas or the Greeks. Yes, this is my pantheon, and when I need courage, I call upon the figure that symbolizes courage, and when I need strength or patience, I do likewise."

"Why don't you just kneel before a mirror and pray to yourself?"

"What a novel idea."

"It's possible that God is a woman. It's also possible that there is no God, that we are all gods . . ."

"I can see you've given the subject a lot of thought." Pastora looked impatient.

"I was raised as a Catholic but I've talked at length with the Indians of my country about the beliefs they've preserved despite the imposition of the national religion." He stopped short, but decided to continue his defense. "My grandmother is Mayan."

"Oh, I wondered about the profile . . ." She treated his remarks lightly. Máximo realized he wasn't going to get Pastora to say more about herself, about the altar, about the dreams he had that pursued him to the hours of full consciousness when, even without sleep, the images ran rampant through his head.

"I have a *Greek* nose! Haven't you ever studied Greek sculpture?" he asked. He was quite serious. Pastora refused to be impressed. "I see, you're saying that your family had a Greek milkman about the time you came along. Oh, but you were raised on a ranch, weren't you? Then it must've been the fellow who passed one day selling Bibles."

"No!" Max didn't smile at her attempt to joke. "I am saying this is the nose of Ulysses!" He pointed furiously to the curve of his nose. She was cynical beyond his tolerance. He turned the lock and held the door open. He wondered if she would draw near for a final kiss. "Now that you've pulled out my palpitating heart, what are your plans for it?"

Pastora blinked slowly. She had a habit of pausing before speaking, a taciturn manner that made it seem at times as if she was very slow in comprehending what was being said to her. He waited for the response. "I should shove it back in through your mouth so you'll shut up once and for all," she said at last.

"Why do you want me to shut up? That's twice you've said it."
Máximo was indignant.

Pastora sighed. "You tire, me, Máximo. Leave now. I have to
pray to all my little dolls . . ."

Máximo closed the door behind him instead and followed her.
"You mean pray to yourself!"

Pastora stopped before reaching the bedroom. She faced him.
"Tell me, who is any different?"

"In other words, we're all a bunch of narcissists; once having
discovered our reflections in the clear pond, we believe we are the
ultimate." He thought he had her.

"Máximo, when are you going to end this pathos driven by
superficiality?"

"Why? Why do you call it pathos? Because I am a man satisfied
with my looks?"

"Because you are a poor soul obsessed with the surface of all
things! 'Un mono vestido de seda sigue siendo mono' who looks all
the more ridiculous for it."

"Now you're saying I am a monkey!" At that moment he was not
wearing a silk suit, but he was partial to them.

"We are all monkeys unless we learn to use what we have here to
examine what is in here," she said, first pointing to her temple then
to the space between her breasts.

The discussion had ceased to keep Máximo's attention and this
time he went to the door prepared to leave. There was frustration in
the air for both. Máximo wanted to know what Pastora really
thought of him. He wanted to know what she believed and whether
she indeed had special powers she exercised at his cost. He wasn't
conscious of her frustration, but interpreted her to be bored with
him.

After lovemaking, their meetings degenerated to such nonsensi-
cal discussions, and the aim was to stick each other with vengeful
remarks. They kissed goodbye like an old husband and wife, a peck
on the lips, more habit than feeling.

twenty-nine

He was afraid of stairs. He had always been afraid of stairs, especially this kind that led to attics and creaked when no one else was around.

He'd been afraid of stairs since he was twelve and Mario—his best friend with the lumpy forehead who said it was that way because they were his brains pushing against the skull, and Máximo believed him because Mario was the most intelligent boy he knew—told him about the stairway in the house where he lived with his mother, older brother, the baby, and the widowed grandfather who talked to himself in the back room.

Mario's house was the green one at the end of the street where they went to school. It was old with shutters and furniture that had belonged to the days of his grandparents. They were standing at the top of the stairs when Mario told him the story. He said that the night before, his brother had been standing on that very spot. He was in his underwear, quivering and calling their mother, who came running with her hair in pin curls. Mario jumped out of bed leaving the infant who slept with him crying. Guillermo, who was the man of the family since their father had disappeared and Abuelo had started talking to himself, trembled, white, tears running down his face. His mother brought him in as if he were a newborn calf left in the cold to die.

After a cup of tea and the children were thought to be asleep, (Mario crept and listened from just outside the kitchen door) Guillermo told his mother what had frightened him. He'd heard a sound out in the hall and went out to check. There was Abuela, struggling up the stairs, one hand on the rail, dressed in black and with the faded apron. "Guillermo, son," she called in a feeble voice. Guillermo began to tremble again. "Go on, son," his mother coaxed, her arms around his shoulder, a hand on his head. "Guillermo, help me!" he finished and broke up in tears.

Máximo stood at the bottom of the stairs and looked up to the attic. He decided to go outside. There were the sheets of steel that had been delivered the day before and lay against the house. He would begin working on a new sculpture that afternoon. Laura's garden filled his nostrils with scents that brought back Sapogonia, the squash his grandmother grew, the chili peppers that made food palatable. Don Fernando was coming down the street. He was an old man, retired, and as such, he spent his days visiting neighbors, fascinated by workers tarring the street or cleaning out sewers, the activities of those who still looked forward to things. The two men waved to each other.

Max remembered the mouse, already dead and shriveled when his seven-year-old eyes spotted it stuck between the cushions of an armchair where a friend of his mother sat politely on the edge, back erect. What were they doing there? He didn't recall. His mother was always making excuses to visit someone in town. She had probably hoped the lady would offer tea and cake, but the woman in the dim house without a bathroom never brought out anything. While the two women chatted, Máximo's eyes were stuck on the mouse's head and blank eyes that seemed to stare out at him.

Don Fernando opened the gate and went into the yard; he wore a billy goat beard and always had the stub of a cigar stuck between his false teeth. He had black shredded wheat for lungs and was dying of cancer. "How about some café?" Don Fernando grinned, baring his woodlike teeth. Máximo patted him on the back. "Of course, come in." He yanked a few twigs of cilantro out of the ground. "Let's have some breakfast to go with it. I'll make a salsita for the eggs that tastes better than your wife's."

"Oh, my wife died. It's been ten years," Don Fernando smiled wistfully. When Max hesitated to lead the way, the old man put a hand on the rail and worked his way up the stairs.

thirty

In the new condominium there was a profusion of light in the afternoon. Pastora lit the white candle of paraffin and placed it carefully on the clay brazier on the bureau. From the top drawer, she took out figurines of both sexes, in various ancient gear and descriptive positions. They were imitations of ancient relics. White flowers in a glass of water perfumed the air. Pastora prayed.

She began her requests for guidance by addressing Santa Clara, who was not represented by any image before her. Then she prayed to her spirit guides, whom she had not paid heed to undeservedly for too long.

To Santa Clara, she relayed the precariousness of her recent behavior. She had been too frivolous and materialistic. Santa Clara had no objections to material gain, but Pastora had forsaken those guides who watched out for her welfare for the sake of tentative things.

Of her principal spirit guide she asked for solace and consolation. She had not forgotten the abortion of thirty-two months earlier. In nature, creatures never ended the lives of others except to survive. To women, abortion was self-defense and preservation of the species. Abortion was not a fancy borne out of the female mind. Abortion was instinct beyond ideas. Abortion was fear (the cat that devours its litter when a predator nears). She thought that her spirit guide knew this, but she prayed she be given peace of mind.

Finally she addressed the spirit guide whose purpose was to aid her creativity. This guide was a constant companion. She hoped it would continue to bring inspiration for her songs and compositions, and appreciation from the public. She had not performed in a year and the world was changing too quickly.

Dominant society was closing again. The youth was interested in individual achievement, financial success. No one wanted to hear about their neighbors' starvation, rape and pillage in American cities. No one joined hands and together raised them up like chains of fists.

And she was no different, susceptible to the same illusive temptations invented by those few who had power. She allowed herself to be persuaded by the finer things in life. She frequented elegant restaurants as she had never done before. Her closets now held expensive clothes. In actuality, however, this new lifestyle held less stability than when she struggled to pay the rent. Tears rolled down Pastora's face.

She had left the blinds open. The sun blared through the windows. This was to discourage the atmosphere that was conducive to the negative spirits. They waited for moments such as this, when her soul wavered with debility and indecision. Yet, she was cold and knew at least one was in the room with her. She forced back the tears and stood erect, her arms crossed.

The telephone rang and, instead of answering it in the bedroom, she went to take up the extension in the kitchen at the far end of the hall. It was Máximo Madrigal. She had not heard from him in a year. It occurred to her as they talked about nothing (their phone conversations were always stilted, conceivably pretentious) that she had moved since he'd called last. She didn't ask from whom he'd gotten her unlisted number.

Her voice was confident. While her eyes darted toward the bedroom at the end of the hall, a shadow stirred. She quickly looked away.

He asked, as if they were such good friends and as he always asked on the telephone with a cordial formality lost when they were together, how her career was going. Before she responded, he volunteered that, as for himself, he could not complain. She did not complain, either. "I'm working alone, composing, and I'm studying piano." She wondered if he could tell that her voice strained to sound positive.

"I'm having a party Saturday night," she said. She went along with the pretense that they were always on good terms, that three seasons had not passed since she'd heard from him. "Please come. The theme is tropical, so try to come dressed for it." Max thanked her for the invitation and hung up shortly after with no intentions of attending. He had no plans to put himself in a position where she could demean him by being in the company of another man.

His friend Ricardo Luna, who worked for the local Spanish

newspaper and who made it a point to be in the know about who's who on the cultural scene, had told him that Pastora was living with an American businessman. Ricardo Luna had been invited to the party and he would surely go in order to find out all the juicy details.

Máximo had not mentioned Laura to Pastora, except when he referred to her as his manager. He did not tell of the loft they had just purchased on Printer's Row which they had elaborate plans to renovate. He was burdened with resentment that he longed so much to see her, to make love to her while she was so involved with another man. He'd said nothing of his feelings either. He had picked up in her voice that she was doing as well as Ricardo said. What did she need Max for, who came groveling like a pathetic dog to sleep at the foot of her bed once a year?

thirty-one

She stepped away from the rectangle of light that painted the hardwood floor and studied her face in the mirror. She wore a sunsuit, more clothing than she could stand on an August day. In the oblong shadows of late afternoon, she criticized the reflected rounded features. Her eyes should be wider, her nose more slender, the lips less generous. She let down her hair and shook it as it tumbled over her shoulders and down her back.

The heat made her lethargic and she wondered passively of the whereabouts of her lover. He had the looks of the all-American hero, the contemporary Hollywood movie star, Aryan, well built. He regarded her with sentimentality flourished in romance, his first true love. In his mind, they were one as those who were bound by sacred marriage vows; but Pastora had no intentions of making such a commitment to him. The more demanding he became and the more he tried to dominate her life, the more she withdrew.

The moments alone she now relished. She escaped in fantasy and got her vengeance in fantasy. She slipped out of the sunsuit and lay down on the bed. Eyes closed, she visualized *him*, with the bearded face, the obnoxious man whom she had not seen in a year and neither knew nor cared about his whereabouts. When he made love to her, he inserted a finger, like a bloodhound on the trail of the wounded prey. It dug deep as he talked in husky whispers, telling how he had missed her, had thought of her incessantly since the last time they were together. He locked his eyes in hers as he confessed the urge that drove him back to her again and again, the madness of her smells that overwhelmed him. She moistened, aroused by the memory of the words and the thrust of the finger digging deeper, swimming in her juices.

Then he would dive in, mouth first, beard soaked with secretions and his saliva. Pastora pumped, teasing the little knob of flesh that titillated with mere touch. He was calling her name, hastily pulling open his shirt, removing the rest of his clothes, then he stretched himself full on her and entered. She burned inside, the stimulated clitoris took her higher, higher, in a self-gratifying voyage. Where was he? Where are you, Máximo Madrigal, that my vagina pulsates imagining you worshipping it as you do whenever we are joined? Pastora tried to suspend the orgasm to bathe in the ecstasy an instant longer, but gave up when the tension was painful.

She relaxed. Her eyes still closed, the fantasy was gone. Madrigal was gone, vanished into the oblivion of the world that swallowed him whenever he left her. She stirred with the sounds of a key in the lock. Her lover came in and thought she had been napping. She stretched lazily. He removed his jeans and summer shirt and eased his body over hers. Just as he entered, Pastora saw two Guatemalan men who'd been watching from the fire escape of the building next door. She lifted her legs and wrapped them over the muscular buttocks of her Viking.

thirty-two

In the lamentable role of Tosca, Laura left for Europe. The presumed purpose was to investigate the possibilities of shows for Max, but she took advantage of her sabbatical to escape another marriage that had served only to demonstrate that the dichotomy of artist as lover hadn't resolved itself with any more finesse than in Puccini's opera.

thirty-three

She had been pacing the floor with breathless sighs for weeks. His dirty looks and nasty comments didn't discourage her. Motherhood welled up inside and she was obsessed as if in a hypnotic state. She let out long sighs from the diaphragm. They reached across the loft to where Max worked on the plumbing. "I want a baby, Max. I'm thirty-one years old! There's a woman on the faculty who's going into the hospital with endometriosis. I don't want it to be me next. I don't care if you don't want children yet, Max. My body can't wait until you're ready!"

"Cómo chingan estas mujeres," he muttered, not looking up, but the sounds of the unknown language caused her to shrink and she went to the bedroom to watch t.v. He threw down the wrench he had in his hand and went out.

After a shot of tequila and a beer, he went to the pay phone to call her, whose number was a neon sign in his brain. It flashed in his dreams. It frightened him out of daydreams while he worked. She answered on the third ring, her deep voice like crushed orchids, disinterested in the caller.

"Are you alone?" he asked her. He had not even said hello.

"Yes."

"I'm coming over."

"Why?"

He started to hang up, then decided to reply. "Don't you want me to?"

"Fine." She hung up.

Máximo left his car parked near the bar and walked the three long blocks, the length of the cemetery that ran along past the street where she lived. He had gone to that bar on purpose, because when he had had the shot and beer to calm himself down from Laura's recent campaign for motherhood, he knew he would want to see *her*. And before she would ask anything, before they had had a drink together or ended with slamming doors and striking retreated warrior poses in separate rooms, they would make love.

A cat on the window ledge inside Pastora's apartment sneered at Máximo, who was on the outside. She lived in the basement apartment in the back of a house where one had to reach out to cold walls in the dark descent of the cement steps to her door.

"One day I will buy you a castle like Dalí bought Gala. And like Gala, you won't let me come without a formal invitation." He laughed as if the remark he'd just made didn't hurt him to know it was false. His fingers were caught up in her hair; they curled like the cat on the ledge, felt adored as if they were all her pets.

"Buy it for me and find out," she said. She never rebuked his fantasies. A leg folded over another and he remembered that she had perfect legs. Nothing about her body was Indian, except for the small ass. He came again. "I leave you my child," he said under his breath, exhausted. She was still, silent.

He woke just as he started to snore, before she gave him a second knock on the head and sent him home to sleep.

thirty-four

Why don't you face yourself and admit it once and for all, Máximo Madrigal? You're a selfish wimp, no more willful than that kind of pussy-whipped husband with a yoke about his neck that you detest so much as to laugh aloud in the poor sucker's face when he stops himself from having one last drink, pulling himself off the stool to head directly home, like a good boy, to his mamacita.

Admit it, Máximo Madrigal, Pastora Velásquez Aké has you by the balls, los puros huevos, those two nitrate-filled nuts you lug around like a pair of trophies: the world's greatest lover, el gran chingón. Face it, Max, she's got you whipped.

Máximo unscrewed the cap from the silver flask and, tipping his head back, drank the last of the burning scotch in one swallow. He studied himself in the mirror, an antique piece that once hung behind the bar of an old establishment, now propped in his studio for the use of his auto-appraisal.

Pastora Aké. Aghh! He shuddered as the pungent alcohol worked its way through his bloodstream, sending chills along his flesh. Pastora was a witch, an unequivocal bruja who'd undoubtedly used her wicked powers to hex him; a drop of spitballed wax on the back of his neck one night, his hairs left on her pillow, pulled from his chest the moment he'd drifted into a heavy sleep after coming. Somehow, she had managed to take something so vital and potent from his being, like the umbilical cord his grandmother had severed with her teeth the dawn he was born; the remains, shriveled ten days later, wrapped and hidden away to protect his soul.

Pastora Aké had severed something in him with her bare teeth, like a savage monster acting upon a primal female instinct, because what bound him to her was unquestionably physical, had nothing to do with the human brain, but stemmed from the acts performed by all species before man became biped and shed the fur on his back.

Máximo let himself drop on a chair, a bulk drawn by gravity to the center of the earth. He was drunk. He was either drunk or hopelessly and passionately in love. He raised an eyebrow toward the direction of the telephone and cursed the instrument for its temptation to make him want to call her. She would answer, her breathy voice caustic as the liquor, intoxicating, not resigned, not receptive, but commanding with its indifference, and he would have to run to see her.

In minutes, he was travelling in a cold-engine car with just enough gas to make the journey, his heart pushing the pedal until he got to the street where past three, four houses, the second one past the alley, the light burned in her apartment, a haunting amber glow guiding him to her door. He would rap once, listen for her movements inside. The locks turned.

Máximo felt the biting sensation that those who are ardent claim has direct association with the blood-pumping organ, a rapid pushing against the inner walls of his chest. He imagined her half-dressed, her hair like a tangle of silk thread over her shoulders, a satin night robe—unlike other women who thought to allow a man to undress them was enticing enough, Pastora was an adept seductress.

What would life be, packing his bags, showing up at her door, surrendering once and for all? Paradise? The depths of total oblivion? To the proverbial heaven and hell he'd heard all men who succumbed to such a woman were destined? It was a decision Máximo had to make, the very one in which he would have to let all superstitions of supernatural possession give way and resign to the constant thrill Pastora gave his relentless ego by not allowing herself to be the conquest. It had unfailing persistency, because now that he knew she would never, ever give in, it actually thrilled him. That was love, after all, was it not? A man truly loved the woman with whom he knew he could never be completely confident.

That was why a yellow streak crawled up his back when he thought of giving in to her. How could he make love to other women if he were living with Pastora, never knowing what she was up to? He ground his teeth at the mere thought of a sickening bastard hopping into their bed the moment Máximo was out of sight. And she was just the type. She would never require proof that Máximo had other women to provoke her into having other lovers. She wasn't insecure enough to worry about the faithless lover. She did as she damn well pleased. She'd look him in the eye and tell him to leave the instant he tried to make a claim. Máximo shuddered.

Where would he go then, he wondered, carrying out the imaginary scenario. He'd have to find another woman immediately, first, to lick his wounds, and second, to take him in, because he couldn't afford to be left out in the street. He might be forced to accept a woman he didn't respect. Certainly, it might be argued that Máximo didn't respect women; but in his own paradoxical way, he did. Surely he did.

Nothing left to drink; winter, an enemy that waited outside. Máximo let his head drop back against the chair and went unconscious.

thirty-five

Eduardo's apartment consisted of a room in the basement of a modest frame house. An attempt at making the place anything more than functional was not evident. An old bed with an iron headboard dominated one side of the area; a hot plate, a small refrigerator, and a tiny laminated table with leaves that could be folded out at each side, along with its two chairs, completed the furnishings. On the table were an outmoded typewriter and notebooks that were scattered about.

Pastora took a seat at the edge of the bed. He offered her a cup of ginseng tea and she accepted. Shortly, a couple and a man joined them. Pastora hadn't met them before, but it seemed that perhaps she had seen their faces in the days when she was a college student. Gloria and Jaime Meléndez, both short, one as dark as the other was light-skinned, were naturalized citizens. Octavio, whose surname she didn't catch, was lanky, and his clothes looked as if he had slept in them. The three were pleasant to Pastora, but a cautiousness devoured the atmosphere.

"I heard you sing at that benefit on 26th St. last month," Jaime told Pastora. His wife nodded. Pastora nodded. Jaime nodded. They smiled at each other uneasily. Eduardo took up a notebook and sat down on a milk crate.

"Some people came in today, about four or five in the morning. We were still asleep when we got the call," Gloria addressed Eduardo. Eduardo jotted it down. "Yeah, I think they're from Sapogonia," Jaime added. "Men? Women?" Eduardo asked.

"I think it's a family," Gloria hesitated, as if she tried to remember what had been said during the telephone call she'd received when she had been half asleep. "A man, his wife, an in-law. I think there's a kid with them."

"They have a child with them?" Jaime turned to his wife. Gloria nodded. "I think so. I may have misunderstood." She laughed nervously. "I was still sleeping at four a.m. when we got the call."

Eduardo turned to Octavio, who shook his head. "I have to go to work tomorrow, man, I start at six. I can't make it."

"We got an address; some lady, a doctor's wife, I think, needs a gardener and someone to help her out around the house. She lives in Lincolnwood." Jaime pulled out his wallet and searched for the paper with the address.

"But she's not gonna want a whole family, is she?" Gloria asked her husband.

"We'll have to see. I'll call her. Is there some place we can put them up meanwhile?" Eduardo asked.

"I already got two guys staying at my place," Octavio said. His eyes were underlined with dark rings. He looked malnourished and he chainsmoked. "But maybe one of them can stay with me," he added.

Eduardo continued to take notes. He jotted down the information from the scrap of paper Jaime had given him. He, too, looked under the weather. Pastora thought his body was fighting a cold, although he had yet to complain. It was Eduardo who volunteered to go for the family that had been driven up to Michigan the night before. The three left and Pastora and Eduardo sat in silence for a while.

Pastora felt the weight of his commitments. He was concerned about the welfare of four people whom he had never met. To Eduardo they might be simply human lives to feel compassion for or symbols of a particular situation. Pastora wasn't sure. She knew little of his activities. Because of their nature, the less anyone not involved knew, the better it was all the way around. Eduardo offered scarce information and she asked almost nothing. She was only present at the meeting because they had had a late dinner together and he had asked her to stay a while. They had only known each other a short time, but they felt at ease in each other's company. There was an honest quality to Eduardo that was disarming. It intrigued Pastora.

He made tea and readied for the six-hour drive to the town in Michigan where the people from Sapogonia waited. Pastora commented that he looked sick. He admitted he had been combatting what he thought was the flu with antibiotics and vitamin C, but since he hadn't rested, it was getting the better of his health. In addition, he, too, had to go to work the next day.

Pastora recognized the catalyst that brought people facing potentially fatal conditions north from Sapogonia, just as those who had fled across the Bering Strait during the Wisconsin Ice Age migrated to where they could continue to breed and survive. She didn't question Eduardo's dedication to his work on the basis of morality, but as an artist, she wondered how one could be so selfless. She sacrificed for her song, it was true, and her lyrics and performances were motivated by the same politics, but she also expected recognition for her dedication. People like Eduardo were anonymous even to those for whom they risked their own safety and well-being.

Pastora put the back of her hand to Eduardo's neck. He was running a fever. "How long have you been like this?" she asked. He swallowed a couple of vitamin C tablets. He said he'd been feeling especially warm all evening. "You can't spend the night driving back and forth from Michigan; the temperatures are dropping. Plus, you're planning on going to work tomorrow."

"I have to," he insisted. "We've had a machinery break down that my partner and I have been working overtime to repair." He was laying out the cards of his dilemma and Pastora knew he had taken her into his confidence for the benefit of her possible aid. She didn't think she had anyone whom she could confide in who could pick up the family in Michigan. She thought of Perla; she always thought of Perla like a silhouette reflected in all of her own activities. Perla had to work in the morning, too. But she also knew that Perla would find the situation pathetic and temporary efforts useless in the face of a greater problem necessitating more important acts to make the real difference. Pastora also recalled, but only by way of association, that Máximo Madrigal was from Sapogonia, from a town called San Co. In basic ways, he was no different than these strangers in question, but he could be no further from them in ability to survive on his own.

Pastora left her friend under warm blankets with a cup of yerba santa brewed with lemon and eucalyptus. She drove that night hoping the snowstorm that had been forecasted wouldn't catch up to her coming or going. She followed his careful instructions to the broken-down ranch house where four shabby individuals piled in her car, scarcely breathing a word. She dropped them off at Eduardo's and went on her own way through the density of morning rush-hour traffic.

She repeated this work on various occasions during that winter, telling herself that she had been appointed by Providence to do so because she had a fairly decently running car and had the time to take the trips that were often made at the last minute. She almost suspected, in addition, that she was motivated by a growing esteem she held for Eduardo Madero, who she knew had ample conviction for both.

It was near the end of winter and it had almost stopped snowing altogether in the Midwest when Pastora first noticed a strange car parked across the street from her basement apartment. Two men sat inside and openly watched her as she entered and went out. She told Eduardo and they decided she should make no more trips to Michigan. She had never brought any of the undocumented workers/refugees to her place, but because of her reputation of singing protest music and the public positions she took during her performances, she knew that the federal government could very well be suspicious as to what degree she was willing to fight policies she objected to.

Finally, they knocked at her door. They were the epitome of formality and asked to come in. Pastora was alone but, believing she was protected by her civil rights as a citizen, allowed them to enter. She told herself she had nothing to hide, at least not literally. She also reminded herself that if she betrayed anxiety, they might use it to harass her. A last thought that floated across her mind on the brink of panic was that she had no one to call if they wanted to take her off for questioning.

"Miss Velásquez, are you aware that it is a federal offense to harbor illegal aliens, punishable by imprisonment and fines of $10,000?" one of the men asked. He was exceptionally tall and made Pastora feel like a child who had to look up to meet his eyes. She shook her head. The other man scanned her studio with a scrutinizing expression. Pastora wondered if she had left any information on scraps of paper about, as she had the careless habit of doing, using the kitchen table as a desk. If he saw the names, he might associate them with the people she had been helping to find work and shelter.

The first man continued, "We're looking for some people who are here illegally from Sapogonia. Perhaps you know them." Pastora was about to deny having any knowledge of such persons when he handed her a slip of paper with a list of names. There were a good deal of them, and since she never concerned herself with names, hardly seeing the faces of those she transported at night, she was able to tell him with facility that she didn't know them.

He then produced photographs. "Have you seen any of these people before?" She examined them, as if she were prepared to admit she had if she did recognize anyone, and returned the pictures repeating that she knew nothing. What right did they have to be asking her these questions? She thought of demanding this information from them, but she was on the defensive, feeling intimidated, and waited.

She hadn't asked Eduardo what she should do if the men who kept a vigilance in front of her place ever approached her, because for an inexplicable reason, Pastora never believed it would happen. She felt she had been so naive about her activities, she didn't believe there would come a time when she could be accused of illegal behavior.

The men left presently, repeating the same warning as when they came in, and telling her that she was obligated to report anyone she knew was an illegal to the immigration office. Pastora mustered up the courage to speak up. "What I don't understand is, with so many criminals running around this city every day, how can we afford to spend our tax dollars searching out innocent people, who really aren't here to hurt anyone?" She hadn't intended to initiate a debate, but to imply that people from Sapogonia, like the refugees from other countries who were given political asylum, were here in search of refuge.

"Some of these people on this list are criminals, Miss Velásquez; murderers, in fact. They're wanted for killing American citizens in their country." The men went away and she didn't see their car near her house again.

"Dear Prince, . . . it is not easy to attain paradise on earth, and yet you seem to be counting on it. Paradise is a difficult matter, Prince, much more difficult than it appears to your beautiful heart . . ."

—*The Idiot,* Fyodor Dostoyevsky

thirty-six

The day before Eduardo went away, he and Pastora had breakfast together. They went to a Mexican greasy-spoon in the same neighborhood as her apartment. Pastora was generally apathetic about food, but when she did take time for breakfast, it was usually spicy: orange rice, scrambled eggs with diced serrano peppers, hot sauce spooned over refried beans.

They were both more quiet than usual. The hindrance of his imminent departure, the details of which she knew nothing about, encumbered the air. It seemed to be the cause of the clouds that scarred the sky, the lethargic drizzle. When they finished eating, he took her home and she asked him in.

It was the first time they made love and Pastora referred to it as that afterward, because a tough membrane had formed between them over the past months and their physical expression solidified it. Eduardo had never been romantic, never spoken to her of a joint future or of a bond between them.

It was dark when she heard him readying to leave, trying not to disturb her light slumber. He bent over and kissed her forehead. "I'll call you when I get back," he promised. She reached out and caught his hand, pulling it to her lips. Then she let go.

Several months later, Pastora performed at a Christian church for a Nicaraguan benefit. When the benefit was over, the clergyman came to thank her. Pastora was growing weary of performing at such events, settling for an empanada prepared by the women of such and such committee, or at best, given transportation money to compensate her for her lending her name to the effort. Still, it would be a contradiction of her beliefs if she never acquiesced to any of the requests that came to her unfailingly throughout the year.

She was about to leave when the clergyman hesitantly brought up Eduardo Madero's name. The man with a receding hairline looked about making certain that what he wanted to say wouldn't be overheard. "Pastora, we have people in Michigan that we need to get here to the church for asylum right away; they're waiting to be picked up." Pastora sensed the urgency in his voice; she sympathized and yet, because of her personal experience with the federal investigators, she wanted to tell him she no longer worked with the underground railroad.

"I think you should know I was suspected of . . . helping out before," she started to explain.

"I realize that, Pastora, but this is a very special case. I wouldn't ask you if there were someone else I could trust to go out there tonight . . ." he entreated.

Pastora waited for him to convince her. Her curiosity was tempting her. "It isn't a criminal or anything like that?" she asked, almost under her breath. She knew this label under the circumstances was relative, but she knew that philosophically she wouldn't know how to come to terms with it. The clergyman assured her shaking his head, "No, nothing like that. It's a woman, Eduardo's wife."

Pastora went pale. Once, when she first met Eduardo, he told her that he was married. Never hearing about a wife again, and more importantly, not seeing any trace of her, Pastora relegated the idea of a wife of Eduardo to the vast realm of abstraction. Now, her head welled up with loose ends wanting to tie together. Was this a clue now as to where he had been in the past months? She felt the heaviness of the possibility that she might never be with Eduardo again pull her down as she stood ambivalently with her inseparable guitar in hand.

She took the money the clergyman gave her to fill her gas tank and left the church to drive out to the house in Michigan where she knew the way well enough to go blindfolded. On the dismal road, she bombarded her mind with questions. Like most women, because women were made to place part of their value on their birth-given looks, their fate on genetic whimsy, she wondered if Eduardo's wife were better-looking than she, and whether during the past months Eduardo had been with his wife. When he returned to Chicago, would it be to join his wife? In which case, would he remain her friend? The questions expended her energy more than the concert she had just given and by the time she reached the dilapidated ranch house where she had never entered, she was fatigued.

She honked once and waited. Ten minutes passed, then a woman emerged. To stave off the cold, she wore only a sweater and unstylish bell-bottom jeans; she made her way slowly to the car with a child who slept in her arms. It looked like a boy of about four years of age. Pastora did what she had never done before and, in fact, had been advised not to do: she got out of the car. She felt inclined to help the woman with her human bulk and eased the child carefully so as not to disturb his sleep, into the back seat.

Both women smiled self-consciously at each other and, after they settled in, Pastora drove off. As she had been instructed, she did not ask the woman any questions, not so much as a name. She turned the heat up, hoping it would make the woman and her child comfortable. Eduardo's wife folded her arms and tried to look as if she weren't apprehensive. The child, who slept with the tranquility of the innocent, was wrapped in an old blanket. Its colors, although faded, were used by the indigenous people of Sapogonia who made their livelihood for centuries through textiles; a pattern alternated with each color, eagle, tree, fish, eagle, tree, fish, air, earth, water.

Shifting hands on the wheel, Pastora managed to take off her coat; underneath she wore a heavy sweater over a turtleneck. With scarcely a glance at the other woman, she handed over the coat. The woman tried to decline the offer, but Pastora insisted in Spanish. "Thank you," the woman's acceptance came in English.

"You speak English, then?" Pastora asked, mildly surprised. She grew irritated with herself for having submitted to her curiosity about the woman. Eduardo's wife nodded, smiling somewhat. "Yes, I lived in the United States for many years." She spoke with only a trace of an accent.

Pastora took the opportunity to examine the woman's face without making it obvious, a glance that lingered only a second or two longer than necessary. She tried to determine if the woman's warm-toned complexion was darker than her own. Her hair was thick and its ends curled independently around her shoulders. Her eyes were deep-set, not slanted like Pastora's, which held the traces of ancestors who'd travelled thousands of years before in canoes from the tip of one continent to the next. She determined that the woman was more attractive than herself. Unlike a female who'd met up with a rival and become competitive, she enjoyed the company of such a woman, to look upon her beauty, to admire it.

They were in Indiana and nearing the toll booths when Pastora first noticed a brown Ford following close behind with two male passengers. In retrospect, Pastora realized it was when she decided to go to the lane where she could deposit exact change and the Ford also switched lanes to stay behind her that she knew they were in trouble, but by then it was too late.

A few meters after continuing on after the toll, a light appeared on top of the car behind her and a siren blared for her to stop. She pulled over. Her teeth chattered from the cold and from fear as she rolled down her window. She wiped her perspiring hands against her jeans and waited for the men who were getting out of their car to come over. She didn't dare look into the face of her passenger, who reached behind to adjust the blanket covering her son.

The man who came to the driver's side didn't move to speak with her. Instead, the other, going directly to the passenger's door, opened it and told the woman to step out. She wavered; her eyes seemed to beg Pastora to think of some way to help her. "M'am, we'd like to see some identification," the man told Eduardo's wife, holding the door open. Pastora and the woman stared at each other trying to read each other's thoughts. Pastora reached down near the woman's feet where she had left her purse. "Here," she told her. "You dropped your purse." The woman took it and stepped out.

While the woman fumbled around in Pastora's bag looking for a piece of identification of Pastora's which she could show the agent and convince him it was hers, Pastora stared straight ahead. Outward calm disguised her panic. She swallowed and spoke directly to the man nearest to her. "Can," she swallowed again, "we see your identification?" The man reached into his breast pocket. They were federal agents. The other man also showed his ID to both women. Eduardo's wife continued to search in the purse.

"We'd like to see the car's registration." The man next to Pastora ducked his head in the window. She was about to reach automatically in the glove compartment when she realized if Eduardo's wife was to identify herself as Pastora, the car was hers, and she would be the one to know where the registration was kept. Edwardo's wife signaled to Pastora with her head, as if giving her permission to retrieve it for the agent. Pastora pulled it out from the glove compartment and handed it over.

Eduardo's wife finally found a utility bill Pastora had been carrying, meaning to pay, and showed it as a form of identification. She had noticed Pastora's license floating in the bag, but hadn't brought it out obviously because it had her photograph. Then she found a gas credit card; she gave this, too, to the agent. He looked at both, unpersuaded. "I'm afraid this isn't enough. Don't you have your driver's license?" The woman pretended to search for it. She was too nervous to have thought of replying that she didn't have it, which was why Pastora was driving, but this would have only led to what happened next.

The agent leaning on Pastora's side asked to see her driver's license. Pastora pretended to dig into her sweater pockets. She smiled nervously at him. "You're not going to believe this, but I think I've lost my wallet!" He moved back and pulled opened the car door. "Would you mind stepping out?" Both men were polite, but they maintained a mocking air. They were aware of the charade and had been humoring the women to see how far they would go before admitting who they were. "If you can't find your license, we're going to have to take you in," he told Pastora.

"But why? I mean, my wallet's obviously been lost or stolen. I had it earlier."

"That may be, but you don't have it now."

"But I haven't done anything, I mean, I wasn't speeding or anything. Damn, I dropped the correct change into the toll box, didn't I?"

"Do you realize it's a violation to drive without a license?"

"And your friend here doesn't seem to be able to find hers, either," added the other agent. Now he could hardly hold back a satisfied grin. The other woman went into Pastora's car for her child, who by then had awoken. His mother kept the blanket around him. He wore no coat. Pastora locked the car and they all followed the men, silently getting into the back seat. As Pastora was about to step in, the agent waiting to close the door behind her said with a smile, "Nice try, Miss Velásquez."

thirty-seven

Dora couldn't sleep. It wasn't the heat, although it was hotter than hell. This was the dawn of the day she began her journey back to the U.S., back to Eduardo.

She had sent him a letter months before and never received an answer. All this meant, of course, was that she had not gotten an answer. Times were such that nothing was certain but the material. He may not have gotten the letter. It may not have been delivered. He may have answered but his letter was intercepted.

She had not seen him since he left California the year before when she had asked a lawyer about requesting political asylum for her in the U.S. He told her citizens of Sapogonia were not granted political asylum. In addition, he advised her in such a way that she should know it was for her own good, but that none of what he had discovered could be proven, that Dora Sierra Madero was considered by the U.S. as an undesirable. She was married to an American citizen, but she did not want to apply for citizenship. She wanted her status in the U.S. to remain a symbol of the political status of her country.

Since returning to Sapogonia, she had witnessed and experienced the debasement of humanity men were capable of. Each morning was a new chance for her to think of something to do—to bring about change, to end the atrocities; but while she remained in her hometown in Sapogonia, the most she could manage was safety and well-being for herself, her son, and aging parents. If she spoke out, if she behaved in any way that might be proven against the new government, only God could help her.

She made the necessary plans to leave. Unlike others who travelled the route, who went by night, who risked their lives in hopes of improving their chances of survival, who separated themselves from family and homeland, she had sufficient money, the connections, even the language skills to get to the United States, but the risk was that her identity could be detected.

First she was to head for El Salvador. This in itself was not to be an easy task, since she no longer had a passport and wouldn't be able to leave Sapogonia easily. But the way had been made and explained to her. She would be travelling with Eduardo, Jr., in a pickup truck with a man who would transport them as his own wife and child, using his family's documents. He didn't do this for money, but out of moral commitment. She would give him money anyway, if he accepted it, because she knew he lived in poverty.

In El Salvador, the same pickup would be loaded with cargo of some type, produce perhaps, driven this time by another individual. Dora and her son would cross to Mexico buried temporarily beneath the cargo. In Mexico, she would meet friends. In a few days she could travel with Eduardo, Jr., to Nuevo Laredo with false documents, depending on her fluent English to dispel any suspicion. There would be a car waiting for her to take her to the state of Michigan. These last people knew Eduardo. They would help her get to Chicago, where she could look for her husband. It was possible that he didn't want a reconciliation. But she wouldn't think of that today. There were important motivations behind this journey.

Eduardo, Jr., missed his father, and this was a fact that both parents had to consider. The boy also worried her; she had taken him to the doctor to see about his hearing problem, but nothing the doctor had suggested or prescribed seemed to help the child. He was having trouble hearing even normal speech. It was imperative to get him to a place where he would be treated before the problem got worse.

And she needed to talk. She needed to tell what she knew, what she had seen.

How does one look up at the stars just as they fade, knowing that that was the day chosen to run and that to be caught meant indescribable consequences worse than death? Dora was no Joan of Arc. She was no saint, not a nun or missionary. She had married for love. She had had a child for the ordinary reasons that women in love want children. She had wanted to give her parents a grandchild. She had longed for, at times—despite whatever else she had been driven to do—a pretty house with lace kitchen curtains, a life of routine and such regularity as to call it mundane, but with the tranquility of the rhythm that such things brought.

Dora became afraid the day the rhythm of the new government of Sapogonia began to synchronize with that of the neighborhood's activities. She no longer expected the soldiers who took permanent post on the corner of her street to go away. If she didn't see them in the morning when she went out for milk, she wondered about them. If someone in the community wasn't picked up for routine questioning on a given day, she felt listless at not having an event to mull over that night.

When Dora had left Eduardo, she didn't care if she saw him again; their relationship as lovers, as husband and wife, was definitely over. And perhaps it was. But she needed to return to wherever he was, like following a thread to a snag in a sweater to find the place where one can hope to pull the threads so that the imperfection disappears and the weaving appears as it once was.

Dora got up to take a shower. She tiptoed across the house so as not to disturb her parents' sleep. Eduardo, Jr., also slept, but on the patio where it was thought to be cooler, on a hammock and covered with mosquito netting. She glanced out the window and saw the child's slumber undisturbed by the occasional ringing of gunshots in the distance, the cackling of an insomnious chicken or one being called upon by the rooster who'd just sounded off its announcement of the new day

She had told her parents and no one else that they were leaving. Her mother and father had given their blessings. Dora turned on the cold water. A tiny lizard ran across the cement wall, rudely jolted by the spray. Dora threw off her sweaty nightgown and stepped in. It was the dawn of the day she began her journey back to the U.S., back to Eduardo.

thirty-eight

You wake on your own in the morning, gather your things set at the foot of the bed the night before, and make your way to the bathroom at the far end of the long room. You urinate, brush your teeth, wash your face and hands, run a brush through your hair. You wear no make-up; even the dashing of black mascara, rouge, and lipstick that you were once accustomed to in the world of men has been discarded, deemed unnecessary and a worthless expense. You slip on the panties and bra, and one of your three button-down blouses or one of your three T-shirts, each stenciled with one slogan or another, and one of your two pairs of jeans or your cotton pants. You always wear athletic shoes. Because it is chilly these mornings, you throw on a windbreaker to run across the courtyard to the cafeteria.

You are on kitchen duty for the breakfast shift. This is your assignment. It is your job, although you don't get paid. Most of the women working with you are silent because sleep, like cobwebs, inhabits their brains and they're dwelling on dreams, which are private and luxurious.

Only Mary Lou Acevedo talks. She chews gum, she talks. She smokes a menthol cigarette and talks. She talks and doesn't care if anyone listens. You listen to Mary Lou because she is the one familiar object that reminds you of where you come from. Mary Lou told you on your first day on kitchen duty that she lived many years before on Peoria St., one block from where you did as a child. She is five years your senior and moved before you started school. She left to 18th St. with her parents, her twin brother, and six other brothers and sisters.

On 18th St.—it was 16th and Racine actually—just past the viaduct, the Acevedo family lived in an old shingled house upstairs from the junk store her father owned and made his living from. Mary Lou's mother found him on the toilet seat one morning, his eyes lost up in his head, his mouth wide open, dead. Something inside him had burst open and poisoned him.

Mary Lou's older sister dropped out of high school pregnant and got married to her first boyfriend, who was black and always had a lot of girlfriends. They have six kids now and live on 17th and Racine. Her husband helps run the junk store.

Mary Lou's twin brother shot himself in the head three years earlier, leaving a Boricua wife and baby daughter behind. No note. His widow went to a spiritualist in Puerto Rico who told her he killed himself because he had another woman who'd put a hex on him when he refused to leave his wife for her.

Mary Lou's younger brothers and sisters had all grown up too fast, learning too much about the wrong things and not enough about what was good for them.

Mary Lou was put in jail because she had kidnapped her own kids. Her ex-husband had warned her, do it again and I'll call the authorities on you. She took the children to Florida. Nearly a year later she was found and put away. But her husband had gone one better. He had let the police know that Mary Lou in part made her living from selling dope. She was also given time for possession of a quantity of marijuana and cocaine sufficient to keep the partiers of any swank NY night club satiated for an entire weekend.

Mary Lou looks younger than her age. She is dark, small with thin legs, no calves, and has a black mole right on the corner of her chin and the distressful eyes of a caged rabbit. It is the look in those eyes and the incessant chatter that tell you why Mary Lou found it necessary to attach herself to a *stud-broad*.

After breakfast there is the meeting with the counselor. The rest of the day, you work as the college advisor's assistant; for this you are paid forty dollars a month. On designated evenings, you attend an aerobics class. In the dayroom late in the evening when you can't sleep, you stay up talking with one or two of the women. At night, sometimes, you go into the laundry room, closing the door behind you, and play your guitar.

On Sundays, you have band practice, which specializes in rhythm and blues, but in the laundry room, where no one's preference of music overrules your own, you play sixteenth-century Spanish music with the principle of variation. You play the compositions of Fernando Sor, his *Variations on a Theme by Mozart, Opus 9*. The theme was from *The Magic Flute*, whose music also provided Beethoven with a theme for one of his sets of variations. The music makes you happy.

Human beings are creatures of habit and it has been barely six months when you have already accustomed yourself to the routine, the lack of privacy, the snoring of the woman who sleeps on the cot next to yours. You have trained yourself to be only so friendly, and never to not be friendly, whether the person presented before you in your personal estimation deserves your attention or not.

When Mary Lou was with her husband, she got involved with a woman. Her husband found out, threw her out, and sought an immediate divorce. He was given custody of the children. The judge, a woman, told Mary Lou that she wasn't giving the children to her husband's care because of her lesbian tendencies, but because promiscuity for a married individual was a bad example of morality to give to children, regardless if it was with the same sex.

Mary Lou's outside lover was kind and attentive. She was like a mother sometimes, when Mary Lou needed mothering, and she was a loyal sister when Mary Lou needed a confidante, and she was very warm and very good to be with. Mary Lou received a letter from her once a week.

Mary Lou, who is older than you, you first regard as a younger sister because of her character, which always makes her easily persuaded, unsure about her own opinions. She tells you one morning that Elaine McElroy, one of the most notorious stud-broads around, wants to marry her.

Mary Lou and you are in the day room one evening, smoking and talking. "I've got eighteen months to go," Mary Lou says, exhaling a puff. "You think I'll make it?" She laughs that little nervous laugh of hers.

"You'll make it," you respond solemnly. You yourself have seven months left, each day marked off in your head the moment you open your eyes in the morning.

"Think my kids'll ever forgive me?" Mary Lou doesn't laugh this time, but plays with a hangnail.

"Your kids have nothing to forgive you for, Mary Lou," you say quietly. "What have you ever done wrong? You left a man who beat you?"

Mary Lou shakes her head, "I left their father to be with a woman."

"She loves you, doesn't she?" you ask.

"I think so, but it's been so long. And now Elaine . . ."

You look away from Mary Lou. In a corner is a group of black women dancing to the radio, in another, a group of white women playing cards, at the far end, a few brown women talking in Spanish. "There's that one who said something to you yesterday," you whisper discreetly, noticing a haughty look being sent your way from the group of Spanish-speaking women.

"You mean la puertorriqueña?" Mary Lou asks. You nod. "She's always saying something to someone!" Mary Lou says. "I just ignore her! Ignore her. It's the best thing, Pastora."

You nod again. Elaine McElroy walks in. She calls to Mary Lou and Mary Lou gets up to go to her.

"Wait," you say, and the spontaneous gesture of your hand on her forearm surprises you. Elaine is intimidating because of her size, but you pity how your friend's docility toward the woman is so obvious. Mary Lou hesitates. She doesn't want to go to Elaine, but she will. She only needs a reason to stay.

Tell her to stay. Elaine is big and tough, with at least six residents as lovers. They give her cigarettes and money. She has sex with them and when they have a problem she gives them protection. They run to quake beneath the great wings of their very own guard. It is because marriage seems so unlikely for Elaine that you have been persistent to have Mary Lou reconsider marrying her.

"Wait," you repeat, quietly, hardly moving your lips. Mary Lou sits down. Elaine McElroy is watching from across the room. She lights a cigarette. "Let's go," you say to Mary Lou and you both leave the room together.

Someone whispers in your ear in the cafeteria the next day, "Watch out! Elaine's mad at you, honey, for messin' with one of her women!" Nothing happens that day. Days pass. At band practice on Sunday, someone else repeats the warning, "Elaine says she's gonna kick your ass good for trying to steal Mary Lou from her . . ." Nothing happens.

One morning you can't find one of your T-shirts. You think you may have misplaced it, but several of your commissaries are missing, too: a new bottle of shampoo and a fresh pack of cigarettes, as well as the porcelain box you keep the hair bands and barrettes in that hold your hair up when you scrub pots, when you play your guitar. One of the residents in your cottage hints that she knows who has been in your things, but she won't say who.

After breakfast, another woman tells you that she saw one of Elaine's women wearing your T-shirt. There was no mistake that it was yours because on the back was stenciled *"Música de las Américas,"* and no one else in the entire state has one like it.

Elaine works out in the gym, lifts weights. She is known to give a hard punch. It isn't her size or her strength that makes you ignore her instigation. You are being considered for a work release program in Chicago. It's almost as good as being home so long as you maintain a clean record.

Mary Lou knows where to find you when you aren't in the dayroom in the evening. In the laundry room, she smokes a cigarette while you play that fancy music she thinks you are a genius for knowing. She liked Elvis Presley as a kid. She also liked María Victoria because her father took her and the family to the Teatro Zenith when they were children and María Victoria was there performing live. "Do you know 'Paloma negra?'" she asks you, and you sing it for her.

"¿Te vas a casar con ella?" you ask without looking at her, who smokes a cigarette and stares at her gym shoes. She sticks the butt under her shoe and puts it out, her small hand lingering along the shoelace. Her eyes are on the foot; your eyes on her hand, the fingers playfully walking over to the tip of your own shoe. She pulls at it and laughs a little. She shrugs her shoulders. "No sé."

"And your friend, the one who's waiting for you outside?" you ask. You are aware that your voice is unsteady suddenly, awaiting her response. She feels your need to know. If Mary Lou were someone else, she would lie. But she doesn't know how to lie. "She seems so far away right now."

Mary Lou has said this looking at you, right into your face, that kind of innocent directness that invades all your barriers. *Look at her, meet the dark, open face, and as you do, it is now only inches away from your own.*

Mary Lou's mouth is very small and thin against yours. Her dishwasher's hands are hard against your ribs and hips. You taste her with your mouth, your hands, her smell, the texture of her hair and skin.

"And who's waiting for you out there?" Mary Lou whispers, a gruff voice in your ear, along your neck.

"No one," you answer, your throat full, so that the words are hardly uttered, "But I won't forget you." And Mary Lou has entered you, so that you haven't had to say that.

You will take Mary Lou with you. Mary Lou, who is the abandoned buildings you explored with a child's courage; rooftops jumped; fast double-dutch tournaments; black girls who pulled your red-ribboned braids; pink and white roses offered to the Virgin the month of May; Christmas pilgrimages which taught you the hymns that gave you the gift of song; urban renewal and the upheaval of your Mexican world; white city workers who relocated each family after its building was marked with an X in a circle, the next one to be torn down; your father who left, and the mother's new husband who never spoke your name or looked you in the face until you were thirteen and he tried to have you in bed; your mother, who stopped being Catholic after your confirmation and went to Protestant church meetings in a storefront every night; Abuelita who took care of you from the age of three months and taught you about the healing of the body with herbs and of the soul with your own; Mary Lou, who banished the devil of your childhood.

Elaine's animosity continues in the form of hurling personal insults when she happens to run into you. Others overhear her and you are constantly assured by witnesses that you must maintain your calmness, that you can't let Elaine's acrimony get the better of you. And you don't.

It happens in aerobics class one Wednesday night. You're near the instructor, facing her, when others, who see her coming in, report later that Elaine rushed toward you like a bull who saw red. She threw her whole weight on you, who were caught completely off guard, knocking you to the floor immediately. By the time officers were able to get hold of Elaine, she had bent back your right foot and left arm to the point of spraining them both.

Elaine is ticketed and sent to the floor for two weeks. Because of your previously unblemished record and because of the vast testimony on your behalf that Elaine had been wanting a fight with you, who repeatedly avoided it, you are not put in segregation, but you are ticketed, temporarily restricted from being in the band, going to aerobics and to the dayroom. You have also lost the hope to be put on work release. It is the committee's assessment that you could have avoided the whole incident had you not insisted on advising Mary Lou Acevedo when you knew what the possible consequences were.

thirty-nine

And there were dreams. The dreams that saved her from endless hours of monotony; hours and periods of light and dark and outside the sun shone or snow fell and one day someone would come to tell her she could go home. The dreams carried her through the nights, and in the day she lapsed into them so that the two-dimensional world of the incarcerated was given breadth.

Before the dreams came a depression that manifested in despondency, long crying bouts, an impulse to recoil. The crying hadn't stemmed from self-pity, but self-reproach. She had been foolish to the point of stupidity. She had risked the safety of another woman, knowing that she'd been suspected already of transporting illegals. Further, Dora Sierra, she'd heard, was to be tried for criminal acts against her country. She had been deported for this purpose. Pastora cried, imagining what lay ahead for Dora in Sapogonia before she would get to trial, if there was a trial.

She remained on this plane of self-deprecation until the day that that woman started a fight with her. While this attack was not intended to be a positive experience for Pastora, inadvertently that was what happened. Pastora realized she had to have courage, the same courage that Dora had. This brought on the next phase in Pastora's emotional and psychological state in that twenty-four-month period.

The last phase came shortly before her release and this began with the dreams. With the anticipation of returning to her life, her music, she had trouble sleeping. The first time she dreamt of the old woman, she didn't know she had gone to sleep. It seemed she had been lying awake most of the night. Then she found herself in the prison cafeteria. There was a piano there that no one ever used. It seemed that she was about to give a concert and was waiting to be called when a couple of women brought in an old woman, shriveled and the color of a prune. She wore an unusual costume, embroidered with many colors. Her black braid came down to her knees. When Pastora saw her, she was ridden with sentiment. She ran to the old woman with widespread arms and embraced a soft sculpture in the form of a grandmother. "Abuelita," she whispered to the old woman, "finally, you've come for me."

They sat and were left alone to talk. It seemed that everyone knew it was a long-awaited reunion of loved ones and watched from the other side of the dream. The old woman spoke to Pastora in Yaqui, Pastora's grandmother's tongue. At this sign, Pastora sensed that this had to be her mother's mother who had died before Pastora was born. "They told me you were dead," Pastora said, holding the old woman's hand tight in her own. The grandmother nodded. "Yes, but as you see, I'm still kicking up dust." She laughed and Pastora loved her prankster's laugh. "You're very pretty, hija," the old woman declared. She pronounced daughter in Spanish.

The old woman became serious. Pastora felt a chill and realized they were no longer sitting in the cafeteria but were outside, breathing fresh air and there was nothing but trees, land, and sky as far as she could see. "Save his picture," the old woman proposed, "this way he will always come back to you."

Pastora began to cry with the relief of one who had believed she was never loved and had found she was loved beyond expression, unconditionally and beyond this world, and while still crying, Pastora was back in her cell again, in the dark and alone.

First there was an involuntary sense of separation from one's heaviest burden: the body. She couldn't be frightened then; as the spirit lifted from the body, the mind had to maintain decisive confidence. In this way she learned that Dora was released and allowed to return to her family until her trial. This was unusual treatment for such a case, but the government of Sapogonia was careful in this instance not to cause international criticism and planned on treating the Sierra woman with kid gloves.

The old woman Pastora later perceived to be not her grandmother, but a new spirit guide who lived in Sapogonia. They met once at a river and visited without speaking for a long time. The old woman told Pastora that the beaches of Lake Michigan in Chicago would bring the same peace of mind whenever she required it. Pastora was skeptical because the river of San Co was the most sublime body of water she had ever seen. It was like a balm for soothing the mind. The old woman persisted about Lake Michigan and the shores of

Fullerton Beach, Addison Rocks, and North Ave. (she referred to the beaches by their names). "You'll see, she said, "you'll see, mi Pastorita." The old woman no longer spoke Yaqui, but Quechua and sometimes Spanish. Although Pastora didn't speak Quechua, she had no trouble understanding what the old woman said to her.

In total, there were three dreams. The visits Pastora didn't count as dreams, although it would have been clearly debated had she chosen to discuss them with anyone. Initially, what the old woman said to her was obscure. Pastora analyzed the experiences as having resulted from a need to fabricate a nurturing figure.

When Pastora in spirit went to see Dora and, upon returning, met the old woman in Sapogonia, she knew who the man was whose picture she had been told to keep. They talked a long while about Máximo Madrigal.

The last dream Pastora had of the old woman of Sapogonia horrified her. The old woman appeared at the entranceway of a ranch house. Her cotton nightgown was blood soaked. Pastora didn't see herself in the dream, but watched as one views one's own dreams at times, from a privileged front-row seat. Pastora awoke with a scream. She spent the rest of the night sobbing; she knew she wouldn't dream of the old woman again.

forty

When Pastora returned to her apartment in the basement, it was late fall and a newly born winter whistled through the cracks beneath the door and windows. The place had the alien feeling of the abandoned, although her few pieces of furniture and her things had been kept as they were and someone had come and cleaned recently. The dog, cat, and birds had been taken into foster homes for the duration of her absence.

She had no job. She mailed a letter of resignation to the community center where she had worked as a family counselor. Her director would have been sympathetic, as the organization involved itself in supporting the rights of Spanish-speaking peoples, but for the security of the underground railroad, she had to disassociate herself with any source inclined to give public attention.

Pastora lay down on the couch and listened to soft jazz on the stereo. She'd made plans with Perla to see her the following night for a good drunk, but that first night home she was going to stay in to put together her thoughts on the future. A letter from Eduardo waited for her. It was brief, apologetic, and pledging indebtedness to her. There had been no return address.

Pastora took off her turtleneck and jeans and ran a hot bath. Hot baths in times when there hadn't been hot water or a bath would have been a supreme luxury. Since the age of eleven and until she went to college she'd spent summers in the tomato fields in Indiana. Among children who knew nothing of sanitation or the privacy of a bathroom, she felt inhibited. Now again, as a woman just out of incarceration, the tiny bathroom of her apartment, its clean tiles, the pine scent of disinfectant, the medicine cabinet with a disposable razor ad inexpensive soaps all for her exclusive use, were the realm of a countess.

After her bath, in which she soaked for an hour listening to a tape of her own music, she put on a pair of flannel pajamas and decided to go to bed. A light rap at the kitchen window and then at the back door sent her suspiciously to ask who it was before opening. "Máximo," the deep voice responded. Curious that on her first night home he should happen to wander by, she wondered if he had by some chance heard what she had been through since they'd last been together.

He came in, the personification of the night wind, Tezcatlipoca, dressed in a black evening coat and tuxedo. "What're you up to?" he asked aggressively, hurrying past the utility room that led to her apartment and into the kitchen. He looked around, smiling broadly. He was exhilarated. Pastora smiled, but said nothing.

"Are you going to bed already?" he wondered, aware that it was late and it shouldn't have been unusual to find her in pajamas. She nodded. "Yes, I'm a little tired." Awkwardly, because time had a way of making strangers of lovers, she went to the stereo and switched on the tape that had been playing earlier. Perla's voice came on, sweet and abundant with memories from what now seemed another life. "Do you like that singing?" she asked Máximo, suspecting he didn't know that it was Perla, as he had probably never bothered to buy the album.

He nodded pensively. "Isn't that a Spanish singer? She sounds very much like one I've heard." Pastora shook her head, but didn't tell him who it was. Máximo had brought with him an opened bottle of cheap wine. He looked in the cabinets above the sink for glasses. Pastora watched. There weren't many places to look and eventually he discovered the glasses and poured the wine. With unabashed assurance he opened her refrigerator. It was completely barren; the motor running, the shelves spotless, but not a trace of a morsel. "What's the matter? Don't you eat?" he asked in Spanish. "Or don't you live on food like the rest of us poor souls?"

Simultaneously, they both fixed upon a bottle of champagne on the shelf inside the door. "Ha!" He sounded victorious. "Champagne! What luck! Who bought this for you, a lover?" He smiled and yet his remark held the tone of accusation. Pastora had no idea that the champagne was there. She assumed it was Perla who knew her weakness for the stuff and it was a dear thought, but now Máximo dumped out the wine he had poured into the kitchen sink drain and proceeded to pop the cork on the champagne. Pastora went to the couch and accepted the glass.

He sat next to her. If Pastora had allowed herself to think of it,

198

she would have known. Máximo was excited for only one reason, to have finally found her there. He had tried many times to see her and always she had been out. But out of stubbornness he returned again and again. "You look well," he said, assessing her. She was still flushed from the hot bath, and the flannel pajamas camouflaged the weight loss. "Where've you been? Touring? Off to Río?" He pretended her quietness wasn't deflating him. "Well?" he pressed. "Did you go on vacation or what?"

Pastora shook her head and sipped the tingling wine. "You wouldn't believe me if I told you," she said without expression.

"I've just had another show in New York," he volunteered, since she had not asked about his activities. "I'm getting ready now for one in San Francisco. You've been there before, haven't you? How is it? Do you think I'll like it?"

Pastora marvelled at how well he now dominated the new language. His accent was notable, but he didn't speak English like most native Spanish speakers. He had an affected continental flair. He used words like "bloody" and "infernal" to dramatize situations. His extensive vocabulary in his first language paved the way into the new ones.

"You'll like it," she said. The champagne relaxed her and she stretched out her arm, indicating that she wanted her glass refilled. He did so, then threw off his jacket. "It's warm in here, isn't it?" he asked, sitting again, closer to her this time. "Maybe it's you," she said in Spanish, in the sardonic tone he was used to hearing. She eyed him steadily. He ran his fingers through her wet hair. "I think it's you that's making me warm," he whispered and pulled her head close so that he could kiss her.

Pastora reached over to switch off the lamp next to the couch and returned to his arms. In the dark, he wouldn't see the tears that went down her face. "What's the matter? Do you have a cold?" he asked.

"No, I'm just happy to see you," she replied.

"Ha! I bet . . . and to how many others do you say the same thing?" he asked, switching back to Spanish. Yet, he sounded pleased, ever the grand rooster strutting about the chicken coop.

It was the only occasion Pastora fell asleep in my arms as well as not waking me up when my snoring got too loud. I was so overjoyed to have found her once again, having tried so often at her apartment that I thought she might have moved away, that I hardly slept that night. I tiptoed to the bathroom to wash up. Her medicine cabinet was practically empty and there was no sign of a man's residency. I wondered if she had changed her telephone number, because the one I tried had been disconnected, but there was no telephone in the place at all.

It was visible that she had been away. Pastora was always so secretive, like a damn spy, as if it would cost her to say where she'd been. I'd thought she'd gone off to live with some bastard again. I asked around among those who claimed they knew her, Diego Cañas, among others; no one knew anything. Cañas guessed she had gone on tour to South America. Pastora had often talked about wanting to live there. She was just the kind of woman who would have done it.

Her friend Perla was so protective of Pastora, she told no one anything. Those two women were fanatical in their loyalty to each other. I had more reason to suspect she did have a lover that she didn't want to reveal. I wanted to venture to her bureau for a clue—letters, a telephone book—but I worried she might awaken and find me going through her things. The altar with its figurines and candles was covered with a piece of linen.

When I made love to her she felt thinner, more frail than I'd remembered her. I tried to turn on a light, but she wouldn't let me, which was odd, since making love with the light on had never mattered to her before. She was small in my arms and yet she'd given herself to me with such fervor that she felt strong, like a feline whose muscles cannot be seen, but who is lithe, agile, and firm.

I dressed and Pastora heard me readying to leave. "You're going?" she called from the darkness of her bedroom. "Yes," I said, feeling a little remorse. I couldn't tell her that Laura was waiting for me to turn up before dawn. I'd left her at the party earlier because I'd been irritated about something that now I suppose must've been due to the alcohol I'd consumed rather than to anything else. Having walked out on Laura, I was on the street, where I called a cab and, without thinking about it, I asked to be dropped off near Pastora's house.

I never dreamed she would be there, that I would finally find her, that she would let me in, and that I would have her again. Or rather, I had dreamed it countless times and wondered if I wasn't, in fact, a victim again of that dream and would wake in the morning knowing it had never happened.

forty-one

The wedding was a small, conservative affair, upholding what white, suburban, middle-America considered good taste. The bride wore ivory; a bodice of lace climbed to the neck and offered a Victorian look. In her hair was a delicate crown of rosebuds and baby's breath. The maid of honor, the groom's sister, wore lilac and the groom and his best man wore black tuxedos.

The ceremony was held in an ornate Lithuanian Catholic Church on the far west side of the city. Pastora's heart palpitated, overwhelmed by the ostentatious designs and elaborate frescoes that covered the domed ceiling and walls, not to mention the parish's own miraculous Virgin statue that cried real tears. Afterward, the party went on to the country club of which Perla's new husband was a member and whose grandfather had been a co-founder. Pastora attended the festivities alone, moving about in isolated symmetry of distance and observation.

She was seated at a table with persons whom she only guessed were related to the groom as friends or business associates. He was a man loyal and endeared to his personal and professional community and it wasn't surprising to see that those whom he esteemed had not only been invited, but had also attended. They were polite couples who talked in whispers to one another as the platters of rare roast beef and potatoes au gratin were passed from caterers to guests.

Now and then, Pastora glanced toward the front table, where bride and groom clinked glasses and smiled for an animated photographer. Pastora looked for them, but noticed that Perla's mother and the boys weren't present. Her youngest sister, who was fair with green eyes and bore no superficial semblance to the mestizo blood from which she descended, but appeared likely to be related to the groom, sat happily at the far end of the table engaged in flirtation with a bland-looking fellow whom Pastora sized up as most likely to be the groom's accountant. *May the girl marry well,* she thought to herself wryly, sighing heavily. She felt hypocritical altogether for having come to the function that for many months had plagued her with its imminence.

"How did you like the food?" Perla asked Pastora when they were actually near each other. Pastora nodded, implying it had been satisfactory, although she had hardly gotten a few morsels down. Pastora took the opportunity to inquire after Perla's relatives. Pastora asked about Perla's twins, whose absence at their mother's wedding was obvious.

"Oh, they're with their father today . . ." Perla's eyes got that black, fiery look of anxiety. Pastora knew Perla well enough to know their absence hurt her. Whether it was because they had to spend the day with their father or because the presence of the bride's two frizzy-haired children was objected to by someone, Pastora didn't dare to ask. The women fell silent.

Perla tried to brighten and turned to watch her other guests mingling around the hall. She put a hand the color of a peeled almond with a stunning band of diamonds interlaced with gold on her groom's hand, who at the moment was involved in a discussion with the accountant. Pastora turned away and saw nothing for a moment, waiting for the cold chill the awkward exchange with Perla had sent through her body. As soon as the combo had set up to play its first waltz, to announce the newly wedded couple and their wedding party, Pastora left.

Bob, Bob, Bob, Bob, Bob, oh, excuse me, Perla, Robert. When Pastora had finally met Perla's dashing lover, the great wooer of her heart, a savvy, continental charmer, a man of the world as Perla had described, Pastora had encountered instead a dry, spectacled man of medium height and uninteresting features, always in three-piece suits that looked as if they had been tailored for someone else and shoes that hadn't seen a decent shine since the day they left the factory.

On the other hand, it was probable that what the man lacked in savoir-faire he made up for as a shrewd businessman. Perla made him out to be an up-and-coming tycoon of sorts. This was an area as remote to Pastora as social activities on the moon, so she couldn't fairly evalute whether Perla's Bob was destined for the unlimited future of the astute entrepreneur that Perla professed. While it was true that Perla may have married Bob because she was so impressed with the side of life and culture she had not known before, Pastora was never convinced that Perla was also very much in love with him.

Pastora knew Perla as an enthusiast, obsessed with new passions and impulses. Pastora resigned herself to

Life Without Perla.

The better part of a year passed before they met up with each other again. Perla was her usual bubbly self. She talked about their investments, her recent projects. Beneath the hyper façade, Pastora knew the other woman was troubled. She invited Perla for a drink, eager to take advantage of the moment when Perla was inclined to turn to Pastora for help.

Since the beginning of Perla's relationship with Bob, he had occupied the roles of guide, mentor, and sole companion. Pastora sensed, even as they sat across from each other, looking directly into each other's dark eyes, that Bob was even at that moment pulling Perla to him, placing her integrity on a loyalty that went beyond sexual fidelity to emotional and intellectual dependency. He held in his power the influence of the Great White Father.

Pastora asked after the boys. There was a tug of regret that she wouldn't see the identical imps with cherrywood skin growing up. Perla told her, using a tone implying that great thought and a sense of maturity had been employed in making the decision, that they had been sent to a boys' school on the East Coast. "But what are they going to do out there?" Pastora blurted out, while knowing she was treading on sensitive ground. "They were born and raised in Chicago! This is their home!"

"Yes, but when we moved into Robert's house, the boys were getting into trouble at the new school." Perla's eyes got blacker and Pastora decided not to say anything more, no matter what. Boys with their Caribbean looks in a school of Aryan-type children in a community such as the one where Perla now lived—Pastora understood what trouble they had been having. Pastora broke the intense contact with Perla's eyes; it seemed as if minuscule flames vibrated inside her pupils. She drank down her wine and lit a cigarette.

"I-I've been thinking a lot about you," Perla gushed out. Pastora looked up and was at once hooked into that hypnotic focus. "I've missed our times together, my old drinking chum . . ." Perla tried to laugh. Pastora raised her glass and forced a smile.

They parted at the step of the restaurant; a kiss on the cheek, a warm embrace, a tacit promise to get together more often. Future attempts were aborted by sudden matters of ultimate importance. Their places in each other's lives had changed irrevocably and neither tried any longer to deny it.

Pastora spent a while after the encounter with renewed resentment for Bob as a symbol of men's indispensability in women's lives. She brooded over her own particular reliances on men. She wrote of this preoccupation in her journal, now her confidante, but it didn't find its way to her music. She stopped writing lyrics and concentrated on composition.

Some months later, Perla came to see Pastora without warning. Pastora offered her old friend tea, and she accepted it graciously, used to Pastora's sparse lifestyle and indifference to homemaking. She talked about every imaginable topic: the new Italian haistylist she went to, the boys' amusing letters, the incorrigible diet her doctor insisted she go on, high blood pressure, etc. Pastora tolerated the incessant chatter, asking few questions until they reached the point when Perla was at ease to say what was on her mind that had provoked the visit.

"You know, Sunday, when we were coming home from Mass . . ." Perla started, her eyes flashing toward Pastora slyly, taking note of her expressions. Pastora was adept at concealing her reactions. The mention of Perla's going to Mass was a surprise in itself, but Perla went on. "There were two men in suits waiting at our front door. At first, I assumed they were associates of Robert, you know, he knows so many people . . .

"Then they looked at me and said, 'Mrs. Bodilla?' I nearly panicked. I think Robert's mouth dropped open, but I was too afraid to look at him when I nodded and had to say, 'yes'!"

"What?" Pastora asked. She was lost. She had never known Perla to be married before now. She had by her own admittance never legally married the boys' father and his surname was not Bodilla. "Who the hell is Bodilla?" Pastora asked. She felt her brow screwed. It was plain that Perla had never mentioned it before because she had not intended for it to be known. Perla took a deep sigh.

"My uncle, Tío Eloy, came to me about . . . two year ago with his son, Eloycito, who . . ." here she sighed again, "had come to this country wanting to start a business of some kind with his father. My tío Eloy had some money. However, Eloycito didn't have papers, you know; he was at the point of being deported. It wasn't a big business, just a mechanic's garage, but he's a hard worker. Anyway, my uncle asked if I wouldn't do his son the tremendous, pretty please, favor of marrying him so that he could legally establish residency."

"And you said yes and now Immigration wants to know why you're not living with your husband . . ." Pastora finished drily. Only Perla . . . !

"Right. They wanted to know why, in fact, I no longer share the same address with my husband, Eloy Bodilla, Jr."

"Wait a minute. Was all this said in front of our friendly Fuller Brush Man?" Pastora didn't know why she had referred to Perla's husband in that way, but at the moment it fit with her image of him on his doorstep and she was unable to resist the attempt at humor. It worked to produce a grin, however briefly, from Perla.

"Uh-hmm. Only it was real strange. During all of this, Robert didn't say a word. I let the men assume what they wanted. But Pastora, if they had found out that Robert is my husband, I could've gotten arrested for bigamy—couldn't I?"

Pastora laughed aloud. Only Perla . . . could end up in trouble for bigamy or for counterfeiting or some such ludicrous underhanded scheme to undermine the system. Then Pastora sobered, because Perla wasn't telling it with the intention of being humorous. "What'd Bob say when they left?"

"That I have to file for an immediate divorce."

"From him or your cousin?" Pastora couldn't deny that she was enjoying the story.

"From my cousin, the poor guy! He's got another year before he goes up for permanent residency. If I divorce him now, he'll have to give up everything here and go back!"

"And has Bob considered this?"

"Yes, but he doesn't want his wife married to another man! He's Catholic!"

Pastora wanted to remind Perla that Perla, too, professed to be Catholic. She wanted to say that as long as the marriage between her and her cousin was only a legal matter, Bob shouldn't be concerned with the Commandments and the sacred laws that guided behavior. Bob held the cards, of course, because he could decide whether he wanted to force a decision on Perla's part if she didn't act readily upon his request. Pastora frowned. From the back of her mind, she brought forth the urge to ask if Perla hadn't helped out her cousin for the sake of material gain.

Perla watched Pastora from the corner of her eye. She was considering whether she should finish the confession. Pastora waited. Perla told her, "You know my car?" Pastora nodded. "My uncle got it for me."

Pastora wanted to rescue her friend, to dive in and keep her from drowning from the predicament she'd unwittingly gotten in with full awareness of the possible consequences. "Oh, hell," she said, groping in the air for the words, "you can always give the car back. You can afford another one now anyway, can't you?"

Perla was relieved by Pastora's response. "Yeah, but what about my family?"

"What about your family? They'll have to understand! It's your husband who's forcing you into this position, after all! They'll surely understand a woman going along with her husband's wishes."

"Yeah, but I'd promised my uncle and cousin I would stick to this . . . until everything was all worked out. It was before I even imagined I'd marry Robert! Robert pressured me so much, I couldn't put him off or he would've demanded a reason; and . . . I didn't want to lose him!"

"Better that he would've been suspicious than have evidence that could land you in jail, no?"

Perla agreed, miserable again. "Robert would never report me. He might leave me, but he would never want to see me in trouble."

Pastora turned away. In the end, it was Perla's fear of losing her man. She would risk a great many consequences, but not that one. Pastora wished she had money, enough to wave in Bob's face, to show him and his segregated world that they could not run a Latina woman so easily and she would buy her Perla back.

forty-two

When Ruthie was sixteen, she had grown taller than her older sister. She was built very much like Pastora, but leaner. She belonged in a tutu. Pastora lamented that her baby sister had no interest in the arts. She was just hanging on to her last year in high school by a thread. Ruth was adventuresome, ready for a thrill and fun. She didn't have time for study, for thinking about what lay ahead.

Pastora took the task of hoping to influence Ruth in some way that would help mold her future, so she spent as much free time with her as she had. One night Pastora invited Ruthie to a film at the Biograph and they rode down afterwards to an outdoor café on Clark St. Pastora had a glass of wine and her sister ordered a soda, although Pastora divined that Ruth was not a stranger to liquor.

She felt estranged from her sister, whom she loved to a degree of being maternal rather than a sibling or friend. She corrected her sister's posture, straightened her hair, adjusted her clothes. Ruthie shrugged her shoulders, pulled away uneasy, but was not apt to resist overtly.

They were talking about this and that when Pastora noticed a familiar face coming up the street. She knew by his walk, a confident gait of long strides on not necessarily long legs. The beard confirmed her dread. He had also noticed her, but she had a hunch Máximo had no intentions of stopping any longer than to say hello, until his eyes registered on Pastora's companion. The sweet face of innocence. Ruth, sixteen.

Máximo took a seat and Pastora felt transported to another world where she was made to watch a scene in which she was not present. Máximo ordered himself a beer. He was studying Ruth's hands. Oh? Is this your sister? I didn't know you had a sister . . . ! He opened a pocket-sized sketchbook and began stealing Ruth's spirit in quick, leaded strokes onto the white paper. Ruth blushed; she laughed melodically. Ruth was sixteen.

Pastora heard something come through the screen: "You should be a model!" Máximo was saying. "I want to, but," Ruth was looking into her glass of cola and ice, her chin held up by a hand, "my father wants me to study nursing. I can't stand the sight of blood, ugh!"

Máximo was amused. He was charmed by the seraph in a short cotton dress and white sandals. He was irresistible, too. Ruth and Max were laughing together. Down the street Pastora saw a squad car moving slowly up to where the car she had borrowed from her parents for the evening was parked illegally. She would get a ticket and towed. Anxious to stop the police, she ran off without saying a word to Max or Ruth, although it was plain as to where she was headed. She managed to get to the car in time and it took another twenty minutes to find parking that was legal.

When she returned, Ruth was sitting alone. Máximo was gone. "God! He's really cute, isn't he?" Ruth was bubbling over, "I mean, he's kinda old, but he's not bad. How old is he—about 30? Pastora, do you know?" Pastora reached for what she believed would be her last cigarette in the pack she'd left on the table, but she found it empty. Ruth informed her, "Oh, Max smoked it. I told him you wouldn't mind." Pastora looked solemnly at her beloved sibling, the angel in her life. She felt Max walking off in a rejuvenated mood, feeling smug.

On impulse that weekend, Pastora went to her mother's house. She knew she wasn't going to visit her mother so much as making an excuse to see Ruthie, to observe her, to feel for the change, an indication. When Ruthie saw her sister coming in, she went into her bedroom and closed the door.

Pastora talked with her mother in the kitchen for a while before knocking on Ruthie's door. Ruthie was listening with earphones to her stereo. Her legs, smooth and tanned, were exposed by a pair of skimpy shorts. Ruth smiled, but didn't turn off the stereo. Pastora looked around and pretended to find the display of Polaroids around the teenager's mirror intriguing. She noticed that Ruthie now had her own telephone with a private line.

"What's new?" Pastora said. Her voice was kept low so as to force the young woman to remove the headphones.

"Wha . . . ?"

Pastora gripped the dresser behind her. She knew, just by the way

Ruthie refused to look at her, that something had already happened. She felt so ambivalent by her paradoxical emotions that she didn't know how to behave, but she was physically affected. Her stomach turned; she was lightheaded. Ruth's long legs, her hair, lustrous over her bare shoulders.

"What's new?" Pastora repeated. She was certain Ruth couldn't realize that Max was her older sister's lover. The paranoia of youth that makes it fear reprimands for experimentation prevented Ruthie from thinking of anything but her own behavior and how it would earn Pastora's disapproval. Ruthie's eyes filled with tears. "Don't look at me that way, Pastora! I didn't do nothing!"

"Then why are you about to cry?"

"He wanted to . . . but I, you know."

"No, Ruthie. Tell me." Pastora knew she was intimidating Ruthie. It was the only way she would find out what there was to know.

"Is Mom out there?" Ruth indicated the kitchen. She wouldn't say anything if she thought her mother was in listening range. Pastora shook her head. "She's gone to church." Ruth sat up and she wiped her nose with the back of her hand. The urge to cry had gone away, but she twisted a strand of hair nervously. She wanted to confide in Pastora, but she was still reluctant. "He called me," she said finally.

"When did you see him?" Pastora maintained a firm grip on the dresser behind her. "The next day. He called me and I went out with him. We didn't go nowhere, I mean, he didn't take me out or nothing. He said he didn't want to go somewhere where someone might see us or you might find out and get mad because I'm your kid sister and stuff." Ruth stopped to check her sister's reaction. Pastora remained expressionless. Ruthie decided to go on. "He took me to his studio to show me his work, you know, his sculpture and stuff."

Pastora wanted to laugh. Máximo, on the prowl for a fawn, a wolf without enough imagination to use a ploy other than the oldest in modern history. Pastora didn't laugh. Her sister, with her childish expressions, fidgeting with her hair, picking on an invisible scab on her lovely knee, was discovering the world firsthand. Ruth didn't read in books of artists and their garrets, or of men who considered themselves the greatest cocks in Western civilization. She had to meet them personally on a stage set for a Grimm's fairy tale.

"He said he wanted me to model for him. He said I had a beautiful body and stuff like that, and you know, I took my clothes off after a while, then, right away he, you know. He said he couldn't help himself, that I was so beautiful and stuff!" Ruthie's voice was high-pitched, as if she expected her sister to rebuff her any moment.

"Speak English for God's sake, will you?" Pastora barely controlled her temper only by reminding herself that her sister wasn't guilty of anything. Ruth's eyes flared, brightening with moisture. "I never did it before . . . and, and, he couldn't get it in!" Ruth let the tears roll down her warm cheeks.

"You stupid little . . ." Pastora muttered, stopped herself, and tried not to cry as well. She left.

A half a year passed before Máximo called Pastora. She knew he had waited for the time to lapse so that his involvement with her sister would be forgiven. She could tell by his sloppy enunciation that he'd been drinking. He said he wanted to see her and she told him she was busy. He apologized for disturbing her and hung up.

forty-three

When Laura filed for the divorce with the intentions of taking the co-owned studio, all the items we had purchased, the new van with power steering and brakes—in short, everything but the invaluable works of Máximo Madrigal and his clothes—I was miserable as I had never been before in my life. I was miserable, too, because I realized that Laura really was a good woman. When it dawned on her that my diverse thirst for women was not about to cease and that her tolerance of it wasn't going to carry her through the better part of a lifelong marriage, she got up one day and left. When I was away from the studio, she came and took her things. Her lawyer advised me that Laura expected to have everything, but for the time being, until I found another place to stay and store my work, I could remain in our place.

During this period, I confused the idea of having lost Laura and her devotion with the actual feelings I had for her; I didn't know if they would have been so pronounced if it wasn't for the fear of what life would be like without her. I saw other women, but there was nothing serious. I was plagued by the sense of ultimate rejection, the feeling of being stripped of my manhood by Laura's North American idiosyncratic decision to simply stop loving me.

I was able to see Pastora on a few occasions during this depression. Surprisingly, she was accessible. I invited her to the studio, I cooked for her or served expresso, which she showed a fondness for. It was pleasant, soothing I would even say, having Pastora sit in her reserved manner, smoking a cigarette as I worked. We always made love. It was nearing spring, but the days were still short so that it seemed in no time it was dark and she went out beneath the refuge of night to someone else, to something; I never asked to where or to whom.

Pastora and I got on well on these rare occasions, that were, as I say, a handful at best. She said she enjoyed my cooking; of course,

I'm an excellent cook. The specialties of my country's cuisine are not as simple as one would like to think. We listened to music. We talked very little about important matters. I told her that Laura was divorcing me and, of course, being Pastora, she said it was overdue and that Laura deserved whatever recompense she sought.

"She spies on me," I told Pastora, determined to get her sympathy in this instance. "She comes to see if she'll catch me with a woman." We both looked to the front door as if Laura had been waiting for her cue to barge in at that instant and catch us on the couch.

"But what difference does it make now? She's divorcing you. She doesn't even live with you any longer," Pastora said. I didn't respond. What could I tell her? That I had ALWAYS denied having been with other women? Naturally, I wouldn't tell Pastora this outright. She already knew I was with other women besides herself, because Pastora just *knew* these things.

Nothing I could ever say to Pastora would be taken at face value. The woman had an uncanny way of seeing beneath every layer of a lie I told anyone else without blinking an eye and without being suspected of it. And because of her insight into my manipulating ways, she would have been the end of me. I would have stopped working. I would never have let her out of my sight. Because as much as I was incapable of physical fidelity, so was Pastora . . . but why go through all this again? How many men had I overheard talking about her—but not in a derogatory way. They never said, "That whore . . ." or winked at each other as if she were the main pussy of the red-light district. They spoke of her with reverence, with tremors in their hearts. They had loved her or they had desired her, but they had also feared her.

"That witch!" they said, and I knew by the tone of their voices that they relished the very idea of having been hexed by the woman. "Watch out for her!" they warned each other, and I, who had made love to her body, had tasted the butter and salt of her skin and touched every inch in search of a hint to her secrets, cringed. I, too, was convinced I was possessed.

I left Chicago. There was nothing for me in the United States. I packed a bag and returned to my home for solace, for refuge. I went to Sapogonia.

I hadn't heard from my grandparents in months and only one letter had come from my mother. At that time she told me that things were very bad in my country. She said she was terribly frightened. But she was never specific; my mother was never a letter writer. Like most mothers, she exhausted me with endless questions and opinions regarding my career, my marriage, my successes and failures, with her wistful sighs, resignation to life, and frequent references to heavenly beings and our dependency on their whims.

To say that I was in very low spirits is a major understatement because I was abysmally sad, and I thought I would take refuge on my grandfather's ranch. I would try to work, perhaps not in metal, but in wood. My last agent had dropped me and I had no exhibits planned. What I felt I needed was new work, something fresh that would startle the stagnated critics in the U.S. so that they would die to have the masterpieces of Máximo Madrigal.

forty-four

Since Pastora couldn't leave the state and had to be most conscious of the places where she gave performances, she spent a good part of the next months looking for full-time employment. The inability to admit where she had been the last two years, stating instead that she had been out of the country on tour, only made her out to be an undependable risk and by December she was still without income and with no money to live on.

"Get a bag boy's job at the supermarket," her mother suggested coolly once. Her parents never hid their disapproval of Pastora when she had been arrested. Pastora knew she might end up having to seriously consider her mother's advice, assuming she would be hired for that kind of work. But she wanted so much to return to her song that she preferred the dismal life she led.

One day she went to Hyde Park to visit Yvonne Harris, a blues singer she was close friends with before she "had been taken away," as she called it. Yvonne, although a brilliant talent who, in addition to her blues forte, sang scat like no one Pastora had ever heard before, kept herself within a circle of black friends and negated the possibility of appealing to a white audience because of her own political beliefs. Her charismatic personality betrayed her deep Southern feelings that left her not trusting white people under any circumstances. She accepted Pastora, whose skin was the color of a mulatta's, because of Pastora's own struggle against racism.

Yvonne made chicken gumbo with what, as far as Pastora knew, were her last rations. "Don't worry about it, girl," Yvonne laughed heartily. "We got to eat to keep up our strength, you know. How else are we gonna keep fighting all this bull around us?" Yvonne had stopped drinking, so Pastora finished the bottle of wine she'd brought for their reunion celebration alone. As she drank, she shared snatches of her experiences in prison and, before the evening was through, they both sang together, in harmony; one, with a raspy, spiritual yearning and the other, soft and haunting. And they both cried.

On Christmas Eve, Pastora decided to find Eduardo, although she hadn't realized it was the holiday until she heard it on the bus on the way to the neighborhood where he had lived before. She doubted he would have returned to the same apartment, but she didn't know how else to trace him. As she anticipated, peeking through the bare windows, it was abandoned, looking even more dismal with his modest furnishings gone.

Just as she was about to walk away from the house, a woman called to her. Pastora recognized her as Eduardo's former landlady. She was coming out to shovel the snow. In Spanish she asked if Pastora was looking for Eduardo and Pastora answered that she was. "I think he lives down the street, in the brick house." Pastora thanked the woman and went there. Pastora was glad for her luck to have met up with the landlady, otherwise she would have gone off thinking the world had swallowed Eduardo Madero while, as life would have it, he was only a block away. Pastora went to the designated building and, seeing his name on the first floor doorbell, rang. Eduardo answered immediately.

In T-shirt and work pants, he looked as if he had been napping. In all probability, he had worked that day. When he saw it was Pastora, the sleep in his eyes disappeared and his face brightened as if he'd found what he'd given up as lost. They embraced in the entrance, a welcome-home locking of arms.

He made tea and they talked. Their meeting was different than Pastora's reunion had been with Madrigal, who always had and always would prefer that she remain a mystery, a personification of sensual fantasy. Eduardo, on the other hand, both feet on the earth, the Taurus, prepared to move boulders, insisted on bare facts.

Presently, having exchanged bits of news—that he had returned to his old job with the help of a sympathetic foreman; building inspectors had prohibited his former landlord from renting out the basement apartment he'd originally had—she told him she was looking for a job and if he should hear of something, anything . . . They fell silent. A light Christmas snow brushed the city streets and they watched it drift against the drapeless windows, drinking tea and content in each other's honest company.

"Thank you, Pastora," Eduardo said, finally.

"Oh?"

"My wife thanks you, too. She asked me to tell you if I ever saw you . . ." Eduardo looked awkward, Pastora thought, speaking to her of his wife. When he had said "wife," the words burrowed into her eardrums. She remembered Yvonne's consoling words, "You know the man loves you. Eduardo's a nice man, so he's just stayed married to that woman because they have a child together."

"Actually the time wasn't as futile as it might seem," Pastora referred to her imprisonment. "What I have regretted was losing my car. It was already paid up!" As part of Pastora's penalty for transporting a refugee, her vehicle had been taken away. She coughed a little, as if to clear her throat, but said no more.

"Dora is back in Sapogonia. She's fine." He was clearly uneasy with the subject at hand.

"How's your son?" Pastora also forced herself to talk. She knew Eduardo wanted it in the open. It was better to speak of these people who were part of his life, make them real and not abstract, as they had been before that night when she had had them in her car.

"He's fine, too. I wanted custody of my boy, but his mother wouldn't permit the separation. She wants him raised in her country."

Later that night, Eduardo would hold Pastora and tell her that he and his wife were legally separated. It had been inevitable because of their mutual dedication to their convictions. He would tell her that the child was his wife's choice. She'd had the baby against his judgment, as he already felt they were drifting apart.

Because he left her with the child, Dora grew enraged and returned to her family in Sapogonia. The awareness by the authorities in Sapogonia of her past activities made it impossible for her to return to the U.S. with proper authorization. She was returning to find Eduardo, whom she thought was still in Chicago, when Pastora picked her up.

"Did you ever get to see her? Or your son?" Pastora asked. In the dark, she could ask without fear that the pain would show. "Yeah," he said. "Before she was sent back, I flew in to see them both."

"And now?" Pastora held her breath for the answer.

"And now? You mean, where do we stand, Dora and me?"

"Yes."

"I'm not sure. She wants a divorce now. I guess it's the best thing."

"And you? What do you want?" Pastora asked, stroking his stub-laden chin.

"I don't know, I don't know what it is that I want," he replied in Spanish. Pastora froze. This was the shield she protected herself with and didn't allow anyone to penetrate, the same one Máximo Madrigal and the likes of him crashed into whenever they tried to get too close for their own advantage. She got up from the bed and went to smoke a cigarette in the living room. Eduardo called to her, but she couldn't bring herself to answer. Isolation had surrounded her. Finally, he came and asked if she wanted him to take her home. "Yes," she told him.

It had been a queer holiday. Forgetting that it was a holiday was not odd, because she had been in such a bleak state of mind. Then the comfort of being with Eduardo again, who had taken her to eat in Chinatown. She asked if he minded buying groceries for her friend, Yvonne, who was almost as glad to see them together as she was to have the food. Pastora remembered another friend in Hyde Park, an Argentine woman who was in the process of a divorce. They took her a bottle of wine. They'd spent the evening with her family, but her stepfather drank too much and became insulting to everyone, especially to Pastora, so they left early.

But it didn't matter. She had had someone to share Christmas with, and when she had fallen asleep next to him and a nasty dream crept into her sleep so that she awoke crying, he had soothed her. Then he reminded her that their time together was limited and imposed upon by priorities; other people more important in his life, ideas more important than the people, work that meant more than ideas.

forty-five

As soon as I arrived at the airport in Puerto Sapogonia, there was something changed. It was in the air, the aroma of guayaba trees replaced by the smell of gunpowder. In place of the sun pouring onto the streets, mourning filtered through the air. Signs of the military were everywhere. Men and women passed each other on the street without a greeting, the tipping of a hat, the tickling of a baby's chin. Beggars were more humble than ever.

It was the first time since I left Sapogonia that I felt the significance of Horacio's death. I felt the loss of a compatriot. He had foreseen this. He had had the soul of the poet and the mind of an historian. He had known what was going to happen within our lifetime because he knew that governments, being what they were, were predictable. We had had civil wars over the centuries, over the decades. We had not learned from our mistakes.

Six months earlier, the president of Sapogonia was taken into custody and imprisoned by the chief of the military. The military claimed that the president had been vastly incompetent as leader of the country and blamed him for the fifty percent inflation over the past year. Three days after the *coup d'état*, it was said that the president shot himself in the head. At his funeral, the casket was covered. It was rumored, not then, but months, years later, in the United States, because no one dared to breathe it at home, that the president's body had been bullet-ridden. The joke ran that he had been so incompetent that he had not been able to point to his head and shot himself a hundred times before he managed to hit the temple. Those who didn't laugh, shuddered.

I went to see my mother, who was at her new home with her husband. They told me that he had lost his business and they had been living off her endowment. They had let their servants go. They no longer went out. My mother had sold most of her jewelry and silver.

218

"And what about my grandfather? And my grandmother?" I asked my mother. Hadn't she heard from them, seen them? Couldn't they help her? She shook her head. "I haven't gone to see your grandparents in a month. Things are very bad for them, too, but they still have a little help at the ranch. No one answers the telephone; I'm afraid the lines in the area have been cut off . . ."

"But you haven't gone to see them—to find out exactly what is going on?" I was amazed. My mother and her husband shook their heads and lowered their eyes, embarrassed by my surprise at their lack of initiative. "It's too dangerous, son," my stepfather told me. "The roads are barricaded; you can't go anywhere without being stopped." I stared at my mother's husband. It was absolutely absurd to me that he hadn't tried to find out how his wife's aging parents were, particularly when he was living off my mother's money and was literally indebted to her family. If it hadn't been for my grandfather, that man would've been out on the street begging for alms! He seemed to read my thoughts and continued to emphasize the dangers of travelling. "Really, son. An innocent person could get shot for no reason on the road these days. It's advised constantly on the radio not to travel unless it is an emergency."

"And you don't consider this an emergency?" I asked sarcastically.

"It's just that we don't know there's any reason to worry ourselves, son. I'm sure that they're fine . . ."

"Do me a favor . . ." I told him.

"Anything. What is it, son?" he asked, believing he had convinced me that he hadn't shown himself to be the son of a bitch that he was.

"Don't call me son again—ever."

My stepfather's jaw dropped, and before my mother could get a word of defense in on his behalf, I was out on the street and had taken his car. I drove without stopping until I reached my grandfather's ranch. I saw several jeeps and soldiers along the way, but except for hard stares, they hadn't stopped me, but waved me on. I didn't stop except to fill the tank with gas and was astounded that gasoline, a natural resource in my country, was at an exorbitant rate, three times what it cost by the gallon in the United States.

I drove with fury once reaching the back roads that wound through various small villages, including San Co, and out to the ranch. Night fell and the phosphorescent creatures for which my country was named, addled by the modernization of their environment, made their way to the road. They croaked a pious song to their ancestors and never knew what plastered their glowing bodies to the asphalt as the tires of my vehicle ran over them, giving off a series of popping sounds.

I hadn't gotten out of the car and already I knew what to expect. There was no sign of the animals; stench reeked. I trembled from inside the car and put a handkerchief over my nose. My stomach felt weak. I considered turning the car around and driving off, but at that hour I would have to cross the soldiers posted along the road that possibly wouldn't treat night drivers with the same casualness as they had done to me when it was light. I steadied myself and got out of the car.

Everything was black and I reached back inside the car to search for a flashlight in the glove compartment. Luckily there was one and I went ahead toward the house. It wasn't a large house, although when I was a child I thought it was immense.

I looked toward the window of the room that had been mine. It was dark, but I could still make out the familiar curtains. My mother had made those curtains just before I left home. They were blue with a peculiar design which reminded me of mushrooms, or penises floating about in water. I felt my knees weaken as I put my hand on the doorknob. I was broken out in a cold sweat. There were soft steps behind me and I turned abruptly. It was difficult to see because the grounds were lit only by the stars and a half moon, but the silhouette several meters away looked to be that of my grandmother. I pointed the flashlight at her just as she called out, "No, hijo. Leave it off."

"¿Mamá Grande?" I uttered. It was an eerie meeting from the start. She didn't move any closer, but stood where she was. I wondered what she was doing roaming about in the dark. "How good that you came back, son," she said. Yes, it was the voice of Mamá Grande, but she remained still as if her feet were dug in the ground where she stood. She wrapped her shawl tighter about her little body as if she were cold. "I knew you would come back soon."

"Mamá Grande, what are you doing out here? Why don't you go inside where it's warm? Come . . ." I motioned, and now that the fear had passed, I went toward her to help her into the house. She put out her shriveled hand. "No, Mimo, don't come close." She added something else in her native tongue, forgetting that I didn't understand, but she went on, "Tomorrow you must go and tell your mother what you found here, but it's better that tonight you stay. It's dangerous to travel at night. *They* came at night." She whispered the last sentence.

"Who came, Mamá?" I asked and found I had obeyed her request rather than persist that she go in and not stand outside in the chilled weather to talk. "Go in and rest. We're in our room, on the bed. But don't go in there, son. Tomorrow, you must make the arrangements. Your grandfather would like a Mass. God bless you." My grandmother's voice made me ache, knowing she wasn't coming any closer because she didn't want to touch me with death. I obliged her and went in. I didn't want to leave her outside, but I knew she was there to protect the grounds while I slept. She had been waiting for me.

The moment I stepped into the house I was pushed back against the wall by the stench of rotting flesh. I trembled and thought to run, but I remembered that it was my grandparents who were lying in their room waiting for the dignity of a burial and, when I was able to overcome the nausea, I went about opening windows, avoiding going into their room as my mamá grande's spirit had told me, and then I went to my former bedroom.

It didn't make sense, but only in my room was there no smell at all except for a warm, welcoming one and, although I thought I was mistaken because of my hunger, it smelled like hot food. As soon as the light flooded the room, I found a bowl of rooster soup on what had been my writing desk. It was the kind of soup my grandfather always insisted I have whenever I complained of feeling ill. A spoon, napkin, fresh bread, and a carafe of wine waited. I looked around, then ducked a head outside the window to thank my grandmother, but there was nothing there but the silence of transformation and the invisible creatures of the night.

I ate and finished the wine immediately and, right afterward, I needed desperately to sleep. I was tired from the plane ride, followed by the tense drive to the ranch, and finally the shock of my grandparents' deaths. Yet, it wasn't as if I had arrived at all, but was having a terrible dream. I thought I would awake in Chicago, in my studio with the cot by the window facing the elevated train platform that let in nothing but a grey ray of light.

I believe I was engulfed in dark serenity for hours before I began to dream. I was making love to Pastora. I had awoken and she was walking outside, past the window of my room on the ranch. When I looked out, she smiled at me. She was dressed in an ankle-length costume, the color of Sapogonian sky in summer. Her hair was loose and long, the way it was when I first met her. "Come in," I told her and the next thing I knew she was in the room and naked on my bed. I took a drink of wine from the carafe on the desk and when I kissed her full lips I delivered it into her mouth. She smelled sweet like honeysuckle and I was lost in the scent of her skin.

Something woke me from my dreams. Perhaps a jeep backfiring as it passed down the road or the shout of a shepherd herding his goats. I could tell by the position of the sun that it was no longer early morning and I jumped out of bed. I was overwhelmed again with the knowledge and fear that my grandparents' corpses were in the other room. I got up and, wanting to have one last sip of wine, was dumbfounded that all traces of the meal I had eaten the night before were gone. My heart pounded. Was it possible that someone was in the house and had taken the things away? Was the housekeeper hiding, afraid to show her face, afraid of also being killed?

I put on my boots and jacket and stomped out of the room to be bombarded again by the morbid reek of decomposing flesh. I started to go to the bedroom, the one I had been forbidden to enter, and hesitated. A chill ran along the back of my neck and I think the hairs stood on end. I knew I wasn't alone in that room, but now, even telling myself that it was only the spirit of my grandmother and that I had already seen it the night before, communicated with it, didn't make me any more at ease. I left immediately and drove until I reached my mother's apartment.

She was red-eyed and probably without sleep throughout the previous night when I went in. She awaited the confirmation of her greatest fear and I sat down at the dining room table before giving her the benefit of a word. "Well, son. Tell me!" She was frantic. I couldn't look at her. "Tell me, are your grandparents . . . ?" Her hand was cold on my shoulder.

"My grandmother says to tell you to take care of things . . ." My voice was strained.

"Then they're all right! Oh, thank God, thank Holy Mary!" My mother crossed herself and sighed with relief.

"They're both dead."

My mother stared at me as if I had just made a bad joke. She backed away, her mouth open. "What are you saying? You just said . . . ? What happened last night?" I was glad my mother had taken it so well. I actually thought the news would send her to hysteria, but she only looked stunned. "They're both dead, and alone. They need to be buried. My grandfather wants a Mass."

"My father wants a Mass?" My mother put her hand against her cheek. She started to get that glazed look mad people have. I thought I'd better steady her, and I sat her down.

"Last night my mamá grande's spirit appeared to me at the ranch. She told me she had been waiting for me. They're waiting for a decent funeral. As the automatic heiress to my grandfather's money, you should go to the bank as soon as possible and prepare the funeral. I think they deserve that much," I told my mother, who was still dazed.

"Money? What money? Your grandfather's properties, stocks, everything was taken away. But maybe there's a little money in the account . . ." Yes, yes, of course I will bury my parents and make sure they have a Mass. My God, poor things, how long?" Mamá was coming back to her old reasonable self.

"I don't know, Mother," I told her, stroking the fine hair along her brow. "The house really stinks. I don't even know what condition their bodies are in."

"You didn't *see* them? Then how do you know?" She looked at me directly for the first time, hoping I was mistaken.

"Because I told you, my grandmother's ghost appeared to me; just as I was about to go in the door, she appeared and told me where the bodies are and not to go into the room. So I didn't. She prepared a nice meal for me, too."

My mother searched my face and felt my forehead, a maternal reflex. I, in turn, felt her forehead, an insolent one. "Why are you feeling if I am feverish? I'm not the one speaking nonsense!" she yelled.

"You don't believe me? Go to the ranch today. See for yourself."

My mother stared at me for a long time. She knew her mother and her capacities. Then she looked around as if someone might overhear. "Don't say anything to your stepfather about that. We'll just tell him you found the bodies and that's that." I nodded. She had a point. I had often noticed him regard his wife as if he believed she wasn't quite all there. There was no reason to encourage him to conclude that it ran in the family.

My stepfather and I called upon other relatives and made our way out to the ranch that same day. The bodies of my grandparents, decayed and smelling of many days expired, were taken to the nearest undertaker. They had both been shot. It seemed to be a case of theft, as many of their valuables were taken and the drawers of desks and cabinets were pulled out. It was a puzzle to me how I hadn't noticed this when I was first there; everything seemed to be in order then. In the dining room, the lace table cloth and silver tray once on it were gone, and the centerpiece of artificial fruit (someone brought it from the United States for my grandmother decades before) rolled on the floor. The cabinets containing silver and china were opened and the contents gone. The strangest of all was that in my room, the bed I'd slept in had been made.

In the kitchen there were no traces that food had been cooked for a while. The fruit and vegetables left in the bins had spoiled. A slab of beef in the icebox was also putrid. I checked the room that belonged to the housekeeper and it was empty. Her body was found later in the chicken coop, slaughtered along with the chickens.

My stepfather and the relatives who had come out with me were ill over the whole scene, the smell of the bodies, their condition. I didn't blame them, but all the while that we were on the premises I kept remembering the vision of my grandmother the night before. I knew she watched us and I made sure she didn't see me overcome by the tragedy. When I got back to my mother's house in the city, I went to bed and didn't wake up for twenty-four hours.

Although I had loved my grandmother and treasured her as a mother as well as a doting grandmother, as the diviner of secrets and medicine woman, it was my grandfather's death that struck me like a sword that pierced through to my very soul and out between the shoulder blades. How many years had he asked me to return, to work on the ranch, to take over, to protect what he had worked for to leave his children, and how many times had I denied him that request? Yet I knew if I had to do it again, I wouldn't have made any other decision.

I would have left as I had done that morning when my heart was broken by the bowlegged Marisela. I would have dropped out of the university to explore Paris with El Tinto. I would have looked for my father in Spain and stayed with him to give me whatever Pío Madrigal had to give his bastard son. I would have gone to the United States to seek my fortune. I didn't want to live on the ranch; I didn't want to live a life of anonymity. I didn't want to exist within the sixteenth-century provincialism of the people of San Co.

I was sorry my grandfather's wealth was taken from him. I pitied my mother, who would have to depend on her husband to provide for her and to make her happy without the comforts she had been used to. I was sorry for myself that I would never again be able to count on financial help from my family when times were bad. I was now and forever on my own.

Then, when Sapogonia itself had turned into a living nightmare of chaos and the macabre as even Horacio couldn't have predicted, I remembered that Laura had left me and wouldn't be waiting when I returned, and at my grandparents' funeral I wept inconsolably, the tears of the loneliest being on earth. I thought to send her a telegram. I was sure that if I told her what had happned, out of sympathy she would postpone the divorce and would return to the studio to reconsider being my wife. She would consent to organize another show for me so that I would have something to work toward and not be drenched in such despair. Telegrams were enormously expensive and had to be approved by the authorities.

My grandparents are dead. They lost everything. I feel
lost. Please don't leave me. Love, Max

I waited for her response for weeks. I went out to my grandparents' against my mother's wishes and decided to stay there for the duration of my retreat to Sapogonia. My mother feared that whoever killed by grandparents would return and, finding me alone, would finish me off. But I thought that there wasn't much chance that lightning would hit the same place twice and I was safer there than where there had been no vandalism or attack.

I worked for months, gathering wood, carving large pieces into shapes of agony and sorrow, of tremendous losses and regrets. I drank and cried and wished my grandmother would appear again, but she didn't. I was sorry that the last time I saw her alive I'd left knowing I would never see her again. I hoped she didn't hold it against me. I prayed my grandfather *wouldn't* appear, because he would certainly drive me over the brink with reproach.

I called Jacobo, who was living in New Mexico, but he wouldn't hear of coming to Sapogonia, even for a visit. He had heard too many stories and the news of my grandparents only convinced him that what he read about the state of my country was true.

I'd begun to refer to Sapogonia as my country for the first time in my life. Home as represented by a territory set off by political borders became Sapogonia when it not only gave to me, but took away. My country didn't consist of individuals each making their own way through life, seeking their own fortunes or destined to have none at all. My country now consisted of groups, clusters, large numbers of people all subjected to the same horrors day after day, all destined for the same maltreatment, the same theft, whether the deprivation was of food or family heirlooms. My country was the home of a university that no longer offered philosophy courses, political science, social science, or psychology. My country now had one national newspaper in synch with radio and television news.

The university paper was obsolete. I walked about on the campus moved by memories of an age no less than a decade before, but which seemed to have taken place in another life, and happened to another man. Out of curiosity, I looked into my old records. The young student working behind the counter was reluctant, but I had gone on about what a successful artist I was back in the United States and how I had had my humble beginnings right there on that campus and smiled and asked if I might invite her for coffee, and she said she had a boyfriend, but perhaps later, and at last looked up my file. It was all there, the record of the classes I had taken, the transcript showing I had completed none of the final courses.

I asked if she didn't mind looking up Horacio's file. I don't know why I had the need to see it, but I felt compelled to be close to what was then and now seemed as if it never had transpired at all. It was agonizing to think all the signs were there so many years before and so few, like Horacio, noticed. She looked all over the place but found no such records. Was I sure he had attended?

I asked her if it was possible that his records would be anywhere else and she said that every so often people came to revise the files. As far as she knew, all the records of past students were kept in her office, but it was possible it had been removed for some reason. Then I thought, hoping the invitation to coffee with a famous artist from the Untied States would suffice as motivation to extend herself a little more, to ask if El Tinto's record was there. It should be with the same file as my own records, I told her. We had attended during the same years and had been taking almost all the same courses. She didn't find El Tinto's records either. No, she was certain, there was no one there by that name.

I went out for a walk. I looked around, behind me, behind trees. I recalled those characters who had harassed students, chased them away from the university, caused them to drop out of debates or quit the newspaper staff. I went back for the girl, who was ready with fresh lipstick and her tinted blond hair brushed, and asked if she didn't mind looking up just a few more names. She looked a little put off, but she complied. With the exception of one name, none was found in the files. "Are you sure any of these people existed?" she laughed.

"No," I answered, and took her to a restaurant off the campus for lunch. I couldn't stand to be at the university any longer. When we returned to her office (I was only being a gentleman escorting her to her desk, you understand, she hadn't interested me that way at all), we saw her supervisor through the glass panel waiting for her in her office. "Do you suppose she will ask what I wanted?" I wondered. Even from the distance, I could see the supervisor's visit to the girl's office wasn't friendly.

"Yes. They always want to know when someone asks to see a file. I'm not sure why, but they seem to disapprove." Her voice was apprehensive.

"Will you tell them what I was looking for?" I asked. She studied me, then she smiled and put her arms around my shoulders. This was very surprising since she had made no such move before then and I hadn't planned anything like it myself, but shortly, I realized what she was doing. She put on a little theatre for the benefit of the spying supervisor. "I'll tell her that you're a former student and you're thinking of returning to finish your studies. I'll tell them because we've been going out, and I liked you, I took the trouble of looking around such a long time in the files. I'll tell them your name is Raúl Martínez, the name on one of the files I ran across when looking for yours. I don't know who Raúl is, but I hope that by the time they find out, you are gone and out of sight and never return here again . . ." She finished with the same artificial smile and we kissed goodbye.

She turned on high heeled sandals and waved as she went into her office. I waved back. I was worried for her. For the first time I knew what El Tinto had felt, why his brother Horacio had panicked. I left that afternoon for my grandfather's ranch and, from then on, only came to the city on weekends.

forty-six

On one of these occasions when I travelled to Puerto Sapo-gonia—it was a greater drive than to San Co, but without going into much detail I'll say that the atmosphere of the small town was distressing and I chose to avoid it completely—I ran into a cousin, the son of my godfather-undertaker, whom I stayed with when I attended the university. He wasn't an actual blood relation, but this is how we always referred to each other. José Luis was several years my senior and it seemed he had been married for an eternity. His oldest son was already working and planning a wedding. José Luis invited me to have a few drinks with him and who was I to refuse? He seemed glad to see me back, even if it had to be for the funeral of my grandparents, assuming right off that that was why I had returned. Which reminded me, why hadn't I seen him at their funeral?

"I don't like funerals . . ." he said with a shudder.

"But your father has always worked in that business."

"I think that has something to do with it. It's a pretty weird business for a child to be around, and I remember how it frightened me when I was young. That's why I prefer my own line of work . . ."

I never knew what it was that José Luis did for a living, but it seemed he was doing well for himself. He had a decent car, he wore new suits and gold watches. "I dabble in this and that . . ." he always said when asked. He smiled this time and gave me a peculiar look, as if debating whether to confide in me or not. Then he decided, "Well, you're not a snot-nosed kid any more; I suppose I can trust you to keep your mouth shut."

We were riding in his car and I could tell we were driving toward the red-light district at the edge of the city, a section that catered to lowlifes, sailors, and a certain kind of tourist. "What are you talking about, man?" I asked casually, lighting a cigarette. I began to make mental guesses about José Luis's occupation: dope dealer, pimp? I looked at the diamond ring on his pinky. Whatever it was, he managed well.

"I have a little business, sole proprietor. I don't run it, you understand. I don't have time to involve myself with those people, you know what I mean. But they pay their rent and they come up with their share of things." He waved the diamond on his pinky as he talked, the stone catching the light and sparkling so that I made a mental note to get one of those someday. It would be much bigger, of course, and wouldn't have flaws as his probably did if one were to examine it closely . . .

José Luis owned a first-rate sleazy night club with rooms along the side for the girls to take their customers. When we drove up, I could tell from the looks of the women that José Luis ranked up there with God, maybe third or fourth in command. They didn't dare get near him, they just worshipped him from afar. I wondered if his wife knew where the money came from to pay for her shopping sprees in Dallas when she bought those dresses she wore to gatherings with the rest of the high-society hypocrites of Puerto Sapogonia.

We went in and we were brought a bottle of scotch without José Luis's having said a word. He explained that the scotch was there specifically for him and no one was to touch it or bring it out for anyone else. We had a shot and then another and we talked. I told him about my travels, my father, Pío, Spain, life in New York, my gringa wife in Chicago. He poked fun at me, saying she was going to take me for every penny I had, so typical of the gringas. I told him the truth that every penny I had ever had was hers to begin with— except for what I made from my work, but that always went right back into it, either for materials or promotion.

Every now and then a girl would give me the eye and, since I didn't look interested, José Luis would send her away. They were the least appealing as far as women in Sapogonia went. Their frumpy bodies with broad backs gave them the appearance of middleweight boxers, who were out of shape at that. They were usually very dark-skinned with caked make-up shades lighter than their complexion, meant to give the illusion that they were not as dark as they were and instead only gave them a humorous mask-like effect. Their hair, which came in bulk weight, was as black as a bull's hide, piled high. In other words, I wasn't drunk enough to go off with any of them.

There was one in particular who was persistent. She stood out from the rest only because she wore an unusual dress. It wasn't one of those fake satin or sequined things with spaghetti straps that accentuated the masculine figure, but the typical indigenous style and of cobalt blue, closer to anything in nature I'd ever seen. It was rare that one of these women would be wearing a native costume for business. I might not have noticed her still, if it wasn't for the fact that she kept giving me the eye.

Finally she came over and asked, "Aren't you going to buy me a drink?" The word she used for drink was not one a minorly cultured individual would use even in that ambience. In fact, it was downright crude and I had only heard men of mean caliber use it. It was slang for "bull's piss." Lighter drinks like beer or wine were referred to as cow's piss. She said "bull's piss."

"Only because you have on such a beautiful dress," I told her and signaled to the bartender. "But I'm not interested . . . I'm just here having a drink with my cousin," I told her and dismissed her by looking back to José Luis as if she were no longer there, but she didn't go away. "As you like, but you didn't seem unhappy with me the last time you were here!" After this, she sauntered off and went back to the bar where she sat and, sipping on her bull's piss, continued to watch me.

José Luis was giving me a crooked grin. "¡Ah! ¡Muchacho! So, you've been a patron of my establishment before! Why didn't you say anything? Never mind, a lot of my city acquaintances come here and, since they don't have any idea that I am the owner, would die if they knew that I knew . . . It's nothing to be ashamed of, the girls here are specialists and we all have our needs."

"They're grotesque! They're circus clowns!" I spat, insulted that he was treating me with such condescension, as if I had a special problem with sex. "I've never been in this rathole before in my life!"

"No need to get offended, Máximo." José Luis patted me on the shoulder and poured me another scotch. "There's no problem. Obviously the young lady is mistaken." We both looked over at her and she winked. She was very sure of herself and only waited for me to finally invite her back. José waved her over. She got off the stool and returned with that sultry walk that moved parts not seen because of the sack shape of the dress.

"My cousin, uh, says he's never been here before. I know he's pretty handsome, but maybe you're wasting your time. Go on and find someone else to keep company . . ." José Luis told her, giving her a gentle pat on the ass. She smiled and we looked at each other.

230

"Whatever you say, boss, but I never forget a face like that one and that's not all I don't forget." She laughed facetiously, "The night he came in here it was my birthday and he was very good to me—the whole night. I even had to send him on his way so that I could get some sleep!" She started to go off when I called her back.

"You say I was here on your birthday? And when was that? Not that it was me, but just to prove to you that I was nowhere near here on that day!"

"The twelfth," she answered, very self-assured. "The twelfth of last month and it was a Tuesday. But forget it, if you say no, then it's no. Who am I to argue? Right, patrón?" She glanced back at José Luis. He approved. The woman went off and in a moment approached a potential customer. I was left to think. The twelfth, in fact, was the same day that I had arrived in Sapogonia. That was the night I went out to my grandparents' ranch and found them dead. Then again, it hadn't been until the next day when I actually saw their bodies, but I had driven out there nevertheless and spent the night.

I began to recollect the other incongruous details of that visit. I had had a meal that no one but a ghost could have prepared with food that apparently materialized from the spirit world, despite that it tasted fairly substantial to me then. Yet, the next morning, all traces of it had disappeared. The condition of the house was different than how I had found it the next day. I had slept throughout the night. I even remembered my dream of Pastora. It was as if she were there in Sapogonia, on my grandfather's ranch, then in my bed, and she had tasted of the sweetness of honeysuckle.

I called the woman in the blue costume. She winked at me and made me wait. The customer she was working on was reluctant to go off with her, preferring one of those with the tits hanging out over the dress. She finally came over. "What is it? Did you remember finally when you were here? An old woman came in that night selling flowers and you bought a bouquet for me . . . You had the guitarist serenade me in honor of my birthday. It was a night I won't forget . . . !"

"Come here," I told her. She drew near, believing I was about to kiss her, but instead I smelled her neck. "What do you use? What kind of scent is that?"

She laughed and even looked a little shy. A shy whore. A shy whore who wore her native costume to work. This was really an original. "I don't wear perfume. I bathe every evening in flower-scented water. It's a custom practiced by the virgins in my village. They bathe in it on the eve of their wedding day. You see? Every evening I am a virgin!" She laughed wickedly. It was annoying because I knew she was hiding her true feelings and, unlike the other women, she managed to get my sympathy. In another moment, she might have me going off to a room with her.

"If you like her . . ." José Luis interrupted, suggesting, like the scotch, this one was on the house. She was waiting for me to say yes. She was sure of it. I shook my head and declined the offer. "Go and have another drink," I told her. She gave me an angry look, but said nothing and left us alone.

"So did you remember her?" José Luis probed. I didn't care for his attitude and told him. "Don't insist. I've already told you this is not my kind of place. Anyway, the night she claims I was in here, I was at my grandparents' ranch. I slept alone . . ."

"Too bad," José Luis laughed and we had another double scotch.

forty-seven

The horrid winter of the North, a season I had never been able to tolerate—and yet without cold to remind a human being of his vulnerability to nature, he would not be pushed beyond his presumed limitations—had abandoned Chicago by the time I returned.

I couldn't bear to go to the studio. I had left all my things with Miguel Spanudis, one of my better friends in the city. Since he lived alone, he said I could stay with him until I found a new place. Laura and I agreed to sell our property and divide the profit rather than continue the spiteful fight over who would get what in the end, and I figured with my share, I might have enough to put down on another loft or rent a store front in a yet-unexploited-by-the-real-estate-prospectors area.

Miguel, or El Griego, as I liked to call him (his father was second-generation Greek and had married a Mexican girl back in the days when Halsted St. was the port of entry for immigrants in Chicago), and I had studied music together. We played at the same restaurants. Miguel got bored with the Bohemian scene that in reality was only a washed-down version of Bohemia in Chicago, where it was always more appealing to have a steady job, and he went to work for a real estate firm. He was able to get hold of property in the Wicker Park neighborhood just before the prices skyrocketed while youth gangs and heavy drug traffic still pretty much kept control. This was where I stayed with him on the second floor of his always-under-renovation building.

The kitchen was a disaster, but he went on about the plans he had for extending it by knocking down the wall that divided it from the back porch. But this would require insulation and storm windows, etc., the total cost of all being just a bit more than he cared to spend at the moment since there were building code violations to see to first, an eyesore of a garage that needed reparation, and on

233

and on. All I wanted was to settle down to work and the atrocious nonfunctioning kitchen became my temporary studio space.

I had sent my work special delivery two weeks before I left Sapogonia and two months later, we had yet to receive any hint that the parcels were on their way. I inquired every day with the local post office, but they knew nothing. Expediency was never a quality of my country's postal system, but two and half months with no sign of anything was enough to worry me to a state of panic. It was months later when my sculptures arrived at last. I had almost given up. The loss would have been greater than anything I could imagine because I had used wood from my grandfather's land and the works I produced were indisputably my finest work thus far. They were the beginning of a series that surpassed all my past work and I could never duplicate them.

As I opened each of the three boxes, I was horrified to see that not one was left undamaged. Anyone might have attributed the destruction to careless handling, but I had wrapped each with the care of swaddling a newborn child. I could tell the boxes had been opened; half of the shredded paper I stuffed in the boxes was gone. Worse than this was the intentional vandalism done to my work! What resulted was not from stupid handling from tossing about on a plane or down conveyer belts. They were hatefully smashed so that what was left could not be salvaged as the original piece.

"Will it at least serve as good firewood?" Miguel asked grimly. I was so upset I could hardly see. My eyes clouded with rage. I shook my head. The work would be salvaged despite the vandals' desire to destroy art. I would work on a series of small pieces. The bastards who damaged my work should have kept it for firewood for themselves if they didn't want me to succeed. "An artist will sculpt out of toothpicks if he must," I told El Griego. And that's what I did, not work with toothpicks naturally, but from what remained of my damaged pieces.

Miguel admired my ambition and agreed to work as my manager. Although he had never managed an artist before, he figured it was very much like selling houses, a field he had displayed quite a talent for. He got me into a group show and, once I had made a little money, I wrote to my mother to come to Chicago. She had been ill since the death of her parents. It must've been her nerves, anxiety with all the distress over the circumstances, you understand. She confided in me that she had been dreaming that she had come to the

United States to live. "I think I shouldn't stay here any longer," she wrote to me, "I have these terrible nightmares that I will end up like my parents, killed in my own home, in my own bed!"

I wrote to her to plan on coming and to bring whatever she valued, but not to anticipate anything that was left behind to be recuperated, not from the safes in banks, not from relatives; no place could be counted on for safekeeping. El Griego said that we could rent his first-floor apartment. It wasn't in as nice condition as his own apartment, but at least the kitchen was usable. I didn't think I would like to live with my mother and her husband, and I decided they could have the apartment and I would stay with Miguel until I scraped the money together for a building of my own. In any case, I had begun to be partial to the sunlight in that demolished kitchen of his.

Miguel, being more Chicagoan than anything else, took an avid interest in the gladiator sport of local politics and began to work on the campaign for a new mayoral candidate. The tío was a Latino by the name of Alan García. I didn't know much about his track record as a politician, but Miguel was placing all his faith in this tío's being the savior of the Latinos of Chicago. Miguel worked on his campaign and donated a great deal of his time, which wasn't any of my business, but I had to remind him that Máximo Madrigal also had a career and I needed more than just a group show once a year. With his regrets, Miguel resigned from his job as my manager.

He invited me to the fundraising events, the banquets, and so on, but unless I got a free ticket, I never went. On most occasions, Alan García didn't show up, too busy campaigning elsewhere and vying for the black vote, the liberal Lake Shore Drive vote, the Polish vote, and on and on. Latinos would just have to keep the faith. His face was seen on television news more often than that of the present mayor. He was certainly a sincere-looking fellow and, because of his candidacy, he made the news in relation to all his other community activities.

As a lawyer, he kept an office in the Mexican community of Little Village. He was involved in the undocumented workers' plight, with gang problems, with the issue of bilingual education. He stuck his nose in every aspect of community life and had something to say about everything.

What caught my eye, however, was not Alan García talking about policies and proposed plans and if he were the mayor he would

. . . but rather the woman who, more often than not, was seen at his side. She hung on to his arm and smiled and shook hands in the spirit of the politician's wife, the future first lady of Chicago. One would think he was running for president and she almost tasted life in the White House. Miguel told me Alan García was not married. "Maritza Marín-Levy is not his wife. Supposedly they're engaged," he informed me.

"Do you know her?" The way he spoke, it sounded as if there was more to the story.

"EVERYBODY knows Maritza Marín-Levy. She's been around a long time. Her Jewish father was a lawyer with the Daley administration—the Levys have a lot of money."

"So she's not Latina?" I thought it was peculiar on the part of the politician who boasted so much pride about his Latino heritage to choose a woman who was not Latina. Of course, as a politician, he had his own theories about diplomacy.

"She says she is," Miguel shrugged his shoulders. "She says she was adopted by the Levys, but she used to say she was Jewish, before it was popular to be Latino. I don't know, but if you ask me, she's not going to marry Alan García."

"Why do you say that? If he becomes mayor, don't you think all kinds of women will be killing themselves to become his wife? Why not her?" On television, while they were only glimpses, she seemed content to be in the public eye, to relish that kind of attention. Her dresses revealed one part or another of her anatomy and her hair was like that of the Hollywood actress Ann-Margret, flaming red and full.

"Have you ever seen Maritza?" Miguel asked. His tone during this conversation maintained an edge of sarcasm. I nodded and said I had seen her on television. "That woman's been engaged to eight different men—that I know of, maybe more. She's lived with who knows how many others. When that girl was born and the doctor slapped her on the ass, she cried, 'Ooh! Do it again!' ¿Entiendes, Méndez?" Miguel couldn't have been clearer, but he continued, "She's not marrying Alan García, man! The guy's got no life! He looks like a wooden dummy. His lips hardly move when he speaks— granted, he has my vote, but I don't sleep with him! Maritza's only with him because today he is the man of the hour. Once he's in office, she'll drop him. If we were talking about Perón or Marcos— but not García. She'll continue to be friendly with him to take advantage of whatever he'll have to offer, but she won't be around to pick up the pieces every time he screws up. It takes another kind of woman to be the wife of a politician. Maritza just likes to be in the limelight."

I hadn't interrupted him because I was lost in thought about how sexy she was and I wondered if that García fellow ever got enough life into him to satisfy her in bed. If I ever got my hands on her, I knew I would make her forget his name, mayor or no mayor. The fact that she was rich only enhanced the fantasy. That was the kind of woman I needed. If anyone required his career to be flashed around in the faces of the who's who, it was me. Laura had done as neat a job of dissolving all my contacts as she had in giving me recognition to begin with. When a woman chooses to knock a man down and keep him down, there is no underestimating her.

At the next fundraising dinner that Miguel invited me to for Alan García, I went. Fortunately, he managed to get a ticket for me, but it meant that I had to sit at the table of the company that had paid for it. I didn't mind pretending I worked for an insurance company. Whenever anyone asked what I did there, I told him I was a sculptor. They must have thought that it was an unusual position, but the caliber of imagination at those functions lacked the initiative to pursue the issue and they simply smiled.

I spent the better part of my evening eyeing Maritza, the main object for my having attended. She was sitting at the front table with her fiancé. "Don't they make a great couple?" one of the women at my table whispered to the one across from her. The other made a face. "Are you kidding? They're like night and day!" "That's what's so great about them!" the optimist beanhead insisted. After the succession of boring speeches, the bland boneless chicken dinner with something disguised as wild rice, the music began.

I watched Maritza leave Alan García to walk across the dance floor (she could have gone another route and not been so conspicuous, but that was not Maritza Marin-Levy's style) to the lounge area, presumably on her way to the powder room. I got up and went in that same direction, helping myself to a drink from the tray of one of the waiters.

Alan García in the meantime was busy shaking hands and making promises. I knew that they probably were not going to stay long, so I had to move quickly. It took an eternity for that woman to come out of the ladies' room. She was with two others, flocking around her like ladies in waiting in their tulle and synthetic silk evening dresses. Maritza was dressed incredibly. I say incredibly because it was incredible that the fiancée of a man in the eye of the critical public would dare to wear such a scanty piece. Her tits, white as flour and rising like loaves of delicious bread, came out at the top, while her ass, like ripened melons, was carved by the red fabric. She glanced at me as she passed and I got my signal. I knew she had noticed me.

"Excuse me," I said to her, stepping right in front and halting the little train of women that grew as it went. They all stared at me, but it was clear I was addressing her. "Would you like to dance?" One of them giggled and the others, with a semblance of decorum, went on their way, leaving Maritza alone. "Well, I was just about to leave, but if you want to . . ." she purred.

I took her by the arm, careful not to raise too many eyebrows as we walked out on the dance floor. It was crowded, so I didn't think Alan García could get a good look at us. "If I wanted to . . . ? And what about you? Didn't you want to?" I whispered. Her ears were studded with rhinestones. Her hair, pulled up, came loose around the pink ears and white neck. She was infinitely sexier in person. I pressed very close and she felt my hard on.

"Who are you?" she asked, not pulling away.

"Máximo Madrigal. I'm an artist. Haven't you ever heard of me?" I said, rubbing my chest against those lucious breasts.

"Yes, I think so. But why haven't I seen you before?" She smiled. Her green eyes were ablaze.

"I was out of the country. Look, when can I see you again?" I detected one of García's men coming toward us.

"Tonight, if you want," she answered.

"Tonight?" I repeated.

"Yeah. I'll meet you at Fullerton Beach." She saw the guy waiting for her and went with him. I stayed until they had all gone, Alan García, Maritza and the entourage, then I made my way directly to Fullerton Beach. She hadn't said the exact time for our rendezvous and it was possible she wasn't going to show up at all, but I didn't want to miss the opportunity.

It wasn't a bad night for sitting at the pier. Occasionally a drunk or a few delinquents went by. I didn't like the idea of being there alone at that hour, but I was carrying my trusty bone-handled switchblade and I was ready if anyone wanted to give me trouble. I must've waited two hours before I saw her coming toward me; the red dress and the orange hair weren't hard to miss, even in the dark.

"Is that you?" she called, still some distance away. Of course I would have answered yes, whoever I was. "Yes. It's me. Come here!" I called and she came, taking careful steps with the heels digging into the damp earth of spring and getting caught in the little cracks of the weather-beaten pier. "How long have you been here?" she asked, out of breath when she had reached me.

"Never mind," I said and put my arms around her to kiss her. I had waited long enough and there wasn't time to waste. I must say this, the woman was in full accord because it took every ounce of willpower to draw away from her to catch a breath.

I looked around. There was no one in sight. I put my suit jacket down on the cement and had her lie on it, all the while kissing her, the full mouth like a dish of oysters; the skin, goose paté luminous beneath the amber street lights. I removed her stockings and kissed her feet, and calves, moving up until, pushing her dress high around the hips, I could bury myself in the nest between her legs. I went crazy when I saw she wore crotchless panties!

She was moaning and pulling on my hair when I stopped and decided that was enough for the time being. It occurred to me that this one had always gotten her way. Of course, I was a man who had always had his. There was going to be a problem. I knew that she had come specifically to have sex with me. She needed a man to make love to her. Alan García, whatever else he may have been to his public, was not even in the most generous imagination a lover. Once I made love to her she would go off into the night content as a milked cow and go back to her future mayor-fiancé. What would I be? Nothing but a grub that was left to crawl back into the cracks of the rocks she was now lying on.

"Is something wrong?" She sat up, her hair everywhere, her dress practically coming apart. Her breasts were staring out at me, her legs were spread. It was all I could do to hold myself back. I put my head down. "And what about him?" I said, referring to García.

"Don't worry about him! What does he have to do with this?" she asked, stroking my temple. Her hand moved down quickly, over my shirt, down to my belt. I put my hand on hers and stopped her. "Are you going to marry him?"

"I don't know!"

"What's the matter? Don't you love him?" I nagged. I was squeezing her hand. I knew it must be hurting her, but she said nothing. "I don't know! I don't know!" she repeated.

"Doesn't he make love to you?" I asked finally. I pushed her away and got up to light a cigarette. I knew what I was doing. I didn't want to look at her, however, because she also knew what she was doing and she was sitting with her body bidding me to come back and take it. "Look, I don't want to talk about Alan García. He's a nice man, but . . . to be honest, he acts like he's not interested in women. What do I know! Maybe he prefers men." She adjusted her hair, but the rest remained the same.

"You want to say he's homosexual?" This surprised me. García looked dull, not gay.

"I don't know. I only know I need something more! And if you think you can give it to me, you'd better come here and do it or I'm going home!" Maritza put her arms out to me. I moved toward her to kiss her; I teased her a little, calculating to bring her to the point of orgasm and then I stopped again. "I'm not going to make love to you until you're mine. I'm not going to share you with Alan García or anyone else . . ." I said cockily.

Maritza stared at me. Her huge eyes moved back and forth to mine as if she thought I was joking. "Do you mean that?"

I pulled away from her and straightened my disheveled clothes. "Excuse me," I said, easing my jacket from under her. "Do you want to come to my place for lunch some day next week?" I asked nonchalantly. "I'm practically a chef," I added. She nodded. She was buttoning up and shifting fabric until most of her was back in concealment. It was all I could do to allow it, but it was part of my strategy.

"What day?" she asked, falling right into my hands, figuratively speaking, of course. I thought of a time and day for the following week and told her.

"Can I get you a cab?" I asked her, helping her up the slabs of concrete and back onto the grass where we would have to walk a distance to Lake Shore. She declined. "I live across the street," she told me. I looked beyond. High-rise buildings, apartments, and condos at the city's highest prices. She really did have money. Of course, Miguel had told me. It was just that it was always hard to imagine money until it became material form.

I kissed her again. "When you're mine . . ." I promised. I watched her go off and disappear past the circular driveway and the doorman of one of the buildings I had been awed by. Life was too sweet, I thought that night, already tasting Maritza Marín-Levy as my woman.

forty-eight

She was going to have a baby. She had known for only a few days that she was seven weeks along. Pregnancy had not occurred to her before. She had been careful to use a contraceptive and the intra-uterine device was checked regularly to make certain it was in place. Worried that she was suffering from an illness, she went to a doctor and was given the unexpected news.

She rejoiced over the child that was sprouting from her very soul, whom she would offer all that she had to give. She whispered the secret to friends, although she had yet to tell her family. Motherhood without marriage would mean only hardship in her mother's point of view and endless criticism from her stepfather.

It was just before her birthday when she heard from Eduardo. The contact came in the form of a post card. It didn't surprise her since Pastora's telepathy was sharper than usual recently, possibly because she now was accompanied by the spirit guides of the new soul she carried within. She had had Eduardo foremost on her mind for several days. He inquired as to how she was and asked if she would call him collect someday soon. He was now living out-of-state.

That weekend, on the telephone, they made small talk until Eduardo told her what had been on his mind. "I'm divorced now." There was a pause; she didn't know what to say. Divorce meant many things, but it didn't obliterate love. "Who wanted the divorce?" she asked.

"We both did. We both decided it was time to go our own ways. She's with her family and our son in Sapogonia." He sounded lonely.

Pastora felt unsure. "Eduardo, maybe you should have written to Sapogonia, not to Chicago."

"What do you mean?" he asked, after a pause.

"I mean, you seem nostalgic, but I don't know why exactly you wanted to hear from me."

"I missed you, Pastora," Eduardo's voice was still distant, but now it was also melancholy.

"Now that you're divorced, you miss me." Pastora, too, was sad.

"It's not that way at all," Eduardo protested gently. "I've missed you for a long time. I just didn't have the nerve to tell you sooner, I guess. I was afraid you would say just what you're saying."

All that swam through Pastora's head during the conversation was that she had a secret. If Eduardo was proposing a future with her, would his political convictions allow for family? "What did you expect me to conclude?" Pastora asked, getting hold of her emotions. "It's taken quite a while for you to admit that I am important to you and it comes when you are unequivocally alone."

"I've known how I've felt about you from the beginning," Eduardo insisted. "But I didn't have the right to tell you as long as I was married. Pastora, can I ask you something?"

"Yes."

"Will you give me the chance to show you I'm sincere?" Eduardo's request tore at her, and before she could let herself be persuaded because of sweet words that came when she, too, was alone, she told him it was too late and hung up.

At the end of the week the entreaty resumed. It took the form of another letter. He asked if he could fly in to see her. He explained again how he had been in a difficult position when they first met and, although he loved her then, he had thought it would've been selfish to speak of it when he was still married to another woman. As soon as he was certain that he was on his own, he began to allow himself to think of her again, to wish, hope, that it wasn't too late as she said on the telephone. Could he come to see her?

Pastora didn't look pregnant when Eduardo appeared at her door. It was her birthday. He didn't bring flowers or a gift, but in his practical manner asked what it was that she would like, and what she felt like doing on her day. It was a nice day for a picnic, or how about a day at the beach? He'd brought along his swimming trunks. Did she want to dress up and go have dinner? What did she need? New clothes? New tires for her car? Pastora laughed. Eduardo made her glad with his amiability and his good humor, and she was pleased that she let him come to see her; but she was very anxious over the fact that she had yet to tell him about the baby.

She didn't know what happened to the joy with which she had planned to share her news with Eduardo. Instead, she spat out all the fears that crept up like harpies in the night. She would be reproached by her mother, criticized as being careless, not to mention immoral. She protested against society for being so latent in developing safe and sure contraceptives for women. She condemned nature itself for placing on women the sole responsibility of the production of humankind. Pastora cried for a long while in Eduardo's arms.

"Look on the bright side," he said when she'd quieted down, stroking her brow. "You're going to have a baby, Pastora." Pastora looked at him, needing to understand the simplicity of the statement because, in its simplicity, she knew there was the consolation of truth. She was going to have a baby. She would have a son, or a daughter, made of the stuff of her body and soul. She would send out into the world no less a human being than all those who walked about the streets, who talked, who questioned, and who sometimes responded, who became the friends of some and the enemies of others. She would teach it to fly.

Eduardo appraised her face, his eyes with golden flecks drawing upon it as if she were the sun itself. "Do you think we could make a go of it?" he asked. She hesitated to speak. "The three of us?"

Eduardo ran a hand through her hair. "Of course! I would've loved you if you had had *five* children when I met you. Why shouldn't I love you now?"

Eduardo Madero returned to Chicago the following month and they were married in city hall.

When Pastora had reached her fifth month, she gave up the plan of having the child at home with Eduardo and the doctor without the interference of routine hospital procedures. She was sent in an ambulance to a hospital that had a special intensive care neonatal nursery. Pastora's body was threatening to expel the baby. She was affixed to an IV; there were fetal monitors on her belly and in her vagina, oxygen in her nose; she was an octopus of modern technology. She remained calm. She meditated.

In a week she was allowed to go home; she was to stay off her feet. The danger of losing the child was persistent and without question. She called a curandero that she knew and together they meditated on their respective spirit guides. On Tuesday and Friday nights, Don Fernando and two or three other believers of healing gathered to pray for Pastora's health and the well-being of the child-in-utero. They bathed her in herbs and oils, cleansed her spirit, as well as projected their own energies into her body to give her will.

During one of the sessions, Pastora communicated directly with a spirit guide. It was said she exchanged nine years of her own given life for the secure delivery of a healthy and sound child. When Pastora recovered from the trance, one of the women present gave her a startled look, but no one told her that sprouting dead center from the top of her scalp was a thick strand of hair that had turned brassy yellow. In a few days, it became silver as a lunar crescent.

During this episode, she was hospitalized again and, in the seventh month, it was decided she should remain in the hospital for her own safety as well as that of the child that was so anxious to make its entrance into the world. She was in isolation and Eduardo, as the husband, was the only visitor allowed. After work, Eduardo came with new books—he knew her favorite authors—or he brought a treat not available on the hospital menu. He never realized how it grated on her nerves to wait, hours on end, to not be allowed to get up, to be made to lie on one side to keep from going into labor, to be awakened throughout the night to have her vitals taken or the baby's heart monitored. She fell into quiet crying spells to comfort herself. When a nurse came in, she wiped her eyes. If anyone called, she allowed herself to sound irritable rather than depressed.

The bag had broken by the end of her seventh month and the doctors predicted the birth could only be staved off for a few days before both mother and child would be infected by the unsterilized environment of the womb. Although Pastora wasn't allowed to stand at all, the amniotic fluid dripped out at a steady flow and the child, with less fluid to keep its cord afloat, was in danger of strangulation. In the last days while they waited for the first sign of infection in her daily blood tests, the child's lungs matured at an accelerated rate and it moved into position. It was determined not to wait. A four-pound human space capsule prepared for launch into the vastness of life.

Eduardo was alerted that his wife was having the baby and he came to stay with her in the labor room. He changed the disposable sheets as they became soiled. He massaged her thighs and lower back and his talk soothed her twelve hours of labor. She meditated to get over each wave of pain and, when they came close in succession, she and Eduardo thought of a name for the baby. They had not discussed it before as other parents, who plan with anticipation, because of their dread of losing it.

"Do you want a daughter?" Eduardo asked, stroking the damp brow and moistening her dry lips with ice chips. Pastora licked her dry lips and without opening her eyes said, "It's a son . . ."

The rush of her labor was coming on again; she tried to sit up and, leaning over the table, vomited.

A short while later she was wheeled into the delivery room and people materialized from every direction: pediatricians, residents, nurses. A woman's voice was shouting, "Open your eyes! Watch your baby being born!" Pastora was concentrating on the doctor's instruction and didn't look up at the mirror. When the baby came out, easier and with more magnificence than a sunrise, he was crying bloody murder. The chief pediatrician who had promised Pastora she would be there to take charge, called out with relief, "Can you hear him? His lungs sound wonderful!" He wouldn't need to be attached to a respirator.

The male infant was examined, cleaned, dressed, and brought to its mother wearing a little cap and newborn clothes much too large for its four pounds. Four pounds. A human being complete with functioning brain, heart, tiny arms that waved about, the swollen features of a homely elf, all the weight of a large melon. Then he was taken away, sent to the neonatal intensive care nursery and placed in a warm incubator with the label: Baby Boy Madero.

Eduardo left after Pastora was taken to a room to sleep. He had to work that day and Eduardo wasn't one to take a holiday, even on such an occasion. He had a family to support. Pastora stayed up, exhilarated from the experience. She had given birth to a human being. She had felt it become a human being and grow in her womb, sucking from her body's resources, creating itself, and determining on its own that it was ready to come out to see light, to know firsthand the bodies attached to the voices it had heard from within its mother-domain.

Buried in Pastora's back yard, in a tightly closed jar, wrapped in a plastic bag, was the remedy she had prepared to heal, cleanse, and contract the expanded womb. It was made of rum, crushed garlic, the flowers, stems, and roots of rue, and was to be taken before breakfast every day for nine days. She had given birth and now she knew in the same way that death would be as magnificent a transformation to another existence.

forty-nine

The invention of a telephone apparatus that included a small screen so the caller and callee could view each other had existed since the mid-twentieth century. Surely the new century would find no self-respecting North American home without one. As late as the latter part of the twentieth century, however, even the most contemporary of homes resigned themselves to telephones where only a voice was linked to the desired party. In the voice was placed the influence of fantasy, illusion, emotion, and concentration.

Once Máximo called Pastora at one a.m. on a Tuesday. Her hair was in dozens of plaits; there was night cream on her face. She wore a pair of flannel pajamas in which nothing close to a body seemed to occupy them. He wanted to come to see her. She hid the sleep from her voice and consented. He was on his way. Pastora ran a bath, remembering the jasmine-scented oil. She douched with a half teaspoon of white vinegar in warm water. She pulled and tugged at her hair until all the plaits were unraveled and her long mane was free. She changed, slipping on a pastel camisole and a satin robe. When she opened the door, the robe parted.

On another occasion, a year earlier, Max had called Pastora and she was in bed with a man whose name was also Max; but it was his last name and was spelled with a double x. He asked if she was busy. She said she was. They hung up.

They had not seen each other for some time. One late August afternoon, Pastora lifted herself with considerable effort to answer the telephone. Her mother reached for it, but Pastora put her hand on the receiver first. It was Máximo's pungent hello, which spoke of so many things without having said them, on the other end. Pastora couldn't talk to him then, she said, and hung up. Her mother wondered but didn't ask about the brief conversation. Pastora made her way back to the rocking chair and eased herself down. She was in labor and awaiting an ambulance.

fifty

One day, my mother was at my door. Miguel and I had barely touched the first floor apartment with a paintbrush or mop, but Mamá seemed ready to do her share and rolled up her sleeves to get her new home in the U.S. into a presentable state. She came alone, by the way. Her husband adamantly refused to join her. "You'll return," he told her. "I might like it enough to stay," she warned him.

"If you prefer to be with your son than with your husband, so be it," he quipped, in the truly resigned manner of the Sapogón.

"I never said I was going so that I could be with my son. I'm going to the United States to start a new life," she corrected him in the true fashion of the feisty woman, who is universal.

This is exactly what she was intent on upon arriving. My mother, who had never had to work a day in her life, got a job in a small shop as a seamstress. Of course, the pay was abominable, although at least it was minimum wage; and the hours, if she wanted to make it worth her while at all, were from dawn to dusk. But along with the other women in need of the work, she did her job and did it well, and even earned bonuses for producing beyond the designated quota of gloves. Oddly enough, she appeared satisfied. It hadn't occurred to me until one evening when we had a little talk after dinner, but it was the first time that my mother was on her own.

I always assumed she enjoyed her role as the princess of the household, or as she was referred to by everyone, la niña. The only daughter, her brothers set out to protect her, her mother sheltered her, and her father, she said, oppressed her. "I know you loved your grandfather," she confessed to me that night, "but I always resented him; if it wasn't for him and for your uncles, your father would've married me. It was very difficult in those days to have a baby without being married. People talked about me and never did get over the fact that I didn't even try to hide you."

248

"What do you mean?" I wondered how one would go about hiding me.

"You know, send you off to stay with other relatives. But your grandfather wouldn't hear of it. At first he made me keep you as a way of making me face up to my sin." Mamá never talked this way before. In fact, Mamá had hardly ever talked to me about anything so pertinent to our lives before. "Then, no man wanted to marry me. Since I had a child, they thought I was one of those kinds of girls. You know. Well, anyway, none of the men that passed through that hole."

"Is that how you looked at the ranch, at San Co, as a hole?" I was mildly surprised, although I concurred.

"You don't know how long I yearned to move to the city." Mamá had that faraway look in her eyes. She wasn't talking to me, just saying things she had thought many times without telling anyone. "When you went off to Puerto Sapogonia—and then afterward to Paris . . . ah! I thought, if only it was me!" She laughed at herself. "That's why I never told you, like your grandfather did, to come back. As long as you were away, exploring the world, seeing things, learning new things, I was, too!"

"And what about when I told you I had found my father?" My mother never asked about Pío Madrigal. She frowned. "I loved that man, but I was young. I should have waited for him to marry me first."

"Do you really believe that? Or is that what your father told you?" I asked.

"I knew Pío wanted to go away . . . that's why I went ahead and did what I did. I thought that if I got pregnant he would stay, but even that didn't hold him. You're just like him. It's good that you got to know him."

"Life is curious, isn't it, Mamá? One is always waiting for it to surprise one, but it's not surprising at all. Do you want to see Pío again someday? You're practically a single woman again, you know!" I teased her. She laughed a girlish laugh, but she replied, "No. What would he see in me now? I'm old and ugly! Forget it!"

"You think *you're* old and ugly! Pío is the one who got old and ugly! I hope I take after you and not him in regard to aging! He's uglier than a tomcat hit by the atom bomb!" My mother gave me a look of disbelief and I considered that perhaps I had exaggerated; but I put my arms around Mamá and she laughed, letting me convince her that she was still the beautiful girl who had mesmerized the roaming gypsy from Galicia.

Mamá didn't like Maritza from the beginning, or perhaps it was the attitude that mothers can't help having when meeting the amours of their sons. Maritza stopped coming by and we had our rendezvous in her apartment. She was still engaged to Alan García, but it was irrelevant to me. I knew it was a matter of time and calculation. I never asked about him. I never displayed jealousy or the least concern for her public appearances with him. She found this contradictory to my original behavior, but could never get me again to say I wanted her to leave him.

You see, I knew that if I persisted, she would stay with Alan. It would mean that I was desperate to have her, and while a man is desperate he's not in a position to make demands. I made my demand once. She had heard it and that was enough. When she intentionally went on about him, or if he called while I was there, I pretended to completely ignore his existence. When she asked if I loved her, I dodged around the question until she gave it up. Sooner or later, she would get the idea.

Sooner or later that whole matter of Alan García as her fiancé was going to end anyway. I agreed with Miguel. Maritza was not the type to stick with an Alan García type; but she was the kind who would do anything for the man she loved. Finally, the day came when she told me she had called it off. She was still wearing the diamond he had given her. She was going to keep it, she said, stating that she had earned it for putting up with his banality as long as she did. I asked her if he had ever suspected anything about us and I was fairly let down when she said no. He never had the slightest clue that he had me as a rival. Actually, it was for the best, since later, when Alan García became mayor and he appointed Maritza the public relations person of Women, Aged, Disabled, and Special Affairs, he never objected to my presence and eventually even became friendly with me.

"I'm sure his people will find someone to replace me soon enough," she said sarcastically, lighting up a joint. Maritza smoked grass when she was agitated, then she would eat. "They'll pick some nice mexicana with long braids and the docility those women are known for and they'll be super happy together!" She tried to laugh despite her resentment.

"Why do you say that about Mexican women?" I asked. "I know Mexican women who are not docile in the least."

"Go with one of them then!" Maritza snapped. She fumed and left me alone. Presently, she calmed down and came over to me, purring and back to her old self, and I accepted her attempts to reconcile. I may have been calculative in many ways with Maritza, but after that first night on the beach, once I found out what it was to make love to her—I never held myself back for any reason, regardless of the consequences. It had taken days for me to have my first fill of her.

Unlike Laura, who was the daughter of a socially prominent family but who preferred discretion, Maritza made herself visible at every opportunity, using to her full advantage any notoriety she had been able to gain as a result of her background or activities. She was extremely active in every Latino issue in the city that was guaranteed to make the news. She joined the boards of various grass-roots organizations. She continued to campaign for Alan García; she went to parties in his honor and attended all the receptions. As much as I could, without forgetting that I was an artist and had to work—I was right there with her, shaking hands, making new and vital acquaintances. I had unwittingly joined in the famous tournaments of the gladiator sport I had once criticized Miguel Spanudis for taking too seriously.

Maritza immediately set to work on helping me get connections that led to free-lance work. I needed a larger and better place to work than Miguel's kitchen, which was where I still went because Maritza's studio apartment was out of the question for a sculptor. When I complained, she decided she would move with me and we found an ample-sized apartment located in a Latino community rather than a high-rise building on Lake Shore Drive. She said she knew her father wouldn't like it, but, after all, she wasn't going to live there alone.

Everything was going well again in my life when, just before the mayoral election, I got the symptoms: Pastora was festering beneath my skin once again. The last telephone number I had for her was disconnected and no one that we mutually knew could tell me if she even lived in Chicago anymore. Someone said she was in Mexico. Others said she was on tour. I even heard she was back in prison.

Then I heard of a concert that was to be broadcast live on public radio. Miguel was going to play a number on the program. It was for a benefit for a new home for underaged unwed mothers. Miguel had two tickets and offered them to Maritza and me. No sooner did Maritza hear Pastora was among the performers than she reacted with hysterical opposition. She looked at Miguel as if he had just suggested that she take hemlock. Miguel and I didn't understand.

"I'm not going to listen to that bitch!" Maritza was never one to skirt around an issue, tact being of the least consideration. "What has she ever done for the Latino community? She sings a song here and there and that's supposed to change things?" She was flushed with vehemence. I wondered if the two women were, in fact, mortal enemies. "I think it's a question of culture as a vehicle for change," Miguel said. "You're underestimating the value of culture as a contribution."

Maritza glared at him, with eyes like that of an animal when about to pounce. "You call what she does culture? I can sing better than she does when I'm down with a case of bronchitis!"

"Now, now, Maritza, darling. Let's not get catty. Pastora is talented and, regardless if she doesn't get involved in local affairs, she's paid her dues. She was up in prison for helping refugees from Sapogonia," Miguel informed her. Maritza looked surprised by this, but recuperated quickly. "And what does that make her now, Joan of Arc?"

"No, but . . ." I started in when she interrupted me. She flew up and waved a finger at me. "Don't defend her! Don't you dare defend her! You don't really know why she was put in jail! I've known her for a long time—she's vicious and doesn't give a damn about anybody but herself! All she's ever cared about is her image!" Maritza was in the heat of rage and I was taken aback at how she'd transformed at the mention of Pastora. Miguel and I both silently deduced that Maritza was acting like a jealous woman, although she would never have admitted this if we'd said it.

Miguel, on the other hand, was an ardent admirer of Pastora. He not only admired her guitar playing, which was in fact exceptional, as well as her songs, but he had also once been infatuated with her. It was Miguel who had come to me recently with the rumor that Pastora had gotten married. Neither of us wanted to believe it, but it seemed to be true. Others were beginning to whisper it as well.

"If you want to go see esa india fea sing her shit, you go without me!" Maritza ranted as she left the room. Miguel and I looked at each other. A few minutes later, Maritza came back into the room with a bag of marijuana and rolling papers. "What did you mean by that?" Miguel asked. I could see he was about to lose his own temper. "I wasn't talking to you," Maritza snapped. "I know," he said, "but what did you mean by 'ugly Indian'?"

"It's just an expression. I just mean that she's ugly," Maritza replied, looking embarrassed by Miguel's obvious determination to make a point.

"Máximo's grandmother was Indian, you know," Miguel continued. I suppose his logic told him that since Maritza had me on a pedestal as the adored lover, she would have to contradict herself to show prejudice against my background in the case of others. Maritza gave me a coy smile. "I know that. I already said I didn't mean to say Indian, only ugly."

"Pastora's always been proud of her Indian heritage. She's never tried to be anything else, but I can't say the same for everyone . . ." Miguel told her with insinuated accusation. I didn't see why he wanted to argue with her. She bid him on defensively, "Like who, for instance? Huh?" Maritza wanted a fight as well. Miguel had become for her the best friend in the lover's life that she couldn't help but resent, needed to compete with, wanted out of the way. If she ended up angry with him, she would be able to justify the ostracism. I went into the kitchen to serve myself a drink.

"When I first met you, Maritza, supposedly you were born in Cuba. That was during the days of the Venceremos Brigade, the popular left. It was cool to be associated with Castro. You were just a little cubanita taken away from your island home and adopted by gringos . . ." She started to interrupt, "That's . . ." He raised his voice over hers to continue. "That's since I've known you. But before then, you might've been Jewish, a typical little Levy going to private schools . . ."

Maritza got up to leave the room and saw that I was watching from the kitchen entrance and she halted. Miguel continued to talk, his voice raised. "Later, you became Puerto Rican. That was about the time of the Humboldt Park riot. You got involved in all the hullabaloo that followed and you were telling people you were from Mayagüez. You may have gone on vacation to Mayagüez with a Puerto Rican boyfriend, but I doubt that you were born there!"

Maritza's eyes reddened. "I was born in the county hospital in New York. The Levys adopted me right afterward and I don't know if

253

my mother was Cuban or Puerto Rican, but it doesn't matter! I'm still hispana and I'm not trying to pass for anything else!" Her jaw was set and I knew that if Miguel hadn't managed to get her where she was most sensitive, she wouldn't have conceded to his accusations.

Miguel was out for blood. "Of course, you're Latina *now*, Maritza! It's cool to be Hispanic, whatever that means! It's so damn cool, we're gonna have a Hispanic mayor running things around here and guess who had to be seen all over town with the future mayor of Chicago? Why little Miss Maritza Marín-Levy herself! Proud to be Hispanic from her head of red hair to her red painted toenails!"

"That's right! And what of it? When Alan gets elected, you better believe I'm gonna have an office at city hall! And if there's anything I can do for any of my *friends*, I'll be more than happy to go out of my way!"

Miguel shrugged his shoulders, unimpressed. He had accomplished what he wanted and he was satisfied.

"If you feel that way, we won't go. Don't worry about it anymore. It doesn't matter. Miguel will understand if we stay home and listen to him on the radio," I told her and winked at Miguel. He turned away. "Hey, I don't care if you listen to me or not . . ." he muttered.

"Just as long as we don't have to hear that whore when she comes on!" Maritza got in the last word and I never again mentioned the name of Pastora around her. It wasn't surprising that Maritza reacted so strongly at the mention of Pastora. It seemed that everyone I met had something to say about Pastora and it was sometimes hostile. Aside from the proverbial "witch," they called her man-hater, castrator. Women said she was egocentric. And Maritza had just called her an ugly Indian.

Pastora was part Indian, in fact, but far from ugly. If she hated men, men didn't hate her. They feared her. Far from castrating them, she made their passions rise. I, for one, found it harder and harder lately to get an erection without thinking of her. As much as Maritza dressed and behaved so aptly in lascivious ways, it was Pastora's subtlety, her illusiveness, that tormented me. And she was egocentric, but, after all, why wouldn't she be?

254

fifty-one

Until the last day of the year, Chicago streets were oddly barren of precipitation. On New Year's Eve, a storm began that eventually left residents stranded at whatever place they chose to see the old year out.

Máximo, dressed in a velveteen tux and patent leather shoes, went with Maritza to celebrate the new year at Adolfo Zaragoza's residence in the Gold Coast area, seventeen stories high, in a two-room apartment, where the walls were covered with clippings, posters, etc.: mementos of a lengthy career as a director of Latin American theatre.

Zaragoza, a short man in his late fifties, had had little success outside of his own country and, with the exception of one or two off-off-Broadway opportunities, was virtually unheard of and much less regarded by the North American public. As discouraging as it was to an individual in the creative arts not to be recognized by the new grande madame of *art nouveau*, he accepted its dismissal gracefully, moving to Chicago to dedicate himself to writing critiques for various magazines. His new business of winery outlets (with a partner of questionable repute who spent most of his time on the East Coast) was his financial salvation. Nonetheless, in particular circles, Adolfo Zaragoza was arguably a man to know, because he made it a point to know everyone worth knowing. This, of course, was Max's evaluation of the situation when Maritza told him of the party.

"But why didn't he address the invitation to both of us or send one to me?" Máximo sulked, pretending that he would not go unless he was assured that his own reputation as an important personage of the Latino celebrity set of Chicago had not been underestimated.

"¡Ay m'ijo!" Maritza ran a white hand with manicured nails of fuchsia color and tropical illusion through Máximo's beard. "Adolfo doesn't know you live here too! He probably doesn't even know that you're in Chicago right now! Everyone knows you had an exhibit in Brazil. They probably think you're down there now."

"What shit!" Máximo pushed the caressing hand away. "If it wasn't for you, I WOULD have been there right now!"

"Look, Máximo, don't start with me. ¡Coño! I already told you it was a simple misunderstanding. I didn't receive the calls they claim they left on my answering machine about your expenses being covered to fly down there for the show! At least Mario is taking care of things!"

Mario, a Brazilian friend of Maritza's, had promised to keep abreast of the particulars of the exhibit. Máximo had serious doubts about her friend's ability to follow through but, under the circumstances, he could do no more than hope for the best.

"What are you saying? You mean that if you had a show in Brazil, you wouldn't want to be there? Didn't you think I was worth having my expenses paid so that you would have taken the initiative to organize that, insist on it? ¡Caramba, mujer! Why do I need you if all you can do is screw me up?"

Maritza stood up. She pulled down her skirt, which had slid up around the fleshy thighs and accentuated the high ass. "Go to hell, Máximo. If you don't want to go to Adolfo Zaragoza's party, I'll go by myself . . . and I'll have a good time, too!" She went out of the room and down the hall. Máximo listened to her footsteps. If they stopped midway in the corridor it meant she was getting her coat and would go out to who knows where. If they continued, she was going to the kitchen to eat, a lesser reaction than running off whenever she was upset. They continued.

He lay back on the futon rolled out in the middle of the bedroom. After she fed her face and calmed down, she would be back. He would give her ten minutes to stuff a piece of roast beef into her mouth that her mother had sent over the night before, or the cold yucca leftover from dinner. She liked Corn Flakes, but usually had them only at night before going to bed, dashed with plenty of sugar and pieces of fruit. All of it first went to the ass, then to the round face. He noticed Maritza wasn't looking quite the same as when they met the summer before, but then he, too, had been putting on a little weight, he had to admit.

If she didn't come back in the room and didn't implore that he go with her to the party, he would go anyway, without her. He would rent a tux and take a bottle of Dom Perignon, the one in the

256

refrigerator waiting for an occasion, and he would send Maritza to hell. As long as she did nothing extreme, like show up at Zaragoza's with another man or leave the party with one, he would ignore her as coolly as if they had never met. In Maritza's case, this was all he could say that could be considered extreme because it was certain that between the time she arrived and left, she would not be alone for one moment. Maritza exuded sex. She smelled of her own musk.

Máximo got up and went to the kitchen. He took out a can of beer from the refrigerator and popped it open without looking toward the counter where he knew Maritza was standing up, eating. "Well, chico, are you going to the party with me or not?"

"Oh, the question is am I going to go with you? Are you sure your boyfriend, Adolfo, won't mind?"

"What are you talking about? Adolfo and I are just friends."

"No one is just your friend, Maritza. What do you think, I'm stupid? Make a fool of Adolfo but not me!"

"I don't have to make a fool of you, you do it yourself. ¡Coño, hombre!" Maritza slammed her fork against the plate and, as she passed Máximo, he blocked her way, thrusting a blown-out chest before her. "Where are you going?"

"Get the fuck out of my way!" She pretended he didn't intimidate her and that she didn't love him as she did, but Máximo knew his effect on her.

"Do you want me to go with you?" he asked, putting his arms around her. Maritza put her hands around Máximo's back, under the shirt. She loved him without comprehending him. In fact, Maritza understood much less about much more than he realized and sometimes the reverse, which is to say that neither understood the other.

They took a day for shopping and it was Max who selected the dress she would wear to the New Year's Eve party. It was kelly green of a new synthetic fabric that was reminiscent of fake leather. He thought the color would bring out her eyes. He instructed her specifically, as well, to do something about the roots coming out in contrast to the auburn hair.

They were in a good mood throughout the day of the party, but Máximo, having had half of a six-pack of beer on an empty stomach, began to have the delusions of the jealousy-ridden once again as soon as Maritza happened to mention Zaragoza's longstanding friendship with her father. Máximo declared that if Zaragoza had actually been around Maritza for that length of time and had never made a pass at her, he had to be blind. Maritza responded that while it was undeniable that Zaragoza had his eyesight in tact, she believed he was homosexual. She had never known him to be romantically associated with any woman and she, like other acquaintances of his, suspected that his business partner was also his lover. Máximo called her a liar. It was the classic excuse a woman gave her man to reassure him he was not being cuckolded under his nose. "Watch yourself tonight," he warned her as they left the apartment.

They arrived at the party fashionably late, as one could be inclined to say of this celebrated couple. They had to stop at Maritza's father's house first. He was ill and they were asked over for dinner. The snowstorm made driving hazardous so that they proceeded on the road at a snail's pace. Máximo considered Maritza a reckless driver, but he also knew he had had enough to drink, so he turned the keys over to her.

One look at Adolfo, whom he had not seen before, and Máximo was convinced that the man was a pedophile. He was reasonably attractive, although visibly out of shape and aging without finesse. "He's wearing a toupee, the vain idiot," Máximo muttered to Maritza. She gave him a repulsed look and went off to help herself to a drink.

"I didn't know that Maritza and you are friends! I've known her father for years, yes, and her mother, of course. Yes, many years." Adolfo had an expression that deceived the charming smile of piano-key capped teeth. His eyes closed partway like that of a cobra sizing up its victim. "I've heard of you, you know!" Adolfo continued. Max concentrated on trying not to appear drunk. "Times are not good, Máximo, otherwise, I would happily purchase one of your works! I've heard they're quite good . . ."

Máximo moved away so that the hand Adolfo had placed on his shoulder slid off. "But you're a businessman now. Times must certainly be better for you than for the artist."

"Don't kid yourself, Max. It's hard on everyone these days." Adolfo looked around at his guests, feigning distraction. Máximo sensed Adolfo didn't like to be pressed. He also suspected they had felt a mutual dislike for each other and the first reason that came to mind was a green blur in the other room at the bar. Adolfo turned back to Máximo. "So tell me, how long is it that you know Maritza? I've known her since she was a child, you know."

"Were you screwing her since then?" Max inquired vindictively under his breath. Adolfo cleared his throat and adjusted his tie. "I don't know what the problem is, Max, but I look upon her as a daughter. Maybe you've had too much to drink."

"Like a daughter? Is that why you didn't invite her father to-night? He didn't even know you were having this . . ." Máximo waved a hand, challenging Adolfo. The best way to be rid of his demons was to have them out in the open right away. Why shimmy around all night pretending that each held a secret from the other? "Enjoy yourself, mi amigo. Any friend of Maritza is welcome in my home, but remember that you're drinking and you don't want to regret anything later."

Adolfo sauntered off and went directly to Maritza. Max watched the decrepit fart whisper something to her and she looked over her shoulder at Max, nodding, and shortly came over to him. He waited for her reproach, a scolding, a hypocritical display of indignation. He would pick up his coat and leave her there with the flea's turd, but she kept silent. She locked an arm into his and smiled pleasantly at the crowd.

He tugged away from her and went to the next room, where his host had a lavish buffet and bar with a decent sample of liquor. He poured himself a glass of scotch and looked around to see who he would recognize in the crowd. There were several familiar faces, but no one he knew personally. A news anchorman, who he believed was a Chicano from Texas, was very smug in the company of a blond gringa with luscious breasts. There were two or three academic types he had seen at a recent music conference at Northwestern Universi-ty. He saw a woman whom he didn't really know, but whom he had asked once to go out with him. She worked at a gallery on Ontario Street. She had turned him down. Her husband (he hadn't known there was a husband at first) was with the Museum of Contemporary Art and kept a close eye on his wife. Max thought it unnecessary. She was no great beauty and apparently she was one of those women who lived for the sole purpose of being devoted to her man.

For a while Max made conversation with an older man who sported a distinguished salt-and-pepper beard. He seemed genuinely intrigued by the fact that Max was an artist. He said he was the president of his own computer company; computers, of course, were the hottest investment since real estate. However, when Maritza found Máximo, his new friend lost immediate interest in Max's elaboration on his technique and made it evident he found the fake leather dress infinitely more fascinating. The computer man was alone on New Year's Eve. Max felt an unusual twinge of compassion and walked off, leaving him in Maritza's company.

He continued to guzzle double shots of scotch until his paranoia that Maritza was deceiving him with Adolfo Zaragoza became vague. In the living room, which was crowded, he set upon taking women out to dance. He was too inebriated to consider if any one was with a male escort. He simply took a woman by the hand; if she came along, fine. If not, there was always another one who would. He showed off his physical agility with salsa steps, mambo, rock, anything that played on the stereo. Finally, he was doing palmas and imitating the dance steps of the flamenco artists he had played for in Spain. Although he'd never taken lessons, he danced now from memory of what he thought they had done on hard wooden platforms, a stilted angling of the arms, elbows in the air, a tilt of the head, eyebrows arched, heels constantly stabbing the carpet to the chanting of an internal rhythm. Some clapped and did what they thought were palmas, but then Max was only doing what he thought was flamenco. He was in the heat of the motion when he thought that the scotch might move its way back up from his stomach. He lost his footing and toppled over the woman who had bravely stuck with him throughout his performance, although he'd seemed incognizant of her and without need of partnership.

Máximo slumped down in a chair and accepted another glass from someone who congratulated him on his dancing. He waited until the room had ceased to spin and drank down the liquor. By then it no longer mattered if it was one thing or another, but he perceived he was drinking champagne. He was sweaty and loosened his tie. Maritza now took over the dance floor, gyrating with a combination of African tribal steps and belly dancing. Her partner couldn't keep his eyes off different parts of her body that vibrated independently of each other. Adolfo Zaragoza, from where he stood and watched, had a perfect view of her backside.

I got up and went to the kitchen, where a lively group was indulging in what I presumed was cocaine. One of the women offered some to me, but I shook my head and stepped away. The truth was I had abused my body with so much contamination that evening that one more substance would have brought on a short circuit. Then I saw someone who for the life of me I wouldn't have imagined went in for those kinds of gatherings. She was dressed in a

260

turquoise Oaxacan costume, embroidered with white and yellow flowers. She wore a necklace of beans and nuts.

I was provoked to question my senses. Pastora was looking directly my way, yet I had the feeling I was seeing not Pastora at all but an aberration. Not solely because she was so ethereal, but because for a fraction of a second, the time it takes to blink, she *was* transparent. I went over to her nevertheless. She leaned against the broom closet door, holding a wine glass, and she took a sip, giving me the chance to think of something to say. "What are you doing here?" I asked. I realized that it didn't matter, but it would have been disappointing if she was with someone. What mattered was that I hadn't seen her in months, indeed, perhaps more than a year. I tried to remember what was the last rumor I had heard of Pastora, but I was too drunk. I preferred to kiss her, but I didn't dare.

"Are you alone?" I asked, hesitant to look over my shoulder for fear of seeing someone about to claim her. She shook her head. She smiled as if she enjoyed discouraging me. "No, I'm not alone. How could I be alone on a night such as this?" She smiled again. The question wasn't intended to be answered. I felt a combination of jealousy and insecurity, as always when a woman let me know I had competition and she knew she had the advantage in the game. "Of course, how could a woman like you be alone tonight?" I agreed, bitter with the fact. It sounded insincere, but I didn't know how else to say how enticing I found her.

Then I got an idea. I gestured to open the broom closet and she moved aside. It was empty, except for the broom, and large enough to walk into. I looked around; the cocainers were oblivious to me and I pulled Pastora into the broom closet. She came willingly and as soon as we had adjusted ourselves in the dark cubicle and closed the door securely, I kissed her and probed beneath her costume. I was delighted by her complacency and I debated only momentarily whether I should make love to her in the closet. It was possible that her escort might find us, or heaven forbid, Maritza, but this only heated the embers. No one would have thought to look for us in the broom closet, I concluded, so long as we remained *very* quiet . . .

Maritza slapped me, holding my head under her arm. "Wake up, love. Please!" I heard her from fifty kilometers away. She wasn't even in the same room. Where was Maritza that she sounded so far away? I came to and saw twenty other faces in addition to Maritza's encircled above me. I was startled suddenly because the only thing I remembered was being with Pastora in the broom closet. I sat up and ran my hands through my mussed hair. I gathered I had been unconscious, but I didn't know what had happened between my lovemaking and the fainting spell. Pastora was nowhere in sight. From Maritza's concern for my state, I deduced that she hadn't seen Pastora and we hadn't been caught in a compromising position. "¿Qué pasó?" I asked Maritza.

"I don't know! You passed out! How do you feel?" She was genuinely distraught and I could see that she was totally confused as to what I had been up to. I got up, with her insistence to help, where I would have a better view of things. "You fell out of the broom closet!" someone told me. Someone else added, "Yeah, like something out of a Charlie Chan movie. We thought someone had killed you and hid you in the closet . . ."

I listened, but I heard nothing mentioned about Pastora. I didn't want to let on, so I couldn't ask either. I told Maritza to get me a drink, but she refused. "You passed out from drinking too much," she whispered. "Look, you spilled your drink on your tux. You smell like a damn brewery." I gave her a dirty look, but I felt self-conscious and furtively wiped the wet spot on the jacket.

"If you were looking for the bathroom, mi amigo," came Adolfo's voice from behind Maritza, "it's down the hall and to the left . . ." He looked disgusted with me and went off to attend to his other guests. "Why would he say that?" I asked Maritza. She looked a little disgusted with me herself and sucked her tongue, "¡Coño! You really are drunk; let's go home." "What's the matter?" I asked indignantly. She signaled down to my fly with her eyes. It was opened. "I think you went into the closet to take a leak, but you passed out before . . ." she said, and walked off.

It was well past midnight by then, the event taking place about the time I had been told I was fumbling around in the broom closet looking for the light switch to use the services I believed were there. Pastora wasn't anywhere in the apartment. Given her sly ways, I concluded she had cleverly evaded detection and left.

fifty-two

Two weeks later, Miguel called to remind me of the public radio concert. Despite Maritza's antagonism, I set upon hearing it, trying to make her understand that since Miguel and I had studied music together, it was important to us to give each other this feedback. She reluctantly resigned herself to it. I no sooner turned on the radio than we heard Pastora's voice on the broadcast. It was that same droned speech she was noted for. I was able to hear her say she had just returned from California, where she had given a concert over the holidays and had attended some conference or other, before Maritza came in with seething intolerance and turned it off. She actually leered at me and I got up and left the apartment.

At the neighborhood tavern, I asked if I could turn on the radio. The few customers there were watching a fight on television and the bartender advised me not to insist. I had a beer and went out to the car to listen to the rest of the program. Miguel was in good form and I was proud that he managed so well, as it had been a while since he'd played for anyone. There were readings by local poets and again, Pastora was introduced. She was allowed one last song. It was an original composition. "Mi amor es un quetzal." When she finished, I went back into the tavern to get drunk.

It was closing time, the favorite in the ring had lost, and the place was sullen with depressed patrons. In my wallet I carried a paper with what Miguel had assured me was Pastora's new number. I went to the back to call her. It rang several times before she picked it up. She could have been sleeping by that hour, but it didn't make any difference.

"I heard you were in California," I said to her. I hadn't asked if she could talk at the moment, how she was, or if I had disrupted her sleep. I was obsessed with one thought.

"Yes," she answered calmly. If she was bothered by my call, she didn't indicate it.

"How long were you there?"

She paused, then, in her concise way, answered. "I spent Christmas in San Francisco, then I went to a conference in Sacramento."

"So you were back by New Year's Eve?"

"The conference took place after New Year's and I flew back in January. Why?"

"No reason. By the way, I heard you this evening on the radio, with Miguel Spanudis." I felt lightheaded and I hoped she wouldn't detect I had been drinking.

"Yes?"

"You should work out that song of yours a little more. I think you could do more with it. ¿Entiendes?"

"Máximo?"

"What?"

"Is that why you called?"

"No. I called because I have nightmares of you, because you are permanently engraved in my memory, because . . ."

"Please don't call me anymore, Máximo," she said in a steady voice and hung up.

I slammed the receiver down and went home. The apartment was empty. I took off my clothes, letting them drop by the side of the bed, and went under the covers. My eyes had just closed and drunkenness had set the room in motion when the telephone next to the bed began to ring. I reached over for it, but no one answered on the other end. I knew there was someone there. I wanted to say, "Pastora, ¿eres tú?" but I thought again. There was a better chance that it was Maritza checking to see if I had gotten back, so that then she could return too, having shown me that she was no ninny to sit home waiting for me. I went to sleep.

That night and the six nights that followed, I was seized by the worst nightmares I ever had of Pastora. They were so vivid that, after the second or third night, I was reluctant to go to bed. I made love to Maritza, hoping to put out the images that were so convincing that I questioned the possibility of another dimension taking place simultaneously, but it didn't help.

In my nightmares Pastora's husband—whoever he was, whose face I wouldn't even know in my waking hours, but in the dream, it didn't matter—came after me. In self-defense, I killed him. In one dream it was hand-to-hand combat. In another, I took the gun he had away and shot him with it. In the next, we struggled and I stabbed him. In each dream I killed her husband and then the nightmare really began. People pursued me, they hunted me. I was tracked down like a monstrous beast, and no matter where I went, someone finally discovered me. I would escape, but the pursuit continued until I awoke.

Now this was probably the simplest of dreams for any therapist of average intelligence to analyze, but I didn't interpret it to be the result of guilt, jealousy, or even fear that her husband was the type to go after a man for desiring his wife. I *knew*, because, as I said, the dreams were three-dimensional—they had breadth, dialog, and vibrant color—that Pastora was provoking those dreams. And I didn't call her again for half a year.

fifty-three

"Tell me about your son." There. He had said it and, having said it, he had banishd the enigma, the mystical androgyny by virtue of his verbal acknowledgment that she had given birth; yes, that she had been with another man, other men. She was not of stone.

She was the personification of the diety Earth Mother, tied to the land by vastness, umbilical cords, penises. She had given birth to a man. From her body had come forth a being with testicles and brain, with heart and hands. Yes, that might still qualify her as a goddess, but not the objective one of once, not of the heart of granite detached from mundane mortality. For she had given birth to a male child and from then on she could no longer see into the eyes of a man and look upon a stranger.

"Tell me about your son," he repeated. She glanced at him for a second, like a bird. Pastora, taciturn in character, had never been one to say what wasn't necessary. She said things once. They were stated. She never volunteered information that wasn't vital at least to one of them, or both.

He regarded her now, slightly fuller. Although her arms were almost boney and her hands and bare feet showed protruding veins, as if unaccustomed to wearing shoes and familiar with hard work, they still had a certain gracefulness about them, like that seen in statutes of martyrs and saints. He looked away, because he did not like to entertain such comparisons with Pastora. Her breasts had been pulled down by gravity from nursing; the nipples no longer stood perpendicular. Her hair was cut rashly along the shoulders, like that of a Tupi Indian. Pastora ceased to be the exalted celestial being. Pastora now labored and toiled like every woman.

"Tell me about your son." This time she said it, in monotone parroting. "And what would you have me tell you, señor?"

"What is it like?"

"One's wings are heavy."

"Why did you have him?"

She smiled; her eyes were off at a distance. She smiled to herself because she kept her secrets for her private pleasure. "To lighten the weight of my heart." He laughed cynically and longer than was natural. Was this a romantic message she'd interpreted from a propagandist women's magazine? She sounded worse than the Spanish soap operas that played faithfully for wide audiences throughout the Americas night after night. Where was it carved that a woman had to have a child to be fulfilled, to accomplish her life's purpose? Granted, it was true for some, perhaps even most, but Pastora had always been testimony to the exception.

Máximo was enraged. Had he wanted her wings weighed down; it would've been with him, riding on her spirit, energy, and compassion—because now he knew she was capable of self-sacrifice. He would've used her for his own purposes, wrung her. He sighed heavily. His rage passed to a sensation that brought a tremor to his voice. He remembered when he first heard her sing. He had flown with her song, not her mind or body, but on her spirit, which was transmitted to the visible world through her music. Sing for me, Pastora, for me alone. He had never implored it. He had sat in the back of an auditorium where he was among the sprinkling of an audience. Later, he had made sure when she was leaving that he was at the door where he could manage to catch up to her.

That night he kidnapped her and took her to his place. He criticized her black dress, "You always look like death," her mutton coat, "You look like a bear," her performance, "When will you learn to pronounce Castilian correctly?" and in the silhouettes of his room, he undressed her. She never asked if he loved her. How could she have dared? She, who never pretended to have sincere affection for any man. He had never told her he loved her.

Máximo swallowed hard. He was overcome with emotion. Too much had passed between them. How many times had he been with other women, any given one of whom, at that moment, he couldn't so much as recall a single detail about, as compared to this one whom he had only made love to, at best, a dozen times? Years gone with sparse remembrances and the solid one of her initial rejection implanted like a motor that drove him to her periodically where he was reminded again and again of her strangeness and its lure.

Now she had a son and the son was not him nor was she his and it was all intricate and inexplicable, but they had been alienated forever by that single fact.

He cleared his throat. "Do you still sing?" The moisture in his eyes made him blink repeatedly. If she noticed he was moved, she made no sign of it. "Now and then, in the shower!" A small laugh, a laugh without humor. She added, "I have a concert later this year in New Mexico."

Pastora Velásquez Aké had a concert, one, in New Mexico. Well, let us all sing the praises, the woman was on her way to stardom! We shall hope that fame and fortune shall not spoil our modest lass from home, but she will be remembered fondly by all those she left behind! "And what will you do meanwhile? Are you singing anywhere locally?"

"I don't have the time."

Máximo's patience wore out. What took her time? What possibly could take the time from an artist to do her work? Was it because she was a woman? Because women, in their inevitable pining for motherhood and the true love of a good man, gave it all up in exchange, considered it an even forfeit? "Are you working at anything else, then?"

"I take care of my son."

"And does that take all of your time, taking care of your son?"

"It takes a good deal of energy caring for another human being. I have pupils; I earn a small income. It helps to feed him, clothe him, to keep us in a warm house in winter and an airy one in summer. When he is sick, I stay up nights with him."

"Pastora, from any other woman I could accept it, the glorification and martyrdom of motherhood! But from you . . .?"

"Máximo . . ." She stood up and sighed. He became alert. "I may have asked to be born with this." She patted her lower stomach and then pointed to her crotch. "I may have asked before entering this life to return here to learn what it was to be a vessel, to be biologically bound to all things, to be bound beyond will, because operations and interferences in that course do not separate a woman, they do not free her."

"But are you freer as a mother?"

"I was not free before and I am not saying that I only conceded to a biological destiny. When you came to have sex with me, possessed by a need that it be me you violated . . . you went off afterward,

268

relieved of that need and charged with creative energy. You diffused it in your work, pursued your individual dreams. I, too, went on with my work. I pursued my ideals. But in my subconscious, I began to count the days, keep track of the internal cycle. And like any mechanism, the moment it failed, when it was out of synch, it was out of my hands."

"How—out of your hands?"

"It's humanity, Máximo. The moment you and I acted like mating animals, that is when we submitted to our mortality. We're not here forever, Máximo. And my son is not a continuation of you or me, who've considered ouselves exceptional individuals among the species, but a continuity of the species, a simple and humble fact."

"You aren't saying he's mine, are you?"

"There are societies in which children born into them belong to all. All are mothers and fathers of the child, all other children its siblings."

"But in reality, it has only one mother and one father . . ."

"No, in reality, there are no mothers and no fathers . . ."

Máximo fell into a silence, interrupting the discourse. He was unusually drained. If it were his child, his son, how would he feel? What difference would it make in his life? Would he insist on having part in raising him? Would he negate her claim? Somewhere deeper in his mind, he knew this contemplation was futile. Neither would she tell him if the boy was his nor did he care. It was, as she had said, the procreation of the species. The discussion on mortality only made him feel the urgency to pursue his goals. They were a way of preserving his notion of immortality, much more than a son, who grows to become a stranger, or worse, betrays you, your ideals.

"Sex and death are one, Pastora."

"Man has believed this."

He rose and left.

fifty-four

She went through her closet with the same objective as when she dressed for a stage performance. Pastora reluctantly admitted to herself that her image mattered no less to her than to the others who were attending the new mayor's press conference at the Daley Plaza. The ultimate in fashion, even in Chicago, was a visible sign of a person's success. Readily, it was a standard pressed much more upon women than it was on men, since the female mode accelerated in change, while men maintained subtle, classic looks. Latino professionals, a new breed in white-collar America, now like their white American counterparts, were enjoying the impressions made by tweeds, herringbones with patched elbows, and wing-tipped shoes, although these were occasionally substituted by personal taste with polyester, synthetic blends, and unorthodox colors and patterns.

Dressed in her best, like a country woman on her way to a Sunday service, she left the security offered by the refuge of her home and went to the meeting where she was invited to attend and to possibly address the mayor—at what feared to become a zoo. Since García's election into office, Latinos had become visible at all levels of local government in an unprecedented manner. From city hall to the grass-roots levels, García's constituents were demanding his immediate attention to their needs.

As a member of the new Colloquium of U.S. Latinas, she was assigned to go to the first press conference hosted by the newly elected mayor of her city. The CUSL was based in Sacramento, California, and she was its official Midwest delegate. The organization was geared at theoretical debate and exchange and was not at all liable to gain popular recognition. To date, it held a stronghold of only about a dozen active members across the United States. Yet, they took themselves to heart.

The hall outside the conference room was crowded with anxious faces, university administrators, office workers, educators and union leaders, smiling and greeting one another. Beads of sweat apparent on many indicated that the atmosphere was less pleasant than one would have liked to assume. The majority of the faces belonged to Latinos, of every hue and hair texture, but to the knowledgeable eye, nonetheless of Latin American heritage. A fair percentage were blacks. There were also several white and Jewish faces. In Chicago, one would never say one was simply Chicagoan, much less, American, but hyphenated and belonging to a particular ethnic origin.

Mayor García arrived promptly and everyone went in and took seats; some where they would be in the television camera's view; others, where they could observe every action made by the mayor and the members of his staff that were present; and the rest just clamored to get a seat.

It wasn't certain if Pastora would be among those asked to address the meeting, but in her attaché she carried a short presentation she was asked to write. She also brought a copy of the pamphlet they had recently published through a feminist press and were distributing through supportive bookstores nationwide. It dealt with the history and present status of U.S. Latinas. There were issues the group was presently working on for the next publication, but such was the controversy among them that it put Pastora on guard, fearing it would soon degenerate because of it.

In front, at a long table facing the public was Perla, sitting two people away from the mayor. Perla was now co-owner of a reputable gallery. Consequently, she joined boards of cultural organizations and, as a result, was asked by the García administration to consult on such affairs related to the Spanish-speaking communities of the city.

Sitting at the far end of the table, Pastora recognized Maritza Marín-Levy. As Pastora had understood it for a decade, Maritza was attempting to follow in her father's footsteps by attending law school at Northwestern, but she never finished.

Pastora found a seat in the middle of the room and took in the view as nonchalantly as she thought possible. Turning back for a brief moment, she saw Máximo Madrigal. He was standing in the back near the door. He wore a cream-colored linen suit and a conspicuous straw hat. A dapper touch, but one that subtly contradicted his presumed cavalier's manners, since he had not removed it, probably so as not to ruin the total effect of his ensemble.

Diego Cañas was also in the crowd and Pastora suspected that, while he might not have been asked to the meeting at all, he would find a way to get attention. Their eyes met and he greeted her with a slight nod of the chin. She smiled politely in return and hoped he wouldn't think to sit next to her. When he finally decided to break into the press conference, she wouldn't want to be mistakenly associated with him. She had not forgotten the days when she had put so many hours into helping him with his gallery/theatre space project that he never completed.

Near him seated together were two other women Pastora knew only as casual friends from over the years: Teresa, the poet, and Juana, who had worked for the Office of Fine Arts during the past Byrne and Washington administrations.

Mayor García was subdued and carried himself with guarded reserve. He was approximately in his early forties and had lived in Chicago since he'd finished college. He was born in Michigan and had attended law school at Loyola, during which time he immediately thrust himself into community politics. That was during an epoch when it was uncommon for youth not to have interest in social reform. He had been the youngest alderman in the city's history and no less outdone by the fact that he was also a Latino.

The press conference began. Issues were raised and addressed in order of their priority on the mayor's agenda. Various groups in private industry as well as those representing social services spoke up when most unexpectedly the representative for the Colloquium of U.S. Latinas was asked to address the floor. Before Pastora stood up, collecting her thoughts, she could only deduce that someone with a certain influence with the mayor must have made it a point to put the innocuous group on the agenda. There were local women's groups that hadn't been asked to voice their grievances or positions on issues, and yet the CUSL, which didn't do active local work, was being given direct attention before the mayor and the media.

Pastora fished into her portfolio, trying not to betray the nervousness that crept up at the mention of her organization. She was among orators and Pastora was not an orator. She seemed to contradict her shyness with her performances, her recordings and compositions, but without music, she was never at ease addressing an audience.

She stood and was recognized by the mayor. Perla noticed her for the first time and Pastora felt the discomfort of her estranged friend in seeing her across the room without their having acknowledged each other. She also sensed Maritza Marin-Levy's eyes drilling into her face. They told Pastora that it didn't matter what she had come to say. She wouldn't be heard. Pastora knew and sensed this all the more because Maritza Marín-Levy, the newly appointed public relations person for the mayor's new Department on Women, Aged, Disabled, and Special Affairs, had over the years shown an unexplicable rivalry with Pastora.

"Mayor García," Pastora spoke up, clearing her throat and finding her voice vastly lacking in projection, which was very odd since, as a singer, she had often been called upon to perform without a microphone and had always managed to be heard. "I would first like to . . ."

Someone in the back called out, "LOUDER! WE CAN'T HEAR!" Pastora moved as if she were inclined to turn around to see who had yelled so abrasively, but chose instead to ignore it. "I would like to thank you on behalf of the Colloquim of U.S. Latinas for allowing me to address our principal concerns to you and the people of Chicago . . ." Pastora hesitated as her eyes locked with the mayor's. She thought his gaze rather vacant. He was distracted and kept checking his watch every few minutes.

"The Colloquium of U.S. Latinas is primarily a group of theoreticians who hope to study the needs of Latinas so as to address them in an articulate manner before our local governments and on a national level," Pastora said, her eyes still reaching the mayor's. She lost concentration if she looked at Perla or Maritza.

For a moment she remembered her son. Had she left enough diapers with the sitter? Yes, of course she had. She raised the sheet in her hands and reviewed the statement with a glance. She spoke again, "I would like to say that the CUSL is concerned with the needs of the working-class woman in addition to her special needs as a non-white person in America." Pastora stopped again. Maritza was saying something to the man next to her, cupping her mouth so that her moving lips could not be seen. When she finished, she saw that Pastora had been waiting for her so that she could continue, and Maritza stared at her with icy smugness.

It was not Maritza then who took aim at her, but the man to whom Maritza had just whispered. He leaned back against his chair and broke into Pastora's speech, "Aren't you a singer or a performer or something like that?"

"Yes, I am," Pastora replied. He shook his head and smiled

sarcastically, "It's just that I'm not sure who you are here to represent. Do you work in the Hispanic community here in Chicago?" The man, Pastora deduced, thought he was clever the way he gesticulated flamboyantly as he spoke, sure that he was making a pretty picture for the cameras.

Maritza confidently planted both high-heeled feet on the floor, toes pointed outward. One could easily see underneath the table a view to where the thighs met, and with a little effort, to the crotch. She, too, was aware of the cameras pointed in her direction. Pastora's forehead glistened. She was so steaming with anger that her ankles wanted to give way, trembling as they were.

She opened her mouth, putting aside her planned speech, and tried to hide how infuriated they had managed to make her so quickly. "To which community in particular are you referring, sir? Are you referring to the Mexican community of the West Side or to the Puerto Rican community of West Town? Do you mean the new Central American community in Logan Square or that of the Cuban residents on Milwaukee Avenue? Do you mean, perhaps, to use 'community' in a broader sense and refer to all the countries of South America, Mexico, Central America, and the Caribbean—in which case we should not say Hispanic, because there are those territories, including Brazil, which constitutes one-fifth of South America and was not settled by the Spaniards and therefore is not Hispanic. Or by Hispanic, do you simply refer to the Spanish-speaking? Forty percent of the Guatemalan population doesn't speak Spanish and neither did my mother when she came to live here . . ."

By this point the fastidious man next to Maritza had replaced his grin with a cocky smirk, still determined not to be castigated for his offensive interruption. Maritza whispered something in his ear again. There were various comments in the crowd; one or two persons applauded, but in general, Pastora thought her comments brought on confusion. After all, the term Hispanic had been made official by the status quo and was only questioned by linguists, scholars, and anarchists, whose custom it was to question mainstream thought.

"Please go on," said the mayor, encouraging Pastora to get back to the issue. Pastora met with Perla's glance. There was compassion in Perla's eyes. Pastora felt they were saying she was about to be made a sacrificial lamb. She thanked the mayor and, resuming her usual composure, read from the sheet. "The working-class woman, the woman employed outside the home, of which there are increasing numbers by the year, in addition to the burden of having to support her children financially, has the responsibility of child care. To date, in the United States no adequate child-care program has been established to help these women take care of their children, who are the children of this country."

"There are programs with scale rates available for women who cannot afford to pay a private babysitter or a more expensive nursery," Maritza said, not looking at Pastora, but directing herself to the public.

"I am not talking about government subsidized programs, although that is another aspect of this issue that should be dealt with," Pastora continued, now determined to say her piece despite Maritza's intention to undermine her. "I am referring to child-care facilities at the place of employment of women; these employers should not be the only ones responsible for providing child-care services, but the employers of fathers, too. To solely place the responsibility of the children on the women and their employers is to continue to make women a higher risk to employ."

"There are reasons why employers don't provide child care," Maritza said with irritation, to imply that Pastora's grievance was trite, if not one founded on lack of information. "For one, employers cannot afford to have mothers called away from their jobs because the child wants them for something or other." She waved her hand, insinuating that the child would be undoubtedly whimsical, knowing the mother was at hand. "Second, we have long winters in this city and all kinds of colds and contagious flus and viruses, which we have been told in such child-care centers go to the rate of epidemics, especially among little kids. And there's also the problem of hiring sufficiently adequate nursery school teachers . . ."

Maritza and Pastora glared at each other. Pastora was infuriated. Pastora started to sit down. All persons who were allowed to speak were allotted the maximum of ten minutes and her time was up. She finished with a question to Maritza, "What do you suggest women with children do?" Maritza repeated the waving gesture that said the issue was akin to expecting her to find the cure for the common cold. "They're just going to have to find babysitters or make do with the programs that are available. There's just not enough money for such programs!"

Pastora thought of protesting a point that had gone unrecognized, namely that funding didn't have to come from the government. In the case of private industry, it should come from the company's profits. But she was dismissed with the standard response to almost all the grievances that related to needed funds, and someone else was immediately called upon to address the mayor.

When the press conference was over, the crowd flooded back out into the hall. Many went toward the elevators, the press followed the mayor and his staff, and some stayed to shake hands with each other and talk. Diego Cañas rushed over to Pastora and gave her a hug. "You were great," he said. Pastora froze with his touch. "You know, I don't think I had ever thought about the things you said before. That was kind of interesting." Deigo was referring to Pastora's retort on the term "Hispanic." She was flushed. Pastora was short with him and looked around. Máximo was still in the room, rubbing elbows with people who looked as genuine as three-dollar bills. "I'm not sure if I had ever thought to say that, either . . ." Pastora uttered, only half attentive to Diego's conversation.

Suddenly Perla was next to Pastora. She smiled cheerfully and shook Diego's hand while placing the other around Pastora's shoulder. "How are you, compañera?" She sounded upbeat, but Pastora knew Perla well enough to detect her uneasiness with having approached her. It had been at least a year since they had seen each other. Pastora nodded that she was fine. Perla said, "I just wanted to say that I understand what you mean, about child care. Lord only knows what I've been through with my twins . . . !"

Diego interrupted, "But you don't have trouble with child care *now*, do you, Perla?" He was being insidious, inferring that Perla now had the money through her marriage to have her children well cared for. Perla's face grew dark. Pastora recognized that expression. It was of an agitated creature about to defend itself with bared teeth. "If you mean that financially I have no worries, of course I no longer need to worry about my children, thank God. But because they are also now in school all day, unlike mothers of infants, I don't have that problem."

Pastora cut in, "You don't have that problem either, Diego."

Diego knew he was surrounded at both sides and, grinning, backed away from the women. Perla shook her head when he was out of hearing range. "Some people never change!" she sighed.

Pastora let her gaze linger on Perla's beauty, the only thing that remained of the Perla she had loved. "And some of us change too much," she said, her eyes meeting with Perla's just as the latter turned to go off.

fifty-five

I waited until Pastora was by the elevators before I caught up with her. She had been the true emasculator of men in that press conference. But Pastora had wasted her time. No one was interested in anything that was thought by an organization of intellectual women.

If Pastora had forsaken her career as a musician for that of a feminist now that she was a mother, or to be some other kind of reactionary because she had been put in jail for transporting refugees from Sapogonia, she was making an atrocious error in judgment. I told her as much going down in the elevator.

"There are slews of nurseries," I said to her. She didn't look at me when she answered, "You didn't hear what I was saying either, did you?" Her words squeezed out from between her teeth.

"You said that women in need must have support from the government . . . !"

"Not the government!"

"Their bosses, then. What does it matter? The point is, there are facilities and I thought that this colloquium that you belong to had more to say."

"It did, but none of you heard it," she answered sharply. We were in front of the building. It was cold and the wind coming in from the lake whipped around us. I wasn't interested in continuing the topic. I had only wanted to speak to her. She finally looked directly at me.

When I first saw Pastora, she was reminiscent of Mexico's beloved silver-screen actress María Félix. María Félix was the one for whom one of her husbands, Agustín Lara (you know, the composer of "Granada"?), composed the song "María Bonita." She didn't *look* like María Félix, you understand, but she had her manner.

That afternoon, however, in the grey daylight, the wind disheveling Pastora's hair, a new fatigue beneath the eyes . . . she no longer had that haughty María Félix demeanor as she did that night in September when she agreed to meet me right after I had flown in from an exhibit in Miami.

We met at my old studio, the one I had abandoned a year before. There was that soft rain of Indian summer and I opened the windows to ventilate the space. The racket of the passing elevated train, a cat howling in the alley below, and the nocturnal sounds of the city turned Pastora, in her turquoise dress that fell over the brown shoulders and slipped over her head with such ease, into the impeccable beauty of my fantasies. I refrained from admitting how much I had always loved her, but it was she who confidently said to me, "It seems you're still in love with me." I looked away from her, running my hand, which contrasted with the color of her calf, her thigh, over the length of the slender leg, "Quizá. . . ."

Maritza was waiting for me at city hall and I said goodbye to Pastora, who perturbed me with her drawn pallor, although the true motivation to run off was that I didn't want to love her, as her husband must have been loving her then, eating with her every evening, sleeping with her each night, waking in the mornings to find Pastora next to him, the countless opportunities a man will have to set his eyes on a certain woman and say confidently to himself, "She's mine."

I looked at my watch—a birthday gift from the Levys. I hadn't ever made use of a watch before then, but a Rolex was not something to be left in a drawer. In all probability, Maritza hadn't noticed the time at all, but I hurried off. She was downstairs with three of her associates, happily wallowing in the newfound attention one gets when serving in public office.

My eyes summed up Maritza's public image as I stepped quickly in her direction. It seemed inappropriate for a woman in her position to dress as if she were a burlesque dancer by profession. Granted, as a man I certainly relished the bountifulness of her figure and how it was displayed with transparent blouses, the stitched-on jeans, skirts that accentuated the derrière, but this also made the public think less seriously about Maritza than what her position commanded.

It was as important for me to have people respect her because through her my possibilities were heightened to secure commissions that other artists in the city could only hope to compete for when submitting handsome portfolios and impressive dossiers. I had Maritza now to make sure it was *my* work that remained on top of the stack and was selected in the end.

I told her over lunch that I was going to go shopping for her. She needed to wear clothes more in the style of that woman, Perla.

Máximo remembered Perla in the days when she was Pastora's roommate. The two women were inseparable then. He had thought they were lovers. In either case, it now appeared each had gone on with her life. Perla indeed was doing well for herself. Máximo made a mental note to give Perla a call and invite her out to lunch or for drinks. Why he hadn't thought of calling on his old acquaintance before, he couldn't imagine.

After Máximo went on his way, Pastora had walked on to Dearborn and caught the Clark St. bus to Belmont, where she made an abrupt decision to get off to drop in on her old friend, Yvonne Harris. Yvonne now lived in a newly rehabbed apartment building off Halsted.

Pastora mentally reenacted the entire meeting she had just attended, culminated by the few minutes when Máximo had caught up with her to talk. Pastora felt as if her body were covered with a layer of slime from the whole episode, the slime of viciousness of her fellow human beings. She, too, had left some of her own slimy excretion behind.

Perla had awkwardly approached her former companion, Pastora, who vehemently rejected that scene and everything to do with its power-based lifestyle, but they were already severed from each other, and neither was able to console the other.

Yvonne was still in her nightgown, although it was late in the afternoon when Pastora reached her apartment. Yvonne was surprised to see her Chicana friend at her door, although she seemed glad for it. They had seen almost nothing of each other in the past two years. One thing led to another and while Yvonne had moved up to the North Side, they saw less of each other than when she had lived south. Yvonne puttered in floppy slippers over to the stove to put the kettle on for tea. She hadn't even had a cup of tea yet that day, just stayed on in the bed reading magazines and trying not to think about anything, she said.

This information and Yvonne's weight loss were signs that she was depressed. "What the matter? If you don't have enough food, why don't you ever call me?" Pastora scolded Yvonne in that firm way friends who are concerned about friends are forced to speak to each other. Yvonne protested. If she was hungry she could always go to her mother's house for a hearty meal; and there was never anything like Mama's home cooking. Her married brother didn't live too far, either. No, she didn't lack food; she lacked money, but not food.

"And I'm tired of playing these clubs! I thought it would be different up here," Yvonne revealed. "I thought these white folks paid better since they like the blues so much, and that maybe they'd treat their musicians better than those fools who run the clubs on the South Side! They're all the same everywhere. Only the faces are a different color. I'm thinking of moving back to the South Side; may as well."

Pastora studied Yvonne, who was very dark with deeply set eyes, and while she was thin her large bones made her seem bigger than she was. "What's the difference, then? I don't get it," Pastora said. "If they're no better on the South Side, why are you going back?"

"I'd much rather be dealing with my own people if there is no financial benefit for me to be dealing with white folks. At least I know my own people, and I miss them, too!"

Pastora nodded, "I miss my people, too, when I'm away from them . . . but I'll be damned if I can understand why they're so determined lately to emulate the values of the white people in this city who created the problems we have to begin with! Someone is always going to have to be on top and someone is always going to end up at the bottom according to this system!"

Pastora took the liberty of looking around Yvonne's kitchen. She was in bad need of a drink. Yvonne informed her that she had quit drinking again, so there wasn't any liquor in the house. What was the point in it? Your high turned into a hangover and in the end, everything was still the same. She didn't smoke dope anymore, either; it was hard on the vocal cords.

"I used to smoke dope to give my voice that gruff sound that works so well with some songs," Pastora admitted, laughing at her past reasoning. Yvonne looked surprised. "Now why would you want to ruin that sweet voice like that? Your voice wasn't meant to be gruff; it was meant to be just like it is, sweet, like an angel's. You're sounding like those white folks up here, always wanting to sing the blues so they smoke two packs of Camels non-filtered before going on stage and, in the end, they sound like your typical white southern peckerwoods!"

Pastora broke out in laughter and forgot about the drink. She had relaxed with Yvonne's humor. Yvonne changed the subject. "You Latinos are really stirring up city hall these days!" Pastora sighed, looking frustrated. "It's a bigger mess up there than even the media can make of it."

"You think that Alan García is really white?" Yvonne asked, trying to maintain her impulsive laughter. When Yvonne laughed, it was contagious and Pastora knew that in the next second the world would turn into a monstrous satire. She shook her head. "He may be white-looking, but he's not, Yvonne. If you study his features, they could be Indian. He's not very light-skinned, either."

"Oh," Yvonne said, not convinced, "it must be that the boy acts so white he's beginning to look like he is."

"He doesn't act white," Pastora reacted defensively. "He acts like a politician—which, in this country, is a white game."

"That's what I mean," Yvonne persisted.

"I just got back from a press conference downtown with Mayor García's new team." Pastora exhaled loudly, as if she preferred to let out a scream. She sat in the high-backed rattan rocker near the window. She hadn't taken off her coat. The apartment was cool. She noticed Yvonne was wearing sweatsocks and a sweater to keep warm. "Doesn't your landlord give you heat in this place?" Pastora had never gotten used to the Midwest cold. If human beings were meant to live in such weather, they would have been born with fur.

"No!" Yvonne answered. "Now don't change the subject, girl! You mean you're going to be on t.v. today?" She curled up in her bed. The kettle whistled and Pastora got up to prepare the tea. "What're you doing at a press conference with the mayor, anyway?" Yvonne called to Pastora in the kitchen from among her pillows and afghans.

"I doubt that I'm going to be on t.v.!" Pastora yelled from the kitchen. Yvonne's only three cups were dirty and she had to wash a couple before being able to make the tea. "Some fool crony of Maritza Marín-Levy pissed me off and I went off on a tangent about the term 'Hispanic,' forgetting what I stood up to say in the first place!" She brought Yvonne the tea and took her seat by the window again.

"Now nobody is going to tell me that that woman is not white!" Yvonne said, referring to Maritza.

"She's very white, even though I'm sure she dyes that orange hair of hers with saffron," Pastora conceded. "But she says she's Cuban or Puerto Rican or something like that. If you really look at her, you can see the strains of African blood. The problem is that, since she has a Jewish surname, people assume those are Semitic features."

"Was she there? I bet she was!" Yvonne seemed in the mood for good gossip.

"Oh, you better believe it, giving her usual show with her skirt up to her panties! And her new boyfriend, Máximo Madrigal, standing in the back like a dog waiting for his bone, or a wolf, waiting for his share of the mutton!" Pastora interrupted herself, recalling her own image at the conference. She said aloud, "Perla was there, too. She looked at me as if I were a sacrificial lamb."

"That's her way of saying you have principles, babe. I saw Perla on the t.v. news one evening. The girl was wearing what looked to me like *mink!*" Yvonne exclaimed. She remembered when Perla was Pastora's roommate, too, and hardly had a decent pair of jeans to wear!

"It was," Pastora confirmed. "She was wearing it today."

"Too bad the girl had to get it by marrying a white man!" Yvonne put her hand over her mouth afterward, as if what she'd said had slipped out unintentionally, and then laughed out loud.

"Máximo Madrigal comes running after me when it was over and his girlfriend was out of sight," Pastora said dully.

"Oooh! Some men never stop. Doesn't he know you're married?" Yvonne clearly had never liked that character, Máximo. She admitted he was a talented artist, but from a picture in the paper she had seen, she didn't like his looks.

Pastora never confided much of her relationship with Máximo Madrigal to Yvonne. Yvonne believed in the institution of marriage as a holy commitment. As a devout Catholic, she was against abortion and birth control.

"Of course he knows I'm married. He knows I have a child. He didn't have much to say today, just the same bullshit." With this, Pastora decided to change the topic of the meeting altogether. It was too disheartening. She inquired more about Yvonne's life and, shortly thereafter, left. She had to catch another bus to get home, but first she had to pick up her infant at the baby sitter's. She would get home, toting baby, diaper bag, toys, attaché case. She would tend to the child's needs, then change into the clothes she usually wore at home, a pair of jogging pants or jeans and a T-shirt. Then she would be herself again.

She would never again go to one of those press conferences. In the morning she would write to Sacramento and report that in the future, other means to express their ideas to the Chicago political circuit with its new administration would have to be found, but setting themselves up beneath the circus tent was not the way to go.

She had seen Máximo again as she probably would as a matter of norm if she pursued the city hall clique, since he was currently related to it through his girlfriend. She relented at the thought that she *had* derived pleasure from seeing him, talking to him. He had said nothing of meeting with her in a more suitable atmosphere. She would have liked to believe it had nothing to do with his relationship with Maritza. Pastora pitied Maritza; living with Máximo was no enviable position.

Pastora didn't know why she had given Máximo and Maritza so much thought that afternoon. She put them out of her mind and went to cut up a chicken.

fifty-six

Not far from my grandfather's land, a shepherd brought his sheep out to graze. He had a small daughter and, when she was old enough, it was she who went out each day. She always wore the same little dress; she was shoeless, usually, or she had sandals with soles made from an old tire. She crossed her legs and sat in a cove playing her harmonica until the sunset.

One morning, riding past, I was shocked by what I saw: a massacre of sheep, their carcasses slain and bloodied across the expanse of rich green. The girl, a light breeze rustling through the faded dress, was motionless, as if traumatized.

I went over to her and, gripping her by the shoulders, I demanded, "Who's done this? Who would dare do such a thing?" She looked me in the eyes and at first said nothing. I thought she might not understand me. I repeated the question, "Pastorita, who has done this to you?"

"You have," she answered. I didn't know why she told me this. I knew nothing about the slaying of the herd. "It's better that you don't deny it. It will go worse for you, if you do." She walked off, her little sandals catching blades of grass. Her sunburnt legs like two pieces of wood in the distance. Her shabby dress, the pathetic flag of her existence.

It occurred to me that she was on her way to report me. Her father and neighbors would be after me. Why would she think that I was the one who committed such an act of madness? I ran and found my grandmother before her shrine in the guayaba-scented garden. Then again, I'm not certain where we were, in the garden before her shrine, or just somewhere on the ranch. The air was cool but the sun was the brilliant one of midday so that we squinted in order to look at each other. "Abuelita, abuelita!" I was out of breath when I caught up to her. "They're coming after me! Where am I going to hide?"

"It's better that you go," she answered. "At the university, they won't find you. That's where your friends are hiding." I took this to be a prejudicial remark on my grandmother's part against my pursuits of an academic education.

"My friends aren't there anymore," I corrected her, and surprised myself at the news. She shrugged her shoulders. "Then tell the pastorita to leave you alone. You were supposed to marry her, but since you didn't . . ."

I ran until I found a cave not far from my grandfather's ranch. I hid where I could peer out and listen for the sounds of the expected posse. My heart pounded as loud as hoofbeats, as I was sure they were going to kill me. They had dogs to sniff me out. I hadn't brought along a gun or so much as a hound to sic on them to give me a running head start if they found me. The telephone rang and I awoke.

There was never any shepherd so close to my grandfather's property and I don't know why I had that dream. I was living in Barcelona at the time. It was shortly after El Tinto and I parted ways. I always remembered the little imaginary shepherdess and how she had killed her herd of sheep to avenge my rejection.

Later in my life on an occasion when I was with Pastora, I recounted the dream. "Pastorita, would you kill your sheep because I told you I was going to marry you and changed my mind, then say that it was me who did it so that I would get hanged?"

"You dream too much," she replied. "You're not worth slaughtering one sheep for a barbecue on Sunday." She laughed at her joke, not loud, just enough to let me know she enjoyed insulting me, and I laughed, too, but I wasn't convinced that she hadn't been the pastora in my dream.

I also wasn't convinced that Pastora wasn't capable of violence.

She left a message with Laura on one occasion that she called. Since I hadn't told her that Laura was my wife, but went on with the story that she was mostly my agent, Pastora must have thought nothing of calling—although Pastora rarely called, anyway. When I got home that night it was late, about a quarter of eleven. I had hardly closed the door behind me when the phone rang and it was Pastora again. It rang several times because Laura was detaining me by relaying the message that a mysterious female had called for me earlier.

Pastora said she had something for me. She wouldn't say what it was, but she insisted that it was urgent. This was most unlike her, but coincided with an episode in which I thought of Pastora constantly. I was trying to see her more often than she would permit and when she said she wanted to see me, I too, was ready to go to her. But I had the problem of Laura, who was standing next to me with arms folded and who would not understand if I had to leave at that moment.

On the telephone, I tried to find out what it was that Pastora had for me. She said she had been thinking about my choice to settle for mediocrity in life, specifically in love and sex. If I didn't settle for mediocrity in my work, why did I settle for it in the person whom I chose to share my life with? I told her it was simply a matter of practicality. All my energy went into my work. There was nothing left over for extreme passions. "I won't accept it," she said, meaning she expected greater things from me, not that she would volunteer to be my woman—replace Laura, who did everything for me but warm my underwear before I slipped into them on chilly mornings.

"Come, it won't take long. It's important that I see you," she insisted. Never, never had Pastora implored me before and never did she say that to me again. It goes without saying that I was compelled by the rare overture. I had a sense that I was going to miss my moment if I didn't go. Laura went to bed, implicitly letting me know that she didn't appreciate what was going on beneath her nose, and this was before she even had a hint yet that I was going to take her car and slip out.

I told Pastora I would see her but that I could stay for no more than an hour and she agreed that that would be enough. I went into the bedroom and informed Laura I needed her car for an emergency; a friend was stranded on the highway and needed a ride, etc. No woman in her right mind would have believed it, and Laura sat up hurling insults at my family and nationality as I walked out.

I drove as hurriedly as I could without getting a police car on my tail. It was almost midnight when I reached the building where Pastora lived. Her light was on and, before I knocked, she opened the door. She wore a mango-colored camisole underneath a shimmery kimono. It was summer and she padded around the apartment barefoot with lithe footsteps that hardly touched the floor. Her hair was loose and flowing and she smelled like the air after it's rained. I was intoxicated by her presence as soon as I got in the door. She held me off and sat me down in the living room, where I saw that she was about to make a gift of a song to me.

The music was not spectacular, but it was extraordinarily mesmerizing, a kind of lullaby. The words were in Spanish. Although you must remember I've only heard it that once, it went something like this: When night comes, I slip you on, silk against my skin, a part of me. Cream against my coffee skin. You are like me, son of my country, white as I am dark. I slip you on and we are as one . . ." I don't remember it all.

We talked. I told her, as we sat next to each other on the couch, the lamp contouring Pastora's face, that if I sought a special woman, she would be like Eva Perón, a woman who would stop at nothing to bring me to the very echelon of success. In the meantime, I preferred to live with the woman whom I didn't love because it was safe for my mental stability.

"Pastora, when I make love to you, I carry with me—all of it— until the next time we're together. Your smell, your legs around me. But you would be the death of me if I surrendered myself to you . . ." What I wanted to say, what was the truth, was that if we were that close, I would do anything to destroy her, destroy the influence she had over me. I would aim to destroy her in order to recreate her as mine, no longer Pastora, willful and resilient. She would not be the Egyptian cobra that wrapped itself around my neck, about to strangle me in the midst of an orgasm.

I went to the door and kissed her. I didn't want to leave, but in the back of my mind I kept foreseeing the scene I was up for with Laura as soon as I returned. I ran my hand beneath the camisole, felt the abundance of her pubic hair, and dropped to my knees before that daughter of highland jungle, to lose myself between Pastora's thighs, Pastora's scents, Pastora's moistness. I couldn't go without lowering her to the hardwood floor, smooth as her own brown skin, and having entered her. I left immediately afterward, hardly taking time to wash.

After I parked Laura's car, walking back to the loft, I noted something very weird in the empty lot next to our building. I'm not sure what it was exactly that initially caught my eye. It seemed like a flash of gold against the dirt. I had to look very closely because it was difficult to make it out until I was standing right above it, and I realized I was looking down at a pair of upside-down claws that stuck up from beneath the ground. Surrounding it was an assortment of things like offerings, coins, some paper currency, orange rind. I scanned the area, there was no one in sight. I picked up the money, thought again, left it there, and hurried home.

The next morning I was unable to get out of bed, running a high fever which alternated with terrible chills. Laura, of course, had no mercy on me as a result of my ghastly behavior with her the night before and said as much before she went to work without even preparing a cup of tea for me. She had diagnosed that I had come down with a twenty-four-hour virus, just punishment for being out at all hours, and left before I could ask if we had aspirin in the place. We did have aspirin, as it turned out, and I made my own tea before going back to bed to suffer miserably alone.

Later that morning, and this was the indisputable evidence that Pastora had to have had something to do with my illness, she called. She sounded very casual. That was *twice* that she had called me recently and now, how could she pretend to be innocent? The sacrificed rooster downstairs said it all! "WHAT HAVE YOU DONE TO ME?" I tried not to sound too hysterical, but the sickness depleted me so that I scarcely had the will to raise my voice. Still, the way I asked let her know I was at the very least anxious about how she played with my fate.

As one could only expect in this tale of bizarre lunacy, she pretended she didn't have the slightest idea as to what I was implying. I told her about the rooster buried in the empty lot next door and how that morning I awoke sick as the devil. She told me, as Laura had, that I probably had nothing more than a slight case of the flu. "You know how you drive yourself to exhaustion." She sounded fairly rational, objective, and somewhat coy. I remained miserable and in severe doubt. "YOU did this to me."

"Don't be ridiculous. I am not into those practices. Whether you believe it or not, I don't try to hurt anyone, either. Why would I want to harm you?"

"I don't know," I lied. What woman in my life didn't have an excuse to want to see me end like that decapitated bird rotting in the ground? "By any chance, did you touch any of what you found—the money, for instance?" she asked.

"I picked up something, but I put it back," I groaned.

"You should have left it alone. It was surely not meant for you, unless you know any fanatical mountain people who are devoted to their old rituals in the city. I wouldn't tamper with it anymore, if I were you."

"Who was tampering with it? *You* left it there, next to my house!"

"I had nothing to do with it. Don't be so paranoid," she asserted. I was too weak to enter into a full-fledged argument. "Fine," I told her. We hung up at a stalemate.

The illness did not last twenty-four hours but seventy-two before I felt able to get out of bed and walk about without sensing the room reeling. The first thing I did was dress and go outside to see if the buried rooster was still there and what it looked like in broad daylight to the unsuspectiong passerby. It wasn't as if animal offerings were a common sight in downtown Chicago.

As I anticipated, there was nothing there, not a trace. Perhaps some winos came by and took the money as well as the dead bird, thinking only what good fortune it was that such an odd thing be left lying around only to have been run down by a garbage truck right afterward, with the bird and money stuffed underneath their shabby coats.

This type of occurrence did not improve my relationship with Pastora nor did it help convince me that I should forsake mediocrity for what, at best, left me sexually peaked and, at worst, was bound to drive me to one form of insanity or another.

fifty-seven

When I was a boy I went with Mamá and Mamá Grande to see Jorge Negrete in *Peñón de las ánimas*. I seem to recall Mamá was escorted by a suitor, but as suitors came far and few between in Mamá's boring life and none ever lasted long enough to make an impression on me, I can't say for sure. A suitor for Mamá, to begin with out in the sticks where we lived, had to be snatched before he went on to the city. It wasn't as if San Co could attract many outsiders. Second, the suitor had to pass the inspection of my grandfather and finally, of Mamá Grande. Mamá usually had nothing to say about the men who were considered prospective husbands. All this pressure on Mamá was made worse by the constant reminder of me as a transgression of the faith her parents had once had in her to behave with the morals and dignity of one of her upbringing.

Peñón de las ánimas was not the latest Jorge Negrete film, but San Co wasn't exactly the cultural center of Sapogonia, or even of the region, for that matter. In fact, it had only recently opened its only movie theater. So whatever it featured was fine for the town and its patrons of nearby ranches and miniscule communities.

We dressed up that Sunday as we always did to attend Mass, had a delicious Sunday dinner, and then we were off to catch the evening feature. Jorge Negrete was one of Mamá's favorites. Mexico at that time was producing the best popular films, as far as we were concerned, and everyone in Sapogonia dreamed of the gallant Mexican cowboys and the beautiful women with satin shawls and golden hooped earrings.

This particular film was engraved in my mind because it was when I first fell in love. If love had to come to a boy of twelve, why not with the most sublime woman of the day? And that was Jorge Negrete's leading lady and later real-life wife, María Félix.

Mamá came out of the theater that evening rather snub-nosed about María Félix. She thought the young star was perhaps too full-lipped and how vain to have the camera constantly on that black mole on her left cheek, which was so utterly obvious since it did it every time it had the chance! Mamá looked nothing like María Félix, to be sure. She was petite like her mother, a full-blooded Mayan Indian. Mamá had walnut-colored skin and those wondrous slanted eyes that sometimes stared out as if they had been painted on by Diego Rivera. But Mamá was not María Félix.

María Félix was big—in my adolescent's estimation and compared to her leading men. She had the rich mixture of Spanish and indigenous blood so that yes, her luscious mouth was abundant like ripened berries that burst as soon as they're between one's teeth, and her dark, tearful eyes were like the fog that clung to the mountain peaks of Sapogonia.

In *Peñón de las ánimas* she fell in love with Jorge Negrete, who was the last surviving member of a rivaling family. She had been promised to René Cardona, who played her cousin and who also truly loved her, but whatever they had had between them before she went to Europe to become a lady was just children's play in her opinion. This was especially true after she met Jorge Negrete, who showed her he was not any ignorant cowboy but as cultured and refined as the next snot-nosed aristocrat, and he proved as much by reciting a poem from memory. She was really impressed. Then he told her that they had known each other always. He meant for centuries or in past lives. A halo appeared behind María Félix's head after the rain stopped and she lowered her perfect gaze because he'd managed to touch her pure soul.

He told her he'd wait for her every day at the same hour in the same spot they happened to have crossed by chance or by fate the first time. She prayed they would never see each other again. "I'll be waiting," he told her, relentlessly. You see, Jorge, being of stubborn blood, was determined to have her. I don't think that the knowledge that he was playing with fire helped María's protest, since it seemed to just provide ammunition. She, on the other hand, being of Catholic faith and a woman, knew the chances a gambling man took and that death was undoubtedly on the horizon.

Jorge Negrete sang a ballad or two, serenaded her discreetly, boldly took her out to waltz to Chopin at a society ball in the presence of her fiancé and fuming male relatives, and in the end she had no choice but to run off with him.

They didn't get very far before the grandfather, an old fart patriarch, took out his gun and shouted, "IF HE IS GOING TO TAKE HER, THIS IS HOW IT IS GOING TO BE!" and shot her dead. María Angela's (that is her name in the movie) cousin-fiancé followed suit by then shooting Jorge Negrete, who thanked him with his last breath, saying he wanted to join María anyway. Then the fiancé went one better, replying to the dying Jorge Negrete, "Not before I do," and carried María's body to the edge of a cliff and threw himself off with her body in his arms.

If this material rings vaguely of Romeo and Juliet with a hint of Orpheus, you can see why the movie made such an impact on me, which reached new dimensions years later when I became so fond of Shakespeare's work. I imagined myself serenading María Félix and had countless battles with my archenemy for her love. She'd met me clandestinely and kissed my hand, begging me on her knees to run before my enemies caught up to me to kill me.

I was living with Maritza when I saw Pastora without premeditated planning, but fate threw us in each other's path in the most awkward of circumstances, just as Jorge Negrete and María Félix were in *Peñón de las ánimas.*

Maritza had gone to the ladies' room at the Trompeta de Gabriel, a Latin night club not especially classy but known for featuring excellent dance music, when I noticed a familiar face at a nearby table. It was of a woman poet, Teresa. She was with a male companion and another couple. I thought I would go over to say hello. It never hurt to be courteous to people who in the future could then be called on by you for a small favor, a recommendation, a piece of advice, or a contact, because no matter what vehicle one needed to meet his objective, there was always someone there to serve as a stepping stone. I thought she had noticed me, too, but she turned away before our eyes could meet.

Then my blood ran cold as I recognized who the other woman was at the same table. It was Pastora without the slightest doubt, although I could only see one-quarter of her face from where I sat. She was dressed in black with her hair styled in such a way that one side fell over to cover an eye and the other brushed behind an ear, over which was pinned a gardenia.

How I wanted her to look my way! I got up and stood at just the point where she would have to see me, if only she would turn in my direction. She didn't! I walked toward her table, but she kept her eyes lowered or turned in the direction of the man she was with. I passed behind her. When she didn't acknowledge me, I lost my nerve to go up to her to say hello. I hadn't seen her in months, nearly a year, and how wonderful it was to see her again, so close, so delicate and intangible as always—except when I had her in my arms . . .

I passed the table again, and a third time, and finally just stood at the place where I knew she had to see me if only she would look up! Finally, it came to me that she intentionally wasn't acknowledging me. She knew what I was enduring and yet, she refused to allow me to approach her! Why? Damn her. I gritted my teeth ruefully. Just because she was with her husband—although I had never seen him before, I knew Pastora wouldn't be seen in public with any other man if she was married, and from all indications, she was indeed married—there was the proof, sitting next to her, his arm around the back of her chair, which was saying to me and every other bastard in the place: Don't you dare get near her, son of a bitch—I was condemned to oblivion!

I should go right up to the table that was suddenly forbidden, as if a taboo surrounded it, a quarantine forbidding me to get near Teresa and shake hands with her companion, whoever he was, and then casually turn to Pastora . . . Then I thought of her icy stare that had more than once left me like a frozen sausage. All someone had to do was push me down and I would've surely cracked in two as I hit the floor. I stood where I was and left matters alone. When Maritza came back, she saw me standing. I told her we were leaving.

All this and I was remembering the time when Pastora had cried. She was actually capable of tears. I didn't exactly see her cry because it was much too dark in the room to see anything. We had a hard enough time finding castaside clothing, much less making out facial expressions and tears, but I heard her sob. Until then it seemed as if I would never in my humble lifetime know that Pastora, like any other woman, like any human being, cried. She cried because I told her that she should never have gotten married. She reproached me also for having married. I told her that marriage for me, a man, was much different. It would not interfere with my career. I would continue with my plans to travel and stay away as long as I desired. I would continue to produce as much as I could, promote it as far as I was able. I would set my own limits. Getting married for a woman meant the end of art, that which demanded by its very nature supreme and continuous sacrifice.

How many women artists had history preserved for us? I am no feminist fanatic, or to use Pastora's term, *non-sexist*. Nor do I feel convinced that they are truly equal in every capacity to men, but I know that there are those who are unique. In one way or another, they manage to excel. Pastora showed true promise as a singer, a composer. She had the conviction to make her name in the United States and, as a descendent of Latin American heritage and devoted to her people, among Latinos, too. She should have moved in with the man, let him support her, put a roof over her head, pay her expenses, and continued to work on her music. She didn't have to commit herself to him in such a radical manner!

"But *you* did it!" she retaliated. It was then that I believed she began to cry. The display of emotion was alarming to me. "I only married for reasons that were advantageous to me," I repeated. "They were going to throw me out of the country! Understand? It is the only way I would marry—by force or trickery! Why didn't you wait until I was divorced—?"

I stopped; I didn't want to get carried away. I had thought of being married to Pastora, imagined the tremendous couple we would have made, one to surpass all artistic couples in history. Diego Rivera and Frida Kahlo? Virginia and Leonard Woolf? They would become insignificant compared to us. I reasoned that Pastora was crying only because she'd had a lot to drink; if the truth be known, we both had. She wouldn't even have been in that room had I not practically kidnapped her. But she made love to me of her own free will and we lay there afterward, wrapped in each other's arms and talking almost tenderly to each other for the first time since we'd first come together.

I didn't admit to her that night, either, that I was in love with her and that that was the reason why I resented her marriage. If she had just lived with that man, I could have hoped to continue to see her and perhaps one day, if I was truly convinced that life with her was possible, I would have spoken up.

How can I explain to you what it was to be in love with Pastora—and to be Máximo Madrigal? You don't know, or perhaps you do, how it is to wake every morning, a tremendous clamp pressing against the temples, telling me to go on, to push a little harder, that it was all at my fingertips, only a bit further, at the next bend, just don't give up. Hilda, Laura, and Maritza were women made to make men ready each day to go on. They made him into a demigod so that when he got an erection, he thought he fucked the world.

When I made love to Pastora, I wasn't even on earth. I don't mean to be cliché, you understand. I don't want to say I was on a cloud or anything like that. I lost my substance, became the molecules of which my body was made and became formless and erratic. I don't know if Pastora evoked this sensation or if it was a result of all the doubts that came to my mind when I was inside her, unlike with the women with whom I felt I could challenge anything. I was Goliath himself with them, and the clever David did not exist. With Pastora, I was only a man.

I didn't tell her that night when she cried that I had loved her for such a long time and loved her even at that moment. I feared, above all, my vulnerability with such a woman. I said nothing because she might expect me to behave like Jorge Negrete, willing to lay down my life for her, and that just could not be. Our similarities ended when fantasy became reality.

I went home to my wife and I was seen with her in public as Pastora was being seen with her husband, as husbands and wives of other lovers would be seen and had been since time ad infinitum—while no one and nothing but our consciences knew any differently as to what our inner desires directed us to do without witnesses.

fifty-eight

Of course I wore a tux with tails. The bride was in a white, fitted gown. The mother of the bride, so ecstatic that her darling daughter had finally decided to settle down, was pacified with a guest list of little more than two hundred "personal friends and relations." Mr. Ben Levy, while in poor health, had the proud joy of giving the bride away.

I, for one, did my part by getting so stinking drunk rather early on in the evening that I relinquished responsibility for my behavior. The waltz, the Levys' friends smiling and hand-shaking, the platters of roast beef, the sweet table, and the five-tier cake with the spouting fountain—nothing was spared to make the wedding day of Maritza Marín-Levy the event of the season.

We were united by the holy bonds of matrimony the following June after we had moved in together. When I think of it, it seems it couldn't have fit in better with Maritza's long-range objectives than if she had begun the arrangements for the wedding on the night we met at that banquet when she was still engaged to Alan García. It's possible that she and her mother had so often planned weddings that were never realized that when the time finally came to really go ahead with one, they were able to pull it off without much ado.

It was spring when Maritza had announced to me that she was actually going to be married this time and that the groom, incidentally, was to be me, Máximo Madrigal. She did this by using one of society's oldest and most successful ploys for duping an innocent fellow who relishes his independence. She said she was pregnant. Well, of course, I know and you know that Maritza was no victim of seduction. She had always taken the pill with apparently no ill effect. I saw the flower-printed compact in her handbag, with its precise rows of miniscule pills; at any given opportunity when she happened to think of it, she popped one in her mouth.

In addition, Maritza gave every indication of being of the frame of mind that if she did get pregnant "by accident," as it was said, she wouldn't have an unplanned child. She wasn't religious and she didn't consider life's variables outside of how they revolved around her. Yet, one day in April, Maritza told me over dinner that she was pregnant. Furthermore, she said, *we* were going to get married.

Well, this news was all very well for an imbecile like Alan García or any of the myriad of lightweights she was with before, but Máximo Madrigal had other plans for his future that didn't necessarily include the permanent arrangement of a family. I had still to pave the road to my own fortune, to follow in the footsteps of Dalí and Picasso. Let me have my riches and fame first, then I would acknowledge the children of my many mistresses!

"I am pregnant, Máximo. And you and I are going to get married." Period.

This announcement coincided with another when she informed me of an attractive position in the city's department of urban planning. Although I didn't have a background in architectural design, Maritza guaranteed me that with a word to the right people, the position was mine. The yearly salary was stupendously alluring. I didn't think it was something I would want to do as a career, waiting to collect a pension and all that, but it was certainly an item that would look extremely impressive on my vita.

As an artist without his own means, I could have told Maritza that there was no way I would be able to support a family. Of course, in Maritza's case this argument would have been futile. We were already making plans to take over her parents' home in Rogers Park. They had bought a condo on Lake Shore and, of course, we would have to pay absolutely nothing but the upkeep of the property. Even if I didn't get a permanent position, money was not an issue with Maritza.

Perhaps this was the reason that financial success wasn't of utmost importance in her criteria for a man. She liked men who attracted attention. She hadn't attached herself to Alan García because she believed in him or because he could show her the town, but because at the time they were engaged he was the most popular guy around. After the election, well, we know what happens then. It's touch and go with the popularity of these politicians. She once dated a very well-known black football player, but after he was dropped from the team, Maritza wouldn't even take his calls. She also dated several nobodys, but with Maritza, who could say what the motivation actually was—sex never being a factor to undervalue.

After she made her proclamation, I began to review my life, and assessed my accomplishments and my present options. I could have disappeared, gone back to Sapogonia—an unsavory thought that I quickly eliminated. Perhaps I could return to Spain, but the future just didn't have the same appeal as it did for me in Chicago right then. The idea of a child was too abstract for me to even consider, although from what Maritza said, the concrete evidence would be before my eyes in a matter of months.

With the house, the position with the city's architectural department, and all the contracts at the Levys' fingertips, it was only a matter of time before gringo Chicago society and I would be on a first-name basis. My English was by then fair enough so that I felt comfortable conversing with anyone, and I must say, I always had my charm to win the ladies, if not their husbands.

One month after the wedding, I realized there wasn't going to be a child. I was duped one hundred percent and deserved nothing else but to know that Maritza had only told me she was pregnant so that we could get married. Maritza, having experienced what thunder and hail my fits of temper brought on, didn't confess. I had to find out through other sources and the sloppiness of her attempt to convince me that she had had a miscarriage, an act not well thought out; she showed none of the anguish or regret of women who have miscarried in their fourth month.

It was all just as well. I hadn't planned on children playing a role in my life's agenda. My career was under way. The job with the city was still being dangled before me as it was before various other candidates, despite Maritza's constant reassurances that I would be the one offered it. In the end, I wasn't all that sure that that was what I wanted to do. It would mean I would have to give up sculpting full-time.

And all of this change and disorder had taken me away from creating so that it was then that I went back to it, producing pieces that surpassed previous pieces and that sold very well. There is nothing bad from which good does not come, the Spanish proverb goes. I am certain that somewhere in this account there lies a true tragedy, but I can't find it, except that María Félix was shot in the back by her grandfather, and that was only a movie.

fifty-nine

The exhibit in São Paulo was the epitome of disaster. Its only redeeming value ultimately became the fact that it was held so far from the curators and gallery owners that I had made contact with in the United States since my career as a sculptor began that they probably did not hear of the ridiculous blemish placed on my name and reputation.

As you might divine, the party on whose head I placed all blame and vowed henceforth to prohibit from active participation in matters of my career, and who, had she not herself reminded me of the advantages of her friendship (indeed the show in Brazil was due to her personal connections), I might have banished to the ends of the earth without a moment's hesitation, was none other than my woman, Maritza Marín-Levy de Madrigal.

It pains me still too greatly to go into excessive detail about the particulars of this episode in my ever-progressing career and I am reluctant to entertain you at this time at the cost of my pathetic recollection, because it did have, as all sad tales tend to, an absurd side to it. For example, when we heard from the gallery that my work was missing, yes, missing without a trace, I for the first time understood that Maritza had not seen to its being insured in Brazil. Later, we were relieved (an understatement considering the panic that befell me) to find out that Mario, Maritza's protégé and man on the scene, having acted on her explicit orders to keep his eye on my work as much as it was possible, had taken it all back to his apartment the day after the exhibit was over.

He hadn't the enlightenment to let us know this, however. He considered it much too expensive to call (the effort was probably discouraged further by the fact, as we already know, that Maritza had difficulty returning messages left on her answering machine) and too much trouble to send a telegram or write a letter. He simply waited to hear from us, presuming we knew he had possession of thousands of dollars of my original artwork.

In the event that you, dear confidante, have the slightest doubt as to how it was finally transported back to the United States and brought to my safekeeping, Maritza flew to Brazil and saw to it personally. I reimbursed her in part for the trip—all the income I had made on the one piece that was sold. Had I had the capital to take such an excursion myself, I would have gladly done it. After having strangled that neanderthal-brain friend of hers, I would have comforted myself at the mouths of the Brazilian beaches and bikin-ied conchas for a good length of time before returning.

Maritza left for seven days. She couldn't risk being away from the city any longer because García had passed the word on to her that she was about to be promoted to an important position in the Department on Women, Aged, Disabled, and Special Affairs. She was evidently resentful that I was responsible for her having to leave at an inopportune time, risking an important career advancement, but I let her know in no uncertain terms that our entire relationship was at stake, as it had been her insistence that I have this show in South America to begin with.

My sculpture, regardless of her or anyone else's opinion, was priceless—and if I sold it at all, put price tags on it, it was because I was nothing but a wretched genius scarcely being honored in his day because the world being what it was, was overpopulated with the blind and the ignorant.

She went, wearing a white cotton outfit, the skirt slit halfway up the thigh in the front, and five-inch stiletto heels accenting curva-cious calves as well as giving her short frame the much-desired height. I left the airport after her plane departed for New York, where she had a flight leaving that night to Brazil, reflecting on that Mario Son-of-a-bitch friend of hers, not giving either one the bene-fit of the doubt to behave on his or her honor in my absence, and swearing that he'd better not come to Chicago soon if he knew what was good for him.

I was unable to work that day, and when I heard the pleas of the one area of my body ever pampered, my stomach, I took Maritza's Avanti and drove north on Milwaukee Ave. I felt nostalgic for the area where I once found refuge, and thought of the Warsaw at Night, the lounge-restaurant where one could have a full meal at a relatively inexpensive price, drinks included, a very tempting prospect; that is, if one was partial to sausage and sauerkraut.

I was passing the Mexico Theater, automatically reading the marquee without special interest, when I was forced by the powers of melancholia to make an abrupt stop. One of the two features that evening was *La Generala*, starring . . . you guessed it, my friend, María Félix playing the lead role. It was a film produced when the star had long made her name, years after *Peñón de las ánimas*. By then, she had lost that heartwrenching naïveté of the virginal type and assumed all the pomposity of a very self-assured vamp.

The vanity my mother detected in Félix's early films was pitifully evident in *La Generala*, with the soft focus close-up shots. However, there was no arguing her striking attractiveness, age notwithstanding.

Mariana is her name in the film, the aristocrat sister of a liberal who is killed by the federales during the onset of the Mexican Revolution. It isn't certain whether her impassioned motivation to join the rebels (and thus gain her status as generala) was solely based on vengeance for her brother or if she sincerely shared his sympathies for the peons. Still, she goes on to play her role with fierce aptitude.

By day, among the townsfolk, she remains the European cultured lady, maintaining all of the social graces of the elite. By night, she helps smuggle arms to the motley crew who purport to seek egalitarian rights, la tierra es del que la trabaja and es mejor morir parado que vivir de rodillas, and all that.

As she can ride, shoot, and witness plunder and pillage, (she draws the line at rape, demanding her subordinates leave the female aspect of the spoils alone) she is given due respect by all around, although there is always dissention among the ranks, at least in these revolutionary-theme movies.

When the leader of the rebels, with the beastly eyes of vermin that tell you they'd just as soon eat you alive as kill you first, falls in love with her, his men begin to doubt his capability to continue to man the ship. "I think we have one too many feathers," one of his men whispers to him, which is the Spanish equivalent of, "Too many chiefs and not enough Indians."

As fickle fate would have it, the officer who killed her brother, a philanderer with a weakness for boasting, also has an eye for the same lady, who he in no way suspects is involved with the rebels.

In the midst of all this, another fellow falls victim to her complex affections, a gentleman from her own class who wants nothing but to take her away from the turmoil that without question is not suited for the timid hearts of the refined. His name is something like Alejandro Cara de Culo.

Mariana has allowed herself to be lured—though if the officer had any sense he would have realized such a woman leads if she is going to dance—to a room. While she goes off to undress in modest privacy, he bares his balls in anticipation of her return and the promising interlude that awaits.

It is not Mariana, feisty member of the genteel who comes to him in the shadows, but the Generala in her riding garb. Before he comes to the realization that the act about to be performed will not meet his approval in the least, two of her men, plus the faithful midget (this film, unlike Hollywood versions of the Mexican Revolution, was conceived in the Mexican mind and like Fellini's bizarre cast of characters, it, too, contains the spectrum of personified alter egos), hold the unfortunate scoundrel down as she proceeds to relieve him of his manhood.

I looked to the left of me and to the right. The huge theater was sparsely populated, but those of us in the audience of the male gender, in unison, I would say, compulsively slumped down in our seats. Those who wore them tipped their Texan hats forward to hide their agonized expressions. One or two put their hands over their eyes. There was no explicit castration scene in the movie, but one's imagination sufficed.

This called to mind the Japanese film *In the Realm of the Senses*, which premiered as part of the Chicago Film Festival one year. Anyone who had the opportunity to see that picture, based on an actual love story, will know what I am referring to. The crime of passion for which the woman was allowed freedom, thanks to the compassion of the jury, also managed to gain mine, unlike the present movie I was watching.

I passed on the Polish dinner and went to have a drink instead. After two or three straight shots, there was nothing left for me to do but to get hold of Pastora. She agreed on the telephone to meet me at my old loft. She remembered the location and showed bewilderment as to why I wanted to go there when I no longer lived there. I lied and said I still owned it and was planning on moving back in.

In actuality, it was already sold, but I happened to have kept my set of keys and the new owner had yet to take possession. It had been vacated since I moved out and there was no electricity or gas, although because it was still early enough in the season, the space wasn't in need of heat. There had always been trouble with the plumbing and the loft, by then, was pitiful in this respect.

I went back to my apartment for a bottle of Toro wine, a half-spent bottle of scotch, and two of Maritza's Danish crystal wine glasses. I took the opportunity to change my shirt and to garnish my skin with a little cologne. Just as I was walking out of the place the telephone rang and, while I hesitated to answer, instinct made me go to it. Maritza was calling from Kennedy Airport. Her flight to Río was delayed and she was "just feeling lonely for me."

Both of us knew she called because she expected not to find me home at that hour on a Saturday night and with her out of town, but we sent each other kisses and promises to count the very seconds of our separation and hung up because long distance was long distance, and the telephone company, if anything, had already made substantial profits on the debilitated emotions of estranged lovers.

I looked up and down the street before going in, but I never saw Pastora's dilapidated car, the one she used to drive and defended by saying that, despite its appearances, ran like a swift chariot. Reflex caused me to look up to the elongated windows on the second floor of my former loft. It seemed there was a dim light inside, which gave way to a silhouette standing by the grimy glass. She was there.

Rather than wait for the freight elevator, I took the stairs, two at ·a time, toting provisions appropriate for the occasion. When I got in I saw that she, or at least a woman, because it was hard to make out who it was who had been by the window, was now turned toward me. The hardness I had always associated with her was gone; something like a putty knife had been used to round out the edges. Her hair, the bare shoulders, and the exposed feet in sandals, which were made of fine straps binding up around the tapered ankles, were almost without substance. It produced an effect similar to that on María Félix in the film I had seen earlier that evening.

Out of character, she filled me with questions. I was anxious and it was possible that she was, too, so she asked about trivial things just to break the tension. "Why did you choose this place?"

"Because I am moving back here; I told you on the phone."

"Where are all your things?"

"With friends."

"And those glasses—?"

"I had them . . . in my car."

"Oh, I see. Like requiring a spare tire in the trunk, you carry wine glasses in case of just such an emergency."

"And you see now? Wasn't I right to do it?" I spread out a Sapogón blanket on the floor, precisely where the bed Laura and I once shared used to be, and signaled with an upturned palm for her to take a seat, which she did.

She was absolutely divine. Even the streak of silver hair that appeared now on the top of her head added to the enthralling effect she had on me, like bodysurfing, succumbing to the ocean's force and being thrust back to shore. We drank a toast, I left the wine for her to finish (which I knew she could do easily), and I drank the scotch from the bottle. And I swooned again, telling Pastora all the agonizing truths that persecuted my affairs with other women.

We made love half-clothed, rested, talked, disrobed completely, and made love again. I was dazed with remembrances of *La Generala*, the haughtiness of a cursed woman who would castrate a man and let him live. I told Pastora that she had traces of María Félix, not the way she looked in *La Generala*, but earlier. So many films raced through my mind that the night was heightened by the illusory romance of cinema, of fable and myth. Had she seen *In the Realm of the Senses?* How would she feel, knowing as she tightened the sash around my neck, that she was receiving the last of my energies, my semen surging into her body, hoping against mortality as I gasped my last breath?

"So that I could have your child?" she asked.

"So that I could be swallowed up by your vagina . . . !"

"What would you do in there?" She turned over languidly. My fingers alone were given, at present, the reign of that territory. A chilly October breeze blew in from the cracked window across the way. I was covered with goose flesh. "I would continue sculpting. And each month, instead of bleeding during your menstrual cycle, you would eliminate the rust of my metals."

Pastora sighed and without warning lifted herself up. "Where are you going?" I asked her. She couldn't possibly be thinking of leaving yet. I pulled her gently back down by a lock of hair at the nape and made love to her again and again, inexhaustibly. It had been so long and so many dreams and so many cunts, but none was hers and finally we lay very still and slept. It was almost dawn.

How odd that Pastora slept so soundly, not waking me up the way she always had the inevitable moment I began to snore. It was I who awoke instead, in the netherlight just before dawn. I felt that parched throat of the half repented drunk and sat up wondering where I would find a cool drink of water in that entire building. I swung my feet over the bed and touched the caressive warmth of a rug beneath them. Until then, I hadn't realized that my surroundings had changed.

We were in a bedroom I did not recognize and, as I walked about, I realized I had never been in that house before, this realization being superceded by the thought that I didn't remember going there.

It was a large bedroom, decorated modestly but neatly, and it had all the finishing touches of the creative and tender woman that Pastora felt like to me that night.

On the dresser, the familiar altar of icons of Eastern and Western faiths. On the bureau, an alarm clock, a tin box containing her few cheap baubles, three yellowed photographs in inexpensive frames. I mused over the photographs. Pastora's grandparents? One of the pictures was of an old woman in full indigenous costume. It was damaged, blurred. She was positioned on a chair set outside on what appeared to be a ranch. Mesquite blew beside her. She was reminiscent of my own grandmother.

I glanced over at Pastora, who was still sleeping undisturbed, lilacked by the transparent curtains on the windows, one of which was opened, and I went to close it.

At the other end of the room was an old Singer sewing machine in its original cabinet with foot pedal. There were various pieces of fabric folded meticulously over it. A sewing basket nearby lay opened, flowing over with a multitude of different colored threads. I padded over to it, fascinated by an aspect of Pastora that I hadn't known before: domesticity. *Femme fatale* I called her before we'd fallen asleep in each other's arms.

Femme fatale, mujer fatal, fatal woman—mishu huarmi, in my grandmother's tongue, which she recognized.

I turned over the basket with my foot, spilling out a riot of paraphernalia—thimbles, unraveling spools, cutting shears, a pincushion perforated pitilessly with straight pins, and various sizes of needles. I bent down and picked up the scissors, running my fingers over the edge. They were almost new and gleamed. I tell myself now, nothing else matters. She has not done you the favor of ending it for you. You told her this night, partly in jest, but she knew you can't speak of death without honesty. Why couldn't she have taken your cue, wrapped a belt around your neck, exhausted you for the last, bitter time? No, she refused. She failed.

She has left it up to you.

You go around the bed again, stepping lightly toward her, resisting the sudden occurrence that you have to shit. It is 19—

> Your country has been taken from you
> Your grandparents were taken from you
> Your inheritance was taken from you
> All that is past, is past, and
> all that is lost, is lost

The End

EPILOGUE

The rain let up. A trickle continued, harmless and tepid for the time of year. Pastora watched her son poke into the soft earth with a stick. His small sneakers peered out from too-long pants. He was a quiet child, mild-tempered and contemplative. He hummed a made-up tune and poked the earth, immersed in the thoughts of the pure.

Pastora crossed her arms and leaned against the entranceway of the garage converted into Eduardo's carpentry shop. His large back hovered over a cabinet of rich birch. He, too, hummed with somewhat melodic direction, but more as a sign that he was in synch with his present preoccupation and with life as a whole.

Eduardo noted Pastora's restlessness. "Do you think it's worth the price I quoted?" he asked, tenderly smoothing out the rough edges visible only to the craftsman. Pastora nodded, "I think so." He smiled, silently proud of his work and his ability to produce utilitarian products. Eduardo was anachronistic in a world where people prized time-saving devices: robots to expedite labor, computers to analyze for them.

She looked again at the little boy in the garden in relation to the man with the large back nearby. It was the back of a man in his prime, who had grown up to be diligent and honest, and had the naïveté to not comprehend why or how, or even know that so many people around him wore masks. Many years away, the little boy, having grown, would remember that back, too.

He would recall that insignificant Sunday, because there would be so many others, just alike, when his father hummed as he finished a cabinet with fastidious attention, work that paid for their house, their food, their shoes, his favorite plastic truck that Eduardo brought home one day . . . "Look, son! Look what I got for you!"

He would be sitting with friends, friends whom he had made because they shared a common bond—college students, army

309

buddies, Peace Corps volunteers, derelicts on skid row—and he would smile after a few drinks, imagining the man with the broad back whose hair had once been black as tar with only a sprinkling of white hair. He would be inclined to voice, more for the pleasure of hearing it himself than to discuss the topic, "My dad was a carpenter, you know, a real craftsman."

His companions would turn. Their eyebrows raised, semi-interested. One might utter, "Oh yeah?" That would suffice as encouragement; he would begin to tell how his father's father had also been a carpenter. This would be followed by reminding them that his surname was Madero and it wasn't a coincidence either. He'd analyzed that their name stemmed from "madera," meaning wood. During the days of antiquity, people's names originated from their crafts or the place from where they came.

Pastora reflected on her own surnames. Her father's, Velásquez, must've meant that she descended from a man who lived on the land of a don Velasco. Aké was Yaqui. Her maternal grandfather was born in Sonora, Mexico. There was little need for researching Aké, having inherited the earth-related features, coloring, and instincts of indigenous grandparents.

"Eddie?" She broke the soothing harmony of his sanding and the rainwater that ran down the gutter of the garage roof.

"Hm?" he said, not stopping his work.

"Hungry yet?"

He looked up at her from beneath winglike eyebrows. "Are you?" he returned. It was like a game with them. He never committed himself to anything until he knew what her feelings were—she shook her head and turned back to look on the child.

Carlitos was the name of her first love. He was a handsome first-grader. However, the first heart she'd broken was in kindergarten. The victim's name was Clifton; the whole year he persisted after her. But Pastora fell in love with Carlitos, whose full head of chocolate hair and irresistible smile with the missing front tooth had captured her adoration and left her pining with unrequited love, since Carlitos would have nothing to do with her.

From then on, she continued in her pattern of being a sucker for good-looking men, until she was eighteen and became a woman, in the law's eyes, her parents' eyes, and in her own eyes. Then, all at once, handsome faces, plain faces, pockmarked faces, faces with noses hinged by obnoxious glasses, faces with dimpled smiles, and those faces that were that much more pathetic when they entreated with a smile were all one.

"Don't kick the dirt, angelito!" she called to her son. "I have seeds planted there—semillas." The little boy turned and stared at her, trying to comprehend. "Theas?" he asked, pointing to the ground. She nodded, "Sí, mi amor, semillas." "Mías?" He blinked. She nodded again, enchanted by the sensuous mouth that attempted to form words. They both looked up at a plane that passed preparing to land at O'Hare.

Life goes on, Máximo Madrigal. Pastora allowed the name to filter through the realm of unexplained and private musings. In all the years she had known him, he had never considered to give her even this, the gift of a single moment of tranquility. The phone had rung seventeen hundred times since she last spoke with him and seventeen hundred times it had not been him. Yet, if he was any-where near, he was trying to reach her. He would persist because in his own eloquent speech he had told her before, "I'm so fucking stubborn, I had to try one more bloody time!" Finally, he would get her on the telephone and it would all begin again.

He had to continue returning to explore her, knowing with each cycle he would never fully create her. It was Máximo alone who concocted Pastora and he did not ever want to know the formula. He alone arranged the meetings. Any suggestion on her part was politely or rudely dismissed or cancelled. Motions she made toward him had caused him to retreat. For this reason, if he suggested an ungodly hour, an abandoned building, a car parked beneath the elevated tracks so that at the precise moment the train sped above, their moans would not be heard, he managed to have her without prelude or pretext.

There was no other way. Pastora was celluloid, the chanteuse of the silver screen of silent films, and larger than life. She was all the heroines who had impassioned young men in adolescent novels. She was the biology teacher of the tenth grade forced to resign when she was pregnant and unwed; the pretty nun of catechism class; she was Mother's friend who for some reason never seemed as old as Mother, who smiled at you in a way that sent goose bumps over your virginal flesh. She was that one insolent girl at your first dance who rejected you in front of your friends after you took that painfully long walk across the room to ask her out to the floor . . .

She was not the enigmatic beauty of Di Vinci, but the harsh

enigma of nature's ferocity over man, the thrashing of a tornado, the scorching lava of the erupting volcano, the hurricane that swept away entire villages into the sea. Awesome Coatlicue, whose severed head was replaced with two streams of blood that became serpents' heads; the same blood that gives life demands it through war, the eternal struggle of all civilizations.

She was an invention to make your world tolerable—an idea, not divinity itself, which is and always has been your place, sensing yourself alien to the earth. For if she were divine, she would have been no less an idea, but less than what she was at that moment, tangible. She was the blood that appeared on your penis the first time you entered a woman who was menstruating and you feared it would curse you. She was the breast that, without milk, still comforted. She was the dark tunnel through which you passed and began your first memory of this world.